Dream Healing

Book II of the Oneiroi Trilogy

L. W. Phillips

DRAGAON SCALES PRESS

Coming Soon

Dream Sacrifice

Book III of the Oneiroi Trilogy

By L. W. Phillips

Dragon Scales Press

An Understanding

To believe in legends, one needs to accept there are powers and beings capable of things beyond the human imagination. God, who created all, gave distinct abilities to all entities, such as angels, gods, humans, creatures, and mixtures of each. They lived as one, some mortal, some immortal.

Many millennia ago, humans began to worship immortals, making them more significant than they were meant to be. For that reason, they were no longer able to live as one. Mortals always wanted what the immortals had, and the immortals used them as their minions to wage and fight in wars, not their own. God became disgusted and separated them all into separate realms. Immortals could no longer live with humans but were still tasked to watch over them when called upon, with consequences if rules were broken.

Unfortunately, if a human and an immortal were together longer than necessary, the mortal would become confused and wonder if they are experiencing reality or fantasy, dreaming or awake. This otherworldly confusion often led to insanity and sometimes death.

What happens when immortals become obsessed? When their obsession is a mortal?

Chapter I

Tennessee

"Damn it! How could you?" Nicole shouted at her mother from across the living room. "I'm your daughter; you can't just send me away!"

The shouting was usual; the reason behind Nicole's outburst, however, was new. Kellie and her husband, John, finally decided to send their daughter to Kellie's sister to finish high school. The decision was not easy; after all, their daughter had once been a straight "A" student, on the math team, a regular volunteer at the hospital, and president of her sophomore class. Now it was the second semester of her junior year; her grades, on a good day, were "C" averages, she no longer volunteered anywhere, and no one in her junior class spoke to her, not since she dyed her light brown hair black and purple, pierced her tongue, nose, navel, and eyebrow, and developed a mouth that could make a sailor blush. She went from *Miss Congeniality* to *Miss Wouldn't Want to Meet You in a Dark Alley* practically overnight.

"You can't keep going on this way, Nicole. We told you that if you didn't start controlling your actions, we're going to send you to live with your aunt. You've been sneaking out of the house doing goodness knows what; you even look the part of a juvenile delinquent, and your grades are horrible. What did you think? That we were bluffing." Kellie yelled back, trying, with volume, to convince her daughter that sending her away was for the best.

It was true; she had been sneaking out of the house for the last year. At least once a week, she crawled out of her bedroom window. She had also taken on the stereotypical characteristics of a defiant teen; she'd been so innocent-looking, but now she just looked scary, and she liked it that way. As for the grades, well, what was the point in getting good grades when your life was over?

"I hate you!" Nicole stamped up the stairs and slammed her bedroom door.

She paced her bedroom floor, trying to calm her shaking hands. *I need to get out of here.* She went to her window and tried frantically to lift it. "Shit," her father had nailed it shut. "So much for fire safety." He had threatened to do just that since he caught her sneaking back through her window last weekend.

Kellie sat on the edge of her brown leather couch, dropping her head into her hands, and cried again. That was all she seemed to do lately—cry. She was forty-two years old with three children. Her twin, five-year-old boys, had blonde curly hair and blue eyes. They looked a lot like Nicole, except Nicole had brown hair before her gothic makeover. Kellie was making the hardest decision a parent could, but she knew Nicole needed to get out of Tennessee and start over. She and John had cried together over their decision to send their only daughter thousands of miles away to the middle of the Pacific Ocean, but at this point, they would try about anything.

Amanda looked at the airline magazine in the seat pocket in front of her. She was accompanying her mother to Tennessee to retrieve her cousin. She had no clue how she would be of any help. Since her abduction and abuse three weeks ago by the Greek god of war, Ares, she hadn't been the same person. Her best friend Kallisto and she had escaped the clutches of a scorned goddess and her son, but not before Ares developed an infatuation for her, and when she denied his advances, he beat her unconscious. Kallisto's Greek dream god, Morpheus, and his brother, Phantasos, saved them. *Phantasos...* Amanda closed her eyes and remembered the last time she'd seen him.

Yes, Amanda's life was all but normal. Her best friend happened to be the granddaughter of Zeus, the god-king of the Greek Pantheon. If that wasn't strange enough, the *person* she loathed, obsessed over, hated, lusted for, and despised was the Greek dream god who had saved her. . . Phantasos.

She was flying over the Pacific Ocean to bring normalcy to a teenager who went through a tragedy that changed the core of who she was. Amanda was a lot of things, but a miracle worker was none of them. She was not the *good girl* of the Kallisto/Amanda duo and certainly not one for tact. She was heading into new territory. To top everything off, she couldn't tell anyone about her divine dealings. She wasn't sure how to keep such things from her cousin. Amanda was an only child, so there had never been any chance of someone finding out.

John arrived just as Amanda and her mother, Kathryn, landed. "How was your trip?" he asked.

"Long, but without delays; how's Kellie?" Kathryn asked in return.

"She's not doing so well. Nicole thinks Hawaii is a threat, and I'm sure when Kellie tells her I came to pick you two up, all hell will break loose." John lifted Amanda and Kathryn's luggage into his Escalade. "I hope you're up to the challenge, Kathryn. Nicole's not the person she was before the accident. She's, well, beyond depressed and perpetually pissed."

The ride from the airport to Amanda's aunt's house seemed relatively quick. John continued to fill them in on Nicole's new outlook on life as they drove, making the trip move along faster now they were on land.

"Kathryn!" Kellie hugged her sister and immediately began to cry. "Thank you. This is the hardest thing I've ever had to do."

John took their suitcases inside. The plan was for them to stay a couple of days before returning to Hawaii in the hopes of persuading Nicole that leaving was in her best interest.

"Can I go see Nicole?" Amanda asked.

"She's in her room. She stomped her way upstairs, cursing when she found out her father went to pick you two up at the airport; second door on the right, good luck."

Amanda knocked on Nicole's door. Nothing. She knocked again—still nothing. "Nicole, it's Amanda. Can I come in?" No answer.

"Uh . . . she's not answering her door," Amanda announced as she walked back downstairs.

John and Kellie looked at each other and ran upstairs. John took out a metal key and unlocked their daughter's door. To their horror, but not surprisingly, their daughter was gone. "How could she? I nailed her window shut?"

"I bet she went out the twin's window," Kellie supplied.

"Where would she've gone?" Amanda asked.

"She usually goes to the graveyard and sits by Chase's grave. When she's not there, I don't know where she goes," Kellie answered.

"If you give me your keys and directions, I'll look for her." Amanda put her coat back on and held her hand out for the keys. John gave them to her, plus directions to the graveyard and the mall, just in case.

Amanda's idea of a good time had never included graveyards. In fact, she hated cemeteries; they freaked her out, but here she was on her way to a graveyard at twilight. *Shit.*

"Now would be a good time for my *all-powerful* friends to join me," Amanda said, looking at the ceiling of her uncle's SUV, hoping to be heard.

⟫⟫⟫ ⟪⟪⟪

Nicole sat by Chase's grave with black mascara streaking down her wet face. No one understood how much she hurt, how painful the last year had been. The only person who could have ever understood died a year ago. That was the night her world changed. He was her best friend, confidant, and lover. The latter was part of her distress—*lover*.

"Chase, all I ever think about is that night. How wonderful everything was before the wreck. Why'd we go that way instead of down Main Street like always? Why was that man driving drunk? Why'd you leave me?"

She beat her fists on the cold, dead grass beside his grave. Tears fell to the ground as she leaned over and wept, imagining them absorbing into the earth, closing the distance between her and the boy who lay motionless. This was the kind of pain that compelled her to pierce her body; each piercing seemed to give release. This was the pain that separated her from the world. She was alone in the grief, alone in the despair. The week following the wreck was lost to her, well, mostly. The anguish was there, even in her unconsciousness. How could anyone understand? No one but he could, and he was gone.

⟫⟫⟫ ⟪⟪⟪

Amanda pulled up to the front of the graveyard. The entrance had two brick columns with an iron gate hinged to each. When closed, the gate said, *Rest in Peace*. Just past the brick columns on the inside of the cemetery was a large oak tree, and next to it was a sign showing the layout of the grounds.

"I can't believe I'm about to go in there," she said aloud. Through the gated entrance, she could see the headstones rising out of the grass in the cemetery, and they terrified her.

As she stepped from the vehicle, she got an eerie, familiar feeling, as if she was being watched. The last time she had that feeling was when Ares watched her through an orb. If that evil god of war watched her now, she was not sure what she would or could do.

"Whoever's there, show yourself."

Phantasos appeared by her side, scaring the hell out of her. He caught her around the waist before she slipped. Shocked, she pushed his chest. Phantasos had made it clear that the two of them were to remain— well—nothing. They weren't even friends. The fact his hands burned a sensual caress down her spine enraged her. At that moment, she hated herself for the way her body responded to his touch and the feelings he aroused in her—all except the ones of hate.

"Let me go. What the hell are you doing here?"

"You told me to show myself," he sounded irritated.

"Okay then, why were you watching me?"

"Kallisto asked me to."

"She did what? Why? I'm fine. Why would she send you anyway?" She knew Kallisto could tell the struggles Amanda had when it came to the god standing before her. He made her crazy, mostly with loathing but also with a sexual intensity that overrode the desire to kill him.

"She felt your distress, and because her father was sitting with her and Morpheus, neither could check on you, so, here I am. Believe me, it wasn't my idea. I'd rather walk across hot coals." He folded his arms and glared.

"Well, as you can see, I'm fine. Now leave," Amanda demanded.

Phantasos looked around and realized they were standing at the front gate of a graveyard in— "Where are we?"

"Tennessee—where I'm getting my cousin. There's no *we* because you're leaving."

"Why are you standing at the entrance to a graveyard?"

"I'm meeting a man. What's it to you?" Amanda was hurt by his "rather walk on hot coals" remark, so she decided to twist the knife a little herself.

With a glare, Phantasos inclined his chin, "Really? Why would he want to meet you in a place of the dead?"

"He thought it would be cool to do it in a graveyard." Okay, she knew better than to go there, but she could not help herself.

Eyes widening, Phantasos turned on his heel and walked toward the wrought iron gate.

⟫⟫⟫ ⟪⟪⟪

"I was kiddin'," Amanda whispered loudly. "I'm looking for my cousin. She ran off, and she's known to come here to grieve."

Phantasos stopped, "Is this the truth?"

"Yes, not that it's any of your business. You can't go in there. If she sees you there, you will frighten her, and if she thinks we know each other, she'll be suspicious."

"Very well, I'll watch from a distance."

Amanda rolled her eyes and saluted her nemesis with her middle finger. Phantasos grinned and vanished. She felt his gaze and wished she could choke him—*or kiss him. Shit, I forget he can read minds.*

Amanda saw her cousin leaning over the grave of her boyfriend. She could hear the sobs wrenching out of her. The site was painful to watch. *How could someone so young feel so much?*

⟫⟫⟫ ⟪⟪⟪

Nicole felt a presence. She jerked her head up to see her beautiful blonde cousin walking slowly toward her.

"So, you found me." Wiping her face and eyes, Nicole stood up to greet her cousin.

"Your parents are worried about you. I'm worried about you."

"Why? I haven't seen you in over two years. You never call or text, and suddenly, you're worried about me. Save us both the trouble, stop lying, stop pretending, and leave," Nicole raised her voice in spite of her scratchy throat from sobbing.

⟫⟫⟫ ⟪⟪⟪

The truth was, Amanda hadn't been worried until Nicole failed to answer her bedroom door. Then, she became very worried when she saw the anguish tearing at Nicole's soul while she lay over the grave of the boy she loved.

"I see now I should've been more concerned. I thought your parents were exaggerating. Truth, I don't think they know how bad off you really are." "What the hell do you know about it?" Nicole dusted her pants off and began to walk away.

"More than you know. Where are you going?" Amanda had no intention of going any deeper into the graveyard.

"I'm going where it's less crowded."

"Nicole," Amanda ran up to her cousin and grabbed her arm, turning her so she could look into her eyes. "Please, talk to me; tell me about that night."

"Why should I? I wouldn't want to mess up your perfect life."

Amanda laughed. "Well, I'll make a deal with you. If you tell me about the night Chase died, I'll tell you how wrong you are about my life." Amanda could still feel Phantasos' eyes on her.

"I don't know you well enough to tell you about that night."

"Fair enough. Will you let me get to know you better then?" Amanda asked.

"I don't want to go with you and your mother. I want to stay here."

"Come back with me, and let's talk about it. I'm from Hawaii, and it's freezing out here. Please, come back home with me." Amanda looked up to the darkening sky and admitted to Nicole, "Graveyards scare the hell out of me."

To Amanda's surprise, Nicole laughed.

Nicole didn't want to fight with her cousin. The two had not seen each other in a long time but had always gotten along well enough. She remembered when Amanda beat the snot out of a boy on the playground when they were about seven and eight years old. The boy bullied Nicole on several occasions, and when Nicole pointed the bully out on the monkey bars, Amanda saw red. She marched her eight-year-old little badass self up to Johnny and kneed him right in the crotch. Then she made him apologize to her. She'd never forgotten that, and that's why she turned and left the cemetery with her cousin.

Chapter II

Pain

"Why did you run off?" Amanda asked Nicole about five minutes into their drive home.

"I needed to clear my head, that's all." Nicole didn't intend to tell her cousin anything that wasn't necessary. She no longer gave information about herself and her *feelings* to anyone. She became jaded the moment she woke from her weeklong coma to find Chase was dead and buried; she never had the chance to say goodbye.

Amanda changed the subject. "I have eighty dollars on me, your father's car, and I'm yearning to see the local mall—how about it?"

"Look Amanda —" Nicole continued, sounding annoyed. "I don't talk much, and I haven't spent much time with people lately, so I'm sure my company isn't what you really want right now."

"You're the only person over the age of five and under the age of forty that I know here." She was not counting the dream god that she could still feel watching her. "I need a sweatshirt. I don't have any cold weather clothes. Surely you can find it in you to show me to the mall."

"Fine. Don't expect me to shop with you, though. As you can see, I don't get into fashion anymore."

"Yeah, I noticed," Amanda briefly looked from the road over to her cousin.

"Turn right at the next light," Nicole directed her toward the mall.

"Let me call our parents so they don't send the cavalry after us," Amanda called her mother and told her she and Nicole were going to find her some winter wear.

Finally, they parked, and Nicole reluctantly dragged herself from the car. She had only been to the mall once, maybe twice, since the accident. That's how she defined everything about herself now, around the accident. Life as she knew it was separated into before and after, pre and post, with and without.

"You aren't going to ask my opinion on anything, are you?"

"Well, that depends on whether or not I go goth in the next hour," her cousin winked at her.

They spent the next hour going from store to store looking for a few sweatshirts. Finally, her cousin stopped interrogating her about the accident and her new take on life. She had to admit—she was actually having a good time until Amanda informed her that she was officially out of money, and it was time to go home. She dreaded going back and facing her parents. It was one thing to have intense yelling matches when it was just them, but now there would be an audience. Plus, they were sending her away, and she couldn't understand how they could do that to their daughter. She definitely hadn't been a saint, but she wasn't doing drugs, even though she couldn't convince her parents of it. They thought something other than the accident had to be the reason for her drastic change. What they didn't know was she'd lost everything that night. All the things a teenage girl holds dear were gone in just two hours. Two hours had created the clammed-up, dejected, piercing-seeking person she had become, and it would take a miracle to find the beautiful, life-loving girl she had once been.

"Look, Amanda, I don't have anything against you or your mom, but I don't want to live with you. I'm not going to Hawaii."

"Have you ever thought that maybe if you were to leave for a little while, you could put some of this behind you?"

"Put it behind me?" Nicole glared at her cousin. "How can I put it behind me? I lost so much that night. I'd never expect you to understand." Nicole stamped off ahead of Amanda, effectively putting enough space between them so Amanda couldn't continue the conversation.

⇒≫⟩ ⟨≪⇐

Amanda let out a deep breath. She could see the pain etched across her cousin's face. *How can I, of all people, help her?*

Realizing Phantasos was watching everything, she rolled her eyes. "Why are you still here? Leave!" Amanda let the words leak from between her teeth, not loud enough for anyone but a god to hear. To her dissatisfaction, Phantasos didn't listen. She could still feel his unwanted presence, watching. *Asshole!*

The two girls remained silent, except for the occasional driving directions from Nicole, all the way home. Once there, Nicole practically leaped from the SUV when Amanda pulled into the driveway. By the time she reached the front door, Nicole had already made her way up to her bedroom.

"Thanks for going after her," Kellie said, hugging her tightly when she walked into the living room.

"You're welcome. Nicole's in a lot of pain. I had no idea she was this bad. I'm not sure how to help."

"That's why we're sending her far from the memories. Everything here is a reminder," John answered. "It's the only thing we can think to do, and her therapist agrees."

⇒≫⟩ ⟨≪⇐

Nicole went to her plush window seat and sat drawing her knees up to her chest. She stared out the window, thinking about Chase and remembering the first night he asked her out. That was a great night. Both volunteered at the local hospital. Working with cancer patients was Chase's passion. He wanted to be an Oncologist. Nicole enjoyed the pediatric ward and, like Chase, dreamed of being a doctor, a pediatrician. After work, he asked her to join him for a Coke in the cafeteria. She accepted, and the two hit it off.

Trying to fight the burning that preceded the tears, she closed her eyes tight. She never cried in front of her family; they hadn't seen her cry since the accident. That was one reason they worried so much. But tears had fallen—every night from her eyes and into her pillow. She cried so hard sometimes it felt like her heart was being wrenched from her chest. The physical pain would build and build until she vomited. She refused to let anyone see that side of her, so she wore her armor. Black long sleeves covered her arms, baggy black pants covered her legs, her fingertips were covered in black paint, and her many visible piercings were all to keep people away. No one ever saw her cry; she rarely spoke to anyone, and that was only if necessary. She buried her pain just as Chase had been buried. *If he can't live, why should I?* Her new looks and lack of social interaction had successfully given her the isolation she needed.

Amanda knocked on her door. "Your mother said I was to sleep on the air mattress in here. Is that okay with you?" Nicole could hear the reluctance in her cousin's voice.

Not turning her head from the window, Nicole answered, "Sure."

Amanda looked around the *girly* bedroom. She saw the remnants of a bright young woman who once inhabited the space as opposed to the dark one who sat in the window staring out into the night. There were pictures of friends and family surrounded in white and pink frames, lining her chest of drawers. A purple lava lamp sat on her dresser, and a large stuffed brown bear sat in the fuzzy purple moon chair. Not the stereotypical bedroom of a goth wannabe, or so Amanda thought.

Nicole could only imagine what was going through Amanda's head. *This doesn't look like the bedroom of the "new" Nicole.* Truth was, she touched nothing unless necessary, and most everything was the way it was the night of the accident. She hadn't changed any of the pictures that lined her furniture; she hadn't sat in her moon chair because the stuffed bear occupied it—and had for over a year. The lava lamp hadn't been on since she turned it off before she left for her date with Chase—the night he died. Her mother dusted and straightened up, but Nicole wouldn't allow her to change anything.

"You can move things around if you need to. Just put everything back how you found it when you wake up."

"Thanks, uh, where's the mattress?" Amanda asked.

"In the hall closet. There's a pump beside it." Nicole still hadn't turned to face her cousin, not wanting her to see the tears rimming her eyes. It was bad enough she saw her crying at the cemetery.

When Amanda went to get the mattress and pump, Nicole brushed the tears from her cheeks. They finally fell.

To Amanda's dismay, she could still feel her nemesis watching. "You can leave now," she whispered.

To her utter surprise, he appeared in the hall by her side. Before she could yell, he covered her mouth. Her eyes went wide, and then she squinted. Slowly, he removed his hand and told her to step into the hall bathroom. He smelled of Mount Olympus and Phantasos.

"What the hell do you think you're doing?" Amanda wasn't happy with his sudden reappearance or heavy-handedness.

"I promised I would watch over you until Kallisto could call or come see you for herself."

"Why are you here?" She waved her hands around the room. "You may feel the need to watch over me...Zeus knows why, but I don't have to actually see you."

"Ouch," Phantasos put his hand over his heart and feigned hurt.

"Stop. You know I'm okay. All you have to do is your mind-to-mind thing with your brother, and they'll know I'm fine. What do you want?" Amanda protectively crossed her arms over her chest, feeling the need to close in on herself whenever Phantasos was around. Keeping her heart wrapped in her arms would surely keep it from feeling anything in his presence.

"I've been observing your cousin and feeling her pain. I thought maybe she could use a good night of healing sleep. What if I had Morpheus ask our father if he would help her for the next few nights?" Phantasos suggested.

Amanda remembered a brief conversation with Morpheus about the strained relationship between Phantasos and his father. Hypnos stopped talking to his eldest son when he refused to go into the dreams of mortals and, eventually, immortals alike. He had become a "fallen," or at least a failed dream god, after the mortal woman he loved killed herself on Mount Olympus. She had been driven crazy by the constant pull between realms of existence. She finally snapped and accomplished something no god, not even Zeus, had known was possible—suicide while on Olympus while in her dream state. Humans can't take the pull from one state of consciousness to another too often; they go mad and, as it seemed, suicidal.

⤳⫸⫷⤳

"Why can't you just do it?" Amanda asked.

"I —" For just a moment, Phantasos did something he had been trying not to do. He looked Amanda in the eyes. He couldn't take the feelings her blue eyes caused him. "I can make her sleep deeply, but I cannot heal her. If you would rather, I could summon Phobetor. He, too, can heal. He's just not very charismatic."

"Not very charismatic?"

"Morpheus is the upbeat flirt — or he was; not so much anymore. I'm the sarcastic yet exciting one, and Phobetor is the, well, serious poignant one. At least, that is the way I see it."

"Will you go away if I say yes to this?"

Phantasos swallowed a grin. He could feel the arousal in her body. He knew her words contradicted the heat in her veins, and he knew not all of her wanted him gone. "Yes, I'll leave you in peace, my lady." He gave her a mocking bow. She rolled her eyes.

She stood biting the inside of her cheek as she thought, seeming to weigh the pros and cons. "What could it hurt?"

"Nothing, he will not hurt her. He will just go into her dream and give her mental healing. She will feel a lot better in a morning or two."

"Fine, I'm ready to do about anything. She's so sad." He could see the worry play across Amanda's brow.

"Okay, I will find Phobetor. Call Kallisto when you get a chance. I think her father had her and Morpheus under interrogation all afternoon. He returned from his fishing trip to find his daughter was very serious about her boss." Phantasos allowed himself one last glimpse into Amanda's beguiling eyes, showing things he knew were better left unsaid, and then vanished.

⟫⟫ ⟪⟪

"Mental note, kill Kallisto for sending the only Greek god that I despise," Amanda said aloud before she returned to Nicole's bedroom with the mattress and pump.

That wasn't exactly true, though. She didn't actually despise Phantasos. How she felt about him was...well — complicated. The only being she truly despised was Ares. Amanda shook the memory of Ares from her head—those were memories she was trying very hard to forget. Now, if her dreams would allow her to forget, maybe in time the pain of them would dissipate.

Nicole sat in the window thinking. How was she going to leave Chase? She wasn't crazy—she knew he was dead, but she felt connected to him by going to the graveyard. Her therapist told her that going to his grave would help her to grieve and get over it. She, however, figured out that getting over it was not something she was willing to do. She felt guilty for even suggesting it to her subconscious. Chase was the one she was going to marry. The one she shared all her secrets with, the one she gave all of herself to. At that thought, a tear escaped her eye and wound its way down her cheek, dripping onto her bent-up knees.

She'd always loved it when Amanda came. Now, seeing her again reminded her that Chase was alive the last time she had seen her, and her mind was whole. Another tear escaped the other eye. Her thoughts and emotions were all over the place.

"Hey Nicole, I found the mattress and pump. Would ya mind giving me a hand?"

Nicole closed her eyes, willing herself to stop her emotional breakdown. She learned to hide this part of her *change* by putting on the, *I don't give a shit* attitude, and when the pain came on the hardest, she would get a new piercing, releasing the pain through a different avenue besides crying all the time.

"Sure," Nicole made sure to roll her eyes so Amanda could see her.

After the girls situated the mattress, thankfully not having to move anything around, Amanda went to wash her face, and Nicole climbed back onto the window seat and resumed her stargazing.

Bending over the sink, Amanda splashed the cleanser off her face and felt the tell-tale shift in the air. Not able to look up, just then she hoped, desperately hoped, it wasn't Phantasos coming back to torture her some more. She finished splashing her face, grabbed a towel, and then looked to see the reason for the shift.

"Hey, girl," Kallisto whispered and grinned smugly. She was enjoying her new powers and learning more about them daily.

"Shit, I'll never get used to you doing that." Kallisto had been popping in and out since they returned from Olympus. "What's up with you sending satan himself to check in on me?"

Kallisto grinned, "I couldn't come and check on you, and I had a weird feeling you needed me. Morpheus couldn't leave either. My dad was a little, let's say, upset. He's not used to me dating yet, let alone having a steady boyfriend." Kallisto had never dated until a couple of months ago. Guys were too intimidated by her beautiful looks and notable intelligence to ask her out. Her father made it halfway through his daughter's senior year without having to worry about someone's hands mauling his daughter—he was fine with her becoming a spinster or a nun. He didn't know about his wife's immortality and especially didn't know about his daughter's.

"When are you and your mom going to tell him?" They hadn't told him about their divinity.

"Who knows. I'm not sure why she's waiting. They've been together for over twenty years. Yes, it's going to suck. He's going to get upset, but the longer she waits, the more upset he'll be," Kallisto rambled in her way. "Were you needing me? Are you okay?"

"I'm okay—now. You could've asked anyone else or, better yet, waited."

"You know I couldn't do that after —" Kallisto stopped. Ares and his abuse of Amanda wasn't a topic they discussed.

"I would've screamed if need be. A small plea to the roof of an SUV was no reason to get — him to come check on me."

"Truth is, Phantasos heard you, and when we couldn't come, he insisted," Kallisto admitted reluctantly.

"He said he would rather have walked on hot coals than to have had to check on me."

Kallisto laughed and rolled her eyes. "Believe what you want. He — well, he needs to decide whether life is worth living or if The Fates' forewarning is going to keep him from it."

Amanda let out a breath, decided she needed a change of subject, and then explained to Kallisto how "far gone" her cousin was. She also told her about Phantasos' plans to get Phobetor to put her cousin in a healing sleep.

"He said the sleep would help her mental anguish."

"It will, but I'm surprised he's getting Phobetor," Kallisto looked perplexed.

"He said that neither he nor Morpheus could give her a healing sleep. He offered to have Morpheus ask it of their father, but he felt Phobetor would be a better choice since he is accustomed to people who are usually unhappy."

"Makes sense, I guess. Well, let me know what happens. I'm going to Olympus tonight to see my grandfather. He wants Morpheus to do something for him."

Amanda shook her head. "Two months ago, I was the adventurous one and there was not a such thing as gods of Olympus — or at least, we didn't know there were. Now, I'm boring, and you are a deity. Strange how life can change in just a couple of months."

Kallisto winked, "I'll see ya soon," and she vanished.

"I'll never get used to that," Amanda continued, cleaning her face. She applied her moisturizer and returned to Nicole's room, where she still sat on the window seat staring into the darkness.

"What would you like to do tomorrow," Amanda asked.

"Looks like I have to pack." Nicole's words were delivered severely, and Amanda could tell she had been crying.

Not knowing what else to say, Amanda climbed underneath the covers of the air mattress and fell asleep.

Nicole looked over at her sleeping cousin, wondering why she seemed so different. Amanda had always been quick-witted and a no-nonsense sort of girl. For some reason, and Nicole couldn't quite put her finger on it, Amanda seemed almost as distant as she was. She did talk to her, but not in the same way. Maybe she just didn't know how to take her new abrasive behavior. *No, there's something else.*

Nicole pulled herself from the window, resigning herself to the sleep her body was demanding. She climbed into bed and before she knew it, she was asleep.

Chapter III

Dreamer

"Phobetor," Phantasos called through his father's mansion. He hated coming here. Unfortunately, Phobetor lived with his father when on Olympus. Zeus gave him special permission to live part-time in the human realm, which had always made him and Morpheus wonder what made the king grant such special permission to Phobetor. Three weeks ago, things started making more sense. Phobetor was one of the two go-betweens for Zeus and his ex-lover, Zenovia, who happened to be Kallisto's grandmother and the reason Hera hated Kallisto.

⋙⋙ ⋘⋘

"You don't have to shout." Phobetor heard his brother and appeared, leaning against a column in the vast room with his arms crossed over his wide chest.

"I am here to ask you for a favor," Phantasos admitted.

Phobetor's brows shot up. His brother had never asked him for a favor. Unless you count that one time, he asked him for help playing a childish yet hilarious prank on Morpheus. That prank went down in history, and Morpheus still got angry if it was ever brought up.

"You want to ask me for a favor?" He feigned shock.

"Ha, Ha. I'm here to ask you to go to Amanda's cousin to put her into a healing sleep. She has been through a lot of emotional trauma over the last year and needs help."

"Why me? That's not really my thing."

"You know I cannot go to our father, and Morpheus is busy getting interrogated by his future father-in-law. Besides, you may be able to help her more than anyone."

Phobetor gave Phantasos a sidelong look. "Should I ask what you mean by that?"

"She's young, turning eighteen in a month or so, and she is miserable and sadder than anyone I have ever seen. Her grief has consumed her. I just thought you would understand her better than the old man, that's all. A younger immortal helping out a younger mortal," Phantasos thought they were a lot alike, both reclusive and neither happy, but he didn't want to alienate his brother, so he downplayed his reasoning. Plus, Phobetor was not an old god—by human comparison, he was only in his early twenties.

⟫⟫⟩ ⟨⟨⟨⟨

Phobetor knew his brother meant more by his statement than age, but he couldn't blame him. For the last century, serving as the go-between for Zeus and his ex-lover had made Phobetor the recluse he had become. If Hera knew he helped the couple communicate, they would all go down. As long as he kept it to himself, only he would fall if the goddess found out Zeus still communicated with his former mistress. They had not been together or seen each other, but because they shared a daughter and a deep love, Hera would've killed any mortal or immortal who dared help them. Phobetor wasn't given a choice. Zeus was his king, and he owed him a debt. However, he might not be as jaded if he had known his father was also helping the lovers communicate.

"Why is she so unhappy?" Phobetor asked.

"All I know is she used to be lighthearted, strikingly beautiful, and very caring of others. After a fatal accident where her boyfriend was killed about a year ago, she turned into a gothic delinquent who cares for no one." Phantasos revealed what little he knew from watching the girls that day and what little he got out of Amanda's head.

Phobetor thought for a moment. "Was she hurt in the wreck?"

"I think she was unconscious for about a week of mortal time. What her injuries were, I am not sure. When she woke, they told her about the boy's death and that he had already been buried. She spends a lot of time by his grave."

"So, she was in love, and he died. She changed her mindset on life and is now severely depressed," Phobetor said nonchalantly.

"Well, I think her feelings are a little more complex than that. Her despair is profound." Phantasos tried to stress the depth of Nicole's anguish.

"I didn't mean to make light of the girl's suffering. I was just trying to consolidate the circumstances and figure out how to heal the child's mental state."

"Child?"

"Eighteen? She's a child." Phobetor lacked four centuries, being five thousand years old, which in god years, was young, a teenager even.

"Well, Pops, I guess we should keep you out of the dreams of the elderly women. We would not want you making passes at the frail," Phantasos chided.

Phobetor gave a wave of his middle finger, "Fuck you." Phantasos laughed.

"Where will I find this emotionally tortured . . . *child*?" Phobetor grinned.

⤜⤜⤝ ⤞⤞⤟

"Follow me." The two dream gods vanished and reappeared in Nicole's bedroom. Phantasos had checked before materializing to make sure both girls were asleep. Amanda knew he could appear, but he didn't think he could take seeing her awake again for a while.

⟫ ⟪

As soon as Phobetor laid eyes on Nicole, his breath ceased, his eyes widened, and his mouth went dry. He thought she was the most beautiful being he had ever seen.

Phantasos was grinning, "Do you still see her as a child?"

Again, Phobetor gave his brother a sign of his irritation, this time adding a sneer. Phantasos laughed.

Amanda moaned and turned over. This time Phantasos' breath ceased, and his cheeks reddened; she kicked off her covers to show she only wore a cut-off tee and a pair of black lace panties.

This, of course, was not lost on Phobetor, who eyed his brother questioningly, seeing his reddening face, and said, "You're a Greek god, for Zeus' sake."

⟫ ⟪

Phantasos had no idea why Amanda's lacy panty-clad body embarrassed him. Phobetor was right. He was a Greek god. Notoriously, the gods were not ashamed of the body, but this had been Amanda's body, and he was looking and shouldn't be.

"Well, now you know who Nicole is. I will leave you to it."

"Are you not going into her cousin's dream to make sure she doesn't wake?" Phobetor grinned, gesturing toward Amanda.

"No. If she does, tell her to go back to sleep. You know as well as I do that she knows about us."

"I just thought since you can't seem to keep from thinking about her, you might as well indulge yourself a little. She would think it only a dream." Phobetor smirked at his brother.

"Let me know how things go," Phantasos said, then vanished.

Phobetor knelt by Nicole's bed and lightly touched her forehead, moving black strands of hair away from her eyes. Then, he closed his and entered her dream.

He was at the edge of a lush hardwood forest. The trees stopped about thirty feet from a cliff's edge, where he saw her profile. She was striking. He slowly exhaled. The girl she had been before the accident was now the one he was seeing. Her natural long brown hair blew back from her face in the wind, coming up and over the cliff's edge. Her arms were folded—she looked cold, standing on the edge of the cliff, staring at mountains in the distance.

"Would you like a coat?" Phobetor asked. He walked toward her. He knew he shouldn't speak to her but couldn't help himself. He was supposed to heal her, not converse or be chivalrous. He could not help but continue his assessment, telling himself it was to learn more about her for the healing. He usually never conversed with his dreamers. Only gave them the dreams and healing magic. Light brown hair, long feathery lashes lining baby blue eyes, fair skin, and no piercings except one in each ear. *Beautiful in both forms.*

Nicole jumped at the sound of a male voice and turned to see the most gorgeous man she'd ever laid her eyes on. He stood at least six-five with dark brown, shoulder-length hair framing a chiseled jaw. His eyes resembled liquid gold, and his body was fashioned to a faultlessness no mortal man could achieve, even if they were to spend their life dedicated to the gym. "Who are you?"

"My name is Phobetor. I have come to help you with your dreams."

"Help me with my dreams? I wasn't aware I needed any help with my dreams. Maybe outside of my dreams, but here, in them,

I seem to have more control." Now standing mere feet from her, she could see his thick, dark eyebrows with their centers raised in a slight upside-down "v." They made him appear intimidating.

Phobetor had to admit. He would not have thought her so sad if he had experienced this particular dream without knowing the situation.

"Are your dreams always peaceful?" he asked.

"Aren't everyone's?"

"No, but I'm sure yours are a little less peaceful on a regular basis," assessed Phobetor.

"How do you know that, and who did you say you were again?"

Phobetor allowed himself a laugh. "I'm a Greek god of dreams. I have been asked by my brother, who is also an Oneiroi, to help heal you."

"Okay, let me get this straight." Nicole was shaking her head. "I'm having a dream about a dream god. Your brother is an Ono. ..something, and you want to bring me peaceful, healing dreams. No more caffeine after five," Nicole said under her breath.

Phobetor grinned, which was unusual unless he was bantering with his brothers. He was enjoying her curiosity. Usually, mortals just went with it and tried to figure their dreams out the next day. He told her exactly who he was and who sent him, knowing she would not remember the conversation when she woke. He had also successfully taken her mind off other things. She had not been having a bad dream or nightmare...instead it was a totally different vision, which he thought was unusual, being the frame of mind Phantasos said she was in before she went to bed. Then, he surveyed the scene more closely. She was on the edge of a cliff and very calm. *She is going to jump.*

"You wouldn't, by chance, be contemplating jumping off this cliff, would you?" Phobetor lowered his chin and cut his eyes up questioningly.

"And if I was, that wouldn't be any of your business."

"Nicole, Nicole, have you not been listening? I'm a dream god, here to save you from yourself. It is my business. Besides, you're way too beautiful to jump off this cliff."

"This is a dream; I wouldn't die. Just consider it a practice run."

"If you hit before you wake, you will die, dream or not." Her words, *consider it a practice run,* did not escape Phobetor's notice, and he, for the first time in over a century, was worried about something other than the love life of Zeus.

"Tell me again why this," Nicole waved her hand between herself and the cliff, "matters to you?"

"Well, I promised to help you, and I don't take my promises lightly. And, now that I have had the honor of meeting you, I am curious as to why such a creature as you would want to end such a beautiful life."

Nicole laughed and, to Phobetor's unease, laughed a lot. "Do you always talk that way?"

"What way?" Phobetor's forehead creased.

"With that thick accent and with words like "such a creature as you." Nicole was still laughing. "Besides, my life hasn't been beautiful in over a year." Nicole abruptly stopped laughing.

"Yes, I suppose I do. I am centuries old and well-read, and . . . you're wrong. Your life is beautiful, and you are beautiful, no matter what happened to you a year ago. We all suffer, but to end your life because of suffering is ludicrous."

Before Phobetor's eyes, Nicole's hair and fingernails turned black as pitch. Her piercings appeared as if they were in her own realm, and black circled her eyes and covered her lips. She looked menacing. "Look, I'm not beautiful, I'm not nice, and I want nothing more than for you to leave me the hell alone." Nicole turned and walked away, her form fading with each step.

Nicole woke, eyes wide and breathing ragged, looking around her room, trying to find the man from her dream. She smelled the faint scent of lavender and honeysuckle and maybe a hint of sandalwood. Gently laying back the covers, she pulled herself from bed. After sliding her feet into slippers, she padded to the window. She wasn't sure why the window, but she had a strange feeling leading her that way. When she looked out, she could have sworn she saw a man's tall figure standing beside the streetlamp. She blinked, and the figure was gone. Nicole furrowed her brows in confusion and chalked her strange dream up to just that, a dream.

Phobetor flashed to Phantasos' house on Olympus. He called out for his brother and was thankful to find Phantasos home.

"I cannot do that again, Phantasos. You will have to be her Oneroi, not I."

Phantasos lifted a curious brow, "Why not?"

"I just can't; enough questions." Phobetor vanished, leaving Phantasos confused.

In the hopes of keeping Phantasos from finding him, Phobetor had flashed to the other realm, his home in Greece. To Phobetor's dismay, his brother was right on his heels.

"You're not going to change my mind, Phantasos."

"Just give me a reason."

"Do I need a reason?" Phobetor turned and faced his older brother. His home was beautiful. Stone and marble adorned the floors and walls. Columns holding up the great ceiling where a mural depicting the forests of Olympus, one of Phobetor's favorite places to be when he needed to be alone, *Where I should have gone instead of here.*

"Well, yes. I need to tell Amanda why," persuading his brother had to be easier than facing Amanda for many reasons.

"She was practicing committing suicide," Phobetor's voice lowered, "while in her dream state."

"What? You have to stop her." Phantasos said, a little louder than was necessary. "Amanda won't be able to take that."

"What do you care if Amanda cannot handle it? You cannot stand her." Phobetor stated.

"The girl can't die, Phobetor. She's going to live with Amanda in Hawaii."

"And I ask you again, why do you care?"

"Look, our brother is engaged to Kallisto, who happens to be Amanda's best friend. Nicole is Amanda's cousin and will be a friend of Kallisto's as well. She needs to be protected."

Phobetor arched an eyebrow and considered his brother's plea. "For that reason, we should interfere with everyone's dreams. After all, are not all mortals connected in one way or another."

"What happened to change your mind? You were going to help her." Phantasos asked.

"She, she was so . . ." Phobetor was lost for words. He stood, unable to elaborate.

"So . . . what?" Phantasos asked, trying to bring his brother out of the trance he seemed to have veered into.

"Hopeless."

"What? You specialize in, hopeless."

"Trust me, this is different." Phobetor turned and walked to his kitchen, where he proceeded to make a sandwich. "You want one?"

"Sure." Phantasos didn't care much for mortal food, but he was starving. "How different?"

"She is too...pained. I don't think I can heal her." Phobetor continued fixing the sandwiches.

"You have taken on worse. Why is this girl's pain too much?"

Handing Phantasos his sandwich and taking his own, Phobetor walked to the TV room. "I will think about it. That is all I can offer just now. Give me until tonight."

"What about during the day? You don't think she will—Phantasos couldn't finish his sentence.

"Actually, no. I think the dream state is, for now, the biggest concern." Phobetor took a bite of his sandwich, refusing to believe what he suspected was possible.

Chapter IV

Jeans

Nicole stepped over her sleeping cousin, who was snoring lightly, trying to make it to the bathroom. Once she made it, she noticed her skin smelled of lavender and a touch of sandalwood. While splashing cold water on her face, she tried to remember her dream. She knew it held the secrets to why she found herself staring out the window at the shadowed figure right after waking. The lingering smell and tall figure reminded her of someone.

Nicole finished with her face and decided to take a warm shower. Maybe that would eliminate the strange feeling the forgotten dream gave her.

The strange feeling grew stronger midway through her shower. Nicole wrapped a large terrycloth towel around her and padded her way back to the bedroom. Someone watched her. She knew it. The feeling was different than the ones before. The hair on her arms rose, and tingles went up her spine. Stopping in the hall just feet from her bedroom, with her body wrapped only in a towel, she tried to make out the strange feeling when Amanda emerged from her bedroom and looked at her curiously.

"Everything okay?"

"Yeah, I just have a strange feeling, that's all." Nicole gave herself a mental shake and excused herself to get dressed.

Amanda continued down the hall, wondering how Nicole's dreams turned out. After brushing her teeth, she looked up and stilled herself for what she needed to do in order to find out the answer to her question. She summoned the one being who got under her skin, Phantasos.

To Amanda's complete amusement, Phantasos appeared in dark green drawstring sleep pants, a skintight white t-shirt, and disheveled hair. Until she read his T-shirt and felt her face heat. In bold black letters, it said, *Talk Dirty to Me in Your Dreams.*

"Why did you wake me?" Phantasos sounded irritated.

"I need to know how Nicole's dreams went last night. Were you able to get your brother to heal her?"

"First, try and remember, I, too, am a dream god, and I just got in bed an hour ago. Next, you can call him just as you have me. Last, yes, he visited her dreams, but she will not remember it. It will take several dream healings to help your cousin."

By this time, Amanda's arms were crossed in defense mode.

"You don't have to be an ass about it. I don't know your brother, and I wouldn't summon someone I didn't know to the bathroom with me. You, however, I know won't try anything, so you're harmless."

Phantasos' eyebrows shot up, and Amanda realized she was clad in nothing but black panties and a short t-shirt. She pulled a towel from the cabinet and wrapped herself in it. "Oh shit."

To her complete surprise, and possibly to his own, Phantasos closed in on Amanda and pulled the towel off. He pulled her to him and kissed her much like the last time at the gala—only this time, it wasn't as raw. This time was gentle. Amanda melted and began to return his kiss, then reminded herself of who she was making out with and where. She made herself grab the vanity behind her with both hands and, with great reluctance, pulled away.

"How dare you."

Phantasos laughed, "And you thought you were safe." Then he vanished.

"Asshole!" Amanda shouted and stamped her foot.

"That's not nice," Kallisto said.

"Damn it, Kalli." Amanda squeaked. "What's with you and Phantasos? Stop popping in on me."

Kallisto giggled, then stopped abruptly and spun in a circle, looking around.

"What the hell are you looking for?"

"Your pants. . . Phantasos was here this morning?" Kallisto wiggled her eyebrows.

Amanda rolled her eyes. "I summoned him to ask about Nicole's healing sleep, and then the asshole kissed me when I told him I was not afraid of him."

Kallisto's eyes widened as Amanda continued her tirade, not taking a breath.

"He's a jerk, and Nicole is not healed yet. I don't know what I was expecting. I thought I would wake up this morning with my cousin back to normal. Apparently, it doesn't work that way, and Phantasos is a jerk."

Kallisto started laughing.

"How in the hell is my cousin's mental health funny?"

"It's not your cousin. It's you and your strange relationship with Phantasos." Amanda glared and shook her head while drawing in a deep breath, letting Kallisto know that the subject of the oldest dream god was over.

"I'm just worried about Nicole," *and thanks to Phantasos, a little in need of a cold shower.*

"Phobetor knows what he's doing. He'll help her. She can't be healed of her mental suffering in just one night," Kallisto offered gently, seeing the worry on Amanda's face.

"I suppose, I mean, I know that I had just hoped . . . why are you here?"

"Just wanted to tell you, Mom's going to tell Dad about our . . . divine nature."

"You're kidding? When? Now?"

"No. She's telling him as soon as he gets back from fishing. He left this morning but should be home in three days. I'm going to be there when she does, you know, giving moral support."

"I can't believe it. What do you think he's going to say?"

"Who knows how someone will react to such a revelation? I just hope he doesn't hold it against us."

"What? He loves you, and he would never hold a grudge. He may need a little time to digest the situation, but he'll adjust." Amanda hugged Kallisto. "Let me know how things go, and try not to worry. Now, leave so I can bathe and try to convince my cousin that life in Hawaii is what she needs."

"Thanks, Amanda. Wish us luck."

"Good luck, Kalli," Amanda gave Kallisto a warm smile and another hug before her friend vanished.

"I'll never get used to that," Amanda murmured under her breath.

⟫⟫⟩ ⟨⟨⟨⟪

As soon as Nicole allowed her towel to fall, the feeling of being watched vanished. She couldn't help but feel relieved that whatever was watching seemed to have some form of decency. She got dressed and began to brush out her wet hair. As she looked at herself in the mirror, she remembered the night she got ready for the much-anticipated date with Chase. She meticulously applied her makeup and straightened her hair. She applied lotion on her freshly shaved legs and put perfume behind her ears and on her wrists. She wore her favorite blue jeans—the ones that hugged her bottom perfectly. The jeans the paramedics cut from her limp body, or so her mother told her a few weeks after coming out of the coma.

Remembering those jeans reminded Nicole of the ones she kept in the top of her closet, in a shoebox to hold in their scent. A pair that belonged to the only love she would ever have. Chase had left them at her house one weekend after changing from a day of fun at the Adventuredome Theme Park. The memories brought a smile to her face, something rare for Nicole. She pulled the desk chair over to her closet, climbed up, and stretched to retrieve the shoebox. This was something she had only done two other times, afraid of the day when his scent no longer lingered on the unwashed jeans. Nicole opened the box and immediately smelled Chase. Her smile gave way to a flood of tears.

"I'll take these with me," she cried.

Nicole climbed onto her bed, tears fell on the jeans, as she breathed in Chase's scent, and wished for a different outcome in life. The memories of their last night flooded her as his smell invaded her senses. She lay there only a couple of minutes before she heard her door open. "Nicole? Are you okay?" Amanda walked over to the bed and laid her hand on her cousin's shoulder.

Nicole sat up, rubbed tears from her face, and turned slowly to her cousin.

"Have you ever lost something perfect? Someone perfect?"

Amanda caught the "something/someone" and debated whether they were one and the same. "I . . . well...let's just say that I have been hurt in many ways."

"Do you know what it's like to need, want, and ache for someone who is lost to you?"

"That, I may be able to sympathize with."

"Tell me about it," Nicole requested of her cousin.

"Well," Amanda looked around the room. Nicole followed her cousin's gaze, wondering what she was looking for. "There's this one . . . uh, the person whom I hate, sort of. I hate him because he makes me . . . *want him* . . . or reminds me, rather, of someone I would've enjoyed being around until...well, it's all very complicated."

Nicole laughed. "You make less sense than I do."

"Just trust me, I have been through more than you know, and maybe one day we'll trust each other enough to talk about our problems."

"Well, I lost so much the night Chase died. I will never. . ." she, too, was unwilling to finish. Instead, she wiped her eyes on the jeans and returned them to their box. Little did Amanda know Nicole doing this act in front of her was a sign of trust. She had never allowed anyone to know of the jeans she kept at the top of her closet.

"Nicole," Amanda looked curiously around her cousin's room.

"Hmm."

"I know this isn't something you want to think about, but perhaps we should go down and get breakfast, maybe bring it up here and start going through things you want to take with you."

Nicole was still holding the box with the sacred jeans, "Yeah, I suppose we should." She hugged the box and placed it back into the closet from where it had come.

The girls found only Kellie in the kitchen when they finally made it downstairs. The air was thick with tension, and there were no words spoken between mother and daughter. Amanda, of course, couldn't take the pressure closing in, so she drew on her inner *cheerful Kallisto,* which came from years of weekend sleepovers for the better part of ten years.

"It's such a beautiful sunny day, and the weatherman said the high was supposed to be record-breaking." Nicole glared at her traitorous cousin, and her aunt just smiled and left the kitchen.

"Record highs — since when did you become Miss Cheerful? I remember you as more of a smart-ass."

"Yeah, well, I remember you as nice...so I guess both our memories are failing us at a young age."

"Nope," Nicole grinned, walking from the room with a chocolate chip muffin in her hand. "You're still a smart ass."

Amanda couldn't help but smile as her cousin walked out the door. That had been the closest thing to the real Nicole she had seen since she arrived. Maybe Phobetor's presence had helped her a little last night.

The cousins spent the rest of the morning and into the early afternoon going through Nicole's black attire. "Ya know, Nicole; you could use a shopping trip."

Nicole eyed Amanda, knowing where her words led, but asked anyway. "Why?"

"Well, it looks to me like you're color blind. I thought I could help you with some color."

"I like black."

"Obviously, but you can wear other colors; I promise, black won't get mad."

Nicole glared, "I'm not ready for color." "Amanda?"

"Yeah?" Amanda answered.

"Do you think I'm crazy?"

Amanda stilled at Nicole's unexpected question.

"No. Why would I think that?"

"Everyone else does, and . . ."

Before Amanda could hear the *and*—Nicole's mother called for everyone to come down for a late lunch.

"Can we talk about this after we placate your parents? You really need to try and look at this from their point of view."

"I know they think they are doing the right thing, but I know they aren't."

⇒⇒⇒ ⇐⇐⇐

Phobetor sat on the shores of Italy, thinking about Nicole. The shift in her appearance while in her dream state proved the girl to be a tough mental challenge—mentally scarred, yet strong.

"But that makes no sense."

"What makes no sense?" Phantasos interrupted, again.

"How in Hades did you find me?"

"You've never been very good at masking your presence."

"I guess I should work on that," Phobetor mused.

"Are you going back into the girl's dreams tonight?"

"I thought I could use another good kick in the balls, so yeah."

Phantasos grinned, thinking Nicole must be a lot like her cousin.

"What has you here, in the dark?"

"Just thinking. There's nothing like Italy, well, except for Olympus, and I figured here I would have privacy," Phobetor gave his brother a side-eye.

"As I said, you don't hide your aura well."

"What do you want, Phantasos?"

"Just checking on whether or not you were really going back."

"Would your concern be for Nicole or her cousin?"

"I am concerned for a human girl who may be contemplating suicide."

"Mortals die. You have never shown interest, well. . ." Phobetor knew they were both thinking of Phantasos' dead mortal love, who died by her own hand.

"Just help her." Phantasos vanished, and Phobetor wondered a little about his brother's sanity.

He looked skyward and smiled before flashing to Nicole's street. He stood again by the streetlamp that was now buzzing, trying to come on. He leaned lazily against the lamp with his arms crossed over his chest, waiting for Nicole to look out her window. He knew he should not do this, but Phobetor decided to screw all rules and help this girl the only way possible, and that was not by pulling her consciousness from one realm or state to another, which led to mental uncertainty.

Phantasos did not know the extent of Marissa's mental instability when he repeatedly took her from one realm of consciousness to

another and she deteriorated to the point of suicide. Phobetor did not want to repeat his brother's mistakes and risk Nicole's mental health. So, he decided to go as himself to her in her realm. *The Fates are not stopping me—yet.*

Phobetor stood there knowing he would suffer for what he was about to do, but opposite to what he told his brother, the girl was haunting his every thought, and he had to fix her—and his desire for her.

Chapter V

Control

Nicole and Amanda had finally finished packing her things. Since her goth makeover, Nicole's wardrobe was sparse, but she wanted to take her books, writing pads, and various articles—like the box at the top of her closet. She went through every item in her room, saying goodbye in her own way. She couldn't help but think about the last moments before the wreck.

Chase sat on her bed as she finished getting ready for their date. He watched as she added earrings, the necklace that he had given her, and his promise ring. It was a much-anticipated night, and she wanted it to be perfect. He sat watching her, smiling as she donned his gifts, never speaking, just smiling. She knew he saw the nervous tension as it radiated off her. She, too, could see it in him.

"Hey, Nicole!" Amanda shouted for the fourth time.

"Oh, sorry. I must've zoned out."

"I told my mom I'd drive her to the mall. She doesn't like driving in places she's not used to."

"Why doesn't Mom or Dad take her?"

"They took your little brothers to a birthday party. I think they wanted to give you time to get to know us a little again before heading to Hawaii."

"Well, if you don't mind, I'm not much into the mall scene, so I'll see you when you get back." Nicole's stomach ached at the thought of having to go back to the mall.

"Promise you won't go missing." Amanda held out her pinky finger.

Nicole smiled and wrapped her pinky around her cousin's. "Yeah, I promise."

Nicole looked around her disheveled room. This was the first time her room had been changed since the night she and Chase left for their last date, *their last everything*. That night, everything changed. She felt like she was losing him all over again.

She wrapped her arms around herself as she tried to keep from falling apart and sat on her window seat. Looking out the window, she watched her aunt and cousin back down the driveway and into the street. Amanda looked up at her from the windshield and waved before driving off.

A tear found its way out of Nicole's eye and rolled unchecked down her face. She wasn't bawling her eyes out. The lone tear silently made its way down her face. Feeling someone watching, she wiped the tear from her neck to where it traveled before her interference. She looked over at the flickering streetlamp as it tried to come on. With arms over his chest and propped against the lamppost, was the most jaw dropping man she'd ever seen. For some strange reason, she felt she knew him. She didn't know from where or how, but he was no stranger.

He beckoned with his head for her to come to him, and she realized she was grinning. Not second-guessing herself—she went. First, she stopped by the bathroom and splashed cold water on her face, trying to remove the trace of a single tear. Next, she did something she had not done in a very long time. She fixed her hair as well as she could in two minutes anyway. She squeezed her shaky hands together, wondering what the hell she was doing, as she stood at her front door, about to go outside to meet a random guy leaning against the lamppost.

"Nicole," Phobetor bent his head, bowing slightly.

"Who are you?" she asked.

"Remember, you and I had a glorious exchange last night while you were under the illusion of sleep," Phobetor grinned.

Nicole squinted, thought, and then she glared. "You? You're the dream guy. You . . . no, you can't be. That's impossible. Maybe I've finally gone completely crazy." Looking at the ground, she rubbed her temples.

"You are definitely not crazy, you are . . ." It was Phobetor's time to falter. Nicole raised an eyebrow. "Well, you are in need of someone to show you what life has to offer."

"And you believe you're that person?"

Phobetor grinned, "Well, I am a god."

"You think awful highly of yourself, don't you?"

Phobetor reached out and touched Nicole's hair, turning it back to the milk chocolate it was before she dyed it, and her visible piercings were no longer present. "See? A god." The hallucination grinned.

"Holy shit! How'd you do that?"

"Now Nicole, I happen to know that you are very intelligent, I just told you. I'm a Greek dream god—an Oneiroi."

"You're a Greek dream god?" Nicole felt her face to see if she was awake or had a fever.

Phobetor slowly nodded, then caught Nicole as she fainted. She was beautiful in her peaceful slumber. He laid her on a pillow he manifested on the black sand under a giant palm tree. He smiled and waved his hand over Nicole's eyes and brought her out of her unconscious state.

"Where am I?" Nicole barely spoke, holding her hand to her aching head.

"You, are in Hawaii."

"W-what?"

"You fainted when I turned your hair and skin to their natural state, so I brought you to the first destination on the itinerary."

Still a little rattled, Nicole shook her head, dug her fingertips into the soft black sand, and sat up. She was indeed not in Tennessee.

"I'm certifiable." She blinked rapidly and shook her head.

"No, you're completely sane. Ask your cousin Amanda. She knows about us."

"Us? What do you mean—us? How many "gods" are there?"

"Well, hundreds, haven't you ever studied mythology?"

"Yeah, the mythology of the Greeks, Romans, Vikings...keyword, *mythology*, as in not real—myth."

"Yes, real, see—feel," Phobetor cupped Nicole's face in his warm hand.

᠅

Nicole closed her eyes and took in the smell of lavender, honeysuckle, and sandalwood. Blinking, she came to her senses and began her tirade on the gorgeous "fictional" being sitting before her.

"What the hell have you done to me? Am I under some kind of spell? Who are you?" *This couldn't be happening—again.*

"Again, my name is Phobetor. I've been asked by my brother Phantasos to help you."

"Help me? Help me do what?" Nicole grew more agitated.

Phobetor's grin widened. "Help you know there's more to life."

Nicole stared at Phobetor and nodded her head. "Well, obviously. You said your brother asked you to. . .heal me? Why?"

"Because your cousin, Amanda, asked him to." It hit her then that earlier, he had said Amanda knew.

"What? You're telling me Amanda asked a man to ask his brother, the "dream god," to help me?" Nicole started to stand but was still somewhat unbalanced, so Phobetor held on to her forearm, giving her assistance. She wasn't used to being touched. People had become distant with her new looks and dripping sarcasm. So, she wasn't sure if she liked his touchy-feely manner, but her legs were shaky, and the sand didn't help, so she allowed his support.

"Look, I understand this is new to you, so pretend you're dreaming. Right now, I want to show you something."

"I need to be medicated," again Nicole felt of her face. "Maybe I have a fever."

***

"No, I told you—why are humans so unwilling to believe?" He rolled his eyes and flashed them from the black sandy beach to a rainforest packed with huge, dark green, wide-leafed plants and the sounds of birds all around. The humidity was even thicker than it was in Tennessee, so it took her a minute to adjust.

Sucking in as much air as she could, "Would you stop doing that?"

Phobetor grinned; he thought she was cute when frustrated, now that her hair and eyes were their natural color.

"How am I to show you the world if I don't do . . . that?"

Phobetor's grin just made it worse. Nicole's temper began to spike, and her hair began to darken as it did.

"What are you talking about, and why do you have that grin on your face?"

"I was just admiring how cute you are when agitated."

"Cute?" She huffed, and she went wide-eyed before another ill word came from her lips. She noticed the breathtaking scenery surrounding her.

"Oh, it's . . . beautiful."

"So, you like it here?" he asked.

"Well, what's not to like?"

"Do you realize you are on the island that is to be your home for the next few months? Don't balk at the chance given."

***

As if a cold bucket of water had been thrown in Nicole's face, she jerked her head toward her "captor," and this time, her hair turned back to its dyed state, her eyes once again were circled in dark eye-shadow and liner, and the nose-ring reappeared.

"You brought me here just to make me feel bad for having feelings? For not wanting to leave my home?"

Phobetor looked a little shocked, "No, I brought you here to help you see where you are going is not the hell world you seem to think it will be."

"And you are a god? Well, that goes to show you that, god or not, you're not infallible because you don't know what the hell you're talking about. My world ended a year ago. I don't want to leave him, and I do not want to live with my aunt. I want to be left alone. I never said I thought Hawaii was hell, I was never actually asked what I thought, wanted, or felt. Take me home. Now!"

⇝⇝ ⇜⇜

Phobetor quickly recovered what he thought must have been a per-plexed look on his face. "I thought you . . ."

"Well," Nicole did not allow Phobetor to finish his sentence, "I guess you shouldn't think then because you have no idea what I feel. Take me home."

By her second demand for him to take her home, Nicole's appear-ance went back to its full state of mourning. Without another word, Phobetor wrapped his hand around her wrist and flashed them back to the lamppost in front of her house. Nicole shook her head, trying to clear it, and turned from Phobetor and walked back to her house. He didn't try to stop her—instead, he thought for a moment and flashed himself to her room, where he waited.

"I'm losing my mind. Or maybe I'm dreaming. Yeah . . . that's it, I'm having a nightmare." Nicole mumbled aloud as she made her way upstairs. When she rounded the corner to her room, she heard a car pull into the driveway.

"Surely that's not Amanda back so soon. What the hell!" The god leaning against her bed frame shocked Nicole—again.

"I told you, I. Am. A. Dream god." Phobetor enunciated each word.

"I so need medication," Nicole closed her eyes, trying to clear her head of the illusion.

"No, you need to realize you have no choice." Phobetor's menacing grin was not what Nicole needed to see. She needed to see a doctor.

"I have no choice? Choice in what exactly? Keeping you out of my bedroom? Hawaii?"

"Something like that," Phobetor winked, then vanished.

Nicole sat on her bed, shocked, as she heard her brothers bounding up the stairs.

⤜⤜⤜ ⤛⤛⤛

Phobetor flashed himself back to Greece. He paced his floors, thinking about the last hour with Nicole. It was very rare, almost unheard of, to find a human with Nicole's ability to remember Oneiroi's face from a dream and to control their own dreams, not to the extent she was anyway. She understood she was dreaming and could manipulate her dreams. Where Oneiroi could control anyone's dreams, mortal or immortal, humans with *knowing* talents could only dream-walk in their own dreams, and there, they ruled and were called benders. Phobetor mostly controlled nightmares, either healing the dreamer from their nightmarish effects or giving the dreamer dark, monstrous delusions, whereas his brothers dealt more with happier topics. Morpheus dealt with physical dreams and could control any form of a dream and was the Oneiroi of the gods. Phantasos dealt in fantasy, those crazy, often laughable dreams that made no sense once awake but perfect sense while asleep. Nicole was no god, but a mortal who could override an Oneiroi-controlled dream given to her...potentially anyway, and that was the real reason Phobetor went to her awake. When she started changing her appearance back while in her dream state was the first clue. The second one was her remembering his face, and last—she changed back when she thought she was either dreaming or crazy. None of this should be possible—none.

"I need to speak with Phantasos about this. Hypnos or Morpheus should help her, not me," Phobetor continued to pace.

Chapter VI

Reality

Nicole closed her door before the boys could invade her space. She went to her window seat and tried to calm her racing heart and mind with its revelation of insanity. All she could think was, *wait until Amanda returns, wait until Amanda returns.* After all, the illusion did say Amanda was behind the unwanted visits.

Something kept stirring in the back of her mind. An odd sense of unease, like some strange connection. Flashes of the wreck and afterward, plus a feeling of being watched sporadically, haunted her. Flashes of car lights, Chase screaming her name. . . being held against her will. The scariest nightmares were fuzzy, at best, of a man . . . no, a creature who held her. As a man, he was very tall, supporting a chiseled body with a mane of wavy black hair, eerily beautiful. However, as a monster, he had the head of a lion encircled with a black mane but still with a man's chiseled torso and legs. He roared and paced about her as she screamed and begged for Chase to help. When she finally emerged, she was told Chase would never come for her. He was dead and buried. These were uneasy memories...nightmares? She didn't know, but they caused her as much pain as losing Chase.

Shaking off the troubling thoughts, she decided to do some research and pulled up Google and typed in Phobetor. She searched the deity for nearly two hours, waiting for Amanda. Finally, her cousin entered her room carrying a bag of chocolate chip cookies and another bag with a blue t-shirt sporting the saying, 'I Had My Patience Tested. It Was Negative.'

"Here," Amanda held out both bags to Nicole. "Allow me to add a little color to your wardrobe. It's still in line with your cynicism, so it's a compromise. The cookies are because...well, what girl doesn't need chocolate chip cookies?" Amanda winked.

Nicole sat on her bed when Amanda entered and just stared as she handed her gifts. She could say nothing as her cousin spoke. Still in her hands was the "all-knowing Google" with its search bar holding fast to the name Phobetor. She had learned a whole lot about the recent figment of her imagination. Like he was the god of nightmares and phobias, and she was insane. Now she had the wreck, death, nightmarish memories, and a Greek god on her list of *"Nicole's Insanity Collection."*

"Nicole, are you okay?" Amanda asked, again, since her cousin just stared up at her.

Nicole still said nothing and handed her phone to Amanda to see what she had been up to for the last two hours.

Amanda's eyes grew wide, and she sat on the bed beside Nicole. "I can explain, but you may not believe me."

Nicole raised an eyebrow, "Well, it's better than me letting go of the last string of sanity holding me together. You need to explain."

"Tell me what you know, so I know how to fill in the blanks," Amanda responded, handing Nicole back her phone.

"I have been visited twice by Phobetor, who says he is a Greek god of dreams called an Oneiroi. . . well, he left out he's the god of fucking nightmares. I mean...who wants to admit they've been known to cause fear and madness when they first meet someone." Nicole was pacing the floor, unable to sit still any longer. "He visited me in a dream last night and today outside by the lamppost. There, he gave me an illusion of Hawaii, while telling me we were actually in Hawaii. It felt so real. The sand...did you know you have black beaches? Anyway, I demanded he bring me home, and he then scared me by being in my bedroom when I got upstairs. Yep, that about sums it up. Oh, he said to ask you, since you are the one who asked his brother to have him *dream heal* me. . . now, THAT sums it up."

Amanda's eyes grew wider as Nicole told her strange tale of the day. She was having trouble figuring out how in the hell Nicole knew . . . remembered so much. It took Kallisto months, and she was a demigod, at the time.

"He's correct. I did ask his brother, Phantasos, to help you. Apparently, Phantasos is not capable of healing you as Phobetor can. Why? I don't know. Let me start from the beginning." After all, where else could she start since Nicole was freaking out?

"Kallisto had horrible dreams after her dad went missing. Her mom, who happens to be a god, called on the most powerful Oneiroi, Morpheus, Phobetor's youngest brother, to help with Kallisto's night terrors. After a couple of months, they fell in love. Kallisto almost went crazy because of the realm hopping she and Morpheus were doing, I will explain that later. Ares, the god of war, was asked to spy on Kallisto by his mother, Hera, the wife of Zeus. She had a feeling Kallisto was Zeus' granddaughter. She was correct. Kallisto's mother is the daughter of Zeus and Kallisto's grandmother, Zenovia. They were in love, so Hera threatened Zenovia, and killed her father. Unfortunately, during Ares' spying, he became infatuated with me, so he kidnapped me and Kallisto. Me, because of his infatuation, and Kallisto to stop her from seeing her grandfather or ever going back to Olympus. Morpheus and Phantasos rescued us, and Zeus changed Kallisto from demigod to goddess, just to piss Hera off even more. Well, that sums it up . . . three months in thirty seconds."

Amanda stopped and stared at Nicole, waiting for her to respond or pass out. When she did neither, Amanda let out a breath and asked, for the second time, "Nicole, are you okay?"

"So, Kallisto is a Greek goddess and went to Olympus?" Nicole stopped pacing midway through Amanda's wild summary and stared.

"I just told you the most unrealistic story ever, and what you got out of it was that Kallisto is a goddess and has been to Olympus, and that's it?" Amanda shook her head.

"What do you want me to ask? I must be stuck again. I have to wait until I wake. Until then, I'll just go with it."

"Stuck again? What are you talking about?" It was Amanda's turn not to understand.

"Like I was after the wreck, the week everyone keeps referring to as my time in a coma. I was stuck in, well, I'm not sure. It's all fuzzy. There was a man, or creature, depending on the moment, in the place I was being held. I don't remember that much about it, but I do remember a lot of pain and tears. I will wake up again. This time, I hope I wake up and this whole year was nothing but a nightmare—one BIG nightmare."

"Nicole, I am not sure about you being stuck after the wreck, but you are wide awake now. This is real, all of it, unfortunately." Amanda scooted close to Nicole and grabbed her hand. "Kallisto thought she was in a dream state as well. You have to understand, this is not a dream, nightmare, or fantasy. I know it feels like it and sounds like it, but you're not insane, and you are awake," Amanda pleaded.

Nicole looked away from Amanda, "What else would you say?"

Amanda sighed, unable to convince her cousin she was perfectly sane, well, as sane as any of them were.

"What can I do to help you realize you are sane and not in a dream or coma?"

"Why?" Nicole asked.

"Why, what?"

"Why would I ever believe something so crazy? I mean, I understand dreams and nightmares are not real, and I am able to cope with that reality, but to bring that dream state to real life, I'm not sure there is anything you can do to make me believe I'm not imagining all of this. I am either in a dream state or I must just be crazy."

"Maybe you'll believe Kallisto," Amanda replied.

"Phantasos," Phobetor yelled.

Moments later, Phantasos appeared on the balcony of Phobetor's Grecian home. "What is so important to have you summoning me so loudly?"

"I'm done. I will not help that girl. Hypnos or Morpheus can, but I am done."

Phantasos tried not to roll his eyes, "Why?"

"She has to be a bender and a good one. Plus, there is something there, like she has been raptured by a god before. I cannot explain it. I feel a god's signature, but it is faint." Phobetor resumed his pacing.

"She's a bender? Are you sure?" Phantasos looked at his brother like he was the one insane.

Phobetor stopped his pacing and knocked back an amber liquid about two fingers high, "Of course, I'm sure."

"What happened? And why do you think she has been raptured?"

"Because she was able to control the first dream, even counteracted what I did. Then, I decided to take her, while awake, to Hawaii, which was supposed to be the first stop of an afternoon of adventure. She did not recognize me at first. Of course, she should not be able to. However, after a hint of who I was—she knew. She remembered."

"You did wh...?"

"No, let me finish," Phobetor held up his hand at Phantasos' wide-eyed interruption. "There is no way to keep our existence from her, especially since her cousin already knows, and she *is* a bender. So, I just sped up all the bullshit and went to her awake. Don't lecture me, please."

"Fine, finish your story," Phantasos went and poured himself three fingers of amber liquid.

"Not only does she know she is dreaming and can control them, she can also override what I put in place. She has extensive practice with dream walking and more. I changed her to Nicole before the wreck while awake, too. She changed her appearance back to her mourning state while *awake*, thinking she was dreaming. The only explanation is that she has been rapt by one of us, possibly The Fates. Benders cannot do that shit while awake unless a god has been involved. All I know is, I have no idea how to deal with her."

"Like any human, except she will know we exist."

"How do you heal someone of nightmares if they give themselves the nightmare? How do you heal a person when they control everything? I refuse to go into a dream without the power to control it." Phobetor took another shot of liquid courage.

"Who knows what benders can actually do? I think we need to find out if she was ever taken to another realm prior to you entering her dream or if she has been involved with a god," Phantasos replied. "I will ask for an audience with The Fates, and you will watch over Nicole."

"But. . ." Phobetor started as his brother flashed from the balcony. "Damn it, Phantasos!"

Nicole lay in her bed wide awake and listened to the sounds of her childhood home for the last night before she moved in with her cousin thousands of miles away. She was confused, depressed, and completely at a loss as to why her world was so off balance. It all started with the wreck but continued to spiral out of control. She agreed with her parents that she may not be a hundred percent mentally stable since the wreck, but this was more than that. She had never told anyone about her *coma* experience. She also never spoke of the feelings she had of someone watching her. Now, she was imagining a dream god, flashing to Hawaii at twilight, and the weirdest thing, Amanda was going along with it all, or was she awake for that?

Soft murmurs from her parents and her aunt Kathryn made their way up to her room. She knew the topic of conversation was her.

Amanda's shallow breathing of sleep was background noise, and the streetlamp shined through the window and across the far wall. Yes, this was it, her last night in her home.

Chapter VII

Hawaii

The plane descended into LAX, where they would catch their next flight to Hawaii. Nicole watched as the ground came into view. At least this time, she would board the next plane without her parents' tear-stained faces and her brothers' cries as they watched her go through TSA. Her heart ached, but she refused to cry in front of them. They were making her go, and she refused to give them the satisfaction.

Thankfully, her last night in Tennessee had been without nightmares, dreams, or spying eyes. She woke up rested and ready for the unwelcome journey. Chalking the strange conversation with her cousin up to stress, she decided not to bring up the *god*, afraid the new day would bring a blank look to Amanda's face and possibly a padded room. *There's no way that any of that was real. It was just another one of my episodes.*

"Hey, only five more flight hours to paradise," Amanda grinned.

"That depends on your opinion of paradise," Nicole replied.

"Even you can't hate hot guys playing beach volleyball," Amanda winked.

As the three ladies made their way to their departing terminal, Nicole had that tell-tale feeling of being watched again. Looking around at the passengers she would be spend the next several hours with, she noticed a very handsome man with a thick mane of shoulder-length black hair standing against the wall with his arms and legs crossed casually. He was very tall with a muscled, thick build. She had the strangest feeling she knew him; however, he did not seem to pay her any mind. Not but a few feet down from the familiar man was what looked like a mother and daughter squabbling—that was even more familiar. She continued her gaze, scanning the bored passengers and wondering why they were going to Hawaii. Were they on a long-anticipated vacation, traveling to the island for work, or were they being taken to the Paradise of the Pacific against their will? *Nope*—She would wager she was the only one forced to the land of surf and pineapple. The call to board the plane came as she looked back to see if the mother and daughter were still engaged in their disagreement, and the weird feeling disappeared.

Finally, their trip ended when the three ladies made their way to her aunt's house. Kathryn showed her to her new prison cell, where a soft, full-size bed awaited her tired body. She was too exhausted to be pissed, so she decided to set down her anger—she would pick it up from where she left it—after a very long nap.

⊱⊰

Amanda was glad to be home. She needed a steaming hot shower and a long nap. The last few days were packed with exhausting travel and an emotional rollercoaster. Nicole only spoke a handful of sentences to her and her mother during their trek across the continental U.S. and the Pacific Ocean. She noticed how her cousin constantly scanned the areas surrounding them and wondered if she was contemplating escape. Desperately wishing Nicole would confide in her, she thought up ways to make her loosen up as she busied herself getting her shower ready.

Hot water drifted over her body as she continued trying to figure out her new world. She now had another person to worry over when she herself wasn't fully healed from her time with the god of war. She closed her eyes and tried to erase the memories that constantly forced their way in. The loofah proved to be her armor against her mind. Scrubbing the skin of her arms where Ares grabbed her and her legs where he forced her to kneel, even her face where he forced kisses, and when she refused, he hit her—the first time. How was she supposed to help her cousin when her world was so grim?

Sufficiently scrubbed, Amanda stepped from her shower, trying to decide what she needed the most—sleep or work on getting to the bottom of why Phobetor showed his hand—hell—his whole body. Why would he appear while Nicole was awake, tell her he was a god, and, to top it off—tell Nicole of her involvement?

Yawning, Amanda lay across her bed and drifted to sleep, still wondering what would make a god show himself to a human he didn't know.

⤜⤜⤜ ⤛⤛⤛

A slight spark in the air around Phobetor signaled Nicole slipping into the dream realm. Still unsure how to heal her, he decided, without thinking about it, that he would go to her dream and watch. *As long as I remain unseen, maybe I can gather some insight into her mind.*

Phobetor was not sure what he was expecting, but it was not a dream where Nicole was wearing hospital scrubs and examining a child with a stethoscope. No, this was not what he was expecting. Her hair was still black and purple but placed in a ponytail, her piercings were gone, and she was smiling. Her smile lit her eyes, and he could not help but notice how incredibly stunning she was. *What am I doing, looking at my human charge this way?* At some point, while Phobetor chastised himself, he failed to notice Nicole staring at him. *What in Hades? How? I am invisible.*

He stood there completely transfixed as he watched Nicole stand from her kneeling position in front of the child as the room changed into an abyss, and the child and its mother disappeared. She then started toward him with her hands on her hips, walking on black nothingness, since there was no floor.

"So, am I to never have a private dream again?" Nicole asked.

Phobetor materialized. "How?

"A god of many words, I see."

"You have no idea how unusual you are, do you?" Phobetor looked straight into her eyes.

"Thanks a lot. This coming from my imagination," She scoffed.

Phobetor shook his head. "How many times must you be told? I am not a figment of your imagination."

"Why are you here?"

"I came in hopes of understanding more about you—so I can help you."

He watched as Nicole's hair fell from its tie, and her piercings reappeared. Her scrubs faded into black jeans and a dark gray T-shirt that said, *Bite Me!* in black letters. She looked as mad as she had when she found him in her bedroom.

"I don't need any help."

"Do you know that you are what we call a bender?" Phobetor said. "You know—you are cute when taken off guard."

⟫⟫⟫ ⟪⟪⟪

Nicole was taken aback. She didn't know which was the most startling, Phobetor in her dreams calling her unusual or him calling her cute. *Who calls a girl cute?*

"I'm a what?"

"You are a bender. You can control your dream state, and quite well, I might add."

"Can't everyone?"

With a soft chuckle, Phobetor responded, "No, nothing like what you can do. In fact, I have never met a bender before, and I have only ever heard of them in what you would call–tall tales, myths, fairytales."

Nicole squinted in confusion, "You mean I'm abnormal in my dream state as well as my wake? GREAT!"

"I am saying—you are unique and powerful in your own right." As he spoke, he changed the abyss to the same beach he had taken Nicole to before.

"I see I'm not the only one who can change my dreams."

"Well, yes. I have many abilities in the dream realm. Dream god, remember?"

"Why were you hiding?"

"I wanted to watch you, see what you were like when no one was watching."

"You've been doing that a lot lately?" Nicole glared.

"No. I am not normally one to conceal myself in any realm. I am straightforward."

"I don't mean in my dreams—well—I don't think they're dreams," Nicole said under her breath. "How long have you been watching me?"

"I just arrived moments before you—sensed me—saw me. Whatever you did to know I was there."

"No. I mean, days, weeks, months—perhaps a year or more?"

"Uh—no. I met you for the first time in that first dream where you were on the cliff. Then the next time I brought you to this spot, except then, we traveled here in body . . . physically. Now we are in your dream."

"So, you haven't been spying on me? And what do you mean, we were here and now we are—or I'm—dreaming? Why is it that when you are around, I think and sound like I'm crazy?"

Phobetor grinned, "No, I have not been spying on you. This was the first time I tried—watching you without your knowledge. As for you thinking you are crazy—you are not crazy. You refuse to listen to what I am telling you, and you are trying too hard to make sense of things."

"Then why have I felt your presence off and on for the last year?"

Phobetor's brow shot up. "You have not felt me."

"That's how I knew you were in my dream just now. I felt you as I do when I'm awake. Only in my dream did I not only sense you, but

I thought, *show yourself,* and I saw you. It's the same feeling. I just can't do anything about it when I'm awake."

⋙ ⋘

Clearly, Phobetor was perplexed. He wondered again about his theory of Nicole being rapt before. She was teetering on *realm confusion,* so he questioned her and made her forget before she woke.

"Have you ever had someone watch you in your dream state before?"

"I've had someone watching me while I'm awake. I thought it was you."

Phobetor realized that Nicole had not answered his question, just restated what she said before. He decided not to push it—for now.

"When? When did you feel like someone was watching you?" Phobetor waited as Nicole shifted on her feet, and her eyes wandered the landscape around them. This was odd behavior for a no-nonsense girl. He could sense this line of questioning was bringing her unease.

"Don't worry about it. Forget I said anything."

Before Phobetor could make another comment, Nicole woke.

⋙ ⋘

Breathe Nicole. What is wrong with me? Her palms were sweating, and her head ached. She knew her heart rate would be through the roof if she had taken her pulse. Trying to remember her dream was not proving easy. She remembered catching Phobetor in her dream, and she remembered him changing her scenery, but that was all. *Why am I shaking? What happened?*

Nicole felt a little dizzy and decided to wash away the weird feelings her dream caused with hot, soapy water until a chill traveled up her spine caused by her invisible stalker. The intruder was back.

Fear clutched at her sides. "Who's there?"

In her head, she heard a growl in response, and her fear intensified. "Who's there? Show yourself!" Still nothing.

She looked around the bare room. No sign of anyone or anything. A bed, a chest of drawers, and a full-length mirror were all that sat around her. To her left was a bathroom, also void of adornments. No one there to spy, no one to growl—*Great, looks like my crazy followed me to Hawaii.*

Nicole decided to shower later. She picked her anger back up and took her sullen attitude downstairs to find her aunt or cousin. After all, she needed to see *exactly* where her parents had sent her, and perhaps the company of her family would ward off the growler, even if only temporarily.

Listening for signs of family, she walked the stairs, trying to think of a way to approach this new life she found herself in. All her body and mind wanted was to go to the cemetery and sit by Chase's grave. The more she wanted to go home, the angrier she grew. She rounded a corner, heard voices and dishes clinking around, and walked toward what she bet was the kitchen. There she found her aunt, Kathryn, talking with a beautiful woman with dark brown hair and gorgeous full lips, and her uncle, Alaric.

"Oh, hey, sweetie. I didn't know you were awake." Kathryn acknowledged her niece. "Nicole, this is Thia, Kallisto's mother. Do you remember Amanda talking about Kallisto?"

"Hello, Nicole." Thia held out her hand.

"Hey," responded Nicole. "I didn't mean to interrupt."

"You didn't. We were catching up, waiting for you and Amanda to wake from jetlag."

"How are you, kiddo?" Alaric asked. She had always loved her uncle. He wasn't blood, but you would never know it. He treated her and her brothers just like they were.

All Nicole could think about was the outlandish story Amanda told her before they left Tennessee. Trying hard not to stare at Thia proved almost impossible. It wasn't just her beauty that made you want to stare, but she could not help but wonder about Thia's mortality—or lack thereof. She also noted her feeling of being watched had vanished. *Yep, crazy.*

"Can I get you anything," Kathryn asked.

Nicole didn't want to be nice to anyone—she wanted to scream and throw a fit and make it clear to her aunt what she thought about her generosity. Oddly, she found herself being polite as she watched the blue depths of Thia's eyes sparkle.

"A coke would be great," Nicole tore her eyes from Thia to look at her aunt. When she looked back at Thia, there was a grin on her face.

"Why don't you see if Amanda's up? She's been sleeping long enough," Kathryn handed Nicole a soda.

"I was going to shower first. Unless you need me to wake her right now."

"Sure, she can sleep a little longer."

"Give me a hug, kiddo. I'm heading out of town as soon as I see Amanda. I'll be back in a couple of weeks, though," Alaric said.

Unable to resist, Nicole asked, "Where are you headed to this time? Somewhere fun, I hope."

"South Africa. I'm setting up our headquarters for our three-month watch of the great white shark. I'll be back for a month or so, then back to Africa after graduation."

"That sounds amazing," and she meant it.

"Well, I'm not sure the family feels that way. Our Alaska trip had to be postponed. When you're given a research grant, you take it," Alaric winked at Kathryn.

Phobetor shook off the strange feeling of being forced out of a dream. That was the first time in his existence it had happened to him. No, Nicole was much stronger than he first thought. What was more troubling was her reaction to his questions. She mentioned she felt like someone had been watching her. That could be anyone, mortal or immortal. He needed to find the underlying culprit. If she felt watched all the time, especially while alone in her bedroom, it was most likely an immortal. All the gods had the ability to watch mortals. Many had orbs, which intensified the experience for both parties, the watcher and the watched.

Phobetor needed to speak with his father and see if he had ever heard about some of the weird occurrences surrounding Nicole. He also needed to speak with his brothers. What the Hades had they gotten him into?

Decision made; he went to locate Hypnos. Flashing from Earth to Olympus, he searched for his dad.

Nicole warmed the water before stepping under the spray of the shower. She had to give it to her aunt. The bathroom was beautiful, even without flashy décor. She felt some of the stiffness from the long trip leave her muscles and tried hard to recall her last dream with Phobetor. She failed to recall anything of importance but could remember feeling angry; of course, she always felt angry.

How had her world become so crazy? Her normal dark and brooding attitude was her comfort zone. She knew what to expect from everyone around her since she was in control. But this new world she found herself in was not only abnormal but impossible. There were no such things as gods or invisible stalkers. Of course, the stalker was part of her new world since the wreck and had apparently followed her to her new jail.

Waking Amanda wasn't something she was looking forward to. She had yet to figure out how to approach the strange conversation they had in Tennessee. So, not knowing how to start the rest of her day, Nicole finished her shower and tried to concentrate on one thing at a time. Unpacking, to find something to wear...that would work for about fifteen minutes.

Phantasos made good on his promise to Phobetor. He stood at the Moirai's entrance, waiting for an audience with the three all-knowing sisters. He had not seen them in several weeks. The last time, they delivered the warning that kept him from exploring an intimate relationship with anyone, especially any mortal.

The daemon finally returned and beckoned Phantasos to follow. He was led to a vast room where the three lovely, yet deadly sisters sat, calmly waiting on Phantasos to explain his unexpected visit, which, ironically, they already knew of.

Lachesis, the oldest triplet, sat straight in an armchair with her ebony hair draping over her slim shoulders and was the first to speak.

"To what do we owe the honor of the eldest Oneiroi gracing us with his presence?"

"Honestly, Lachesis, why ask what you already know?" Phantasos grinned.

"We know what you want to say, but often a being, when asked, says something else. We answer what is spoken— if we wish," Lachesis grinned.

"Ah, well, I want to know if dream benders truly exist and if Nicole Wilson, Amanda's cousin, is one. Also, has she ever been rapt to any realm besides the one she lives?"

"Specific questions—someone has learned," Clotho, the youngest of the three, smirked.

"Finally," stated Lachesis.

"The young girl of which you speak is very troubled, no?" Questioned the middle sister, Atropos. Her pale emerald eyes and auburn hair gave her an exotic presence.

"Yes."

"The mortal needs help but warn Phobetor that his methods are unconventional, and we are watching. We are not able to answer your questions, apart from one," Lachesis took the lead.

"I suppose one out of three will have to work."

"Benders are real," answered Clotho.

"Healing her is needed but could come at a price. This road you Oneiroi go down could lead to a deadly end." The Moirai spoke in unison.

That is creepy. "Always a paradox with you ladies. Thank you for what you have given me. I will take my leave.'

"Oh, Phantasos," Lachesis called.

Phantasos stopped and closed his eyes. He didn't want to hear any more warnings about his love life. He was doing all he could to heed their initial warning. Reluctantly he turned and faced the sisters once more.

"Yes?"

"How is Amanda?" Lachesis asked.

"I suppose healing from her abduction," was his only reply.

"You do remember our warning?"

"Yes, I think about it all the time."

"Good—you may leave," the eldest Moirai nodded once.

Phantasos was escorted from the mansion and went to find his brother.

Chapter XIII

Paradise

With all her clothes put away, it was time to face the prison that was Hawaii and, worse, find out how crazy she was. Time to see Amanda. Nicole walked down the hall to Amanda's room to find her cousin already awake and writing in what looked like a journal.

"Hey, think you can show me around," Nicole broke the silence.

Her cousin jumped. "Shit! You startled me. Yeah—sure. What do you want to see?"

"Somewhere quiet and beautiful," Nicole responded. "Somewhere I can be alone to think."

"Beautiful is kinda our thing in Hawaii, and this happens to be a great time of the year to find quiet. Let me change, and we can go to a few places close by."

"By the way, your dad is waiting to say bye. I met Thia earlier. I'm not sure if she's still here." This was Amanda's chance to say something.

"Makes sense then."

"What makes sense?"

"Must be Dad's South Africa trip. The reason you're speaking to me again—Thia must've worked some magic."

Here she goes. Maybe I'm not crazy—or that crazy. "Magic? And yes, to set up camp. Great whites—now that's cool."

"Yes. . . very cool. Thia can read you—literally. If you were projecting attitude or spite, she'd probably calm you."

Under her breath, Nicole thought aloud. "So, it's true."

"Afraid so," Amanda confirmed.

Nicole shook away the unease. "I'll wait for you in my room. Just knock when you're ready." As Nicole walked to her room, she couldn't shake the sick feeling in the pit of her stomach . . . confirmation. Their conversation, in Tennessee, about gods was real. She wasn't sure she was conscious and not dreaming. So, she pinched herself. "Ouch!" *Surely not. Greek gods can't be real.*

Nicole laid back on her bed and stared at the ceiling, trying to think clearly. The last few days and discussions about unbelievable phenomena triggered unwanted thoughts and flashes of memory—headlights, the screeching of tires, and the crunch of metal. Blood everywhere. A large man with thick, raven black hair and chains lined the walls of a dimly lit, damp room. The head of a lion. These visions, or possibly nightmares, were always on the edges of her mind. She tried to keep them at bay—maybe she should just face them. She assured herself that the wreck, and Chase accounted for several of the flashes, but who was the man with black hair, and what was a lion doing in the *visions*? Why were the walls lined in chains? The mind was strange. Instead of protecting her, it worked overtime and conjured scary images—or *memories*.

Her stalker was back. She felt the ominous presence from the top of her head to her toes. *I'm being paranoid.*

"You son of bitch, show yourself or leave me the hell alone," Nicole spoke with confidence she didn't feel.

"Who are you talking to?" Amanda asked from the door.

"Shit!" Nicole jumped from her bed. "I guess you got me back."

"Sorry. Who were you talking to?"

"If I told you . . . you wouldn't believe me. And you'd think I was insane." *Maybe I am.*

"Were you not listening? My best friend and her mother are Greek gods. The god of war abused me, and you think I will think you insane? Come on, give me some credit," Amanda chided.

"I'm still having trouble believing I heard you correctly," Nicole admitted.

"Well, you did. Get used to it. Good lord knows I'm trying to."

Nicole contemplated how to explain what she herself did not understand. "I feel someone watching me. I have since the wreck. You know that hair-raising feeling when someone walks up behind you, and you don't actually see them, but you feel their presence? It's like that, but when I look around, no one is there."

Amanda's eyes widened, and she mistook the enlarged orbs for judgment. "See, I told ya. You think I'm crazy."

"No, I don't. When do you feel this way?"

"It comes and goes. Earlier, I thought I heard a growl. Maybe my parents are right, and I do need more therapy."

"Nicole, I hate to tell you. That's a sign you're being watched by a god or a creature not of this world. I'm no expert, but I think most of them can do it—watch us—that is. Could it be Phobetor?"

"I thought so, but this has been going on for a year. I've weird visions—no—that's not the word. Uh, weird nightmares of some truly strange shit too. The problem is that I'm not always asleep when I have them. Sometimes, the bad dreams are bad daydreams."

"Would you be comfortable talking with Kallisto about this?"

She had trouble talking about this with Amanda. She was in no way ready to discuss her mental instability with a stranger, even if that stranger was—different.

"No, I won't do that. I don't know her. I don't like talking about my coma, Chase, or the wreck with anyone. I feel sick talking to you about this. There's no way I'm ready to talk with anyone else. And I don't want you airing my dirty laundry either. Promise?" Nicole held her pinky finger out to Amanda, waiting for her cousin to enter into their childhood promise ritual.

"Nicole, this could be serious, even dangerous. You need to speak with someone that could actually help you. Kallisto is great. She can help."

"No, Amanda, pinky promise, or I will find my own way back to Tennessee. I'm serious." Nicole's pinky started shaking with anxiety.

"Okay, for now. But you must promise me—if this gets any worse—you'll let me tell Kallisto."

After a long moment of contemplation, Nicole agreed, pinkies were crossed, and another pact was made.

Phobetor did not get a lot of information from his father. Benders were tall-tales for the mythical. All beings had them. Irony at its best. His father knew some mortals could manipulate parts of dreams, but nothing like what Phobetor described to him.

He wondered if Phantasos found anything of merit from the unusual sisters. As it was, the mythology of humans had it wrong. Mortal's fables proclaimed them to be evil crones. In reality, they were beautiful triplets that looked nothing alike but seemed to share one brain, completed each other's sentences, and were all-knowing. One had blonde hair, one auburn, and the last black. All were so magnificent it was hard not to stare...*creepy*.

Most of all, Nicole consumed his thoughts. When he was engaged in other tasks, she still hovered in the back of his mind. She never left. The night he saw her lying asleep in her room in Tennessee, he could not believe how beautiful she was. He enjoyed her snarky attitude and could not wait to see her, even when she did not like him being around. He knew something strange was going on within her. Not because he believed she was a bender but because a strange, heavy feeling surrounded her. If auras existed, he would say she was encased in black, much like himself, but hers was from an outside force, where he was made that way. His came from inside him—the third side of the Oneiroi triangle. Someone had to be the nightmare, the phobia that haunted dreams. He drew the lucky straw.

Shaking the musings from his mind, he decided to see if he could find Phantasos. Fortunately for him, Phantasos had the same idea and appeared beside him.

"Hello, brother. I was on my way to see if you learned anything from the weird sisters," Phobetor grinned.

"Be careful...they may be watching."

"So. What are they going to do? Throw me into darkness? That's where I live. Send Hera or her cronies after me? Well, looks like they are too late for that one too."

"Yeah, well, I am standing here beside you, and I do not relish any of that dark juju getting on me," Phantasos deadpanned. "Did you speak with dear ole' Dad?"

"He has never seen or heard of an actual bender and says he was always under the impression they were myths," Phobetor answered. He went on to explain his last moments with Nicole.

"So, you do believe a god has influenced her mind? Possibly Ares or Hera?" Phantasos asked.

"I do. I have been racking my brain trying to figure out who and why her. If she has felt a watcher around for a year or more, her situation must be a coincidence to Amanda and Kallisto's."

"I agree, even though that is a very strange coincidence."

Phobetor could see his brother stiffen at the mention of Amanda. Curiosity got the better of him.

"What is going on between you and that human, Amanda?" Phobetor just ripped the Band-Aid off.

Phantasos' eyes narrowed at the question. "Not a damn thing. Nor will there ever be anything going on between us. Never ask again."

A mischievous grin spread across Phobetor's face. "Don't be like that, brother."

A middle finger was the only response Phantasos gave him in reply. "Do you want to know what The Fates *riddled*?"

"What did the creepy three have to say?"

"Benders are real, but they would not confirm if Nicole was one nor if she had ever been raptured to another realm. The Fates also confirmed she really needs healing, but for us to be aware that the road we walk could lead to death. Whose death, they did not say."

"And here I thought I was the sick and twisted god on Olympus," Phobetor responded to his brother's message. "Not all gods have the ability to take a human physically, but many have the ability to rapture a mortal mentally. Let us hope this being we think is watching her is not very strong."

"I have no idea, but we need to get to the bottom of this before someone gets hurt. If Nicole has a god following her, she and all around her could be in danger."

Phobetor briefly saw concern etched across Phantasos' eyes. He knew his brother remembered Amanda's battered body and Kallisto lying on the cold ground being tortured. None of them would be ready to face the wicked obsession of another god so soon, but it looked like they had no choice.

"I will watch over Nicole and try to pry more information from her. Can you deliver the information to Morpheus? We need his and possibly Kallisto's help to watch over Amanda and her family," Again, Phobetor watched his brother flinch at Amanda's name. Yes, he needed to know what was up with his oldest sibling.

⟫⟫⟫ ⟪⟪⟪

After Amanda said her goodbyes to her dad, they hopped in Amanda's car to see some quiet places, as Nicole had suggested. Silence emanated from the car. The radio wasn't even playing. Nicole watched the palm trees and wide-leafed plants race by her window as she committed the landmarks to memory. She wouldn't allow the *jail* walls to contain her for long. The only reason she wasn't already by herself was her lack of knowledge. She knew nothing about Maui.

The car pulled into one of the four parking spaces by the road. A sign showing the layout of trails with markers for waterfalls. Still silent, Nicole followed Amanda from the car to the mouth of the trails.

Finally, Amanda broke the thick silence. "This is where Kalli and I go when we need time to unwind from our everyday lives."

Nicole remained quiet and followed as she contemplated how her life had gotten to this point. She wasn't unfazed by the land's beauty.

In fact, she appreciated it, but showing that pleasure would give Amanda the wrong idea. Her cousin would think she was softening to her new life. No way was she going to give any of her family that satisfaction. This new life was only hours old, and no matter how beautiful the landscape, the feeling of betrayal was still a heavyweight in her chest.

After twenty minutes of walking and a little climbing, the girls found themselves at the sanctuary. Nicole tried holding in her awe, but it was futile. Amanda had led her to paradise. Rock cliffs with green vines and giant wide-leaved plants covering the cliff's boulders surrounded a blue pool of water fed by three waterfalls. Birds sang, and the air smelled clean.

Amanda kicked off her shoes and waded knee-deep in the oasis. Nicole followed suit. Cool water assailed her senses.

"Nice?" Amanda asked.

Before she could stop herself, she agreed. "Very."

Calm enveloped Nicole, and she finally felt an ounce of peace, which lasted all of ten minutes before the all-consuming feeling hit her like a wave. Someone was watching—again. The feeling was inky and dark. Clutching her chest, she scrambled from the pool.

⟫⟫⟫ ⟪⟪⟪

"Nicole! What's wrong?"

"Nothing. I'm fine," Nicole barely responded with a voice of terror as she stumbled her way from the pool to a grassy area.

Amanda knew that was a lie. As she watched her cousin fight for breath and composure, she couldn't decide what to do—until all the blood drained from Nicole's face, and she started shaking. Then her eyes rolled to the back of her head, and she hit the ground; Amanda had no choice. She yelled for help.

"Phantasos!"

It only took moments when not only the god she loathed but another appeared, and Amanda pointed to her cousin in hopes the unspoken gesture conveyed her worry. The other god had to be Phobetor. He had a similar appearance to his brothers, except with dark brown hair and the most unusual eyes of the three—liquid gold. Amanda could only stare at the god as he noticed Nicole's distress, and his eyes of gold turned raven black.

"What happened," the deep voice of Phobetor broke the silence.

It took only three strides for the exceptionally tall god to clear the distance to Nicole.

⤜⟩⟩⟩ ⟨⟨⟨⤛

Phobetor was not prepared for what he saw. Nicole was in obvious pain as she writhed on the ground.

"Nicole?" He wrapped protective arms around her. He was not ready for the feelings her pain released in him.

"I'm okay—I'm okay," Nicole repeated on a loop as tremors racked her body.

Checking her eyes, he saw fear. Raw fear. An emotion he had an unusual, intimate relationship with. He was the god of fear and nightmares. He could taste her panic. *Something more than grief has ahold of her.*

Time crawled as he waited for her to come back to them. During that time, all he saw was black. Rage was not a foreign concept to Phobetor. However, this was the first and only time in five millennia he felt rage over a woman's fear.

Rapid gasps turned to even breaths as she relaxed into Phobetor's chest, and her shaking subsided. It was a testament to how frightened Nicole was that she had recovered and not pushed him away.

"What happened?" Phobetor directed his question to Amanda.

"We were wading in the pool, enjoying the waterfall, when she just freaked the hell out."

Nicole slowly removed herself from Phobetor's hold and wiped her eyes.

"I'm fine. I just—" Nicole broke off whatever she was about to say.

"You just—what?" Phobetor's question came out a little sharper than he meant for it too.

"I'm fine," Nicole repeated firmly.

"No, you are not. You are anything but fine. You were shaking and with a look of fear in your eyes. What happened?"

He meant for his words to come out powerful. However, they came out demanding. He could tell by her wide eyes that she was stunned by his tone. It was not a voice to be answered with defiance—it was the voice of a god.

"I—I felt the presence. That feeling of someone watching me. This time, it was different. It was foul and grim—dark. I could smell decay and taste my own grief."

"Did you feel any presence?" Phobetor directed his question to his brother.

"No," Phantasos answered.

"Me either. Who or whatever it was, it sensed us or knew we would come."

"I am taking Nicole with me," Phobetor announced.

Amanda took a step toward him. "No, you're not."

"I will not leave her here and wait for another call."

"I told you I'm okay. It was just different *but familiar.*"

Phobetor heard the "but familiar" comment Nicole said under her breath but did not comment, storing the information.

"Fine. Phantasos and I will walk with you back to your vehicle."

Phantasos and Amanda both protested at Phobetor's compromise, but with one look at the god's black swirling eyes, they both accepted not even the eldest Oneiroi would mess with Phobetor when his eyes were black as night.

Chapter IX

Bender

THIS WAS NOT WHAT Nicole had in mind. She wanted a peaceful day to learn of a relaxing place to escape when she needed time alone. Instead, she freaked out for a few minutes and landed herself in what must be another dream. No way two Greek gods were going to escort her and Amanda back to the road. *I'm certifiably nuts.*

After she and Amanda donned their shoes and Phobetor made introductions, the unusual group started their ascent to the road. They were only five minutes into their walk, and the atmosphere swelled with tension. Strangely, the tension was coming from everyone except her. The hold her imaginary stalker had on her was gone, for the moment anyway.

Her cousin was quiet, unlike her usual snarky behavior. In fact, Amanda looked more miserable than Nicole felt. Anytime the pathway allowed easy walking without the use of her arms, she would wrap them protectively over her chest. Amanda was not behaving like the cousin she knew and loved.

Phobetor seemed pissed. His eyes continued to swirl black instead of gold, and the look made him both intimidating and kind of sexy. *Did I just think Phobetor was sexy? Yep, I'm dreaming.*

His brother, Phantasos, she thought that was his name, had a snarl on his face. *Why is he pissed? He doesn't even know me?*

Nicole left Phobetor's side and jogged the short distance to her cousin. "What's wrong with you?"

"Nothing."

"Well, *nothing* is not what your body language is saying."

"Just drop it," Amanda replied.

Not wanting an argument in front of the *gods*, Nicole returned to Phobetor's side to drill him with questions. She needed answers. The first of which was how and why two deities found themselves in the middle of Maui with her and Amanda.

"Why are you here?"

"I thought it was obvious." He raised one brow. Nicole could not help but stare at that brow. When he did that, her heart skipped a beat. "To walk you and your cousin to the car."

"No, why are you here," Nicole gestured around her.

"Amanda called on Phantasos because you were having a—spell."

"Wait, she called Phantasos, and I woke—or whatever I did—to you holding my trembling body? Something is off there."

"He and I were together when he got the call. I am sure she would have called me had she known me. She must have been truly scared to call for Phantasos."

"Why?"

"My ἔξυπνος ομορφιά, you are not seeing with your eyes?"

Nicole followed his eyes to her cousin as she stomped through the brush on the trail, murmuring to herself. Further ahead of Amanda, she saw Phantasos looking as if he could tear the world apart.

"Do they hate each other?"

"There is a fine line between hate and—well—not hate."

"Do all you gods speak so strange?"

"What do you mean? I know I have an accent, but I would not call it strange." Phobetor looked slightly offended.

"You never use contractions, and you speak in riddles. Also, you called me something in Greek. What was it?'"

"If you mean mortals bad habit of combining two words to make one word, then no, we do not. Riddles? If you think I speak in riddles, you should hear an oracle or one of The Fates. They speak in riddles."

"And the Greek name-calling?"

"It means clever beauty," Phobetor smirked.

Nicole felt her face heat. She bit the inside of her cheek and looked at the foliage they passed instead of him, trying to squelch her embarrassment. *He called me a beauty. A smart beauty. Damn.* "Back to my cousin. What's going on?"

"I am not sure what has happened between those two," Phobetor nodded toward Amanda and Phantasos. "However, I do know that someday, all their issues will come to the surface, and I hope to Zeus everyone knows how to swim."

Nicole felt like she'd just walked into the Twilight Zone. A place where no one fully answered her questions, Greek dream gods were real, and she lived in Hawaii—and was stalked by hell knows what.

"Interesting. Now, what the hell is wrong with me?"

⊷⟩⟩⟩ ⟨⟨⟨⊷

Phobetor stopped on the trail and thought for a second before daring to answer Nicole's question. Nothing was wrong with her; however, there was something different about her. How do you tell a human woman she is the most magnificent being you have ever encountered, but she also has a shit ton of baggage? One of those bags happened to be another deity or creature snooping around.

"There is nothing wrong with you. You do have a flare for the dramatic—" he looked Nicole up and down, taking in pale skin, raven black and purple hair, dark eyes, and lavishly painted full lips that held—*promise*. He shook his head, mentally scolding himself.

"Well, thanks for lying," Nicole said dryly. She had stopped in front of him but now turned to walk away.

He grabbed her arm before she took a step. "I am not lying. I do not lie, even when, maybe I should."

"Then tell me what the fuck is going on," Nicole's shock from the stalker episode was completely gone, and back was the girl he had come to know.

"We are not sure. I have guesses, which just led me to more questions. All I know for sure is that you are a bender. You can control your own dreams like my brothers and I can control the dreams of others. Benders are myths—*were* myths. Looks like you have proven another being exists. Myths are real," he winked.

"What is so damn special about me being able to control my own dreams? Doesn't sound like some great feat," Nicole shook her head.

"Well, there are a lot of myths, but since I nor my family have ever come across a bender, I am not hundred percent sure all the abilities you have."

"Give me the ancient tome version in a modern cliff notes break-down."

"I have no idea what a cliff note is, but I will tell you what the myths tell of benders."

"We have just a few minutes left on this magnificent journey to the car—spill it."

"Benders started out as mythological tormentors of the Oneiroi. They were our scary bedtime stories. Stories the gods told us so that we did not misbehave as children. According to the mythos, dream walking could become deadly if we were to land in the dream of a bender. The bender wielded the control, exceeding the Oneiroi's power. They could trap us or turn our powers around on us. As we got older, the Bender stories were more of a way to make us train to be better and stronger. However, after thousands of years, we never ran into one, so your kind became a myth."

Phobetor had to smile at Nicole's gaping mouth. He thought she looked adorable when she was caught off guard.

"Seems I have surprised you with the truth."

"So, you think I'm one of these mythological beings that can kill a dream god? I have got to get more sleep."

He watched her think. Her eyebrows drew together, and she slowly shook her head. As he watched her absorb the truth of his words, he thought about her face when he materialized beside the waterfall. He decided in that second, he would not allow her out of his or a god he trusted sight—ever again. The deity leaving when they materialized was a good reason to press her not to be alone. The way she shook in the shallow, cool water below the falls. Her eyes rolled in the back of her head. Seeing her like that broke something in him. He did not know her well but felt like he had known her for centuries. Phobetor could not help it. His protection senses were riding high.

"The most important thing is that we find out what is causing you to have those episodes. It seems when you have a god around, the stalking ceases. One of us will have to monitor you—all day—every day."

"What? No damn way is there going to be a god with me all the time. No. No. No." Nicole's voice rose with every no.

With that loud denial of protection, Amanda spun around.

"What's wrong?"

"Your perpetually pissed off god's brother here," Nicole pointed to Phobetor, "has just informed me that a god will need to be with me at all times."

"He's not my anything," Amanda snapped. "Why does she need a god around all the time?"

"Because the stalking seems to stop when one of us is around," Phobetor answered.

"I guess we'll have to tell Kallisto—unless you want one or both of these two watching you twenty-four-seven."

"Screw you, Amanda. I refuse to be coddled. I won't be *watched* 24/7 by anyone, especially these two."

"You may not have a choice," Amanda replied.

⟫⟫⟫ ⟪⟪⟪

Tired from the hike and strangeness of the afternoon, Nicole dismissed herself, climbed into the passenger seat, and waited on her cousin. She watched as Amanda argued with the gods wishing she could read lips.

"Damn bossy Greek assholes," Amanda said under her breath as she seated herself behind the steering wheel.

"What was that all about?"

"Nothing. I mean, why are men such asses? They don't want you but think they can dictate your life."

"Amanda, are you actually asking me or just ranting?"

"Ranting."

"Well, I assume you are talking about Phantasos. He's totally into you."

Amanda glared as she put the car in drive and headed home.

Chapter X

Fear

The next several days went by in a flash. Unable to convince the gods she didn't need them to hang around all the time, Nicole allowed Amanda to tell Kallisto everything—well, all they knew anyway. She did have to admit no weird ass episodes had plagued her since the falls. The biggest stressor in Nicole's daily life was high school. Yep, she was as much of a pariah in Hawaii as she was in Tennessee. The only difference is that these kids didn't know that she was sweet and innocent not too long ago, with dreams of becoming a doctor. She walked the halls alone, except for the constant—god lurking.

"Nicole, right?"

Nicole looked up from her cell phone to the eyes of a nice-looking boy. He was dark with brown eyes and a grin holding straight white teeth.

"Yeah, who's asking?"

The boy smirked. "My name is Pika. We have a couple of classes together."

"And?" Nicole sounded bored.

"You don't make this easy on a guy, do you?"

"Make what easy?"

"Getting to know you." The boy was still smirking.

"Why would you want to know me? I'm not a very exciting subject."

"Wow, someone has really done a number on you."

"What do you mean?"

"I mean—I haven't seen you with anyone but a few senior girls in the afternoon. I never see you talking to anyone. Plus, when someone offers an olive branch, well—you're brash."

"I'm here against my will. I see no need in making friends when I plan on going home soon."

"Well, Nicole, it was nice to meet you, I guess. If you decide you want to talk to someone, I'm always around."

Nicole watched the boy walk away, feeling a pang of regret for being such an ice queen when he was only trying to be nice. But she didn't want *nice*. She wanted to be left alone, which didn't fit into the hovering god's agenda. *I'm at school. You can let up, you know.* She had no idea if the deity could hear her thoughts.

Her next class was an elective and one of only two left since she came into the semester late—creative writing or physical education. Creative writing it was. Kallisto and Amanda were both in the class. Kallisto loved to write; Amanda, well, she loved to talk to Kallisto.

"Hey, Nicole," Kallisto said.

"Hey." Nicole dropped into the seat behind Amanda and across from the goddess herself. She tolerated Kallisto as she did everyone else. They were people placed in her life because her parents decided to send her away. No need to forge friendships. Once her parents decided to let her go home, she would be leaving.

She noticed the watcher was gone. Phobetor must have decided there was no need to continue watching since Kallisto was with her.

"I saw you talking with the junior boy in the hall; what's his name?" Amanda grinned at her.

"I don't remember it," Nichole shrugged.

"You aren't going to make friends if you can't remember their names," Amanda joked.

"I don't plan on making friends."

Before Amanda could respond, the teacher entered and wrote their assignment on the board and discussed the difference between first and third-person POV.

A few minutes into class, Nicole asked the teacher if she could go to the restroom. Alone at last, Nicole decided to make a side trip outside to the gazebo instead. She sat listening to the birds and watching the palm trees blow in the slight breeze. She needed a few minutes to think about her new life and remember her old one. She needed to think about Chase. Slowly the images of her time with him came vividly to her mind. She could swear she smelled his one-of-a-kind scent in the breeze. As she reminisced about the last night they were together, a tear fell unchecked from her eye to her lap.

One minute, she was deep in thought, and the next, she was hearing his voice. Not Chase's—*his* voice.

"Does it hurt?" the voice asked.

Nicole could hear the excitement in the unembodied voice, which echoed as if it was far away. Nicole tried to ignore the voice, but her shivers and goose flesh gave her away.

"I asked you a question. Answer me!" The voice was becoming clearer and more demanding.

"Yes, it hurts," Nicole whispered in reply.

"Good. Let me feel your pain, Nicole. Give me your fear."

The voice continued to taunt her and ask for more. It wanted to enjoy her agony. Her eyes rolled to the back of her head where she saw him. The thick mane of hair surrounded a masculine face and catlike green eyes; damn— he was huge.

Nicole rubbed at her wrists as she shook.

"That's it. Remember the pain? The pain of losing Chase, losing your memories, losing your sanity. Remember how it felt to be with me?"

"No, please, no," Amanda begged. "I don't want to remember anything except for Chase."

"You know better than that little girl. You know you must feel it all. I need you to remember the pain."

"No! I said leave me alone!"

A deep laugh reverberated from the maned man. He was unquestionably frightening, eerily gorgeous, and oddly familiar.

Nicole came to lying on the floor of the gazebo with tear-streaked cheeks. Morpheus watched as she shakingly wiped her cheeks, trying to remove the signs of her tears. Shock displayed across her face when she noticed him.

"You're Morpheus," her acknowledgment sounded painful, almost scared.

"I am."

"Please don't tell Amanda."

Morpheus tilted his head at her plea. "She and Kallisto are the ones who sent me looking for you. You have been gone the whole class period."

"Seriously? I just walked out here a few moments ago."

"Well, if a moment is over an hour, then yes. When I found you out here, you were—what is the word—seizing."

"I had a seizure, and you didn't call the ambulance? I've never had a seizure. I'm so tired," Nicole fought to keep her eyelids raised.

"It was not a normal seizure, as you would call it. You were fighting what we call a rapture. Before you ask, that is when a god takes you somewhere besides your realm."

Nicole took several steps back with fear on her face as she asked the beautiful god standing before her, "You tried to take me? Why?"

"No, I found you here. When I saw you lying on the floor, the presence left."

"Presence, what presence? Someone else tried to take me?"

"A god or otherworldly creature with the power to rapt a mortal left when I presented myself."

"A god or—thing—was here—with me?" Nicole's voice shook.

"Not physically, no."

"I don't understand."

"It is like when you feel one of our presences but cannot see us. We are there but not physically present in this realm."

"How did you find me?"

"I work with one of the history teachers on a project. Anyway, Kallisto called for me through our bond, and I immediately began looking for you. After thoroughly searching the restrooms, I came outside and felt the presence."

Nicole rubbed her head, "Well, Amanda trusts you, and you definitely sound like the other two that are always hanging about."

Morpheus smiled as he watched the mortal. She was still shaking, and he knew she was trying to be brave, but the otherworldly presence still weighed heavy on her mind; he could feel the thrum of energy radiating from her. She reminded him of Amanda. Same eyes and steely resolve.

"Well, I am sorry we have not had the chance to get to know one another. It is my understanding that my brother, Phobetor, has been healing you."

Her eyes darkened at the mention of his brother. Morpheus was not sure if it was out of contempt or something else.

"I guess—he and Amanda won't allow me out of the presence of a—" Nicole waved her hand at him, "—god or whatever you guys are."

"The ladies are worried about you. So is my brother. He, too, was unable to find you. Do you have these episodes often?"

"After the wreck, I had a couple of anxiety attacks that left me weak but not seizing. I've had a few weird events since I've been in Hawaii."

"Do you remember anything from them?"

"Fear. I remember fear."

Morpheus could tell she was not being a hundred percent truthful. She was definitely leaving something out.

"You, Nicole, are a remarkably interesting mortal. My brother believes you are the embodiment of our Legend of the Bender, and you were fighting rapture in the gazebo. Mortals never fight rapture."

"You're talking nonsense. This is all just so damn messed up."

"Come on. We need to get you back to class."

"How will I explain this to my teachers? That's all I need is to get in trouble here, too. There's no telling where my parents will send me next."

"Leave that to me."

Chapter XI

Solution

"Morpheus wouldn't tell me what happened with you earlier today. Why?" Amanda started her interrogation of Nicole as soon as they got in her car.

"I guess he figured you could ask me yourself."

"Well, I'm asking. What happened to you? Where did you go for so long?"

"I needed some time alone, so I went out to the gazebo on campus and enjoyed listening to the birds and feeling the breeze."

"Why do I sense you aren't telling me the whole truth."

"Probably because I'm not," Nicole admitted as she stared out her window in deep thought.

"Nicole!"

"Shit, you don't have to yell."

"I guess I do since I've been calling your name for the last two miles."

"Sorry."

"Are you going to elaborate on what really happened," Amanda's concern was morphing into irritation.

"Apparently, I had a type of rapture seizure."

"A what?"

"Morpheus found me in one of my spells at the gazebo. He said there was a presence trying to take me to a different *realm*. If you believe in that sort of thing. I'm pretty sure this is all a long, very elaborate dream. Shit, maybe I'm still in a coma."

Amanda was at a loss as to what to do. She could feel the god watching them and wondered why he hadn't stopped this presence from messing with Nicole.

"What good are the gods if they aren't keeping you safe?"

"It's not his fault. I was with Kallisto during class. Apparently, everyone raised the red flag when I didn't come back from the restroom. Besides, Phobetor doesn't watch me all day during classes since Kallisto and Morpheus are there. I guess he never thought I would venture outside for some alone time."

Amanda noticed Nicole's immediate defense of Phobetor and found that fact very interesting since she wasn't one to defend a person she could blame. "I guess you won yourself a forever watcher after today," Amanda smirked.

"That's just ridiculous."

"How can you say that when you were literally seizing a couple hours ago? Some weird shit is happening, and after Christmas break, I don't put anything past the gods."

"Then why are you allowing them to follow me around?"

"Because not all of them are bad. The Oneiroi and many others are good, mostly."

Amanda could see Nicole's brows rise from her periphery.

"Even Phantasos?"

"For keeping you safe? Yes." Amanda admitted. "Can you remember anything?"

"I was afraid. Very afraid. That's all," Nicole spoke with finality.

Amanda let Nicole return to her brooding as she thought about what happened. She didn't care that there were two gods at the school. She wanted Nicole watched at all times. Amanda knew the depths of depravity a god would go to in order to get their way, and it seemed someone or something wanted something from her cousin.

Bounding up the stairs, Nicole ignored Amanda's fuming over her escape from the gods' supervision. She wasn't a kid, and she was getting damn tired of being coddled like one. She needed to go home—now.

"Hey, Mom," was all Nicole could say. She surprised herself—not actually meaning to call her parents. Hearing her mother's voice on the other side of her cell phone shook her.

"Nicole! It's so good to finally hear your voice. How are you, sweetie?" Kellie asked.

"When can I come home?"

"Hun, you know you're there until the school year ends. We discussed this."

"I want to come home now. I hate it here."

"Give it some time."

"I want to come home," Nicole's tough exterior cracked, and so did her voice. Her eyes burned with unshed tears.

"I'm so sorry, Nikki."

Nikki was the nickname she hadn't heard since leaving the hospital. Her mother used her full name once she donned her new wardrobe and piercings. When she was especially upset with her, she used her first and last name, which was more often than not. The nickname wrenched her heart and brought her too close to her past.

"I gotta go. Tell the boys I said *hey*."

Nicole stared at the cell in her hand after she hung up. What she hadn't admitted to her cousin or the youngest Oneiroi in the gazebo was that she was extremely terrified. The monster of her nightmares, the one that lurked in her proverbial closet and in the dark recesses of her mind, was back.

She mustered up the nerve to write what she remembered down in her creative writing notebook, hoping that if someone were to read it, they'd think it was a class assignment. Unfortunately, all she could vividly recall was the paralyzing fear of a large man with thick black hair and a roaring voice, one that resounded off the walls. Nicole concentrated hard on remembering—something—anything. She zoned out and started to remember a darker place with a steel table and metal shackles splayed across the walls. The unclear masculine voice demanded—*something*—*what did he want?* Breaking out of her self-imposed trance, she heard Amanda asking to come in.

"It's unlocked."

"Could you come downstairs for a few minutes?"

"Dinner ready?"

Amanda didn't reply, and as Nicole rounded the last staircase, she saw why.

"What the fuck?" Nicole went ridged when she took in the sight of not one, but four self-proclaimed deities and her cousin just a couple steps in front of her.

"Look," Amanda raised her hand in an apologetic gesture, "we are trying to keep you safe. I couldn't stand for something to happen to you."

"Why is everyone here?"

"We have been trying to figure out what is going on with you," Phobetor interjected.

"Behind my back? Then suddenly, you thought, hey wait, maybe we should include the one who needs help?" Nicole snarked.

"No, it's not like that," Amanda said.

With her arms crossed over her chest, Nicole glared at the group who were staring back. "So, tell me what you *all mighty ones* have decided about my fate?"

"We," Phobetor pointed between himself and his brothers, "are trying to figure out who or what is trying to rapture you. This is a big deal. There are a lot of issues with you being a bender and being raptured against your will."

"What do you mean?"

"When a god or goddess raptures a mortal, they take them to another realm. You have probably only heard of a mortal's final rapture. Same premise of taking, but not for good, and you are not dead. You are actually taken to another realm for a small amount of time, usually. Some gods and creatures can only do this by taking you mentally, and others—they can take you physically," Phobetor explained.

"Why am I different," Nicole asked as her stance became less tense and more questioning.

Nicole noticed Phobetor look toward his brothers before he answered. "Mortals do not fight rapture. They cannot. However, you did twice that we have seen. We think it has something to do with you being a bender."

"I'm not this bender you keep referring to. Stop placing me in a separate category than mortal, human, girl, teenager, hell, I'll even take bitch—but stop making it sound like I'm not a person."

"They are saying it wrong," Kallisto glared at the Oneiroi and they had the sense to look sheepish.

"Then you explain it," Nicole suggested, arms crossed.

"A bender is a human—a mortal. They, pointing to the brothers, separate bender and mortal out of awe. You are to them as they are to you—a myth made flesh. To us, you are a person with special abilities. One who fights to control her dreams. Not mythical, just extra unique."

"Well, to me, you're my bratty younger cousin," Amanda winked.

That almost got a smile out of Nicole, but she held strong, not wanting the group to see they were breaking through her armor.

"So, what are you wanting from me?"

"We need you to understand why we cannot let you out of our sight," Kallisto interjected. "We ask that you let us know when you need alone time so we will be prepared. We need you to cooperate with us."

"If you are taken, there is a very slim chance we will find you. There are many realms a god or creature can take you. If the being can only take you mentally, and they decide to keep you—your body would be unresponsive. You would be warm to the touch, but your mind would not be there. Your mind would undergo whatever hell the deity or creature decided to inflict upon you—possibly, forever," Phantasos explained.

"This situation can be, at minimal, dangerous, and, at max, deadly," Morpheus added.

Nicole looked at each being before her. Her gaze landed on Phobetor. He looked upset. Uneasy. She couldn't decide whether it was anger or regret. Whichever it was, she could tell he wasn't happy. His eyes were black as night, and his jaw clenched as his brothers spoke.

With a sigh of defeat, Nicole said, "Fine, but the first god that goes in the bathroom with me gets bitch slapped.

Chapter XII

Maddened

Phobetor waited. Kallisto was with Amanda and Nicole, so technically, he was off duty for the evening. He should work to find out more about benders or put together a list of gods and creatures that are known to have rapt mortals. Instead, he waited for Nicole to walk into her bedroom. He was pissed that she placed herself in danger. Which in itself was not unusual, but this was different. She purposefully went out by herself to have *alone* time. If she had been taken he would never know what happened to her, and for some reason, that realization set his blood on fire. The thought of her taken or gods know what, to who knows where made him shake with a rage he had never experienced. Staying seated tonight while everyone was present proved to be a lesson in self-control. Nicole's lack of understanding of the danger she placed herself in made him want to shake her. Truth was, he was pissed at himself for trusting her to stay in the school building. Now he knew he should have stayed with her all day, no matter what. He will make sure she is watched at all moments, wherever she goes, even the damn bathroom.

"About time." Phobetor walked behind Nicole after she had taken a few steps inside her bedroom.

"Shit!" Nicole jumped, clutching the front of her shirt. "What are you doing in my room?"

"I have decided that I am on duty tonight. I plan on being with you at all times unless Kallisto or Morpheus is with you."

"Kallisto is right down the hall painting her fingernails with Amanda. I believe I'm okay."

"How do I know you will not sneak out to have some *alone* time?"

"So, that's what this is. You don't trust me?"

"Why should I after the stunt you pulled at school? You could be missing right now! If that being has the power to physically rapt you, you could be gone." Phobetor growled. He knew he was being a little irrational, but damn, he could not control his temper, as he made the lights flicker.

"Why the hell do you care? You barely know me. Surely you have better things to do than babysit a mortal."

"Why do I care?"

⋙ ⋘

The glare of anger in his swirling black eyes made Nicole retreat from the god. He stalked toward her, not answering her question, just glaring as he matched each of her steps. When Nicole bumped into the wall, fear ran up her spine as Phobetor continued approaching her with those onyx eyes blazing. He lunged for her, grabbed her wrists in his hands, pulled them above her head, and pinned them to the wall. His hands were hot, burning with fury that matched the ferocity swirling in his eyes.

With what could only be called a snarl, Phobetor said, "Why do you think?" as he pressed his mouth to hers.

Shock rocked through Nicole, followed by desire. Before she knew what she was doing, she kissed him back. Not a gentle kiss, but one fierce with passion, penetrating her shield of anger. He never released her hands, even when he pulled from her lips and placed his forehead on hers. They stood there with her hands pinned beneath his, ragged breaths coming from them both, and if she didn't know better, the air was crackling with electricity.

"For some reason, I cannot allow anything to happen to you. I refuse. I am not the god you think I am. I insight fear, anger, and nightmares. For centuries I have worked to control the darkness I wield in dreams, and you, Nicole, may single-handedly start my struggle back to day one," he kissed her forehead and then vanished. Nicole's arms dropped to her sides.

She closed her eyes and touched her lips in shock. So much emotion. She had never been kissed like that. And with that thought, the realization that she had just kissed someone other than Chase hit her hard—she had just cheated. With shaky legs, she made it to her bed, where she curled up and cried.

⟫⟫⟫ ⟪⟪⟪

"She's in so much pain, Kalli. I'm not sure what to do. Our mothers thought getting her away from Tennessee would help, but I'm not so sure the wreck is the only cause of her depression," Amanda let out a frustrated breath as she painted Kallisto's toenails.

"It'll take time. I think the wreck started her spiraling, but something or someone else is dealing her misery. Maybe if we concentrated on the why, the who will manifest," Kallisto responded.

"Did you see how Phobetor kept looking at her? What's up with him?"

"I think he likes her," Kallisto answered. "I just don't know if that's such a good idea, though. He has lots of issues. Not only is he the god of nightmares and visions, but he can also entice fear and anger. And from what Morpheus says, Phobetor has been different since most of us know about him and Hypnos helping Zeus communicate, for decades, with my grandmother. He's waiting for Hera to put two and two together."

"I have no doubt that bitch and her son already know. I'm sure they've always known. They're too cunning and malicious not to know everything about the ones they see as threats," Amanda replied. She continued to Kallisto's other foot, with the polish, as she thought. "Do you think they have anything to do with this?"

"I thought of that, but I don't see why they would. I mean—Nicole's wreck happened a year ago. Ares just saw you when he started watching me for Hera after Morpheus and I met. Months after. It doesn't make sense they would be after Nicole or even know her."

"True."

"Speaking of the evil duo. How are you?" Kallisto asked.

Amanda stopped painting for a moment as she thought.

"I'm as good as I can be. I have nightmares—"

Kallisto started to interrupt.

"—I know, I know. I don't want them to know. I don't want anything to do with the gods. Present company not included," Amanda gave Kallisto a fake half smile.

"Morpheus helped me," Kallisto reminded.

"Yes, well, I don't need a dream god interfering with my mind. And before you call me a hypocrite," Amanda held up the hand without the polish, "I know they can help; I just don't want Phantasos to see or know."

"Amanda—"

"Please don't, Kalli. I don't want to talk about it—or him. I want to forget."

⇒⇒⇒ ⇐⇐⇐

Phobetor's mind reeled. He almost lost all control when Nicole walked into her bedroom. He needed an outlet, one that did not include his charge. Closing his eyes, he worked to find the perfect victim for his wrath. *There, he will do.*

He entered the sleeping mind of a self-proclaimed asshole. A man who had recently stolen money from his employer. Unfortunately for him, his employer was none other than Hermes, the god himself.

The man was in dreamless sleep when Phobetor entered. With a snap of his fingers, visions of torture danced across the thief's mind. He was shackled to a tree in a deep, damp forest, barefoot and without clothes. Phobetor wove in growls and distant screams, knowing the most efficient way to scare a mortal was by invoking all five senses with fear.

Something wet and furry crawled over the asshole's feet, but all he could see was blackness due to the sudden removal of vision. Pain dug into his leg from thigh to ankle, and the strong stench of copper hit his nose moments later. He felt the warm blood ooze from the stinging wound and screamed in panic.

A grin stretched across Phobetor's face as the man begged to be released. His onyx eyes danced with joy and amusement as he crafted the nightmare. He knew how to control the torment he inflicted, careful not to go too far—as he once did. But he wanted to. Not because the man was a thief, but because the man was just there—afraid— and in his presence. The presence of the god of nightmares.

Just as the thief's tortuous nightmare became almost too intense to bear, Phobetor changed it to a vision of humiliation. The employee saw himself standing before his peers, still handcuffed and dirty from the forest, with his vision intact. The thief's colleagues interrogated him and made him admit his indiscretions. They belittled him. Just before anguish went too far, Phobetor switched his vision to one of absolute loneliness. No one could hear or see him as they walked the same sidewalks and ate in the same restaurants, not even his loved ones and friends. He was invisible to all. Finally, Phobetor allowed the man to wake. Sweat dripped from the human's brow, and he could still smell the copper stench of blood and hear the growls of monsters. Shaking, the man rose from his bed and wept in his *dirty* hands, while sitting on bloody sheets.

Phobetor returned to his Grecian home a little less agitated.

Chapter XIII

Welp

Eyes slightly matted and sore from a night of tears, Nicole woke the morning after the unknown being's failed attempt at complete rapture. That was what she should be concentrating on; however, that damn kiss had her mind in a tailspin. She thought she'd done something wrong by kissing the irritatingly handsome god back. She felt unfaithful. Her brain knew better, but her heart—well, it still belonged to Chase, no matter how far away or how deep he lay. Apparently, her libido had no such issues and was no longer in mourning.

Rubbing her eyes, she noticed the absence of her irritating yet handsome watcher, so she assumed Kallisto was still in the house with Amanda.

She jumped in the shower and allowed the water to cascade over her body, releasing the tension of the night before. It was Friday, and she hoped she could talk her cousin into taking her to get a tattoo over the weekend. One she had been thinking about for the last few months. Knowing Amanda, she would.

Entering the halls of a high school, where she knew only three people, was hard. Even when shunned in Tennessee, at least she knew the people who were rejecting her. The girls gave her a wide berth, and the guys, well, they looked on with curiosity until one of the other girls noticed. Black and purple hair, piercings, and black shadowed eyes did not distract from the fact that Nicole was beautiful. Her armor had effectively done its job. So why did it seem so much harder here? In Hawaii, she could just tell they all disliked her.

Standing by her locker, she felt him. This time, she knew it was Phobetor who was watching. She wasn't exactly sure how she knew, but she did. She continued rummaging through her things, trying her best to ignore the heavy-handed Oneiroi.

"Good morning, Nicole."

Nicole jumped at her name since, typically, no one but her *inner circle* spoke to her.

Oh, damn, what's his name? She could never remember a name, but a face she would always remember.

"Remember me? I'm the guy with the olive branch—Pika. I thought I would try again—since we have first period together."

Nicole just stared.

"Or not." Pika turned red-faced and started to walk away.

"No, sorry—you just startled me, is all. Sure, I'll walk with you." *What better distraction than company?*

Pika gave her that bright white grin she remembered from the day before as they fell into step together.

"Where did you say you're from," Pika asked.

"I'm from Tennessee."

"I wondered where that accent was from," he grinned wider.

"I don't have an accent—you do." And that was how she made her first acquaintance in a year.

"Wanna sit together at lunch? That's the other class we have together." Pika asked as they walked out of their first-period class.

"Did you lose a bet or something? Seriously? Won't your friends judge you for hangin' out with me?"

"I don't care what people think. I'm not a "judge a book by its cover" sort of guy. Why do you think that of yourself?" Pika inquired with a smirk.

"See those girls over there?" Nicole gestured to the gaggle of girls watching them. "See the repulsion on their faces? That's because you're talking to the new *odd* girl."

"They're looking at you because they're jealous. They can't pull off your look. Don't mistake envy for disdain."

"Trust me, Pika—it's disdain." Nicole walked to her next class without answering his question about lunch and feeling an odd sense of shame for speaking to another boy—*will this feeling that I'm betraying him ever go away?*

The rest of the morning, she carried her books and the invisible dream god around campus. She felt his presence but nothing more from the deity. The memory of the kiss still lingered in her mind, and she caught herself thinking about it during her classes.

Without missing a beat, Pika sat with her during lunch and continued their conversation from that morning. She couldn't help but laugh with her new friend. He was quite funny.

That was when her overbearing god decided to make things a little more interesting. Nicole felt warm hands wrapping around her wrists. Releasing a gasp in the middle of Pika's story about a horrific science teacher and frantically rubbing her wrists definitely got Pika's attention.

"Are you okay?" he asked, looking down at Nicole's hands as she massaged her wrists.

"Yes, I just—" *What do I say?* "—I just had a sharp pain. Uh . . . from an old wound."

"Okay. Well, it seems painful. You keep rubbing your wrists, kinda hard."

"It's fine." *What the hell?*

Next, her body sparked with desire. Instead of the commons and lunch tables, she saw herself pinned to her bedroom wall by Phobetor. She felt her own body under his. She was in his memory and *awake. What the hell?* Under his thumbs, she could feel the racing pulse of her own wrists. A jolt of intense need washed over her—his desire—for her—*Holy hell.*

"You sure you're good?" The commons and Pika came rushing back into view. Concern was etched across his face.

Sounding breathy to her own ears, Nicole replied, "I'm fine. I'm not feeling well. I think I need to see the nurse."

She jumped from the table like she was on fire, without a goodbye or disposing of her tray, and ran out. Once in the girl's bathroom, she checked under each stall to ensure she was alone. Then, she did what she had witnessed Amanda do once. She lifted her head to the ceiling, called Phobetor an asshole, and told him to materialize.

"What the hell was that?" Nicole demanded when Phobetor appeared at the far end of the restroom, leaning against the wall with his arms and feet crossed, grinning. He wore all black. Maybe it was because of their surroundings, but he looked more intimidating than she remembered.

"What?" perversity danced in his eyes.

"You know what," Nicole stammered. "Me seeing you—me—us." She realized it was her first time to see him since their kiss. *Shit.*

"Oh. That." He uncrossed his legs and stood straight. "Well, I just thought if you were going to flirt with the guys at school, you should remember where your tongue was just hours ago."

Nicole stood there with her mouth agape, blinking. *He did not just say that.*

"What's wrong, Nicole?" Phobetor winked.

"I can't believe you just said that—or did that. What do you think Pika thought about the way I acted?"

"Is that the whelp's name?"

"He's just being nice. If you haven't noticed, I don't evoke warm fuzzies."

"That is as you want it. Just think of it as me furthering your need for exclusion."

"Most would want me to make friends," She crossed her arms, trying hard not to think about the desire she felt from him just moments ago.

"Oh, I have no issue with you having friends, Nicole. As long as they are not whelps." Phobetor grinned, then vanished.

"What an asshole!" Nicole exclaimed as three girls entered the restroom.

Radiating anger, Nicole flashed the girls a scowl and left the bathroom completely humiliated and a little aroused. *How will I ever look at him again?*

With a grin, Phobetor continued to watch Nicole as she marched from the restroom right before he vanished. Why he made the rash decision to show his emotions to a mortal girl with not one but two displays of vulnerability, he had no clue. All he knew was that she got under his skin. From the moment he saw her asleep in Tennessee, there had been an intense pull to her that he had never experienced before. When he thought she might kill herself, flashes of her standing on the cliff's edge plagued his memory—that moment was when he became worried, and then protective. More emotions he had not experienced. *What is wrong with me?*

"How are things with your mortal," Phantasos asked, leaning against the doorway with a D.F.O. t-shirt that stated, *I've Been Hated by Many and Wanted by Plenty!*

"Damn it, Phantasos. Do you not know how to knock?"

"Careful, you are starting to sound like Morpheus."

"Meaning?"

"Not sure you realize this, but you were speaking aloud. I heard you speak of your new vulnerability." Phantasos flashed his brother a wicked grin.

Phobetor gave his brother a friendly wave of his middle finger and said, "Get lost. And stop listening in on my tirades."

"Now, now, little brother. What are older brothers for if not to lend a listening ear and a shoulder to cry on?"

In Phobetor's hand, he materialized a tennis ball and chucked it with his god's strength at his annoying brother.

"That was not very nice. What if that had actually hit me?"

"Next time, it will, I promise." Phobetor sat on the couch, wishing Phantasos would leave so he could watch Nicole without interruption. A god dividing his time was not difficult, but under the current circumstances, Phobetor would rather pay close attention to only Nicole.

"Are you falling for a mortal? A mortal who might also be a bender. Literally, an Oneiroi's worst nightmare?" Phantasos asked. "Oh, the irony."

"No, I am just curious about her, is all."

"Sure," Phantasos sounded unconvinced.

"Why are you here?"

"I came by to see if you wanted to start putting some ideas together with what Morpheus witnessed yesterday. A list of gods and creatures that could be trying to rapture Nicole and reasons each may have."

Chapter XIV

Zeus

FOR THE NEXT SEVERAL hours, Phobetor and Phantasos made a list of creatures and gods. The list of gods was long, and just when they thought it was complete, they added another name. The creature list was shorter but still had a dozen beasts on it. They further divided them into beings that could fully rapt a mortal and those that could only rapt a human's mind.

"What about Nymphs and Daemons?" asked Phobetor.

"Possible, but not probable. I think we should stick with the list of gods and creatures for now. We should work on the ones who can only mentally rapture a mortal first," Phantasos spoke as he added a name to the creature list. "If she was being mentally raptured instead of being in a coma for a whole week, the being is strong."

⤜⤛ ⤚⤛

That evening, Phobetor was summoned by Zeus. A summons from Zeus always evoked dread. He had been the messenger between Zenovia, Kallisto's grandmother, and Zeus for the better part of a century. He had also given Zeus information about other gods when asked. Phobetor never liked being the messenger and wondered more than once why he did not call on Hermes for the job. After all, he was the messenger and emissary of the Greek Pantheon, not to mention many other things; plus, he was Zeus' son. For some reason, *Zeus only knew why*, Phobetor and his father were the ex-lovers' go-between and the deity messenger.

He asked Phantasos to watch over Nicole, telling him he had a dream issue that needed dealing with. Phantasos feigned reluctance, but Phobetor knew better. He saw the excitement dancing in the eldest Oneiroi's eyes, and he knew the reason behind his brother's concealed gleam—she was tall, blonde, and had a serious attitude.

Materializing before the broad doors of the god king's mansion on Olympus, Phobetor waited to see the deity. A young, very lovely daemon beckoned him in and through the vast atrium, where he glimpsed the statues of the gods of Olympus. There stood his exact replica in marble between statues of his brothers. Phobetor lifted a brow at the sight. He could see his reflection in the pallid marble floors, and the nine-meter ceilings gave an endless feeling to the atrium.

This was one of only a handful of times Zeus called for him to come to his home. Usually, these meetings were done via dreams where Hera, Zeus' wife, and the reason for the secrecy, would never find out her husband was in correspondence with his ex-lover. He found it odd that Zeus would risk their meeting, especially after the revelations from six weeks ago.

The daemon led Phobetor to a room dwarfing the entrance and had him wait for Zeus' return. *Nice of him to be here since he was the one who summoned me.*

Phobetor took in the marble structures lining the walls, gold vases, and oil paintings standing at least two-meters tall. It was curious that some paintings depicted places in the mortal realm. One of Crete, one of Athens, and one Phobetor just recently saw—the waterfall where Amanda took Nicole in Hawaii–*odd.*

The beautiful falls reminded him of how she looked when he materialized after Phantasos heard Amanda's call. That was the second time Nicole scared him. Just as he was reaching out to touch the painting, the doors opened, startling him out of his memory, and in walks Zeus.

"Phobetor, nice of you to come," Zeus bellowed.

Like I had a choice.

"Is it wise for me to be here?" Phobetor asked.

"Leave," Zeus ordered his minions. Once Phobetor and the king were alone, Zeus answered. "My need of you is not of my usual request. I need a dream god to help with a nightmarish task."

"Who or what do you want to frighten?"

"I know you recently helped Hermes out with a thief issue he had at one of his galleries. I need you to dig deeper."

Wrinkling his forehead, Phobetor said, "I do not think I understand what you are asking of me?"

"It has come to my attention that my son Hermes has made some enemies, and he will call on you more often to help dispatch them. I am telling you to report your findings to me before you report them to my son or get rid of them. Chances are you will do things exactly the same as Hermes instructs, but I must know first, not after death."

"Should I not know what is happening before I dream-dive into a bad situation?" Phobetor asked.

With what could only be described as a chuckle, Zeus answers, "You know that is not how this works. I will never show my hand unless it is necessary. I will tell you if it becomes essential for you to know."

Damn him. Again, with this shit. Phobetor glared. He could feel his eyes turning black.

"We are done, Phobetor. You may leave." Before Phobetor walked through the doors, Zeus called out to him. He stopped without turning around. "Oh. Do not speak to anyone about this—including my son."

⤜⤜⤜ ⤛⤛⤛

Something shifted in the air around Nicole, letting her know Phobetor was no longer the god who watched her. Goose flesh rose over her body.

"Show yourself," she demanded.

It wasn't but a second before Phantasos materialized in front of her.

"What are you doing here?" She asked.

"You asked me to show myself."

"No. Why are you here and not..."

"The handsome Phobetor?" Phantasos winked.

"Or...Morpheus or Kallisto..." Nicole blushed. It seemed she was no more comfortable around the jerk eldest brother than Amanda was. She could seriously understand her cousin's angst toward him.

"He had errands to take care of," Phantasos responded to only the whereabouts of the middle Oneiroi and not why the others were not there.

"Deities have errands?" Nicole didn't know why, but that just sounded very ungodlike.

With a half-smirk, Phantasos leaned against the wall and crossed his arms. "We always have things that need addressing. Do you need me to hurry him up for you?"

Nicole mirrored Phantasos' stance by crossing her arms over her chest and lifting her chin. "No, I could just tell someone else was watching me, and after the...incident, I was nervous...that's all."

Still smirking, "He will be back soon, and it will be he who watches you all night."

Nicole decided to get a few digs of her own in. "Phantasos, cor- rect?" She continued without his answer. "What's going on between you and my cousin? I mean...I see the way you look at each other when the other one isn't looking. Why do you pretend to hate her?" She smirked.

His face paled briefly before returning to his snark. *That got him.*

"There is nothing between us, I assure you."

"Could've fooled me."

"I do not hate her. She is just another mortal girl. One who hap- pens to be best friends with my brother's betrothed."

"Whatever you say." Nicole was the one smirking.

"Now that you know who is watching you, I will go back to my observations from Olympus," Phantasos vanished.

"Coward!" Nicole said to her ceiling.

In the middle of reading, Nicole felt Phobetor return to his post. She smiled to herself and immediately felt guilty. It was late, so she decided against an interrogation. *Tomorrow, I will address his earlier behavior.* She sat her book on her end table and turned off her lamp. She could've sworn she heard a deep voice say, good night, my έξυπνος ομορφιά.

CHAPTER XV

Tattoo

FINALLY, THE WEEKEND WAS Nicole's first thought before opening her eyes. No worrying over classes. She sat up and laid out a plan of action. *Tomorrow's my birthday, and I need a tattoo.* "I really need to get my own car," she mumbled to herself as she stumbled from her warm bed to the shower.

The tattoo she was desperate for was of Chase's birth and death dates. She pictured the dates in Roman numerals, arching around a lion's head. Why a lion? She had no clue but felt an irrational need for the creature to be imprinted on her body. The picture came to her two weeks ago while she was in that trance between sleep and wake, that moment when her mind decided to answer her deepest questions and resolve insoluble issues with rationale—when, in wake, all she did was play devil's advocate to her musings. She had not been able to dispel the thought or the defined image from her mind since. All Nicole discerned was that she needed that specific tattoo—now.

Stepping into the bathroom, Nicole turned the shower on to heat up and began brushing her teeth and preparing for her day.

"I can feel your presence. I know you are there, watching me. At least you can do is buy me dinner first—before you watch me bathe."

"There is no shame in the naked body, not for us immortals."

The words were spoken in her mind and not aloud, or at least that was what she thought anyway. *So strange.* She could also feel the grin behind the voice, wherever it came from.

"I'm not immortal, so at least give me fifteen minutes to bathe without your *stalkery*."

No more words came to her mind or ears, but she felt the telltale presence grow incredibly weak but not wholly gone. Not sure what that meant exactly, she had no choice but to remove her nightclothes and step into the warm shower. The hot water felt amazing, so Nicole just stood there for a few minutes, allowing it to seep into her muscles. When she began to wash her hair, *his* presence left.

Maybe immortals were not completely immune to the naked body—because this was definitely different. Phobetor was learning that even after exposure to the public baths of the beautiful Greek gods of Olympus, there was nothing that prepared him for watching Nicole. He even made it where mist covered her most alluring areas, but his mind could not handle it. He was just teasing himself. Once she started moving under the water, he had to stop. He stopped the orb's transmission and prayed to Zeus that for fifteen minutes, her *actual* stalker would not show itself.

Busying himself, trying not to think about *her*, Phobetor picked up the scroll containing the lists of gods and creatures he and Phantasos had compiled. *This is an impossible task.* Most gods had the ability to rapture humans, if not fully, mentally. The list had not accomplished its intended goal of narrowing down the possibilities. As far as the creatures' list, it may help. He scanned the creatures who had the ability to rapt. The first ones on the list were the centaurs, gorgons, and sphinx. Each could fully rapture a mortal. However, none of these creatures were to be trifled with. Each was exceptionally dangerous, and each would gladly bargain with a god if the price was right. After all, it was a sphinx that held Kallisto and Amanda for Aries' twisted pleasure a couple of months ago. Phobetor did not know much about the gorgons, except they were some of Hades' minions. Maybe a trip to see Hades later this week if Morpheus and

Phantasos were up to it. He was not going back to the underworld alone. That was a once-in-a-lifetime mistake he had no intention of repeating. Centaurs could be reasonable-ish. They were easy to anger and traveled in herds, making one-on-one conversations impossible, and all he needed was a pissed-off herd of centaurs out for his blood. The sphinx were solitary creatures, menacing and beautiful. Perfect for manipulating a mortal. They were also cunning, and there would be no way to seek out all. Yes, it looked like the best first course of action was to speak with the dark god, Hades.

Peeking back at his orb, Phobetor saw that Nicole was clothed and heading downstairs. He had not seen her face-to-face since the bathroom incident at the school. He knew he was in for a tongue-lashing and not the favored kind when he and Nicole saw each other in the flesh again. He could not wait.

⟫⟫⟩ ⟨⟨⟪

Nicole decided to put her pride aside and beg Amanda for a ride to a tattooist. She had money—in fact, she had a lot between her college funds, the money she had made when she babysat before the wreck, and the thousand dollars her parents gave her before the flight to Hawaii.

"Amanda, could you take me to the best tattooist on the island? I can't stop thinking about this tattoo I have in my head."

"A tattoo. Where?"

"I don't know. That's why I'm asking you."

"No, where on your body?"

Nicole's eyes momentarily glazed over before answering. "My back, just left of center, behind my heart."

"Well, as long as you keep it from any of the adults that will kick my ass for taking you, I guess."

Nicole was relieved her cousin didn't argue about the tattoo. However, she would probably get a little irritated when she found out Nicole planned to get another piercing while at the shop.

The girls were headed downtown when Amanda asked, "So what art are you getting etched into your skin forever?"

Nicole side-eyed her cousin. She knew Amanda didn't have any issues with tattoos, she was aggravating her. "Just some important dates to me around a lion's head."

"What dates?"

Does she have to be so nosey? "Chase's birth and death dates. Like on his tombstone." Nicole noticed sympathy in her cousin's eyes when she glanced from the road to her.

Once at the tattoo shop, Nicole told the artist what she wanted as Amanda looked through the tattooist's drawings, passing the time. She could never see Amanda with a tat. "I want the lion to have red glowing eyes and a black mane. The dates in Roman numerals" —she wrote the dates out for the artist.

Under her breath, she asked if he or someone else could add a Medusa piercing. She also told them she wanted it done before Amanda had time to interject.

"Why a lion?" Amanda asked as Nicole lay face down with the tattooist diligently working on her back.

"Don't know."

"Don't know? You're getting a tattoo of an animal, and you don't know why you chose that animal. Are you crazy?"

"Depends on who you ask," Nicole replied halfheartedly. She didn't want to answer questions. She wanted to revel in the pain. This pain, the pain of a needle scratching at her or the pain of one piercing her, seemed to be the only thing that allowed the pain of the heart to take a backseat.

"How long will this take?" Amanda asked.

The artist interjected this time. "About another hour. Maybe an hour and a half."

"Then I'm going to the mall to see Kallisto. It's only a mile down the road. Call me when you're ready."

Once Amanda was out the door, the artist gave Nicole's back a break while he pierced her right above her Cupid's bow—*the Medusa.*

Nicole looked in the mirror at her new tattoo, and it was eerily gorgeous. Tears started burning her eyes, and she pressed her lids together to keep them from falling. The stud in her lip looked great, too. There was nothing like the feeling of her skin after tattoos and piercings. The calming effect for Nicole was next level. This was the outlet she needed. The one she turned to in the months following the wreck. Not only were they outlets—they were permanent markers of her trials. She only had a few tattoos, though. This one *was* beautiful and bold. The lion looked real and oddly familiar; the artist was good. The dates were reminders of a beautiful soul. One she had the opportunity to love, even if it was for just a blink in time.

She called her cousin and prepared herself for the berating.

Chapter XVI

Painting

"Let me see. What—have—you—done?" Amanda shook her head.

"I got a tattoo. See?" Nicole turned her back to her cousin. Her tattoo showed since she had forethought to wear a halter top and a ponytail.

"Oh, I see the tat. It actually looks amazing. I want to know what that is on your lip."

"It's a Medusa piercing. Like it?"

"Your mom and dad are going to kill me," Amanda murmured.

"Believe me. They won't kill you. They know how I am. If I want it, I'll move the heavens and earth to get it. You never have a chance." Nicole smiled at Amanda and waited for her to give up, stop worrying, and admit her piercing was badass.

"Thanks. Good to know how little value I bring to the table. Why did Phobetor allow this?"

"You really think he is going to try and stop me, not after—" Nicole stopped. "Never mind. What's done is done. How's Kallisto?"

She could tell by her cousin's face that she noticed Nicole's sudden halt in the middle of her sentence. "After what, Nikki"

"Nothing. I don't want to talk about it."

"Did he hurt you?" Amanda's tone was demanding, even when her volume was low.

"What? No! For goodness sake, Amanda. He's not going to hurt me."

"How do you know?"

"Do you really think Morpheus and Phantasos," Nicole saw Amanda wince at his name, "would allow him around me 24/7 if he was going to hurt me?"

"No. Neither Morpheus nor Kallisto would." Nicole noticed she left off the eldest Oneiroi's name.

"Let's go to the *Gallery of the gods* and show Kallisto." Nicole was ready to show off her new body mod.

Moments before Nicole and Amanda walked into the gallery, Nicole's hovering deity vanished. It was strange. She hardly noticed his constant presence anymore, but she definitely noticed when he wasn't there.

"Amanda, do you feel anyone watching?"

"No, but they aren't watching me."

"He's gone." Nicole shook her head in confusion as she opened the gallery door. He'd been so adamant that she was watched all the time. *Where did he go? No one's there. WTF.*

Her spiraling thoughts were laid to rest as she glanced around the magnificent gallery. The paintings and sculptures were unlike anything she had ever seen. She's been to the Smithsonian and many art exhibitions in Nashville, but nothing held a candle to the art before her. Until the man in the far back corner turned around. *There's where he went.*

Their eyes were locked, and a devilish grin stretched across his gorgeous face. She smiled back until—there's always the moment when surprise overtakes all senses. Like the moment she saw the handsome god before her and was awed—then she remembered she was pissed at said god.

She could tell when Phobetor realized she remembered her bedroom and the school bathroom, and his grin turned to a momentary mischievous smirk. That smirk caused her to see red. Nicole excused herself and hurried to give the middle dream deity a piece of her mind.

"Hello, ἔξυπνος ομορφιά."

"No, you don't get to speak. What was that shit?" Nicole wasn't really mad at him. She was mad at herself. It was easier to blame him for the kiss she felt guilty about returning. The jealousy and his little mind trick in the school lunchroom was his fault, though.

"I love the addition to your Cupid's bow." Phobetor ignored Nicole's outrage.

"Why have you become so touchy and so—kissy? What was that in the bathroom?"

Phobetor just grinned down at her. "The people on the other side of that bust of Aphrodite are concerned for you. They think I am, in your words—not mine—touchy and kissy against your will. Should we inform them all is well, and you were touchy and kissy back—you know, so they do not think ill of me exerting myself on the unwilling?"

"I—I—" Nicole flushed crimson, turned, and stormed to her cousin, who was conversing deeply with Kallisto.

"Was that Phobetor I saw you speaking with?" Amanda asked.

"Yes. I suppose he changed to physical form when he left from watching me." She could barely believe the words leaving her mouth. *How strange my life has become.*

"Why are you so red-faced? What happened?" Amanda asked.

Nicole noticed Kallisto trying not to laugh. *Damn it. She heard us.*

"Nothing. He's just exasperating at times."

"Enough about him. Look at this place. It's breathtaking." Nicole said as she looked around the room full of divine realism. She caught Phobetor propped against the manager's desk in the back of the gallery, speaking with the blue-eyed beauty, Morpheus. Then, from the back office, Phantasos appeared with a t-shirt that said, *Dare to Dream*—the irony was not lost on Nicole.

Amanda and Kallisto followed Nicole's gaze.

"Yes. Yes, it is," Kallisto agreed with a smirk.

"I was actually talking about the artwork." Nicole laughed, and her mood improved immediately.

"Oh, so am I. I mean, those three are works of art. Don't you ladies agree?" Kallisto winked.

Amanda said nothing. She and Phantasos had to be exchanging mental warfare for how they were staring at each other. The looks they gave one another made Nicole squirm. Was it anger, lust, hatred, or fear?

"Well, it looks like they are in deep conversation. Will you show me around?" Nicole asked Kallisto.

"I like your Medusa piercing," Kallisto said. Amanda glared at her. "I'm sorry, I do. It's cute."

"Thank you. I got a tattoo also." Nicole turned so Kallisto could see her back.

"That's beautiful. What are the dates?" Kallisto asked, not knowing the significance.

"Chase's birth and death dates," Nicole replied, but for the first time that day, she did not sound upset by them.

"I'm sorry."

"Don't be."

"What's the lion for?"

"Don't ask her that," Amanda said, rolling her eyes. "She doesn't know."

"You don't know why you got a lion on your back?" Kallisto asked.

"I just thought of it, and I loved the idea. I like it. He's a dark, sinister lion. Kinda like me, don't you think?"

"Dark, maybe—but not sinister. No matter how hard you try, you will never be sinister," Amanda said.

"That's not what my parents think."

"They're wrong," Amanda said as she gazed at a painting of The Fates. It wasn't the ones from the exhibition. This was one of all three sisters together. One holding a thread, one with a pair of scissors, and one looking on, waiting.

"Aren't they stunning?" Nicole asked.

"In a cruel way, I suppose," Amanda answered and walked to the next painting.

"Look at this one of Hermes. He's so handsome. I've always pictured him differently. A little geekier looking," Nicole said.

"No." Kallisto laughed. "He's as beautiful as the rest of the gods of Olympus. I haven't met one yet that isn't absolutely dazzling in the looks department. I've met plenty whose insides were black as night, though."

Nicole and Kallisto turned to find Amanda had disappeared while they discussed the beauty of the gods. She was transfixed by a large painting of Ares in all his "god of war" glory. A thin crown of golden fig leaves and lightning bolts circled the prince's head.

"I'm sorry, Amanda. I begged for them to take it down, but John said we can't. Morpheus even asked Hermes if we could. Apparently, $140,000 paintings must be sold." Kallisto rubbed Amanda's back in comforting circles. Nicole could see the pain in both their eyes.

Nicole wrapped her arm around her cousin when she began to shake. "Kallisto, do you have a place she can sit down in private?"

The girls followed Kallisto to the back, where Amanda could sit on a sofa and have a glass of water. Seconds later, Phantasos and Phobetor entered the office where they tended Amanda.

"What happened?" Phantasos asked Kallisto.

"I forgot to warn Amanda about the painting of Ares. She was standing in front of it, unable to move. Then she started shaking uncontrollably."

Phantasos made a deep rumbling sound from his chest, much like a growl and asked if he could speak with her alone. Nicole looked nervous, but Kallisto nodded and tugged at her arm.

"It's okay. He's the only one that can help her when Ares is the subject. Trust me, please," Kallisto looked worried for Amanda as she begged Nicole to trust the eldest god.

Nicole walked back out to the floor with Kallisto and Phobetor.

"Excuse me. I need to speak with a customer," Kallisto explained before leaving her and Phobetor alone in front of a painting of Hades and Persephone.

"Will she be okay?" Nicole asked Phobetor.

"Yes, she will be fine. Phantasos refuses to have it any other way."

That statement said a lot about the god her cousin claimed to despise.

Chapter XVII

Memories

IN THE DEEP RECESSES of her mind, Amanda sat on the couch, not moving. She had to be remembering her times with the evil god. Phantasos knew of the torture he could see on the outside of her body when he took her from that dilapidated mansion in the realm Ares had taken her and Kallisto to. Amanda refused to tell any of them the entire story. Ares had the ability to rapture both mortals and immortals, mentally and physically. He was one of the strongest and most cunning deities of any pantheon. The god of war had taken her several times. He began small bouts of torment, holding her captive for hours, not revealing himself—she thought those were nightmares. He moved on to revealing himself to her in the mortal realm—*her realm*. He threatened her family and Kallisto. He wanted Amanda for himself, and they knew he had beaten her—severely.

Phantasos kneeled on the floor in front of Amanda. "Amanda, it's me—the asshole. I know you want to cuss me or wave that middle finger in my direction. Please do not let that bastard win. Come back" —*to me...he thought.*

Amanda managed to look down at him, but her glazed, wide eyes proved she was still somewhere else. Phantasos knew she was not being mentally rapt. It was her memories that held her captive. Rapture and torture can cause horrible scars on the psyche. Apparently, even more horrific ones than any of them had known. The only one who might know the extent of Amanda's would be Hypnos since he helped heal her that night. Phantasos had tried to ask his father, but being his father had not spoken to him in a century, Hypnos refused to acknowledge his inquiry. *Maybe he would do it for Phobetor.*

She was still shaking. Looking around, he found a basket beside the black leather couch that held a blanket. Apparently, Kallisto put her touches on his brother's office. He wrapped her in it and cradled her between his legs and against his chest.

He hated with every fiber of his being what had happened to her. If Zeus would have allowed it, he would have killed Ares for what he did. However, Phantasos did have a glorious time beating the sadistic god, almost to death, with Zeus' permission. After all, Kallisto was the king's granddaughter and, ironically, Ares' niece. However, Ares was definitely team Hera when it came to his father's children outside of his and Hera's marriage. *A mama's boy through and through.* Phantasos still might kill him if Amanda continues to relive the horror he caused. Thoughts of finding her beaten and lying on the floor in her filth plagued Phantasos still.

She was so warm, and her hair smelled of oranges, the sun, and Amanda. Unfortunately, he would never allow himself to do more than this. She was out of his reach. The Fates made sure of that with their warning. Phantasos refused to be the cause of death of the beautiful woman in his arms. He would rather keep her at arm's length, banter, and argue with her than have nothing at all. This was how it would have to be.

Amanda fell asleep just moments after Phantasos began holding her. He knew horrific memories of Ares held her mind hostage, and he wanted to be the one to console her through them. Twenty minutes later, she began stirring. He laid her down on the throw pillow before she felt his arms around her. The removal of her warmth struck a twinge of pain where her head had lain on his chest.

⇢⇢⇢ ⇠⇠⇠

"What happened? Why am I here—and with you?" Amanda asked, yawning.

"You had the displeasure of seeing a life-size painting of our nemesis. So, you took a turn down memory lane, and it was a dark road."

Amanda took note of his use of *our*, remembering the painting. She knew how much Phantasos hated Ares. Almost as much as she did.

"Where are Nicole and Kallisto?"

"They brought you back here. Kallisto had customers, and I asked if I could help you," Phantasos answered, but without softness.

"Why?"

"Because you needed me. Whether or not you agree, you did." He kissed her forehead. "I will always protect you."

And before she questioned his intentions any further, he vanished.

⋙ ⋘

"Hey, where's Phantasos?" Nicole asked when Amanda returned to the floor of the gallery.

"I assume he returned to his brooding," Amanda answered. "I'm sorry I freaked out. That hasn't happened in weeks."

"Are you okay? I had no idea," Nicole asked.

"Yes. I guess the offending painting took my mind by surprise. It was like I was there again—in his hold. I really don't wanna talk about it."

"Okay. Uh, Morpheus and Kallisto are helping a customer with a rather large purchase or two," Nicole quickly changed the subject and gave Amanda an update on her friends.

"Where's Phobetor?" Amanda asked.

"He's gone to pick up pizza."

Amanda raised an eyebrow. "You guys sent a Greek god to pick up pizza?"

"Why not? Doesn't he have to eat?" Nicole giggled.

"Yes, I suppose. But you do realize he's a Greek dream god—correct?"

"I do. But he's not God, so he can help out." Nicole gave another laugh, and she knew Amanda was picturing the cluster that was happening at Pizza Palace.

"Well, I have no plans to return to the devil's side of the room. I guess it's good I only work here around the holidays. Hopefully, that monstrosity will be gone by my next shift. I'm not sure seeing his face and body daily would be good for me."

"You know, if you ever want to talk about it, I'm all ears." Nicole gave her cousin a soft smile, hoping she could see the sincerity in her offer.

"Ditto," Amanda said.

Ten minutes into their back and forth, Kallisto returned with a bright smile. "You look better," she says to Amanda.

"I feel better. Phantasos left, so it's just us."

Kallisto grabbed her soda and started taking a sip when Nicole said, "I sent Phobetor for pizza." Out came the soda through Kallisto's nose.

"Are you serious?" Kallisto asked, laughing and wiping her face with a tissue from the desk.

"Yep. He seemed pleased to do it. I'm not sure what all the fuss is about." Nicole said innocently.

"I just never pictured the dark and ominous Phobetor as a pizza delivery guy, that's all," Kallisto snickered.

"Morpheus will be done in a few minutes. Those customers," Kallisto pointed nonchalantly, "purchased two large paintings and a bust of Apollo. Nice sale," Kallisto nodded in satisfaction.

About the time Morpheus sauntered over to them, Phobetor walked in with four large pizzas and a look of triumph. All three girls giggled at his obvious pride in his fetching skills.

Kallisto placed a "Gone to Lunch" sign on the gallery door, and the five of them went to the back breakroom to eat.

"Kallisto," Nicole began with curiosity sparkling from her eyes. "Can you tell me what it was like to be— uh, raptured? I don't want to pry. I just—I know from the stories I've been told that Morpheus took you to Olympus. I just want to know what it was like for you."

"It was like I was dreaming. I could remember some things and not others. I couldn't remember his face, and the back-and-forth pull made me feel like I was going mad."

"Was it painful?" Nicole's eyes were downcast, but she could see in her periphery Phobetor's head snap in her direction.

"It wasn't painful, no. It was more confusing and made me feel out of sorts. Out of control. Is that how it is for you?"

"Why do I remember Phobetor and his brothers' faces, but you couldn't?"

Phobetor spoke up. "Because I did not rapture you. If you remember, the first time we met was in your dream. The second time, you did not recognize me. I told you who I was, and you still did not believe me because you could not recollect my face. I did that on purpose. After I saw your dream, I was not about to only show up in your dreams. I definitely was not going to rapture you since I suspected you were a bender with a haunting past. So, you required a different kind of healing. Besides, Amanda already knew of us, and you were going to live with her. The Fates would have stopped me if they did not want me to show myself."

"Laws, rules, and a vow bound me not to tell Kallisto," Morpheus interjected. "The Fates make the rules on such things."

"So, I guess The Fates don't want me to remember my rapting capturer because I can't remember," Nicole said.

"Dreams are different. And since you are, or we think you are, a bender of dreams, you will remember dreams, but most likely, if the god or creature does not want you to, you will not remember being raptured. It depends on the strength of the being taking you." Morpheus explained further.

"Can these Fates you talk about help me remember?"

"Oh yes, if they wanted to. Most likely, they will not want to. They rarely ever interfere with fate," Morpheus responded.

"Why is this happening to me?" Nicole's voice was just over a whisper, as if for her ears only.

"That is what we are going to find out," Phobetor said.

The certainty with which he responded made Nicole feel a little better about the strange happenings. Maybe—just maybe—the motley crew she found herself part of could finely help her figure the last year of her life out.

Chapter XVIII

Underworld

"You think an audience with Hades will get us any closer to the being who tried to rapture Nicole?" Phantasos asked.

The three Oneiroi brothers stood on the old, stained pier, each in fighting leathers armed with swords, waiting for the ferryman so they could cross the infamous river Styx. The way to the underworld was eerily dark, damp, and ominous. In the distance, blackened rock cliffs rose above the river, dwarfing their surroundings. Morpheus held the three golden coins they would use to pay the ferryman. Each coin bore the picture of Hades on his throne on one side and his wife, Persephone, on the other.

"He may not even see us," Phobetor responded instead of answering Phantasos' question.

"Oh, he will see us. That I can guarantee. Whether or not he is inclined to help us, that is to be seen," Morpheus grinned.

"Should I ask why you are so certain he will grant us his ear? Does it have anything to do with the last time you spoke with him?" Phantasos asked with a raised brow.

"Some things are between me and Hades. That is all you need to know, brother. Heads up, the ferryman is coming." Once the skiff and its eerie navigator approached the pier, Morpheus tossed the gold to his awaiting skeletal fingers. With his head deep inside his hood, the ferryman's face was lost to the shadows. His cloak covered him from top to bottom, with only his bony hands showing as he held the ferry pole.

"That is not unsettling at all," Phobetor said with mockery. "He has not changed in the millennium since I was last here."

"I am sure you will find neither has the Cerberus," Morpheus shivered. "That mongrel is what unnerves me out the most about the underworld. I never know which head to watch."

The brothers stood on the skiff as they glided across the river. The smell of sulfur and a greenish haze hung just above the water, making the journey more menacing. Morpheus could see the black scales of a giant serpent weave through the water, periodically skimming the surface. He saw the white faces of the dead suspended in Styx's depth, but that could have been his imagination. After all, it was the imagination that scared a being, mortal or immortal, the most. The reality was usually never as bad as what a person's mind could conjure.

The closer they got to the other side, the more in focus the Cerberus came. Once at the iron gates of Hades' realm, the Cerberus snarled and crouched, readying to pounce. Each head with its red eyes locked on an Oneiroi—one head for each dream god. Morpheus told the creature of their wish for an audience with its master. Low growls came from each snout in response. He knew it was contemplating whether to eat them or not. *Thank Zeus*, Morpheus thought as the gates swung open for the brothers to enter. The giant three-headed dog sat, almost docile, except for its snarled lips. Its serpent tail swished and drool dripped from its lips—all three sets—into puddles around them. Its overpowering, putrid breath caused Phantasos to gag. They skirted by, dodging the slimy puddles, keeping their hands locked around the hilts of their swords, just in case the massive mongrel changed its mind.

About half a kilometer in, they came to the three roads that divided The Realm of the Shades or, as most call it—Hades—named after none other than the legendary god himself. He was the ruling god of all three. One led to Tartarus, hell, another to the Asphodel Fields, purgatory, and the last to the Elysian Fields, Paradise. A minotaur with the long horns and snout of a bull and a massive humanoid body stood watching. His eyes glowed green as he observed the crossroads. The brothers remained straight toward Tartarus, trying to ignore the beast as it huffed through its nostrils.

It took another kilometer to reach the large black doors with ancient Greek markings, depicting the rise of Hades to the Realm of the Shades, also known as the Underworld. All immortal beings and their consorts went to the underworld, as long as they had two things—an interment and a coin. If they lacked one of the two, they wandered Styx edge until their body was given a proper burial and a coin placed in their mouth. Morpheus was lucky that Kallisto's father had neither, giving Hades more reason to allow her father's return to his family.

The doors were closed, and no one or nothing was around to allow entrance. "What now?" asked Phantasos.

"We wait. Hades knows we are here," Morpheus answered.

Distant screams and moans of pain broke the silence. Deep howls of the hellhounds accompanied the screams. After a few minutes of waiting, growls came from the rock cliffs around them.

⊱⊰

Phobetor glanced at his brothers as the growls got closer. He wondered what possessed him to return to this realm, and the image of a black-haired mortal girl came to mind. After a century here, he vowed never to return, most certainly not willingly. Zeus waited just over nine hundred years to demand payment for getting him out of Tartarus. The payment was him becoming Zeus' personal messenger and snitch.

"Let us hope he opens that door sooner rather than later. I have not fought a hellhound in centuries," Morpheus said.

"What is that mortal saying?" Phantasos asked. "It is like riding a bike."

"Well, that is not very comforting since I have never ridden a bike," Phobetor says as he pulls the sword from his side, just in case.

Red eyes peered in the darkness, slowly closing the distance to the Oneiroi. As the stench of the hellhound began to scent the air, the large doors opened.

Phobetor sheathed his blade, and the three brothers walked side-by-side into the dark throne room of Hades. The ceilings seemed endless, and the rough black slate walls looked damp, giving the ambiance of cold dread. Blueish light spilled over the room, barely illuminating their surroundings. Their boots hitting the black marble floor was the only sound since the screaming and growls disappeared once the doors closed behind them.

At the far end was a giant black throne with the same carved story as the doors. On the throne was the god who once tortured Phobetor for being the only god his instincts allowed him to be. Since his imprisonment in the Underworld, he worked hard to overcome his deepest desires and the instincts of his station.

Hades looked bored, and Phobetor understood why. His thin black crown of obsidian sat slightly above his sharp brow. The lines of the god's face looked to have been chiseled from stone, sharp, almost too sharp. With a straight nose and black hair hanging to his shoulders, no one would ever think of Hades as anything other than a harsh ruler. His eyes were the lightest thing in the underworld; they were pale, shiny green. His looks may give off cruel vibes, but many goddesses fell to them. He was what they called severely gorgeous.

On either side of Hades stood, on their scaled tails, two of the three Gorgons sisters that were left. Their sister, Medusa, was slain several millennia ago by Perseus. The brothers knew better than to look into their eyes. They wanted to stay corporeal instead of the stone the sisters would be more than happy to make them. Out of Phobetor's periphery, he could see the snakes coiling around on their heads. Asking Hades if the minions on either side of him were to blame for Nicole's rapture was going to be interesting.

The underworld was not as full of festivity as one would think. There were no sinful parties. Hades ruled the realm with structure. He hated the damned almost as much as he hated Zeus for making him the king over them. Even though the Elysian Fields fell under his watch, he never visited. Hades' only solace was the six months out of every year his wife was allowed to stay with him. It was Phobetor's understanding that the king of hell loved Persephone more than anything and worshipped the ground she walked on.

Hades' lips turned up in a half grin, one of mischief, as the brothers approached the throne. Phobetor knew this visit would cost. Just how much was the problem.

"To what do I owe this honor? All three Oneiroi in the Realm of the Shades—interesting," Hades deep voice echoed through the chamber.

"We come to ask about some of the creatures homed in this realm," Phobetor answered.

Hades arched his brows in question, and his grin widened.

"Can you tell us which of your creatures have the ability to rapture mortals?" Phobetor questioned.

"Can I? Well, of course I can. Will I? Now, that is the true question. Why do you want to know?"

The snakes moved faster, and low hisses started from the Gorgons. "We are protecting a mortal whom someone or something is trying to rapture, and we neither know who nor why," Phobetor answered, hoping the hissing Gorgons stayed put.

"And you think it is one of my creatures?" Hades' tone became a little more threatening, and the Gorgons started shifting, clearly not pleased with the line of questioning.

"We do not know. There are so many beings that have the power to rapt a mortal. We are trying to find out who wants her."

Hades stood from his throne and walked down the dais to stand in front of the Oneiroi. He looked each in their eyes—for what Phobetor did not know. All three brothers tightened their hands on the hilts of their blades. It would not be Hades who sprung—it would be his Gorgons.

"So, has another mortal woman captured the interest of an Oneiroi? Have you boys not learned your lesson?"

"As you know, Kallisto is not mortal," Morpheus spoke.

"Oh yes, but you did not know my great niece was a demigod when you were pursuing her. However, she is more than that now. My messengers tell me my brother made her a god. Lucky you," Hades said. "What makes mortals so interesting that the gods of dreams cannot seem to leave them be?" Hades' smirk was back.

Phantasos growled at the god, "Does it matter?"

"Phantasos, certainly you are not the one interested in a mortal. Hopefully, after the tragedy of your last one, you learned better than to toy with humans. After all, they are so very fragile. Even at their own hands."

Phobetor and Morpheus grabbed Phantasos before he could do something stupid, like pull his sword on the king before them.

"The mortal is my charge," Phobetor interrupted whatever Phantasos was about to say or do. Phantasos stood with his lip curled and white knuckles on his sword. Phobetor could sense his brother was at his breaking point. He always was when Marrisa was referenced.

"Ah, so the last brother finally fell?"

"She is my charge, not my lover," Phobetor replied.

"Yet. She is not your lover—yet," Hades smiled.

"Are you going to answer us or not," Phantasos snarled.

"Morpheus, you should inform your brothers how it works when you need something of me," Hades looked toward Morpheus, and his smirk twitched.

"What is your bargain?" Morpheus replied, and Phobetor could feel Phantasos stiffen.

"I want to know why my brother is so interested in Hermes' life. What has my nephew gotten himself into?"

Both Morpheus and Phantasos looked taken aback. Phobetor stood very still.

"We do not know of what you speak," Morpheus answered.

"You may not, but he does," Hades pointed at Phobetor.

"You should know Zeus never reveals why he inquires about others. He has secrets, and you know by now I am his lapdog," Phobetor answered. He felt his brothers' eyes on him as he spoke.

"Well, just as I have a bargain with Morpheus, I will make one with you. Once you know, come back and tell me. I will make sure your trip to my realm is less exciting next time. Here, when you are ready to speak with me, rub this coin and speak my name. You will come straight to me, wherever I am." Hades hands Phobetor the coin.

"Your creatures who have the ability to rapture, mentally and or physically," Phobetor pushed, and the Gorgons' hisses became louder like the serpents on their heads. Each began to sway, much like a cobra.

"None. I removed those abilities once I became wed. Never allow power to your minions that could harm those you love."

Phobetor could not believe the god before him used the word love. *The rumors are true, then. Hades finally has a weakness.*

Hades turned and walked back up to his throne. "Now that you have what you want, and I have two Oneiroi under my hand, you may leave."

"Can you give us an easier return?" Morpheus asked.

"What would be the fun in that?" Hades gave them the evil half-grin he was known for. "Oh, Phantasos." Hades spoke to the gods' retreating backs. Phantasos stopped but did not turn. "I am patiently waiting to have all three Oneiroi at my beck and call. It will not be much longer."

Phantasos stiffened. Then, without response, he walked from the throne room.

Chapter XIX

Job

As Nicole expected, neither her parents nor Amanda's mom, Kathryn, had any issue with her new Medusa piercing. She figured they pretended not to see it so she wouldn't get satisfaction from seeing them upset. Little did they understand this had nothing to do with anyone other than her—it was a way to remove the pain from her heart. The memories were now immortalized on her skin instead of always hanging in her thoughts and dreams.

She woke to her eighteenth birthday, grinning at her ceiling, thinking about how much her life had changed in just over a month. Yesterday felt different somehow. It was almost like she was starting to become part of something. She also thought about asking John, the manager of the Gallery of the gods, for a job. She could use the cash instead of her college fund. Plus, she would be around the deities, which would make the crew feel better—besides, it was a cool ass place to work. With the decision made, she went to find her cousin.

Nicole found Amanda on the front stoop watching what—Nicole didn't know—but she looked zoned out. Ever since Amanda saw that painting, she had been strangely quiet. Nicole almost turned around not to disturb her, but she knew how it was to allow your memories and pain to take over, so she decided interrupting her cousin's reflections was a necessity.

"Amanda," Nicole spoke softly, not wanting to freak her out.

With a slight jump, Amanda answered, "Yeah?"

"I've been thinking. I need a job. I saw a sign in the window of the gallery. Do you think they would hire me?"

"Wait. You? Nicole—wants to get a job? Why?"

"Well, I just thought I could use some extra cash, and it's better than sitting around and doing nothing all the time."

Amanda flinched, realizing she hadn't been the best hostess. "You should ask Kallisto what she thinks. After all, she does work there."

"True. Wanna go over and see if she's home?" Nicole asked.

"She's working until the mall closes at nine. What time is it?"

"It's seven-thirty."

"Seriously? Damn! I've been sitting here since five this afternoon. It seems like it's only been minutes."

"Look, Amanda," Nicole decided on some intervention. "You've been so distant since yesterday, ever since you saw that painting. What can I do to help you? I don't want you to end up like me. I mean, you'd look great with black hair and piercings, don't get me wrong—but that's not you. You have so many friends that are here for you."

"And you don't?"

Nicole felt a little uneasy at her cousin's reversal. "I suppose. But what happened to me was the death of the most important person in my life. Don't get me wrong. The things Ares did to you were horrendous, and from what I understand, Phantasos made him pay for them. But you have your life and so many people to help you through it. I wish I had the support group you do."

"You know, you have that same support system now. Everyone loves you."

"I have to admit. As much as I hate to." she raised her head to the sky, "Even though I'm being watched all the time, I'm starting to like this motley crew of yours."

"Does he watch you ALL the time?" Amanda asked with brows raised almost to her hairline in question.

"Not after some embarrassment. Now he flashes to my bedroom and stands guard at my bathroom door. It's better than me trying to bathe with my hands covering myself." Both girls laughed.

"Come on. I'll take you to the gallery. By the way, you shouldn't be cheering me up today—it's your birthday. Happy eighteen, cuz."

***

Amanda thought about what Nicole said on the stoop as she dressed to take her cousin to the gallery. She could not shake the cold feeling the memories stirred in her for some reason. The memory of the horrid dungeon Ares had taken her to several times with its cold, damp floor and musty smell. She hadn't told any of her friends that she had done a lot of research on Ares after the incident. Of course, she knew most of what was written to be fiction, as was its place in the bookstore, but it was books based on the old religion when mortals worshipped the gods of old that she read. She learned more about his lovers, his relationship with his father, Zeus, and even his children. Some were horrific. Especially those two who always rode into battle with him—*What were their names?*

She even knew of Hera's relationship with her son and how she favored him above all. His cruelty knew no bounds, and all the gods knew he had a preference for mortal women and nymphs—*They knew.* She wasn't the first woman, mortal or otherwise, that he had tortured. Not the first one he touched. She found herself lucky that he had not touched her any more than he had, truly believing the only reason he had not was the circumstances of the situation. If she hadn't been the best friend of Zeus' granddaughter, she knew he would have harmed her even worse.

Amanda shook her head, trying to clear the fear his memories evoked, and hurried back downstairs to take Nicole on a job hunt.

"I don't see Morpheus' Mercedes in its usual parking space, so maybe Kallisto is alone, and she will tell us what the boys did last night," Amanda said.

"Whatever they were doing, Phobetor looked sick from it," Nicole said as the two walked to the gallery.

John sat at the desk on the sales floor, and Kallisto was dusting frames and busts when the girls got to their destination.

"Kalli, Nicole wants to discuss something with you," Amanda got the conversation started.

Kallisto looked at Nicole and waited.

Nicole wrung her hands. She had no idea why she was so nervous. Getting a job seemed like a big step since the wreck. The last work she did was volunteer work with Chase. Everything brought her back to that night. *Before and after was still how she defined things.*

"I was wondering, since you guys are looking for help if you might consider me for the position."

"Well, I know John wants someone who can work on short notice on the weekends and evenings when needed, plus close a couple of times a week. It's a good gig for someone who's in school. You could work with me sometimes."

"Do you think he'll be okay with my hair and piercings?"

"I think he would be okay with them. But I'm not sure. Our clientele is sophisticated and can be—judgey. Just ask. The worst he can do is say no."

"Do I need to fill something out?"

"Yes, give me a sec," Kallisto walked to the back offices.

Nicole turned around to find Amanda had walked away. She started looking for her when she spotted her white T-shirt. She was standing in front of that god-awful painting again. Nicole walked over to her, making sure she was okay.

Amanda whispered as if not wanting the painting to hear. "You know, they have his eyes all wrong. Don't get me wrong, this looks just like him. But here," she touched the frame of the painting, "his eyes look inviting and captivating. In real life, they look forbidding and devilish. Here, he smiles. In real life—he smirks. Here, he looks warm. In real life, he's cold—like the dead."

"Sounds like a straight "A" asshole to me. Come on. I really don't think looking at this is helping."

Amanda allowed Nicole to drag her to the opposite side of the gallery. Kallisto stood with the papers in her hand, waiting on a customer. "Let's go look at the pictures of Poseidon and his minions. At least he had cool water creatures."

It only took a couple of minutes for Kallisto to answer the customer's questions. "Fill this out." She handed Nicole the application. "You can use the desk John was sitting at earlier. He's gone to get us sodas before the shop closes."

Nicole sat and filled out the application. She had grown so comfortable with Phobetor watching her that she rarely ever thought about it while she was busying herself. It was when she was alone or in the bathroom when she recognized he was there, watching from his orb. This was one of those times she thought about him. The gallery made her mind wander to her watcher as she filled in the blanks with her life. *He must be bored.*

It was the experience section of the application that brought her musings back to her current task. That was where her mind spiraled from Phobetor to her past. Her volunteer work at the hospital with Chase. A stab of pain shot through her chest, and she thought she heard a low laugh. *Phobetor?*

Chapter XX

Hermes

"I'm so excited for you," Amanda said. "What did John say about your *look*?"

"He's fine with it. Said that as long as I wore nice clothes in blacks and grays, as not to take away from the artwork, and styled my hair, he was good with my *self-expression*," Nicole grinned.

"Wanna go look for clothes tomorrow after school?" Amanda asked.

"Looks like I have to. I only wear black, but not even I can argue they are dressy. Hell, not even sure they would rank as casual," Nicole laughed.

Amanda noticed changes in her cousin. She was now able to laugh at herself. She took strides in changing. Small steps. The Nicole she went shopping with in Tennessee was all but gone. The tattoo and piercing really did seem to let out her built-up tension.

"Do you want to talk about the painting?" Nicole offered.

"No. I'm good."

Amanda internally cringed when Nicole asked to talk about Ares. She didn't want any of her friends or family to see how screwed up she was from that asshole. How scared she was that a god with so much power seemed obsessed with her, even though she hadn't heard from him in two months, she constantly waited on the other shoe to drop, and the god of war to decide he wanted—*Stop thinking about it.* Amanda mentally scolded herself.

"Hermes, what can I do for you at such short notice?" Phobetor asked the god of many hats who just appeared in his media room in Athens without an invite. "Seems as though I should ward my property. What if I was with a lady?"

Instead of his notorious winged helmet, he wore a black Armonie suit with platinum winged-shaped cufflinks. He, like all the gods, had unusual eyes. Close to the same color blue, but slightly lighter than those of Morpheus'. His thick blonde hair was kept short, and he chose the look of a forty-year-old billionaire businessman—which, technically, he was. His looks were otherworldly—it was his lips that set him apart from the other Olympians. They were perfectly full, and with them, he kept the proverbial pot stirred on Mount Olympus. It was not his fault as it was one of the hats he wore. *The messenger.*

Hermes laughed, "I took my chances. I wanted to thank you for the scare you gave my employee. I need you to check into something else."

"What skills are you requiring of me this time? Nightmares, spying, both?"

"I want you to see what is happening with my daughter's husband," Hermes responded. "So, I suppose spying in and possibly out of dreamland is the answer to your question."

"First, which daughter? I only know of a couple, and I apologize, but since only Angelia was raised on Olympus—

Interrupting Phobetor before he made a list, Hermes condescendingly stated. "Of course, it is Angelia."

"Why? What could an elderly mortal man be up to that you need an Oneiroi to spy on him?"

"You know how much Angelia hates her godhood. For Hades' sake, she would not allow Aphrodite or me to meet our grandchildren. We have only been able to see them through scrying. She closed all links to the orbs. Fortunately for us, she never thought about scrying. Her husband does not know of the gods, or so we thought. Angelia swore after her previous husband passed; she would never allow the gods to interfere with her life again. Not that she allowed that debacle."

"That does not answer my question. Why do you want me to check on him?" Phobetor asked.

"They live somewhere in the eastern United States. Angelia finally reached out to Aphrodite because she felt like something was wrong with her husband. *What's his name?"* Hermes looked to the ceiling for answers. "Anyway—Angelia said her husband, Anthony, yes—I think that is his name—was acting unusual around her, like he was scared. They have been married for almost half a century. Their children are in their late forties."

"Still not following why. He is a mortal with an issue with his wife. Why do you need me?"

"Because Angelia told Aphrodite that her husband's uneasy feelings came from an immortal's interference. She could sense it on him."

"So, Angelia's husband, whom she has never divulged her heritage to, came home with a god signature around him?"

"Yes," Hermes said.

"Interesting. Who do you think it is?"

"No clue. Angelia is over nine hundred years old. It was around her fiftieth birthday when Zeus had to intervene, so my daughter's life is a mystery to me."

"I remember, and just another reason the king's life and ours would be easier if he had kept it in his pants," Phobetor deadpanned under his breath.

Hermes did not respond to the slight on his father. "The nymph, Priapus, is still imprisoned for his heinous act upon Angelia. Zeus sentenced him to a millennium of torture for harming his granddaughter."

"How long after the sentencing did Angelia find solace in the mortal realm?" Phobetor asked.

"She left before Priapus was taken to Tartarus. She has only spoken with her mother a handful of times, and those were short. She wants nothing to do with our world—nothing."

"How is she passing as mortal with her family if she never ages? How do her children not know they are demigods if they never age?" Phobetor questioned aloud.

"She has strong magic. She spelled her daughters and herself to look as if they are aging. Someday, she will have no choice but to tell them. Go into Anthony's dreams, hell, to him, and see if you can figure out what god is hanging around?"

"Yes. But it will be a while before I can. I am on an assignment. When I can, I will have my brothers assume charge of with my current assignment and check on him. Send me a messenger with everything I need to get to the correct mortal since Angelia has masked her powers from us." Phobetor said. "Oh, and Hermes."

"Yes?"

"This is it. I will have paid my debt to you once I uncover what is happening with your estranged family. Understand?"

"I wondered when you would finally call it." Hermes grinned widely as he flashed from the mortal realm.

⋙ ⋘

Back at Amanda's, the girls walked into a kitchen decorated with balloons, streamers, and a cake, wishing Nicole a happy 18th birthday. Kallisto was there, so she must have used her godly powers since they were together not long ago. Thia and Kallisto blew kazoos while Kathryn placed a purple birthday hat on her niece's head. Nicole smiled wide and her eyes started to burn.

"Thank you, guys," she said, hugging each one as she laughed at the silly hats and unholy sounds. She felt like she belonged.

After celebrating with cake and laughs, she took a call from her parents and brothers that left her a little homesick. It was her first birthday away from home. She now had a job, friends, and a better sense of self since the wreck. The emotions of the day had been tiring, so she decided to go to bed early.

Speaking to the air around her, she told Phobetor, "I'm about to get ready for bed. Give me fifteen minutes in the bathroom." She hated this. Always being watched and never having a spare minute to herself. She was now eighteen, and she needed her privacy.

Right as she reached for the bathroom door, Phobetor appeared behind her. She felt him before he spoke. Gooseflesh enveloped her body, and a tingle flashed up her spine. *I hope to the gods he can't sense my reaction to him.* She closed her eyes in a plea before turning to face her enforcer.

"To what do I owe the pleasure?" sarcasm dripped from her words and stance, trying not to show her anxiety.

Grinning, "I thought we should talk. It has been a while since you have had any strange issues. I thought you would like to see Olympus on your birthday."

Nicole stood openmouthed.

"Or not?" Phobetor looked uneasy.

"Are you serious? I can go to Olympus with you. Like, Olympus–*Iliad* Olympus? The Olympus?"

"Yes," Phobetor laughed. "But in all fairness, *The Iliad* is a fictional tale of my world. Olympus exists. So, you would not be going to the Olympus of *The Iliad*. You will be in the actual realm of the gods. The largest and strongest Pantheon of any realm."

"Wait. What?" Nicole held up a hand. "There are other Pantheons. Like, other gods—other realms?"

"Oh yes, έξυπνος ομορφιά, many others. Much of your mythology is rooted in facts. Just like you are real, a bender, a myth to the Oneiroi."

Again, Nicole stood there, mouth agape. Shocked. "This can't be real." She pinched herself. "Ow!"

"What did you do that for?" Phobetor smirked.

"Because ever since I met you, my world has turned upside down. It's just all hard to believe, that's all."

"Do you want to go?"

"Hell yes, I want to go. Should I let Amanda know?"

"No, I asked Morpheus to ensure that she is sleeping deeply. She will not wake until he allows her to."

"That won't hurt her, will it?" Nicole was concerned for her cousin, especially since the painting incident.

"No. Morpheus would never allow anything bad to happen to Kallisto's best friend. We will only be gone for an hour or two. Depends on whether you like it."

"Do I have to be asleep for you to take me?"

"Normally, yes. But I will not risk dream rapturing you. We are going with you wide awake."

"Can I wear this?" Nicole gestured to her black jeans and long-sleeved black t-shirt."

Phobetor laughed. "You can wear whatever you like. Now, hold my hand."

She placed her hand in his and asked, "We have to hold hands?"

"I must touch you. I can always hold your waist," brow raised, waiting for her response, which came quickly.

"No. Hand will do."

Phobetor smirked, lacing his fingers with hers, "Hold on tight, έξυπνος ομορφιά."

Chapter XXI

Olympus

Nicole opened her eyes, since the pull from realm hopping was quite shocking, and viewed her new surroundings in wonder. They were in a mansion. *His,* she thought. The ceilings had to be at least six meters high. Gray marble floors and white statues were everywhere. An odd-looking creature of sorts greeted them, just inside the atrium where giant windows overlooked a gorgeous mass of land. She thought she saw a doe and its fawn at the tree line nearest to them.

"Master Phobetor, shall I set the table for three?"

"Three?"

"You, your father, and your guest," the mostly human but with ears of a *fox maybe,* cut his eyes toward Nicole.

"Yes. Please do. I will be taking Nicole around. Tell my father I have company, and she is mortal." The creature, *or servant,* she hated thinking of the being as a creature, stiffened at his request, then nodded.

As Nicole listened to the exchange, three things struck her—*hard.* First, the creature spoke very well. Second, she was no longer wearing her jeans and a T-shirt. She wore a stunning, off-white chiffon peplos with gold fig leaf pins holding the wide shoulder straps together. And third, she was meeting his father. *What the hell?*

Once the attendant was out of hearing range, or what Nicole hoped was hearing range, she spun on Phobetor. "What the actual hell is wrong with you?"

"My έξυπνος ομορφιά, I do not know what you speak of," his grin showed otherwise.

"Your father? You want me to meet your dear ole' dad? I don't think so. Take me back."

"Now, Nicole. This is an example of why I brought you while you were awake instead of asleep. I have no intention of taking you back until after dinner, which will be in a couple of hours—mortal time. So, resign yourself to enjoying your evening and never fret over meeting Hypnos. He loves a challenge, and you, my έξυπνος ομορφιά, present one."

Nicole wanted to slap that devilish grin off his handsome face. Then she noticed he said evening when clearly it was daytime on Olympus. *Interesting.* "What about my clothes? Where are they? And you said mine were okay to wear."

"Of course, they were. I will return them when we are back in your realm. I would have changed them no matter what you were wearing. This is more presentable for Olympus. Everyone can sense your mortality, but from afar, you do not appear mortal." Phobetor took her hand and led her deeper inside the palace. "Look," Phobetor gestured to a wall of mirrors on his left as they entered a great room with chaise lounges, ornate rugs, and beautiful paintings that reminded her of the gallery.

The shock was evident on Nicole's face. She most definitely did not look like herself. If she had to use one word to describe the woman looking back at her, she would have to use the word flawless. He had not changed her hair color back to its natural brown. It was still black as a raven wing with purple highlights. It was woven into elaborate braids with curls around her face and down her back. *Do I have that much hair?* A thin band of gold circled her head, and gold bangles hung from her wrists. Her makeup was nothing she could ever accomplish. Her eyes were lined in black with winged edges, and the shadows made them look big and beautiful. The shade of her skin was perfect, so perfect that any flaws she had were now hidden, allowing her natural beauty to shine through. She had never felt so beautiful. When she turned to see her tattoo, it was gone magically concealed.

"What do you think?" Phobetor's voice betrayed his anxiousness. Nicole gave herself a mental high five. *He knows there's a fifty-fifty chance I may flip.*

"Wow! I've never looked so—

"Stunning?" Phobetor said.

"As much as I cannot stand for someone to toot their own horn, yes, stunning."

"I am unsure what *toot your own horn* means, but this is the clothing of the gods. You are always stunning, no matter what you wear." Phobetor regarded her through the mirror, his godly gold ones locked on her baby blues.

Nicole's heart rate spiked, and she hoped he couldn't sense it. The way he looked at her made her stomach tighten and her mouth water. She inwardly cursed pheromones, unable to stop her body's reaction to him so close. She adverted her eyes to the floor to release the trance. Before she alluded her eyes, she noticed his widened grin. Yes, he sensed it. *Damn!*

Clearing his voice, Phobetor held his hand out to her and asked, "Ready to see Olympus?"

"Oh, I'm more than ready." Nicole didn't hesitate and took his hand. Between the way he looked at her and her excitement to be in the mythical world of her dreams, she was in awe.

⁂

Phobetor could not believe how cooperative Nicole was being. The first place he would take her would be the forest. There, she could watch the animals and experience the beauty that even Maui could not compete with.

"Are you alright?" Phobetor asked when he saw Nicole swayed on her feet. He flashed them to the forest, preferring that to walking, he had hoped to fit as much of the mount in before dinner and their interrogation from his father. He was also confident that he had lost his immortal mind by having the servant taunt Hypnos with the disclosure that his son's guest was a mortal female—nothing *to be done about it now.*

"Yes. I'm good. It's just—does rapture feel the same when awake as it does while asleep?" Nicole questioned.

"That is a question for Kallisto or Amanda."

"I don't want to remind my cousin of such things. There was nothing good about her experiences with rapture."

"Very true. See if you can speak with Kallisto when Amanda is otherwise preoccupied."

Phobetor watched as Nicole took in her surroundings. Her bright eyes were wide with amazement as she looked from the magnificent waterfall to the two young centaurs who splashed each other in the stream down from the falls. Her gasp caused Phobetor to tighten his hand around hers letting her know she was okay.

"Are those—Centaurs? Real live centaurs?" Nicole's eyes were so wide Phobetor had to laugh.

"Yes. Many centaurs live on Olympus. Those twin colts belong to Hippolytus. He and I were close in our younger years. He grew up and had a family. I grew up to scare beings in their dreams." Phobetor said quietly. "Maybe Pegasus will show himself, and I can really see your eyes light up."

"I suppose my eyes are alight with awe. This is amazing." They watched as the colts chased each other out of sight. "The air smells like lavender and honeysuckles. Does it always smell like this?"

"Yes."

"Look at the water. It's so blue. Are there fish in it?" Nicole inquired as she let go of Phobetor's hand and ran to the bank's edge."

"Yes," Phobetor followed.

"There's fish!" Nicole exclaimed. "They're glowing in all sorts of faint colors. They look like our angelfish."

"They are kin to the angelfish of your realm. I am sure Poseidon had something to do with that. After all, he spends more time in the depths of your oceans than here."

Nicole's head jerked to look at Phobetor. "Seriously? Poseidon is in our oceans. Why is it that every time I think I can't be shocked, I'm more astonished?"

"Let us go to the fountains," Phobetor reached for Nicole.

"The fountains?" Nicole asked just before they vanished.

Chapter XXII

Hypnos

"Hello, Father," Phobetor said as they sat down at the massive marble dining table.

Nicole's gaze did not leave Hypnos, as she sat across from Phobetor and to the left of her host. She felt alone without Phobetor at her side. Unfortunately, there were only three of them, and Hypnos sat at the head of the table. The conversation was better in the triangle they formed, but she could not help but feel a little vulnerable. She hoped fear wasn't what his father saw on her face.

"Hello, son. I see you have a beautiful guest. Ms. Nicole, welcome to our home and to Olympus."

Nicole could feel the tension in the air. Was Phobetor going to get in trouble for having her here? She hoped not. *When did I start worrying about him?* That and the realization she hadn't thought about Chase while on the Mount made her squirm more than the handsome yet intimidating deity to her right.

"Thank you. It's all so amazing. Beauty as I have never imagined."

Several nymphs brought out the meal. She wondered to herself who else would be joining them because there was more food on the table than three people could consume in a week. Again, surprise filled her that she knew many of the dishes. Roasted duck, sauteed green beans, potatoes of several kinds, Brussels sprouts with candied bacon and cranberries, the list continued all the way through dessert. "This reminds me of Thanksgiving at home."

"What brought you home, son?"

Here it goes. He's in trouble.

"I hoped you would be here. As you know, I and the other Oneiroi—" Phobetor did not use Phantasos' name, knowing that would only annoy his father, so he put him and his brothers into their god category— "believe Nicole to be a bender of dreams. She has shown her ability to overpower and control hers. She has also been known to conjure and control, with great skill and clarity, dreams without the use of an Oneiroi. I wanted you to meet her. She also has a slight problem I hope you can help with."

Phobetor saw the intrigue on his father's face. "Explain," was all Hypnos said.

"Someone or something has been mentally rapturing Nicole, on and off for over a year. We, the Oneiroi, witnessed it the last two times it happened. When a deity appeared, the entity left. It has the signature of a god or a powerful creature. We have not been able to find more than that."

"Does this entity have a nefarious feeling?" Hypnos asked Phobetor.

"Yes. Quite nefarious."

"What do you remember of your rapture? Has it only been mental rapting?" Hypnos turned his questions to Nicole.

"I'm not sure if it's always been just mental."

Phobetor was surprised by her answer. He and the rest of the crew were under the impression that she had only ever been mentally raptured. Why would she second guess that now?

"What can you tell me about your raptures?" Hypnos questioned.

Nicole looked at Phobetor with pleading eyes. *Don't hate me, please.* For the first time, she wanted to tell someone about her experience with her coma. She knew when she mentioned it now, at the dining table of the god who protected her every day and his father whom she did not know, her protector would think it a slight. Hell, she hadn't even spoken with Amanda about it. *Here goes nothin'.*

"Just over a year ago, I was with my boyfriend. A drunk driver ran into us. All I could hear was tires screeching and then the crunch of metal. Next thing we went airborne and then off the side of the highway. We kept hitting trees as we rolled down an embankment. I heard him scream my name, and blood was everywhere. That's all I ever told anyone of the wreck." Nicole watched Phobetor's reaction as she continued. "I remember a strange man from my dreams—coma—whatever it was. He had a mane of jet-black hair, a menacing grin with fangs—and he was huge. He wanted me to be afraid. Seemed to relish it. For days, he kept me chained to walls or tables. Sometimes, Chase was there, which I'm not sure how he could have been. I remember begging Chase to help me. Anyway, I've dismissed this as nightmares. Then all this rapture, dream bending, and gods stuff, well, now I wonder if there was more to it."

"Why have you never mentioned this to any of us?" Phobetor's eyes were black.

"Because I thought I was crazy. Hell, I still think I'm crazy. I can only remember, or I think it's memories—small snippets of things," Nicole answered with a shaky voice.

Hypnos thought a moment before speaking. "Unfortunately, the time of your coma is nothing we reverse and see. We cannot check for a signature. It is exceedingly important that you let the Oneiroi know if you have any interaction from here forward, even if you think you are crazy. When gods mess with mortals' minds and pull them from realm to realm, they can become unstable. You cannot wait to see if madness takes you."

"Will bringing me here cause me to go nuts?" Nicole's eyes widened. Beginning to shake, she put her fork down on her plate.

"It could, but Phobetor did not bring you via sleep. You have been completely awake the entire time. Whether you remember this, well, that remains to be seen. It is never advisable to allow yourself to be raptured until final death."

"That is enough, Father. She will be fine. I am with her at all times, and if there is a time I cannot be, one of the other deities whom I trust is with her," Phobetor said.

"That is good, son, but not even you nor Morpheus can keep a mortal's mind intact should it decide to break. Just remember, dream bender or not, she is mortal."

"I would like to go home now," Nicole stood on shaky legs. "Thank you for your hospitality, Hypnos. I feel I should leave. Phobetor?"

Phobetor stood, glaring at his father. "I will take you home."

⊶≫⟩⟩ ⟨⟨⟨⊷

"I thought you were with her at all times, my son," Hypnos sat in a leather chair in his library and sipped from a glass of amber liquid.

"Kallisto and Morpheus are with her. Why did you tell her those things about possible madness?"

"Phobetor, you know better than to bring a mortal to Olympus. How many times do things need to go wrong with you three boys before you learn your lessons?" Hypnos responded.

"She has abilities like none we have ever seen. I believe her mind will remain unbroken if she is not in a state of sleep."

"You believe is the problem. You do not know. Stop playing with the lives of mortals. Ask Phantasos if he would ever do it again?"

"There it is. Phantasos' situation with Marissa was different. He loved her, but she was not strong, not like Nicole."

"Kallisto was strong too. For Hades' sake, she was a demigod, the granddaughter of Zeus. The push and pull of realm hopping was too much for even her. You think Nicole is stronger than Kallisto was?"

Phobetor stared at his father. He had not thought about Kallisto's struggles. She was powerful now. A goddess by all rights. She was often on Olympus with Zeus and Thia. How could he not have thought of her struggles? *I am an idiot!*

"You are right. I will not bring her back to Olympus or any other realm other than her own." It hit Phobetor that he wanted something more with Nicole than he should, and that could have caused the girl he was beginning to care for to lose her mind.

"Son, I know the pain you are in. The last century has been arduous for us both. Zeus placed us in an unbelievably difficult situation, between him and Hera. One day the right immortal will come along. This mortal girl is not the one for you. I am sorry," Hypnos returned to his amber liquid and the book on his lap.

⤜⤜⤜ ⤛⤛⤛

"Morpheus, Phantasos!" Those were the only two words Phobetor spoke when he flashed back to his home in Greece. It took only moments before his brothers stood before him. Phantasos wore a t-shirt that said, *I am Ambrosia!* Phobetor pointed at the shirt and rolled his eyes.

"A summons. To what do we owe the honor," Phantasos gave a mock bow.

"I have some things I need to take care of. It may take me a couple of weeks. Between the two of you and Kallisto, do you think you can watch over Nicole?" Phobetor paced as he spoke.

"Why? What is so important you would leave us in charge of watching over a girl you are interested in?" Morpheus grinned.

"I am not interested in her. She was intriguing, but that ship has sailed as the mortals say. She still needs the gods; I am just not capable of watching over her all the time. Will you help me, or do I need to employ a full-time daemon to babysit?"

Phantasos glared at Phobetor. "If she is suddenly no longer intriguing, why would you feel the need to be the one to employ someone for her safety? What happened?"

"Nothing, I just do not have time.'

"Wait a minute," Morpheus said. "When you brought her back from Olympus and left her with us, you went back to see father—did you not? Do not lie. We can tell."

"How did you know we went to Olympus?" Phobetor asked.

"I hate to break this to you, all-knowing one. But Nicole told us everything. She even told us about the quaint little dinner party where she announced her concerns about her coma after the wreck," Morpheus continued. "Amanda is pissed at you for taking her and equally pissed at Nicole for keeping the nightmares of her coma from us when we are all trying to keep her safe while we figure out who is rapturing her."

"She remembers then?" Phobetor sat on the edge of his couch and rubbed his hand over his face.

"Yes. Apparently, taking her while awake is the key. Or so we concluded," Morpheus said.

"Let me get this straight. You, not knowing how it would affect the mortal dream bender, took her to Olympus—another realm. Not only another realm but to the most powerful Pantheon there is after knowing what it did to other mortals, including Kallisto. Who ironically was never mortal. What were you thinking?" Phantasos rarely raised his voice, but rare meant sometimes he did.

"No wonder you and Father do not speak. You are just alike. Yes, I took her. I admit, I was wrong. There—satisfied?" Phobetor turned his anger from himself to his eldest brother.

"I will help watch her," Morpheus said. "But you are the one who will explain your sudden change in interest—"

"We—" Phobetor started to interrupt, but Morpheus held up his hand.

"Do not offend us by denying it. You have started falling for the mortal. If she were honest with herself, I believe she shares your sentiment. I refuse to get in the middle of that," Morpheus stood with his arms crossed.

"Little brother, you are so screwed," Phantasos chuckled. "I, too, will help watch her. Good luck. You are going to need it." Phantasos laughed when Phobetor waved goodbye with his middle finger.

"I will be back. Honestly, I have things to do."

Chapter XXIII

Distance

"Why would he take me to Olympus if he knew it would cause me to go batshit crazy?" Nicole paced Amanda's bedroom as Kallisto and Amanda watched her.

"I still cannot believe you never told us everything you remember from your time during and after the wreck," Amanda interjected again.

Ignoring her cousin—again, Nicole stopped her pacing and stood looking out Amanda's window. "He was supposed to protect me, not throw my ass into danger."

"Honestly, I don't think he thought it would harm you. He didn't take you while you were asleep. From my understanding, every mortal the Oneiroi ever raptured to Olympus was asleep when they were taken. I was always asleep when Morpheus took me. He never thought to take me while I was awake. The only time I was ever taken to another realm without being asleep was when Ares kidnapped me," Kallisto said.

Nicole saw her cousin flinch in the reflection of the window at Kallisto's mention of the god of war. It was still dark, even though it seemed a lot longer than one night. The streetlamp was in full glow, reminding her of the first time she saw Phobetor from her window seat in Tennessee. A surprising ache traversed through her chest as she thought about her parents and little brothers.

Slowly, she turned to Kallisto, "he was supposed to protect me," then Nicole returned to looking at the streetlamp.

"I admit. I had my concerns about Phobetor at first," Amanda began, "but since I've been around him and seen him with you, I think Kallisto's right. I don't think he would ever intentionally harm you. I actually think he's into you."

"No, he's doing Phantasos a favor. The brother you asked to help me chose Phobetor to "help" me instead. He's in this as a favor to Phantasos, who is in this for you. Nothing more."

⟫⟫ ⟪⟪

Phobetor decided he would wait and speak with Nicole after her classes. She had only slept about three hours. He knew this because no matter what he said to his brothers, the truth was, he could not stay away that long. He watched her sleep through his orb, paying close attention to her eyelids as they flittered, giving away the fact that she was dreaming. The strength it took for the Oneiroi in him to restrain from entering her dreams was difficult, but he knew better. She would not be happy, plus he dreaded telling her that he was going away for a while. That was the truth. It should only take a couple of days instead of a fortnight, but that was for him to know and not her or his brothers. He would be going to see Hades and then to see Zeus. *What did I do to deserve this? The snitch of the gods.* He thought as he watched the beautiful girl sleep.

⟫⟫ ⟪⟪

The first thing Nicole felt upon waking was Phobetor watching her. She knew it was him. Lying in her bed, she made a crude gesture at her ceiling and could have sworn she felt his laughter, and against her will, she grinned.

She knew the second he entered her bedroom just after she closed the bathroom door, per their everyday ritual. She leaned her back to the door and thought about what Kallisto and Amanda said. Could he have really not thought going to Olympus would harm her? *Is he into me?* Deciding that was not the case. She huffed and climbed in the shower. Phobetor was gone when she opened the door to her bedroom. She could feel him. Apparently, he didn't want to be seen. *Fine!*

Classes went by in a blur as she thought about where she was the night before. Olympus—so beautiful. Well, until she found out she could never go back since it may drive her to a mental breakdown. She definitely didn't need another one of those.

"Nicole, wait up."

Nicole turned to find Pika dodging through the sea of high schoolers toward her. "Hey, Pika, I haven't seen you in a couple of days. Where've you been?"

"I stayed home with my little sister. She's sick, and my parents are on the Big Island for work."

"I'm sorry to hear that. She, okay?"

"Yeah, just a cold. She's back today, so I am too. Can I borrow your notes?'

"Sure, but you might want to read over the chapters. I'm not the best note-taker." Nicole felt lighter. This was normal. It had been a long time since she felt normal. No wreck, no nightmares, no gods—just a friend wanting class notes.

"You want to get a soda after school?" Pika asked. "Not a date, just a soda. You know, as friends. Nothing more."

Nicole grinned as she watched Pika stumble all over his words. *This, too, is normal.* She thought.

"I'm supposed to go clothes shopping with my cousin after school. I got a job. Tomorrow?" She had no idea why she agreed to a soda, but she said it before she thought.

"Sure," Pika's disappointment was short-lived. "Where did you get a job?"

"At the Gallery of the gods, in the new outdoor mall. Have you ever been in there?"

"Oh yeah. I went in right after it opened. Once was enough. Those paintings cost as much as my house. They're magnificent though.

I've never seen art so realistic. Which is crazy if you consider the subject matter."

It was all Nicole could do to restrain herself from making a smartass remark about how real the subject matter was. "Well, my friend works there, and she put in a good word for me. I start this weekend."

"That's good. I tried working, but since my parents started their touring agency, I became the babysitter. They are good about giving me spending money, though."

"Well, I gotta run to class. See you later?" Nicole asked.

"Sure. See ya at lunch."

Nicole felt the unease between her and Phobetor before she left for school, but that was nothing to the feeling she had now. She knew it had to be because of Pika. It felt like he simmered with anger. *Well, tough.*

⋙ ⋘

Amanda waited in her car for Nicole. This was all her fault. If she hadn't gotten the gods involved in Nicole's life, she wouldn't be worried about her cousin's mental state even more than she was before Hawaii. Now she had to worry about Nicole's emotional state from losing Chase and the push and pull of the gods. Surely, Phobetor would not do that again. It was bad enough there was a crazy god or creature after Nikki—now she had to worry about the gods that were on their side, too. *Ugh.*

She felt it, a watcher. Unlike Nicole, she had no idea who it was. "Who's watching me?" There was no answer. "Who the hell is watching me?"

Still, no answer, but the passenger side door opened before Amanda had time to call on Kallisto. Once Nicole sat, Amanda felt the being leave and replaced with the force that was always around when Nicole was. *That has to be Phobetor.*

"You still have your stalker?" Amanda asked.

"You know it. Where are we going first?"

"How about the mall? Kallisto's working with Morpheus. After we get your clothes, you can take them to the gallery, and you can model them for us. Kallisto can let you know if they'll work," Amanda answered.

Five stores, at least ten pairs of pants, even more tops, and four pairs of dress shoes later, Amanda was relieved her cousin was done with her shopping extravaganza. Both girls had their arms full of bags and boxes as they made their way to the gallery to see Kallisto so Nicole could show off her spoils.

This time, Amanda was determined to stay away from the painting that haunted most of her thoughts since Saturday. Since her little breakdown, she started imagining things. Like in the car, thinking someone was watching her again. She woke two nights in a row with cold sweats, thinking she was back in that damp dungeon and could swear she smelled him—Ares. The scent of lavender and—him. His scent would be intoxicating if it were of anyone else. Unfortunately, the memories it summoned were nightmarish.

Before stepping into the Gallery, Nicole wondered if Phobetor would show himself—he did not. She could still feel him watching, after entering and speaking with both Kallisto and Morpheus. *No answers for me.* She thought.

"Amanda suggested I try some of this on so you can tell me if it is appropriate or not," Nicole said as she gestured between her and Amanda's arms full of bags and boxes.

"Sure. Here," Kallisto led Nicole to Morpheus' office. "You can change in here. Come out when you get ready."

She donned the first outfit, which happened to be her favorite. A tight white button-down black straight-legged dress paints and a thin men's black and white tie with a loose knot, accented with four-inch heels adorned with a small silver skull on the back of each, only visible if she lifted her pants leg. She stepped out of the office to the three of them holding signs. Morpheus immediately held up a sign with the number 10 on it. Kallisto and Amada followed suit. Three tens. Nicole giggled, and the sound startled her.

"You like?" She turned in a circle.

"Nicole," Kallisto said. "You are gorgeous."

She blushed and grinned at Amanda when her cousin gave her a wink. "Now, show them the one that I chose for you."

"Keep in mind, Amanda chose this, and I'm not sure it will work for here. But I love it," Nicole turned and went back to the office.

Next, she exited with Amanda's pick. A short schoolgirl black and white checkered skirt with the same white button-down as before. This time, she had knee-high black socks and chunky shoes completing the look.

Morpheus' eyes went wide, and he excused himself with a cough.

"Uh, I love it, but I'm not sure John will let you wear it here."

"She has a date with Pika after school tomorrow," Amanda's smile reached her ears.

"It's not a date. It's a soda."

"Well, that's when you need to wear that," Kallisto's grin was infectious.

Morpheus walked back in with another god on his heels. Phobetor.

"Ladies," Phobetor bowed while keeping his eyes on Nicole.

Nicole audibly swallowed. She could have sworn his golden eyes flashed black, as they did when he was angry. *Maybe it was just my imagination. I'm the one who should be mad at him, not the other way around.* Spinning on her heel, she went back into Morpheus' office. Once, without everyone's eyes on her, she sent a text to Amanda.

I think that's enough.

Amanda's text came in almost as fast as hers went out—*Party pooper.*

Deciding whether to be a coward or not was her next obstacle. Her choices were one of three. Walk out there and pretend she wasn't livid with the dream god, walk out there and give him a piece of her mind in front of everyone, or her favorite, she could not walk out there.

While turning her options over in her head, the door opened, and Phobetor took all her decisions off the table as he walked in.

"Tell me you are not planning on wearing that to work, school, or anywhere in public."

Nicole glared and decided on a fourth option. *Ignore the oaf.* She busied herself with folding the clothes and putting them back in boxes and bags.

"Are you ignoring me?" Phobetor asked.

Nicole continued with her task. She didn't expect her eyes to start burning. *What the hell is wrong with me? Don't you dare cry.* Her internal dialogue apparently held no sway over her traitorous eyes. She felt his hand on her shoulder, and still, she refused to face him. Nicole had no idea what her excuse would be once all the clothes were bagged.

His hand tightened, and she knew what was next. He spun her to face him. Instead of looking him in the eyes, she looked straight into his chest. *Well, shit, that's no better.*

"Why are you crying?"

"I'm not. I stubbed my toe. It hurt," she lied.

"That so? Well, I want to apologize for last night."

"For what, embarrassing me in front of your dad, placing me in danger while knowing my mental state is why I'm in Hawaii in the first place, or—wait—for showing me a magnificent place I can never return to, but will always dream about? What are you apologizing for exactly, Phobetor?"

Nicole saw him flinch. "I am sorry for taking you to Olympus. Honestly, I was not thinking clearly. I am truly sorry. I also came to let you know that Phantasos, Morpheus, and Kallisto will be watching over you for a time. I have business I must address."

"Well, thanks for letting me know. I'm surprised you did it this long," Nicole tried to keep her voice from cracking to no avail.

"Why do you say that?" Phobetor asked.

"Isn't it obvious?" Nicole turned back to her task. "Again, thanks for letting me know."

For a long minute, she felt his gaze on her back as she fought with those damn burning eyes of hers. Finally, she felt him vanish instead of leaving by the door. She no longer felt his presence in the office or watching over her. *He's gone.* For the first time since the wreck, her tears were not for Chase.

Chapter XXIV

Date

Not wanting to stay in the same realm as Nicole, Phobetor decided to return to Olympus. Weeks of watching her had his mind addled. He thought of that Pika boy following her around the school. *A soda*—even Phobetor knew better than that. He knew what that kid wanted—he saw it in his eyes. If he stayed on earth, he would harm the boy. He needed a distraction. *What better way than the nightmares of mortals?*

Phobetor watched for an imperfect human. One who could use a premonition on how to behave. He played off a being's phobias, their deepest fears. After his time in Tartarus, he now chose those who needed to learn a lesson from his creations. Often, the dreamers he sought were on the verge of becoming wicked. Most were the epitome of fear—therefore, he had to be worse. The nightmares he now wove were worse than the ones he created pre-hell. His time in the underworld made him into something unique. *A little better but a lot worse.*

After his night of terror-filled dreamers was over, Phobetor sat in his bedchamber, twirling the coin Hades gave him through his fingers. Why both Zeus and the ruler over the underworld were so interested in Hermes' boring ass life, he had no idea, but he hoped this was as much as he would be required to get involved. If he went to Hades now, he could continue staying busy instead of giving in to the orb to see what *she* was doing. Not contemplating the "soda" date she had with the mortal. Three terror-filled nightmares and his mind was no clearer than it was when he left Nicole standing in Morpheus' office.

⟫⟫⟶ ⟵⟪⟪

It was fifteen minutes until the final bell and twenty before Nicole would be on her way—on a date. Was *that what a soda with Pika would be?* She didn't want a date with Pika. She wanted a friend. Her mind was made up—she would set boundaries. He needed to know she was not looking for anything other than a friend she could bounce the occasional homework questions off of and someone to have a soda with after school on days she wasn't up to going straight back to her aunt's house. Why she was getting herself worked up over a soda, she had no idea. Maybe it was because the only male she had been around without supervision since Chase was Phobetor. *Phobetor*—

She didn't sleep much after he told her he was going away on "business" —like she believed that. The way his voice sounded—she knew what hadn't really started between them had already ended. Why the lack of his spying eyes bothered her so badly, she refused to contemplate in great detail. *Ugh, get a hold of yourself, Nicole.*

One of the other deities was watching her now. She thought it might be Phantasos only because Morpheus and Kallisto were busy wrapping up their classes. She could always tell when the watcher was Phobetor. It could be anyone now, even the one who wanted to rapture her. Not caring who was watching her, she continued as if they were not.

Well, there goes the bell. The plan was that she would meet Pika outside the school, and they would go to the mall for a soda, and then he would drop her off at her aunt's.

There he stood, next to his car, waiting. A knot formed in Nicole's stomach because he looked so happy, and she was sure she looked like she was tolerating the situation. *It's just a beverage* she recited the mantra in her head as she approached the little red car and the boy with the toothy grin.

"Ready?" Pika asked when Nicole was ten feet from him.

"Yep. I was thinking we could go by the gallery once we get our drinks. That is if you don't mind?" Nicole preferred having others around.

Pika looked a little crestfallen but recovered quickly. "Yeah, sure," he answered as he opened the door for her.

Crap! Guy friends rarely open the door.

She had to admit, Pika was funny and a little charming. He never dared to try and hold her hand, as they walked a foot apart and sipped their drinks while discussing their classes. This set her at ease, not discussing her past or her future, just the present and nothing of world-shattering importance.

"You have a great laugh," Pika said.

"Thanks," Nicole replied, hoping the conversation was not about to get weird.

"You should do it more often."

"Look, I see Kallisto through the gallery window. Let's go say hey," Nicole was thankful to have a quick end to the conversation about her laughter or the lack thereof.

"Sure." Pika followed.

As usual, when she entered the Gallery of the gods, her watcher left. Immediately, she started glancing around to see if Phobetor was in the showroom. *Nope.*

Kallisto came bounding up and hugged Nicole. "Well, hello to you, too."

"Mor— I mean, Ambrose just told me about the new schedule. I didn't know. Are you good?" The look on Kallisto's face was that of sympathy. *Not good.*

"I'm great," Nicole lied. "Kalli, I want you to meet a friend of mine from school. Pika, meet Kalli. The beauty of the school, so I've heard her called," Nicole gave a conspiratorial look at Kallisto.

Kallisto rolled her eyes. "I guess you've been talking to either Ambrose or Amanda. Hi, Pika. It's good to meet you."

Pika shook Kallisto's hand and pulled it back quickly, looking at Kallisto like she squeezed his hand too hard. *Weird.* Nicole could tell Kallisto noticed. "Good to meet you."

"Are you ready to start Saturday?" Kallisto addressed Nicole.

"Can't wait. I could use the money and something to do on the weekends besides staring at four walls. I think I left one of my bags here yesterday. Care if I go look in the office?" Nicole asked, pointing to the back of the gallery.

"Sure. I'll show Pika around. Take your time. No one is back there."

Nicole looked at Pika, who nodded and went to find her missing bag of accessories.

The back was dark, but the light from the gallery allowed Nicole to easily walk to the office without having to hunt for the light switch. As soon as she opened the door to Morpheus' office, a rush of nausea flooded her. Her tongue thickened as saliva filled her mouth. Even in the dark room, her eyes saw yellow spots right before everything went black.

⤜⟩⟩⟩⟩ ⟨⟨⟨⟨⤛

"My dear naughty girl. You and your friends thought you could keep me away forever? You should know better. As soon as I have a proper hold on you, not even they will be able to break the bonds that tie us. You are my source, and I am not only persistent, but I am very patient—Now, scream."

Nicole was without sight since a wrap covered her eyes. Cold, damp stones dug into her back from bracing herself to the wall. She couldn't move in any direction with her hands bound in shackles above her head and fetters around her ankles. The smell of wet earth, rusted metal, and lavender filled her nostrils. On the voice's command, she screamed as sharp nails traced down her arms from wrists to shoulders. Not deep enough to make her scar or even bleed. It was his touch, his breath on her face, and the terror-inducing memories her mind was flooded with that made her scream. She screamed until she blacked out—again.

to shoulders. Not deep enough to make her scar or even bleed. It was his touch, his breath on her face, and the terror-inducing memories her mind was flooded with that made her scream. She screamed until she blacked out—again.

"This painting is of Perseus holding the most infamous Gorgon's head after he slayed her," Kallisto was explaining the paintings to Pika as they waited on Nicole.

"Medusa, right?"

"Correct. You know some Greek mythology."

"My grandmother believes in the gods. Hawaiian gods," Pika added. "She tells us stories of not only them but other Pantheons. My favorite are the Norse legends."

"Interesting. Maybe you should apply for a job too," Kallisto grinned.

"Maybe I should. If my parents ever stay home long enough. They opened a travel agency not long ago. They do tours on most of the islands, so I stay home with my little sister."

"It's been a while since Nicole went to the back. I'm going to see if she needs any help. You can continue to look around. Most of the art has plaques telling about it."

Kallisto heard the thrashing before she entered the office. When she turned on the light, she found Nicole three feet inside the door, on the floor with, her eyes rolled to the back of her head and her arms and legs flailing in jerky motions. Drool ran down her cheek as she shook.

"Nicole!" Kallisto screamed.

"Morpheus, Mom! Someone, Help!" Kallisto yelled at the ceiling.

Moments later, the office was filled with deities, and Pika, who stood still with a look of shock and terror all over his face.

Chapter XXV

Rapture

Phobetor found himself once again in the place he swore never to go back to. He should be grateful since Hades started his journey at the doors to the throne room instead of the noxious river. Now, to get in.

He stood waiting for Hades to allow entrance when he heard a muffled scream. Or he thought he did. Knowing the underworld played on your anxieties, he ignored the sound when a new sound reverberated around him—*Hellhounds.* Looking up, he saw three pairs of glowing red eyes slowly closing in right before the large black doors swung open. "Those damn things are one hell of a welcoming service."

The gorgons grinned as they greeted him and fell in step beside him as he approached the dais where Hades sat on his throne, looking forever bored. The only sounds he could hear once the doors closed were those of the snakes slithering on the gorgons' heads. He briefly wondered if they could reach him should they decide to strike and if so, would it hurt the gorgons when he cut the snakes' heads from their bodies?

"Well, well, so soon?" Hades smirked.

"Hermes came to me asking me to look into the dreams of his estranged son-in-law," Phobetor answered without preamble.

"His son-in-law? Why?"

"All I know is that the man nor the children have never known about Angelia's heritage, and now it seems he knows something. Angelia does not know what, just that he came home acting strange with a god signature about him. She reached out to her mother," Phobetor sounded uninterested, hoping Hades would think the news trivial.

"Have you yet to walk in this mortal's dreams?" Hades asked.

"No. Hermes is supposed to send me some information so I get the right person since he has not been on the gods' radar. Plus, I was to report to you before I did anything. I have not been to Zeus either—before you ask."

"Good. You did well." Hades tossed Phobetor another coin. "Come back when you have more." Phobetor found himself back in his bedchamber, pissed at the highhanded god.

That is when he heard it. The screams and cries for help. *Kallisto!* He knew it had something to do with Nicole. He could feel it. That connection was not something he had time to examine.

He flashed into the gallery office, full of total chaos. At first glance, he only saw her—Nicole, on the floor, unmoving. Frozen, all Phobetor could do was watch in absolute horror as a bright light emitted from Thia's hands where she held them above Nicole's heart, begging her to wake. Morpheus held Kallisto to his chest as she cried, and Phantasos paced, running his hand through his hair. The Pika kid was sitting on the floor against the wall with his head between his legs. Seeing the boy brought on another feeling. One Phobetor refused to think about, however, it did jar him out of his momentary trance. He took three large strides that brought him to the other side of Nicole.

"What is wrong with her?"

"Kallisto came in to find her seizing. The seizures stopped but she's unresponsive," Thia answered.

Phobetor rounded on Kallisto and his brothers with black swirling eyes. He was close to losing control, and he knew it. "How could you allow this? I trusted you to watch her."

Putting up a hand, Morpheus pushed Kallisto behind him. "Calm down and listen, Phobetor. You are no help in your current state."

Phobetor gritted his teeth and took a long breath, trying to reel his emotions back in. He could feel the tremors leaving his hands, but his eyes refused to obey. "Why is that mortal here?"

"He was with Nicole. He was close to losing his mind when Phantasos calmed him and left him against the wall. He won't remember this," Kallisto answered as she stepped around Morpheus. She was here with me. Phantasos watched her all day. When she arrived here, I took over. There is no way with my god signature that this should be, but apparently what or whoever wants her is either a lot stronger than we thought or growing stronger."

"Let me see if I can enter her mind," Phobetor looked at Thia, his eyes still black as coal and swirling like a storming sea.

"Is that such a good idea? Your eyes say it is not," Phantasos asked.

"I am okay. Nicole has nothing to fear from me. Whatever has her is the problem." Phobetor sat on the floor and pulled Nicole's head into his lap. Closing his eyes and placing his hands in her hair, he pulled the tether he had refused to acknowledge earlier— the one that connected him to Nicole.

Nicole, let me in. He could tell the entity that took her was no longer around. She had placed herself in a dream-like state—a stasis. One, he could not go in without her acceptance. This was definitely new territory for the Oneiroi. He never knew a being, mortal or immortal, whose dreams he could not enter without their knowledge. Having to ask permission was not something he knew how to do. The space he was in was like a holding cell of fog with no floor or ceiling. No walls—nothing but the cold, thick fog.

Έξυπνος ομορφιά, let me help you. Open your mind to me. Phobetor stood helpless in the fog. He thought over the last several months, from his brothers learning of his unwanted affiliation with Zeus to meeting the beguiling girl in his lap thrown into his already screwed-up existence. His waning hold over his control, the power it took to not wreak havoc over the irrational fear of others, was staggering. His thoughts whirled. How could he think of helping Nicole if he had such a tenuous hold over his own self-control? All he knew was he had to. *Nicole, please. Please let me in. I promise you will always be safe with me.*

❧ ☙

Nicole lay in the fetal position next to Chase's grave. Tears streamed down her face onto the thick, soft grass beneath her. With every tremor of her body, she curled tighter into herself. She was not quite sure how she was bound by a horrific being one second, and the next, she was with Chase in the graveyard. She still felt the cold metal of the shackles on her wrists and ankles, even though they were no longer there. His voice, she knew his voice. She knew it was the one from her coma.

"Chase, were you ever there with me? Why did I live, and you didn't?" Nicole softly spoke to the dead, wondering if she willed it while in her dream state, would he answer. "My memories of that night and the week following have so many holes. I don't know what's real anymore. Not since the car went down that embankment."

Fog began to fill the graveyard, and it was not of her making. She closed her eyes in fear—resigned—and waited for the shackles and deep, bodiless voice to return. Instead, she heard a plea.

Έξυπνος ομορφιά, let me help you. Open your mind to me.

Nicole, please. Please let me in. I promise you are safe with me.

I am so sorry. I will not leave you again, just let me in.

Opening her eyes, she was unable to see the grave. She could still feel the soft grass, but it was like she was encompassed in a thick cloud. Phantasos wanted in her dream, her safe place. Here, she was protected, even from him. He couldn't confuse her anymore. Her parents couldn't keep her from Chase. The voice could no longer scare her. *Alone. Alone in my dreams, I'm safe.* Nicole mentally communicated back.

Let me help you, Nicole. Please.

She could hear the fear in his voice as he begged for entrance. Did she want to allow him back into her life? Staying in the graveyard seemed safer.

You have control. That will not change. Just let me help.

That was true. If she allowed him in her dream, she could always kick him back out. Minutes ticked by as she contemplated.

Amanda wasn't prepared, even though Kallisto had called her, so Phobetor took the reins and explained everything that happened. She still wasn't quite as prepared as one would think. When she saw Nicole unmoving in Phobetor's lap, she went weak in the knees. The sight before her was unnerving, to say the least. He, too, was zoned out. His eyes closed, and his hands tangled in Nicole's hair, made Amanda feel completely helpless.

"What exactly is he doing to her?" Amanda addressed Morpheus, pointedly ignoring Phantasos.

"He is trying to reach her. All we can sense is the entity that took her is no longer around. Phobetor is looking for her."

"Can't you help?" Now she addressed Phantasos.

"No. If he finds her and needs us, then we can help," Phantasos answered without looking at her.

"Why?" Amanda glared at Phantasos, wondering why he wasn't being more proactive.

This time, Phantasos looked at her. The two's eyes locked on each other. Amanda's heart raced with anxiety. "We do not have the bond they do. It became apparent when he saw her lying on the floor with Thia trying to help her. Your cousin and Phobetor's bond is strong."

"I don't know what that means," She was getting very irritated at the Oneiroi before her.

"He is closer to her and has been in her dream state several times. He has the best chance at reaching her," Morpheus stepped in presumedly to defuse the tension.

"That still doesn't explain the *bond* he speaks of," Amanda turned toward Morpheus and Kallisto.

"It just means he is closer to her and has feelings for her," Morpheus explained. "He is better equipped to help her through her terror. He is Phobetor, the dream god of fear, phobias, nightmares, and visions. This is what he does. With that and his connection to her, he is the one that has to do this."

Nodding, Amanda sat by Nicole and held her hand. She prayed in silence for her cousin as the others sat around waiting.

Chapter XXVI

Truths

Comfortable with her control over her dream, Nicole sat up. Once she made up her mind, the fog slowly lifted, and Phobetor took its place on the other side of Chase's grave.

"I thought you didn't want to deal with me any longer," Nicole quickly stood, wiping her face from the tears and black streaks covering it.

"I never said that." Phobetor's eyes swirled black.

"You didn't have to. I could tell from your body language and the sudden shift from how you were on Olympus."

"It was a mistake. I will not leave you again."

"What if I don't want you around?" Nicole crossed her arms.

"Tough."

"So, this is how you're going to help me? By being unmoving and demanding?"

"One of the ways," Phobetor smirked.

One brow raised in question; Nicole stood in defiance. "What are the other ways?"

"First, I need to know what happened while you are in this state. Before you have time to forget," Phobetor's voice became softer. "Where are we?"

"Phobetor, meet Chase," Nicole pointed at the headstone.

⤛⤜ ⤛⤜

"I see." Phobetor could not help the irritation that flooded his body when he read the headstone. Again, another emotion he refused to acknowledge. "Why?"

"This is the only place I feel safe. And he has answers I need." Nicole's voice was so low, and Phobetor had a hard time hearing her.

Still irritated that her safe place was with another, dead or not, Phobetor responded to her admission of needing answers from the dead. "How will he give you answers that you do not already have? This is a dream—one you control. If he were to answer you, the answers would come from your own mind."

"I know. I'd get pieces to the puzzle I seek to finish. I know the pieces are in my head. But they are too buried, and the ones I have, I don't know if they are real."

"Does the puzzle you are trying to put together have anything to do with the coma you were in?" Phobetor asked.

"Everything. And more," Nicole's words were still very quiet. Unlike the ones she spoke when he first arrived at the grave.

"Where did the entity take you? What do you remember?"

Nicole's eyes glazed. Phobetor could tell she did not want to tell him. Or maybe she did not want to remember. With great reluctance, she told him everything she could recall.

Phobetor walked around the grave as she spoke and took her arm from around her chest to examine her wrist. As he thought—raw, red rings circled it. *Shit!* He snarled in anger.

"Wait, what did you say you smelled?"

"Dampness and lavender, like on Olympus."

"The creatures on Olympus would never cross their king by rapting a mortal, even if they could. A god wants you, Nicole." Phobetor took up pacing as he continued to listen to Nicole's recollection of her moments with the deity.

"Tell me everything you remember from the night of the wreck," Phobetor said.

"I'd rather not. That night is not one I want to share with anyone, especially you."

Phobetor felt like she just slapped him. Yet another feeling he did not want to deal with. "Well, my έξυπνος ομορφιά, if you want to start getting to the bottom of this, you have to."

"It's private, very private," Nicole shifted. "I can't tell you here, beside Chase's grave." The graveyard faded.

Phobetor looked around their new location. They now stood in her bedroom in Tennessee.

⌁⟫⟩⟩ ⟨⟨⟨⌁

"Chase and I had been dating for a year. We decided to give ourselves to each other—completely. She waved her hand at the chair. He sat there watching me finish with my makeup. You have to understand, he was my best friend, not only the lover he became that night. He was the one I told my dreams to—the one I always wanted to be around. My parents loved him too. Life was the best I had ever experienced. I've always heard your first love was strong, but after the wreck, it became all-consuming," Nicole walked around her room, picking up picture frames and tracing the people in each one with her finger.

"Don't get me wrong," she continued. "My feelings for him prior to the wreck were strong; they just weren't as intense. I was hyper-focused on my future. I wanted to be a pediatrician. One of the many things I loved about him was that he wanted to be a doctor, too. We had the same goals. So, I thought giving myself to him would be okay. Neither of us would veer from our goals.

"We had dinner, then spent a couple of hours at a hotel. I refused to lose my virginity in a car." Nicole had moved to the window seat and sat with her arms around her legs as she remembered.

"I get the picture. I do not wish to hear about your hotel adventure," Phobetor growled.

Nicole let out a humorless laugh. "Well, I don't plan on giving you a minute-by-minute, but there were a few things said that I keep going back to."

"Okay."

Nicole looked at Phobetor, still sitting in her moon chair. He looked tense with his hands clenched into fists, his jaw clenching and unclenching, and his eyes turning from gold to black; he looked beautiful—angry—but beautiful. It's so different from when Chase sat there that night over a year ago. Chase was a boy with big dreams. Phobetor was a god who controlled them.

"He kept using words like forever and eternity, very different from the goal-orientated conversations we always had. Oh, there's another one of the words he used—*always*. This was before we became comfortable in the room. After we—well, you know—those words stuck in my mind. For the rest of the evening, until the wreck, I started thinking of ways to make him my forever. Same college, same apartment, same bed. I even thought we could take turns in med school, which is ridiculous. I mean, who wants to wait that long? All those thoughts within a couple of hours. Then, after a couple of hours of the mental restart concerning my future and the loss of my virtue, I suddenly lost that future. It took only seconds." Nicole stared out the window as she told her tale.

"What happened once you left the hotel," Phobetor asked.

Nicole glanced back at Phobetor with tear-filled eyes. "We decided to grab a coffee on our way home. It rained while we were inside. Chase chose to go the short route. It was around eleven fifteen, and I needed to be home by midnight. An SUV ran a stop sign and straight into us. We went over the guardrail. Here's where I get lost." Nicole excused herself, needing the bathroom. Truth was, she was having a hard time talking about that night. To have said as much as she had was more than she'd ever done.

Phobetor stood.

"Where are you going?" Nicole asked.

"Wherever you are," he replied.

"I need to pee. You can't follow me."

"I will stand at the door. This is your dream, Nicole. You can—**not**—have to relieve yourself if you wish. You are stalling."

With a sigh, Nicole returned to the window. "Fine." She manifested tissues instead.

"I heard him yell my name. I saw blood. No clue whose it was, mine or his. Here is where I told the police and my parents that I woke up in the hospital."

"Did you tell them about the hotel and the—conversations?" Phobetor asked wide-eyed.

"For goodness sake, no." Nicole sat on the bed and faced Phobetor. "This is where I remember him—the deep voice, the dark hair, and the godlike body—the fear and pain I was in. Do you see? I was in the same place during my coma that I was in tonight."

"The place you described to me at the cemetery?" Phobetor asked.

"Yep. For a week, according to my parents and the doctors, I was actually in a comatose state. When actually I was being tormented by that man. He loved my fear. I was shackled to the walls, to a metal table, and to chairs. I heard Chase calling for me, telling me it would all be okay. He sounded like he was in horrible pain as he was trying to reassure me that I would be okay."

"How did you wake?" Phobetor asked.

"I'm not sure. I remember he became crueler as time went by. It was like once I reconciled myself to one form of terror or torture, he needed to make it worse. He wanted me to be scared. I can't remember all I went through. I'm not sure I want to." Nicole took a deep breath. "Maybe it was my anger. I got so very damn angry. Next, I woke up in the hospital with its sterile scent and warm blankets—instead of the smell of damp, moldy earth and a cold metal table. They told me Chase was dead, and his funeral had taken place three days prior. That's when I went off the deep end, so my mother says."

⟫⟫⟩ ⟨⟨⟨⟨

Phobetor thought over all Nicole divulged as he tried to put his irrational emotions about her story to the side and concentrate on who the being was and not the ways he wanted to eviscerate him. Learning of her extracurricular activities did not help his anger either, and that baffled him.

"Phobetor?"

"Sorry. I am thinking about the voice. He is definitely a god, but one I cannot seem to get a handle on. Are you ready to go home?"

"Go home?" Nicole asked.

"Yes. Back to your friends."

"Oh. I thought you meant Tennessee. You mean I should wake up?"

"No—home. Even though you are controlling this," Phobetor waved his arm around. "This is not a dream as you know it. You were mentally raptured. You took that realm and have made it into a dream-like state that you can control. Realm hopping is what you are doing, but you have masked it as a dream."

Phobetor watched as Nicole tried to understand his words. "I don't understand."

"As you should not. This is not a normal circumstance for me either. But, for our immediate needs, wake up."

⟫⟫⟩ ⟨⟨⟨⟨

Nicole blinked a couple of times to find herself on the floor with her head in a lap. She could see her reflection in his golden eyes and felt large hands tangled in her hair, caressing her scalp—*Phobetor*.

So much passed between them in the mere seconds before Amanda called her name and began shaking her in excitement. Phobetor helped her as she sat up.

"Nicole, you scared me to death." Amanda held onto her tightly.

"I'm okay," Nicole answered once she got her bearings and noticed the three of them were not alone. Kallisto, Morpheus, Phantasos, and even Thia—*and Pika*—were there, all watching her with looks of worry and relief, and a few tears on the faces of her cousin and the youngest goddess. "All this for me?" Nicole tried to grin. "And why is he here," Nicole pointed to the mortal leaning against the wall.

"When I went to find you, you were in the middle of having a seizure, where you are now," Kallisto started. "I asked him to stay on the gallery floor; however, I heard a gasp, and when I turned, it was him. Once the cavalry arrived, Phantasos helped me out with your date."

Nicole felt Phobetor stiffen and noticed black creeping into his eyes when Kallisto referred to Pika as her date. "We just went for a soda, not a date," Nicole clarified.

"If you have this now, I will take my leave. She does not need to be alone," Thia looked between Phobetor and his brothers, then vanished.

"I will never get used to that," Amanda murmured.

"Tell us what happened," Phantasos demanded.

"Give her a minute to breathe," Amanda snapped. Nicole felt the usual tension and hostility between the two.

"I'd rather talk about this later, but if you must know—Phobetor can fill you in. I need water, food, and a nap. Kallisto, would you and Amanda take me home, please?" Nicole asked.

"I will fill my brothers in on the rapture and be at your home shortly." Then he turned to Kallisto, "Please, stay with her at all times. Even sitting outside her shower. She cannot be alone, especially right now."

Chapter XXVII

Aftermath

Nicole watched as they raced past palm trees and houses on their way to Amanda's. She had a difficult time understanding all that had just happened. Day-to-day life seemed better and more vibrant instead of dull and dark. She missed Chase every day, which the stasis Phobetor found her curled up in proved she still felt strongly for the boy. The difference now was not every second of every day was dedicated to him as it was a year ago or even two months ago. She admitted this revelation to herself. But if she was actually doing better, why did she conjure his grave for her safety from the god who held her captive? *What did the unembodied voice want from me—why me? Who belonged to that voice? Was Chase alive and tormented by the voice right after the wreck?* She shivered. *Why is Phobetor hot and cold toward me?* So many questions plagued her mind.

"Well, I know you don't want to talk about it now, but what the hell is going on?" Amanda gripped the stirring wheel tighter than was necessary.

"If I understood that, I could fix it. I can't fix it," Nicole answered.

"Does Phobetor know how?"

"I think he's trying to figure it out," was all Nicole said, all she wanted to say. She needed to sleep and didn't have the answers her cousin wanted.

"Let's all meet tomorrow after classes," Kallisto could tell by the heaviness of Nicole's eyes that even if she knew the answers, she was too tired to say. "Maybe we can come up with a plan."

Nicole nodded, then closed her eyes. Amanda looked at Kallisto through the rearview mirror with the same eyes as the girl who had woken from her time in Ares' hands. Clearly, by the look in Amanda's eyes, Nicole's situation brought back unwanted memories. *This isn't good for Amanda.* Kallisto thought.

Once back at Amanda's, Kallisto grabbed her friend's arm and told Nicole they would see her in a minute. "The Oneiroi will know more. Nicole is a mortal teenager who, until a few weeks ago, knew nothing of the world we live in," she gestured between them. "She was in a bad place when she arrived here. Pushing her will only send her spiraling back. Possibly further than she was. I know you need answers. We all do, but you can't push her minutes after she returned from a rapture, and the gods know what else."

Amanda only nodded and went straight to her bedroom. Kallisto entered Nicole's room, where she found Nicole already asleep, curled on top of her bed. She sat in the chair watching over her, waiting for Phobetor to finish with his brothers, and thought about the signature she felt when she entered the office and found Nicole on the floor.

Once the girls left the gallery, Morpheus and Phantasos took Pika and his car home and wiped the entire night from his memories, replacing them with memories of homework and TV. Phobetor shot daggers of hatred from his eyes when Phantasos said he would place memories that Nicole and Pika's soda date was the next night. Chuckling, Phantasos vanished with the boy.

Walking the gallery in deep thought about the night's events, Phobetor glanced at the painting of Ares, remembering the look on his brother's face when he returned from kicking the god of war's ass after he abducted Amanda and Kallisto. To the right of Ares' painting was a bust of Hermes which reminded him he had to speak with Zeus, and soon, before Hades had time to taunt his brother and Zeus kicked his ass.

"Kallisto is with Nicole," Morpheus said as he appeared by Phobetor. "I stopped in to see how they were. Nicole fell asleep in seconds. I wiped the boy's mind, and you will be glad to know Phantasos only made sure the memories of his family coincide with the ones I placed."

"Now, brother, surely you know I would never interfere with your relationship like that," Phantasos taunted as he arrived moments later.

"We are not in a relationship unless me healing her is considered a relationship," Phobetor denied.

"Well then, I will be back in a minute," Phantasos grinned.

"You will sit here with us, brother, or the next time you sleep, I will visit." Phobetor's grin widened and was not at all kind. His eyes flashed black as night.

Phobetor went through everything for the next half hour, from taking Nicole to Olympus to when Nicole woke in Morpheus' office. Once finished, the Oneiroi dissected each of Nicole's instances and decided another visit to The Fates Three was in order.

"Morpheus, go with Phantasos to meet with The Fates, and I need to visit Zeus tomorrow. Can you have Kallisto watch over her while at the school when I take leave to visit Zeus?" Phobetor looked at his brother. He knew by the concern on their faces each worried about his state of mind but would never say anything. His mental state was not up for discussion. Not since the day he left Tartarus behind.

"Brother, do you think her being a bender has anything to do with this?" Morpheus asked.

"I thought so before, but now I am not so sure. If the god that is after Nicole knows she is a bender, then he would have to know she would be difficult to manipulate to his will."

"It was Kallisto who found her, correct?" Phantasos asked.

"Yes. She was waiting for her to return to the gallery floor. Nicole went to find a bag she left in my office the day before. As strong as Kallisto and her signature are, the god should not have wanted to try rapture if he could not take her fully," Morpheus answered.

"Did she say what the signature felt like?" Phantasos asked.

"She has only experienced a few signatures. She said it felt a lot like that of a strong male god. Definitely not a creature. The only nefarious creature she experienced was the Sphinx, but the signature did not feel similar to it."

"At least we have that," Phobetor stated. "I am going to relieve Kallisto."

"By the way. Kallisto suggested we all meet after classes tomorrow. Amanda is not dealing with this well," Morpheus said.

"What is wrong with Amanda?" Phantasos asked with an edge of worry in his voice.

"She is a mortal who has sustained much suffering. She is still dealing with the aftermath of Ares' abduction of her and Kallisto, and now her cousin is being tormented by a god. She has to be on edge," Morpheus answered.

"After the beating he took, Ares is the last being she needs to worry about," Phantasos said as he vanished from the room.

"He is in denial," Morpheus said to Phobetor as he vanished, leaving Phobetor staring at the walls filled with images from his Pantheon.

"Which of you is going to die?" he murmured to the artwork as he disappeared in thin air.

⟫⟫⟫ ⟪⟪⟪

Phobetor found Nicole curled on her side as she was in the graveyard when he appeared in her bedroom to relieve Kallisto from her watch. Unwilling to look away from the girl on the bed, he addressed Kallisto without turning his head. "Thank you for watching over her. I have her now."

His thoughts were consumed with Nicole, how he dismissed her the day before, and her refusal to look at him. He thought of the girl standing on the cliff's edge, practicing. She reminded him of himself about a millennia ago. Broken in so many ways. He placed a strand of hair behind her ear that impeded his view of her face—*whichever god is after you will die.*

He was the Oneiroi known for being ruthless. No matter how much he had changed, after his one hundred years in the underworld, the memories of the gods were long. They knew better than to cross him or those he cared for. So, who was brave enough to provoke him?

As the thoughts of the unknown god and all the ways he wanted to kill him played at the edges of his mind, Nicole turned her sleepy eyes to him. He would have thought she was asleep had he not been a dream god and the slight grin that crossed her face. She was awake, barely, but awake. Silently, she reached for his hand and just looked into his eyes. It almost broke him. She gently tugged at his arm, so he climbed in behind her. His large frame enveloped her small body, cocooning her in his warmth and safety. As soon as he settled in, she was out again. He held her all night, wrapped in her scent.

⟫⟫⟫ ⟪⟪⟪

Amanda sat in the dark against her pillows, one in her lap, dripping tears on it as she tried to muffle her sobs. *Why is this happen-*

ing again? Why Nicole? Why me? She was only minutes into her self-deprecating when she felt the presence. *Was it Ares?*

"Show yourself," she insisted.

Less than a second later, Phantasos appeared at the foot of her bed. "Damn, of all the gods. The devil himself."

Phantasos cocked his head to the side and grinned. "That is not a very nice way to greet the god who . . ." He cut off whatever he was about to say.

"Well, I guess said god should knock instead of watching me through one of those orb things. Or are you just a creeper?"

⤜⤜⤜ ⤛⤛⤛

"We are stepping up security. I was merely checking to make sure all was good in here," Phantasos knew bantering with her would get rid of the tears. *Whatever it takes, even if she hates me.*

"Well, the only Greek in here is you. So, it was good until—

Phantasos held up a hand. "Might I remind you, ἀγγελος, that you asked me to show myself. I stand before you because you want me to." If looks could kill a deity, he would be dead; however, she was no longer crying.

"Want you? I think not. By the way, what did you just call me?"

Phantasos' grin widened. "Good night ἀγγελος. Until tomorrow." He vanished.

⤜⤜⤜ ⤛⤛⤛

Amanda sat there, mouth agape, shaking her head. She went from sobbing to mad as hell in seconds. He was the only one who could anger her so fast. Just his presence pissed her off. Looking to her ceiling, she said, "I hate you!"

She could have sworn she heard a low chuckle.

Chapter XXVIII

Fates

A BRIGHT SUN STREAMING through her bedroom window was Nicole's first sign she made it through the night without dreams, nightmares, or—Phobetor in her bed. She rolled over and felt the space behind her. It had been real—the spot, his spot, was still warm, and she could smell his lingering scent. *He must've just left.* Well—he wasn't physically present, but he was watching. She could feel him. With a shy grin, she rose from her bed and padded her way to the bathroom. One look in the mirror and she knew why he left—*Yikes, a little scary there Nicole,* she thought to herself. Black mascara and eyeliner were everywhere, even under her chin. *Ugh.*

Twenty-five minutes later, she emerged from the bathroom clean with her makeup on, hair wrapped in a towel, and one around her body. To her shock, he was there. "Uh, sorry. If I'd known you were actually going to be in my room, I'd taken my clothes in with me."

There was no mistaking the heated look in Phobetor's now black eyes. He looked at her from towel to toe and back up. It must have been the look on her face because she spun around to face the wall.

"No worries," he said. She thought she heard him say, "Glad you did not know," under his breath, but she was already in her closet and wasn't sure if that was her mind putting words in her head.

She couldn't decide which was worse, the embarrassment of him standing in front of her while she was barefoot in terrycloth or the obvious desire in his eyes that made her need another shower—*a cold one this time.*

Dressed, Nicole exited the closet and walked swiftly past Phobetor and straight back to the bathroom, too nervous to look at him. "Give me ten more minutes."

⇒⇒⇒⟩ ⟨⇐⇐⇐

Phobetor grinned wide as he watched the embarrassed Nicole essentially run back to the bathroom with only one towel this time. *This is going to be a fun day.*

Moments later, she appeared fully dressed in her *leave me the hell alone* armor. "So, are you flashing me to school or going back to your eerie-looking glass to watch me all day?"

"I thought about registering in high school for a while," Phobetor tried hard not to smirk.

"You wouldn't dare!" Wide eyes and fear peered back at him.

"I mean . . . it would be easier," he tried to hide his amusement.

"I'm sure Kallisto and Morpheus won't allow anything to happen to me."

"You have been under their charge twice where the deity got to you anyway. I am not sure that is such a great idea. Besides, Morpheus will not be there today."

"Fine. Watch me through your spying ball thingy. I'm riding with Amanda and Kallisto. I will physically see you this afternoon at our *crew* party."

"See you then, έξυπνος ομορφιά," Phobetor said before he vanished. Once in his home on Olympus, he thought about the night he spent in Nicole's bed. He worked all night, keeping dreams from her head. He gave her his strength mentally and physically so she would wake as rested as possible and be able to use her ability against the god who sought her. It was good that gods could go days without sleep when necessary.

He also noticed she failed to mention anything about their night wrapped together in her bed.

"How is it that I get the privilege of asking for an audience with the Moirai—again?" Phantasos asked Morpheus, appearing in his brother's bedchamber. He wore ripped jeans and a tight, dark gray D.F.O. T-shirt that proudly displayed, *Skilled in all Positions — Interview Me.*

"For the hundredth time, Phantasos, you could knock," Morpheus scowled.

"How was I supposed to know you had company?" Phantasos grinned wickedly.

"It's okay. Amanda and Nicole are waiting on me anyway. I just wanted to say bye since I won't see you at school," blowing Morpheus a kiss and winking at Phantasos, Kallisto flashed from Olympus.

"Seriously, knock next time."

Phantasos chuckled. "Are you ready to go see the weird sisters?"

"Are you wearing that shirt to see the Moirai?" Morpheus asked, shaking his head.

"Why not? Maybe I will get lucky. Moirai are demanding and not very flexible. Perhaps I can make them more—flexible," Phantasos smirked.

"With a t-shirt? You have a death wish," Morpheus chuckled, and they both vanished to the mansion of The Fates.

"You're quiet back there," Amanda said, looking in her rearview at Nicole.

"Do you know what happened with Pika last night?" Nicole asked in answer to Amanda's observation.

"Morpheus and Phantasos took care of everything. He nor his family will have any recollection of last night's events. I believe they said he remembers watching TV and studying," Kallisto informed them.

"That's a relief," Nicole said and returned to the quiet of the window and thought. Phobetor hadn't mentioned holding her through the night, and she had no idea how to approach the subject.

***

Standing next to Nicole's locker, Pika smiled wide as she approached. "I'm looking forward to grabbing a soda this afternoon. Wanna meet me in the parking lot and ride together?"

No one mentioned he would think yesterday's *date* was today. Scrambling, Nicole decided. "Yes. I'll meet you after classes." She needed to let Amanda know. A warmth ran up her spine, letting her know Phobetor got the message. The crew would have to meet later that evening instead of directly after school.

***

Morpheus and Phantasos found themselves waiting at the gates of the mansion of The Fates Three. "You seem a little nervous, brother," taunted Morpheus.

"Dread and nervousness are two different things. Every time I see these women, they give me a warning about loving a human. It seems I will never outlive my past." With his admission, the gates swung open, and a daemon led them to the mansion and to the throne room of the triplets.

"Well, well, well, it seems the Oneiroi have more questions. I do not believe you have ever been to our home this much. Seems the company you keep of late have your minds in a whirl," Clotho, the youngest of the three, spoke first. With her long, curly blonde hair and ice-blue eyes, she looked to be the most approachable of the three. That would be a mistake to think, though. Innocent, she may look; however, she was as deadly as her sisters.

"We need answers. Answers that could cost a life if we do not get them," Phantasos said.

"Oh, Phantasos. You know how this works. We know what you want. It is up to you and your brother to ask correctly for the knowledge you seek," Lachesis, the eldest sister, said.

"Would you beautiful ladies take pity on us and answer, without riddles, any question we ask?" Phantasos winked.

With a wide grin that reached her emerald eyes, Atropos answered. "Oh, what a flirt you are, Phantasos, but you know better than that. It is about intelligence. Surely you can figure out our responses."

"Well, yes—but who wants to put that much effort in," Phantasos grinned just as wide.

"Is the bender in mortal danger with the god who is after her?" Morpheus said, putting an end to the banter.

"Mortals are always in danger with the gods, but the one you speak of is in particular danger," Atropos answered.

"Who is the god rapting the bender?" Phantasos asked. It had not gone by his notice that Atropos' answer was more straightforward than they had ever received. *Maybe she is susceptible to seduction. Interesting.* He also noticed her sisters glaring at her.

"The one whose death you seek will change the balance—a war between gods. Take heed how you proceed. Make sure Phobetor does not return to Tartarus for life," Clotho answered.

"So, we cannot kill the god. Who is it?" Morpheus asked again.

"You have all you need to figure this out. Tell your bender not to fear," Atropos answered, with another glare from her sisters.

"What is going on with Hermes that the god-king and the under-lord both want intel?" Morpheus asked.

All three Moirai shook their heads in unison.

"No answers to the Hermes inquiry?" Phantasos looked directly at Atropos. Her straight auburn hair and emerald eyes were stunning, enough to turn his head. He shook his head, removing the spell. *She did that on purpose.*

In his head, he hears Atropos. *Never mistake power for intrigue.*

"As we have told Morpheus before, we are bound to not speak of some things, and that is one of them. Heed our warnings. All of them, Phantasos," the eldest Moirai answered.

Phantasos flinched at the threat.

"How do we keep the bender safe? How do we protect her?" Morpheus asked.

"You do what you can. Fate will have its way no matter what. Be prepared," Clotho answered.

Phantasos looked at his brother. "It seems we need to dust off our armor, brother."

"War can be prevented. Mortals are temptations for the gods. You must know when not to be tempted," Clotho reminded the brothers of their warnings.

"We have answered your inquiries. Now, go warn your brother. Protect the mortals, but remember that does not always mean death," Lachesis dismissed the Oneiroi.

➤➤➤ ⫷⫷⫷

Morpheus flashed to Phobetor to take over, watching Nicole while he went to visit Zeus. "We will discuss the musings of Moirai this evening with everyone. There is much to discuss."

Phobetor nodded and flashed to the doors of the great mansion on Olympus. Without having to announce himself, the doors swung open to reveal a nymph waiting to escort him to the king of the gods of Olympus.

Zeus sat on his throne with its engravings of the beginning of time. "Welcome. Are you here to discuss Hermes or the bender?"

Phobetor knew the king watched, but his asking about Nicole and confirming she was a bender took him aback. Maybe he had answers he would be willing to separate from.

"I come to speak of Hermes, but I would love to discuss the mortal as well," Phobetor answered.

Zeus grinned, "We shall see."

"Hermes came to me asking that I get close to his son-in-law. Apparently, the mortal does not know of his wife's heritage but came home feeling uneasy with the signature of a god surrounding him. Angelia was worried enough to reach out to her mother. I have not gone to the mortal yet."

"Is this mortal girl keeping you from the task Hermes has asked of you?" Zeus questioned.

"No. He is getting the information I asked for. I am sure to hear from him shortly."

"Do not let this bender get in your way of the task Hermes has set you on. I need to know what is going on with my son and granddaughter."

"Speaking of the bender. Who is rapturing her?"

"I do not tamper with such trivial things. If a god wants her, and you do not want the god to have her, that is a problem for you. Now, if my son has not come to you within a fortnight, I expect you to go to him and ask if he has the information you need."

"I will be back in a fortnight." Phobetor flashed from the room and back to relieve Morpheus of his watch.

Chapter XXIX

Gathering

Nicole walked between the cars to where Pika leaned against his. "Ready?" she asked.

"Your chariot awaits," Pika bowed slightly and opened the door for her. She couldn't help but laugh at him.

She thought about the day before and how strange it was to repeat the same thing over. She would have him take her home right after their soda this time. Phobetor was back at his orb, and Kallisto and Amanda were at the mall, not far away. *I am safe*, was the mental mantra that kept her from panicking.

"What's your favorite band?" She knew Pika was trying to keep the conversation going to relieve the awkwardness between them.

"I like old punk bands. Not sure you've ever heard of them," Nicole answered.

"Try me."

"Well, okay. The Sex Pistols, Dead Boys, The Damned, to name a few."

"You're right. I'm more of a pop-rock guy. If it's on the radio, I'm in," they both laughed.

They ordered their drinks and sat and talked about normal teenage issues. It was nice to talk like she had no care beyond schoolwork, social ranks, and the future.

About thirty minutes into their conversation, Nicole looked up to see Phobetor staring at her. He was there, in front of her. Pika's back was to him, but not for long. When she went quiet, and Pika saw her eyes trained behind him, he turned to see what caught her attention. *Shit.* Was the only word to go through her mind.

"Nicole, how are you?" Phobetor asked as he stalked toward them.

"I'm good. Pika, this is—"

"Ty . . . I am a friend of Nicole's," Phobetor said in an American accent, surprising Nicole.

"Good to meet you, Ty. Want to join us?"

"No. I am meeting friends. It was good to run into you, Nicole," Phobetor turned and left as fast as he appeared.

What the hell is he doing? She felt his presence, watching, and his amusement filled her.

"How do you know him?" Pika asked.

"Uh. He lives down the street from my aunt." She made sure Pika could hear that she was done with her soda and sat it down in front of her.

"Would you like some fries or another drink," Pika asked. She could tell he wasn't ready to go. But she was. She needed to see what the guys found out from The Fates and what the hell Phobetor was up to.

"I can't. I have homework, and I promised to spend some time with Amanda and her family. Her dad comes home late this evening. He's been on a work trip."

"Okay," Pika said reluctantly. "Let's head out."

"I had a good time," Nicole said as they started down the road.

"Have you ever had the feeling you were reliving something? Kinda like deja vu?" Pika asked.

"Sure. I've read it's when your eye captures something twice."

"No. Like your whole day has been on repeat," Pika said, sounding confused.

"I can't say I have," *Crap!*

"It's felt like that all day. Until we got in my car just now. I sound crazy," Pika half laughed.

"Not crazy, just not a normal feeling. I suppose we all have weird days."

"Thank you for going with me to the mall. Maybe we can go out sometime?"

"Pika, are you asking me on a date?"

"Would it be so bad if I was?"

"Do you always answer with a question," Nicole giggled.

"Maybe. When I don't want to answer the question," he grinned.

"Ask me again in a week. I have a lot going on this next week. I start a new job, and my family will be doing a lot to prepare for Amanda's dad to be gone for months. Maybe I'll have a schedule by then."

"So that's not a no—I'll take it. This you?" he pointed to the house she came to know as home.

"Yes." Nicole leaned over and gave him a light kiss on his lips, then opened the door and fled to the house, not looking back to his shock.

Phobetor's frame filled the door when she opened it. His eyes were squinted, and his mouth set in a scowl. *Oops*, sometimes she forgot he was watching.

"Is everyone here?" she asked, trying to break the tension between them.

"I feel everyone's signature in the study. Amanda's mom is still out," Phobetor replied, his glare not subsiding.

"Let's do this," Nicole skirted around the massive form that is the god of nightmares and walked to the study.

⟫⟫⟩ ⟨⟨⟨⟨

Morpheus stood next to the desk, his arms wrapped around Kallisto, waiting for the last two to settle in for the debrief of the day's events. There was no mistaking the tension filling the air as Nicole and Phobetor entered. He could tell his brother was close to exploding. The tension in his limbs screamed jealousy and a little disgust. Regret and shame from Nicole radiated off her. *What happened in the last few hours?*

"Okay, Phantasos and I will fill you in on our trip to the weird sisters, and then Phobetor can tell us about his trip to see the king.

Next, Nicole, will you start from the beginning and tell us everything you can possibly remember from when this unknown god raptured you?"

"Yes. I'll try. They're pretty fuzzy."

"The Fates never denied you are a true dream bender. In fact, they answered our questions as if you were a bender, and we had everything we needed to figure this out." Phantasos spoke first.

"They warned that we do not kill the god who we seek. They especially said for you," Morpheus turned his eyes on Phobetor, "not get yourself sent back to Tartarus for life. The warning was spoken of twice in our brief audience with The Fates."

"The most interesting thing said, other than confirming you are a bender," Phantasos added, "is for you, Nicole, not to fear, but also said you are in danger. I am not sure what they mean. It was definitely a contradiction. Unfortunately, they like their puzzles."

Phobetor verified, "Zeus confirmed Nicole is a bender. He actually referred to her as the bender, wanting to know if I came to speak of Hermes or "the bender.""

"Speaking of Hermes, we asked the Moirai about him. They would not even acknowledge what we asked, just continued to warn us," Phantasos interjected.

⤜⟫⟫ ⟪⟪⤛

"So, no killing this asshole who haunts me. I'm a dream bender, and Phobetor is in on the edge of Tartarus—nice," Nicole summed up the discussion.

"I have a fortnight to speak with Hermes' son by marriage, per Zeus," Phobetor added. "I do not think Hermes' situation has anything to do with Nicole's raptures, but we should always keep our eyes open for all possibilities. I will be going into this mortal's dreams over the next couple of weeks. When I do, someone needs to watch Nicole."

Nicole scowled.

She spent the next hour telling them everything she remembered about each rapture, starting with the wreck over a year ago. The gods and Amanda took it all in, only interrupting to clarify sensory words she used in her descriptions. There's a lot you can tell from your senses when you remember very little. The smell of lavender gave away that it was a god from the Greek Pantheon, unless another smelled of the purple blossoms. The sound of her capture's voice also gave away the god was male.

Car lights streamed across the walls of the study. "That's my mom and dad back from the airport. It's best if everyone is gone but Kallisto and Nicole. It's a little weird to have three men that look like—well, it's just a little weird," Amanda looked at her watch, "at ten thirty at night, to have company."

Morpheus nodded and leaned down to kiss Kallisto. Amanda scowled at Phantasos, and Nicole turned her back to Phobetor under the pretense of looking out the window. The Oneiroi vanished.

Chapter XXX

Gallery

"Dad!" Amanda ran into Alaric's arms before he made it two steps into the foyer.

"Well, if that's not a great homecoming. It's only been two weeks." He chuckled and squeezed her tight.

"I know. It's just that my senior year is almost over, and I'm more emotional than usual. I guess I'm trying to capture all the "moments" since Kallisto and I will be moving to the dorms in a few months."

"Like I said, baby girl, it's a great homecoming." Baby girl—that had been what he called her before she was even born. She didn't remember the last time he called her by name. Actually, the only times she remembered him using her name was when she was in trouble. Since she was about grown and no longer the hyper child or the back-talking preteen, he rarely called her Amanda.

"Hello, Kalli," he nodded toward Kallisto in greeting, then turned to Nicole. "Come give your uncle a hug," Alaric reached for Nicole, still holding onto Amanda. He squeezed them both in a bear hug. His thick biceps and wide chest encompassed the girls. Amanda's parents looked like middle-aged supermodels. Both were in their early forties with thick blonde hair, captivating blue eyes, and fitter than most of the people she knew—not counting the deities in her new life. The reason for Amanda's beauty was clear—she had no choice but to be gorgeous.

"How was your trip? Tell us about the sharks." Amanda's eyes gleamed at the thought of great white sharks everywhere.

"We are set up to start in a month. The sharks aren't there yet. So, I didn't have the pleasure of meeting any," her father smirked. "Maybe you three ladies can come to the camp for a week before classes start this fall?"

"I'll be in Greece most of the summer, but maybe my parents will let me fly from Greece to South Africa before coming home," Kallisto interjected.

"Well, who knows where I'll be—Tennessee, Hawaii, juvenile detention," Nicole answered with a mischievous grin.

"Prison is not an option. You like things on your own terms too much," Kathryn laughed. "Plus, the food sucks, and you don't look good in orange." Everyone laughed.

"What have you ladies been up to?" Alaric asked as they walked to the living room.

"I've been trying to decide if I want to work more since everyone else is—Nicole starts her new job tomorrow," Amanda said.

"Oh yeah, where?" Alaric asked his niece.

"At the gallery with Kallisto and Amanda if she will give in and just work," Nicole shook her head at her cousin, tempting her.

"Is your boss sure he wants all three of you—at once? That sounds like tempting fate," Alaric chuckled when Amanda elbowed him. The family and Kallisto sat around until midnight asking Alaric about his trip and his new adventure with the kings of the sea.

⤜⟫ ⟪⤛

The next morning, Nicole rode with Kallisto to her house to get ready for work. It was no more than a ten-minute ride, but Nicole felt the tension in Kallisto rise the closer they got.

"Are you okay?" Nicole asked.

"Yeah. It's my dad. He's fine with the announcement of mine and Mom's godhood. I mean it took days to convince him we nor he were going crazy. It's just, well—he feels betrayed by mom. The air's thick since her confession. It doesn't help that Morpheus and I are together. Dad is super protective of me, and he feels like his world has been turned upside down—I guess it has. He's not the protector anymore. We are."

"Good morning, Mom," Kallisto said as she entered her home.

"Good morning, sweetie. Good morning, Nicole. Are you ready for your first day of work?"

"Yes, ma'am," Southern to the end, Nicole replied politely.

"Good morning, Dad," Kallisto turned to her father, who was deep in his phone reading the daily news.

"Good morning, Kalli. You ladies, have a good day. I'm heading to the docks to prepare the boat for a four-day outing. See you this evening," her father left the room. Kallisto saw the sadness displayed in her mother's eyes.

"He'll come around. He just needs more time," Kallisto reached for her mother's hand and squeezed.

"It's been almost two months," Thia shook her head.

"I'm taking this one," Kallisto pointed to Nicole, "upstairs to show her black is not the only color eye shadow comes in."

Once dressed, the girls drove to the mall, with Phobetor watching the entire time, even though Nicole was with the granddaughter of Zeus.

⁂

"So, let me get this straight," Nicole addressed Kallisto. "Hermes owns the gallery and many others around the world, correct?"

"Yes. It's one of his many hats. He's the messenger of the gods, the deity of trade and commerce, and the conductor of souls—he carries the dead to the underworld, where they then go to one of the Fields or to Tartarus."

"When does he sleep?" Nicole asked as she entered the gallery behind Kallisto.

"He's divine—he doesn't need it as much as mortals do," Kallisto answered as she turned on the lights.

Nicole's breath caught as the illumination of the divinity in front of her now held a different realization. "Are these paintings truly exact? Does that painting really look like Aphrodite?"

"Yes. I have yet to see any that aren't replicas of the deity they depict. The ones of Mount Olympus are also accurate."

"I've seen that place," Nicole points to a painting of Olympus. "When Phobetor took me." She felt sadness fill her, so she turned from Kallisto to look at the sculptures on the far side.

"Let me turn the air down some," Kallisto walked to the back. She returned with Morpheus in tow.

"Good morning," he nodded to Nicole. "Are you ready to get started?"

"Yes. What's first?"

"First, I will show you around. You will need your phone. I will show you the art, and you will take a picture of it—flash off. Then, you will make notes so you can remember everything about each piece. Once you get used to who is who, things will become easier. You will need to remember what was happening in each piece since you will already know who the piece is of," Morpheus answered.

"I'm going to wrap some pieces that were sold yesterday so the guys can deliver them," Kallisto said. "By the way, remember, he's Ambrose while in the gallery," Kallisto winked.

"That's right. Your alias," Nicole grinned and started following the youngest Oneiroi around, taking notes and pictures. It took several hours to go through all one hundred pieces on the floor. *Who knew the gods of Olympus were so popular?*

"It's your lunch break," Kallisto announced. "Morpheus is going on an errand. I'll watch the shop. Can you bring me back a cheeseburger?"

"Sure," Nicole left the gallery and ran into a large man who was about to enter. "Oh. I'm sorry," a chill went up her spine, and her tattoo started to burn on contact with the giant of a man.

"My apologies," he spoke with an accent she couldn't place.

Moving around him, she continued walking. She felt Phobetor watching. Surely, if the man was a divine threat, he would've appeared or something.

With cheeseburger and milkshake ladened arms, Nicole returned to the gallery. "Here, I hope you like chocolate."

"Of course," Kallisto grinned.

The girls sat at the table just inside the back, where they could hear the bell when someone came in. "Did that big guy with the accent purchase anything?"

"What guy?" Kallisto asked.

"The one I literally ran into as he was coming in the door."

"No one came in while you were gone. It's been a rather boring day."

"Are you sure? I saw him," the chill returned.

"I'm positive," Kallisto said.

"Well, maybe he decided not to come in."

"He may've had the wrong shop. We get that a lot. People come in here thinking it's the photo gallery next door."

"Yeah. That's probably it," but Nicole felt differently.

The rest of the day flew by. John relieved the girls and took the Saturday evening crowd, and Amanda picked Nicole up.

"The night's young, let's celebrate your first day of work," Amanda said as the girls walked down the sidewalk.

"What do you have in mind," Nicole asked.

"Well, there's a young adults club close by. I haven't been since Kallisto's dad went missing. Our lives have been different since then. It's fun. You may want to roll up your sleeves and unbutton your top some. Then you will be perfect," Amanda jeered.

"I kinda feel out of my element going to a club, especially with no black shadow."

"Here," Amanda handed Nicole her travel makeup back. "I'm sure you can find something gray in there," she winked.

Once the girls were both satisfied with their club attire, they headed to Maui's young adult dance club—The Dragon's Lair–for ages seventeen to twenty-three only.

Chapter XXXI

Dance

Immediately, Nicole felt foolish. She had never been to a dance club. The only dances she had attended were in junior high school and a couple in high school before the wreck. There, she knew everyone, and the teachers and chaperons controlled the hormone-laden adolescence. Here, teens and young adults gyrated on the dance floor, surrounded by deafening music and darkness, except for the occasional blue and white flashing lights. Some people danced with partners, others without. Sweat dripped down their faces. It was only seven at night, and the place was packed with people getting closer than she thought possible with clothes on—and in public.

"You, okay?" Amanda yelled over the music.

"I'm good, but wow," Nicole called back.

"Let's get a soda. Follow me," Amanda grabbed her hand and tugged her through the mayhem. Apparently, Amanda didn't mind the sweaty bodies bumping against her on all sides since she chose to go through the crowd instead of around it. *I suppose the shortest route is a straight line from point A to point B.* Nicole rolled her eyes as Amanda continued to pull her to the opposite side of the room. *Did that guy just grab my ass?* She thought.

Finally, across the room, Nicole got close to Amanda's ear. "Remember, I dress like I do to keep people away from me." To Nicole's irritation, Amanda just grinned, then leaned close to the guy behind the counter and ordered two Cokes in plastic bottles.

"Never have an open container. Someone could drug your drink," Amanda told Nicole.

"That's reassuring," Nicole responded. She may look the part of a partier, but she'd never been one, not before or after her wreck.

Amanda pulled her onto the dance floor. "You need to loosen up. Just enjoy the music flowing through your body."

Nicole looked around her. Everyone looked happy. She started moving. After a few minutes, she relaxed and started enjoying herself. Three songs in, the guy she could have sworn grabbed her earlier made his way over to them. He winked and held out his hand. *Oh shit!*—was the first thought that ran through her head. The next was—*Why the hell not?* Before she knew it, the good-looking, nameless guy clung to her as she danced between his legs. Both moved to the fast-paced beats of the song. His hands made their way over her ass. She kept moving, too wrapped up in the music to care—until nameless stopped and turned. Phobetor stood there, glaring. He made more than two of the nameless guy. Nameless moved, thanking Nicole for the dance.

Nicole forgot how large the deity was. Her neck craned to see his eyes since they now stood chest to chest. She was sweaty, and her hair was half down, sticking to her face. His lips were set in a straight line, and his eyes swirled black. She looked next to her and found Phantasos with Amanda against his chest with the same look, maybe a little more pissed off, though. *Well, shit!*

Nicole turned to walk off the dance floor, and Phobetor grabbed her arm. "I think not, my έξυπνος ομορφιά." He started dancing against her. Even closer than nameless. There was no more wondering how those fully clothed people got so close to each other—she quickly found out when his body started moving. She also realized his eyes turned onyx and swirled with other emotions besides anger. *Holy hell.* They now swirled with desire. She felt his need and swallowed. *Where in hell did he learn how to move like this?*

⇢⇢⇢ ⇠⇠⇠

"What the hell are you two doing here," Amanda yelled over the music.

"I am trying to keep my brother's monster from rearing its ugly head," Phantasos answered.

"He looks fine to me," Amanda said as she looked over at her cousin, who was putting on an exhibition with the Oneiroi. She couldn't believe that Nicole, who reluctantly came into the club with her, was the one dancing beside her now—and with a god. "Damn! Who knew she could dance like that?"

Phantasos grinned and wrapped Amanda in his arms. "What is the saying you mortals use...If you cannot beat them, join them."

Not wanting to cause a problem, since Nicole seemed to finally be having a good time, she succumbed to temptation and danced with Phantasos. However, she kept him at arm's length and pushed at his chest to give her breathing room. He smirked.

"I refuse to get down and dirty with you," she told him. Phantasos chuckled, and the four danced for over an hour.

⇢⇢⇢ ⇠⇠⇠

Exhausted, Nicole pulled Phobetor to the bar and ordered two sodas. He took the drink from her but never took his eyes off her. Amanda and Phantasos continued to dance.

"Where does she get that energy?" Nicole asked allowed.

"You worked all day. She did not," Phobetor answered.

"I need to get her. I'm tired and ready to leave."

"Let me," Phobetor offered.

Moments later, Phobetor was back. However, Amanda and the eldest Oneiroi continued to dance. "Did she misunderstand you?"

"No, my ἐξυπνος ομορφιά. I told them I had you and we were going," he clasped her hands, and they walked to the middle of the dance floor, and she felt the spinning feeling she got before she—

"Where are we?" Nicole stood gazing about the vast room.

"Athens, Greece. My home in your realm."

"You brought me to your place in Greece? I'm going crazy. What if someone saw us just vanish into thin air?"

"You are not crazy, and no one noticed. That is why we went into the crowded dance floor."

"What about Amanda?" Nicole was overwhelmed by the sudden change in venue and concerned about her cousin.

"Those two will be a couple of hours. I do not think Amanda's parents would like it if you came home without their daughter, especially since she is the one driving. You can rest here. When they are done, Phantasos will let me know, and I will take you back."

"I'm not sure leaving those two together is such a good idea. They may kill each other," Nicole said as she took in the incredible sights before her. His home was just as amazing as the one on Mount Olympus, just on a smaller scale.

"True, but my bet is on Amanda. Trust me, she can take my brother." Phobetor winked. "In all seriousness, with him, she is safer than with any other. No matter how much she hates him."

"Okay, I guess. I've never been to Greece," Nicole changed the subject.

"It is beautiful. When I was young, my brothers and I played on the shores of Greece. It reminds me of good times. Here, sit." Phobetor led her to the massive couch facing a wall of glass with the city of Athens splayed before them. Sunlight spilled into the room through the wall of windows.

Moments ago, she was covered in the darkness of night, and now, she appeared across the world, thirteen hours ahead, in the blink of an eye. *This is incredible.* Nicole gazed at the sight before her.

"Yes, beautiful," Phobetor repeated. "It's beautiful!"

Nicole looked up and blushed—he watched her, not the view beyond the windows.

She cleared her throat, trying to chase away the embarrassment, and asked. "How long have you lived here?"

"Just under a century."

Her eyes widened. "A century?" *I'm way outta my league here.*

"Yes," he smirked. "Unfortunately for me, Hera is an astute goddess. Zeus had me delivering messages that could get me killed by her or one of her overzealous minions. So, this," Phobetor gestured around the room, "was his way of giving me what you call—hazard pay."

"What about Olympus?"

Phobetor rounded the sofa and sat a couple of feet from her. "I live here mostly but go to Olympus every few weeks. The gods need the grounds of their Pantheon to keep their strength up. We are connected to the essence of the land."

"What would happen if you never returned?" Nicole asked.

"I would weaken to that of a sickly mortal, unable to walk dreams, no immortal powers, just immortality."

"That sounds horrible."

"It is. Those in Tartarus live below Olympus, so they do not completely lose their power. They have just enough to continue their miserable lives."

"May I ask a question?"

"Of course. You can ask me anything," Phobetor answered.

Nicole felt heat run over her cheeks, but damn, she felt she needed to know. "The Fates warned you not to get put back in the underworld. Why were you there?"

"My core is not all good. I am the ruler of nightmares and the conjuror of fear—the master of unimaginable visions and anxiety. Unfortunately, I have a temper. There was a time when I took my abilities too far. I became a monster by all standards. I unleashed my abilities on whomever I wished, drawing power from the nightmares I conjured. Now, I only unleash such horrors on those who need to see things in a different light in hopes they will change their course. I have not preyed on the undeserving in a millennium. I walk a thin line. Being the Oneiroi I am, I must remind myself daily that I am a weapon for the good of mortals and gods."

"Do you want to harm people, now?" Nicole asked. She realized she should be quaking after his admission, but for some irrational reason, she felt completely safe with Phobetor. Even if she was half a world away from everyone she knew.

Phobetor looked from her to the landscape beyond the windows. "I have lately. Each time you were raptured, when I saw you with that Pika kid, and when you were dancing with that asshole," he did not look at her, but she could see the worry in his posture and hear it in his voice.

Damn. "Each time was because of me." It wasn't a question, but he answered anyway.

"Yes."

The emotions playing at the edge of Nicole's soul were nothing she'd ever experienced, and she didn't know how to process them. *Ignoring them sounds good.*

"Well, I'll think about that later. Can you take me to see the shop Kallisto and Amanda rave about? I think it's called Designed for Olympus, D.F.O for short."

Phobetor smirked and held out his hand as he stood. "You are in luck. We can actually walk there in less than ten minutes."

Nicole released a mental breath and took Phobetor's hand. "I need a t-shirt."

Chapter XXXII

Leo

Stepping out into the sunshine of Athens was the most surreal moment of her life. Nicole was in awe of its beauty. Phobetor was right. They stood before the famous D.F.O. shop in under ten minutes. It took one step into the shop to let her know she was not in the shop of a mortal—*Lavender and honeysuckle.* She turned and looked at Phobetor.

He returned her grin with a wink. Hermes is not the only god who earns a mortal living in this realm. "Welcome to Phantasos' shop."

"Are you serious?" Nicole exclaimed, not quite believing him.

"Why do you think he is always wearing their t-shirts? I do not think your cousin or Kallisto know he owns it though."

"Wow. I would never have guessed Phantasos owned anything, let alone D.F.O. That's crazy cool." Nicole combed over every inch of the store. The decor was made up of straight lines, tropical plants, and large white columns dividing the sections. It smelled of the mount and felt otherworldly. *No wonder they flip over this place and its clothes.* There was a wall covered in peplos, chitons, and togas.

By the end of her perusal, she had two t-shirts, a pair of black jeans, and cream peplos with gold fig leaf pins to hold the shoulders together.

"Let me see the T-shirts you chose?" Phobetor eyes were back to swirled gold, and he looked happier and somehow lighter than she had ever seen him. *He is absolutely gorgeous,* she thought.

She held up a gray shirt that stated, *I Belong on Olympus,* and a black and white one that said, *I Want a Dreamer.* She smirked in challenge. He grinned in return.

"I might can make one of those happen," he winked.

Before they returned to his house, Phantasos had reached out to Phobetor to let him know Amanda was on her way home. They flashed back to Hawaii and met Amanda as she pulled into her driveway. She looked exhausted.

"Hello, cuz," Nicole smiled wide as she held up her D.F.O. bag of spoils.

"You've got to be kidding me," Amanda shook her head. "I got stuck with my immortal enemy, and you went to Greece to shop? How's that fair?"

"Maybe we can all go soon," Nicole looked to Phobetor for help.

"Sure. I know Phantasos would love to visit," he winked at Nicole.

"Fine, but let's leave him out of this," Amanda said.

"I will be watching. You ladies have a good evening," then he vanished.

"How was the rest of your evening?" Nicole asked as they quietly walked to Amanda's room.

"It was okay until another guy asked me to dance. Phantasos actually growled at him. Growled...like a dog. I seriously don't get him."

"I don't think he gets himself. Other than that?"

"He was nice enough. I just danced and enjoyed myself. He danced and made sure no one else saw me. How about you? Greece? I mean seriously... Greece?"

"Yep. You should have seen my face when I found myself in a sunlit world with the city of Athens laid out in front of me. It was just as amazing as Olympus."

"I've been there, but never with a Greek god. I mean, damn. That's like a dream come true." Amanda grinned. "No pun intended." They both giggled. "Let me see what you got."

Nicole pulled out her shirts, jeans, and the cream peplos.

"I can't wait to go to that shop," Amanda said as she inspected each article of clothing Nicole brought back.

"It was awesome. Uh, Amanda," Nicole folded each article after her cousin finished with them.

"Yes. Your demeanor just changed. You okay? He didn't do anything to you, did he?"

"Hell no. I'm worried about you," Nicole admitted.

"Me? Why me? You're the one with an evil god breathing down your neck."

"It's just...you're not yourself. You haven't been. I can also tell you have mixed emotions where Phantasos is concerned. Like you hate him, but don't."

"He's an ass. When I think he's not, he proves me wrong. And when he proves me wrong, it's usually hurtful. Apparently, it has something to do with those weird sisters and their sight. Warnings or not, he has no reason to be hurtful, but he does it anyway. I don't know. Mostly, I hate myself for allowing his moodiness to affect me. At the end of the day, after what I went through in January, I'm not sure the Amanda you once knew is in here," Amanda held her hand over her heart.

"You're right, I've seen him be an ass, but I've also seen how he looks at you. He's fierce when it comes to your protection. I honestly think he's a natural ass who needs to sort his shit out, but I also believe he cares about you. He may not want to, but he does," Nicole decided to keep the D.F.O. owner's information to herself.

"That's enough about my life. How are you doing? You're taking the whole; *there's a Greek god trying to steal me away,* thing in stride."

"It's weird. Before I came to Hawaii, I was ready to end it. I didn't feel like I had anything good left to live for. Now, I feel different. I've got me to live for, and that's enough. Phobetor hasn't entered my dreams in a long time, but he's been a big part of healing my soul. It's like his presence chases the fear and anxiety away," Nicole admitted.

"Are you catching feelings?" Amanda teased.

"I'm not sure. I'm catching guilt for sure, though," Nicole admitted.

"Why guilt?"

Nicole felt a trimmer of anxiety flash through her, "Chase."

Amanda's eyes softened. "He's gone. You deserve to live. Chase would want you to live if he cared for you as you do him." Amanda pulled Nicole to her chest and stroked her hair. Nicole allowed a single tear to roll unchecked down her face. "Healing takes time. You have time," Amanda said.

"Morpheus," Phobetor called to his brother.

Seconds later, Morpheus appeared in the living area of Phobetor's Grecian home. "You summoned," Morpheus bowed at the waist, aggravating his brother.

"I heard from Hermes' messenger. He sent me his son-in-law's name and a few mental pictures of him. I need to get this over with. Can you watch over Nicole until I return?"

"Kallisto and I can. Are you leaving now?" Morpheus asked.

"Yes, after I inform Nicole of the shift change."

"No need for her to know. We will watch her."

"Well, evidently, another gift of a bender is they can feel watchers. She can tell when it is me, but she can only sense another's presence and not who they are."

"Many mortals can feel watchers, but you are saying she knows when it is you?" Intrigue splayed across Morpheus' face, followed by a grin.

"Yes. I know what you are thinking. Stop thinking," Phobetor sneered at the inquisitive Oneiroi. "I need to get this done so I can get back to Nicole."

Morpheus stood with his arms crossed and a smirk on his lips. "Since you know what I am thinking, maybe you should prepare yourself for the inevitable."

Phobetor shot him what he hoped was a "back the fuck off" look and vanished.

Morpheus chuckled and flashed to his bedchamber to watch through his orb. He sent word to Kallisto, knowing she and Nicole would be at work in a couple of hours, then he would join them. Until then, he would watch over Nicole as she slept and think about who could be tormenting her. The words of the Moirai continued to stir his mind. *You have everything you need.*

Hermes' messenger gave Phobetor a few locations where Angelia's husband could be. It was early afternoon in West Virginia, so the mortal was probably home, hopefully taking a Sunday nap. *One could be so lucky.*

Phobetor stood at the gates of a large cabin built in the mountains where Angelia pretended to be mortal. He had to give it to the goddess. She may not like Olympus and its politics, but obviously, she enjoyed its beauty and the riches it offered. Becoming *mortal* had not removed her eye for luxury. After all, he stood before an enormous wrought iron gate depicting a fairyland scene. With small, winged fairies and toadstools along its bottom. A massive cabin with a well-trimmed yard was set up higher on the edge of the mountain. Reaching out with his gifts, he sensed three mortal signatures and one of a dog. One mortal was awake, busying themselves from room to room. *Probably a servant.* One being was awake but sitting still. The other was blessedly napping. With a little push, he confirmed the napper was male. Phobetor entered Anthony's dream state by drawing on Angelia's memories and photos the messenger obtained.

One would like to think an elderly man's dreams were all peaceful, but Phobetor had no such delusions. He had conjured horrific dreams for all ages. If Anthony's mind would play without him applying pressure, then maybe he would not need to scare the old man. Anthony was not dreaming; he was resting with his mind shut peacefully off. *How nice, but that will not give me answers.*

Phobetor searched through the man's memories until he found what he was looking for—the signature of a Greek god. The presence was cunning. He could tell the deity worked to keep anyone from accessing his mark. Unlike the Oneiroi, he was not perfect at masking his essence. Phobetor watched as the memory played out. To Anthony, he was dreaming about that horrible day at the office.

"Hello, Anthony. You may call me Leo." The god wore a made-to-measure black suit and Ferragamo Oxfords. *He has style, at least.* Unfortunately, the god made his face unrecognizable. *Just a few more minutes, and I will know who you are.*

"How did you get in here?" Anthony asked the deity, looking the god up and down.

"Now that is a funny story. You see, Angelia has been keeping something very important from you. Please do not pass out or have one of those attacks on your heart when I tell you because her secret is a big one."

"I don't know who you are or what you're playing at, but you need to leave." Anthony pressed a button on his desk phone, but nothing happened. Sweat beaded around his hairline.

"Do not be rude. You and I will become great friends. You see, your dear wife is a god. Not a demigod, no...she is the daughter of Hermes and Aphrodite and the granddaughter of Zeus himself."

"You are a madman! Martha, get the police on the phone!" Anthony yelled as he pressed several buttons on the speaker.

"Your secretary is unresponsive at this time."

"Did you hurt her?" Anthony gasped.

"No. Why would I do that? She was just frightened to the point of fainting. She will be out until I stop enjoying her fear," the god delivered each word slower than was necessary, giving time for each one to sink in. "Now, where were we? Oh, yes. Your Angelia. She hates her heritage and has fooled you and your family for over fifty years. Not long for one of our kind, but more than half of a mortal's life. How does that make you feel, Anthony? To be lied to." The god watched as Anthony scrambled to gain breath.

"Again, you are insane," Anthony trembled as sweat dripped along the slope of his nose. "Leave me and my family alone."

"Unfortunately, I cannot. There is one of your family members I need. My time is up. We would not want the Oneiroi to find out."

The god vanished before Anthony's eyes and moments before Phobetor could visualize his face. Tears tracked down Anthony's cheeks as he scrambled to his feet and ran for his office door.

Phobetor allowed the man to wake, noticing his heartbeats had quickened and his breathing was unsteady.

Damn it! Phobetor pulled from Anthony's mind.

Chapter XXXIII

Rapture

Nicole watched as Kallisto typed in the alarm code, effectively turning off the offensive beeping so their day could begin.

"Unfortunately, we have inventory today," Kallisto informed as she circled the gallery, turning on switches to illuminate the paintings throughout the gallery floor.

"I know where the lights in the backrooms are. I'll get those," Nicole said. While turning on the light, she noticed two large paintings propped against the back-office walls, covered in shipping paper. "Do you want me to unwrap these paintings?" She called out to Kallisto.

Kallisto entered the office area and stared at the paintings, mouth agape. "Surely those are not what I think they are."

"I need more to go on here," Nicole laughed. Kallisto stood very still, like the paintings were going to detonate or something equally as crazy.

"Hermes commissioned our paintings," Kallisto whispered, evidently not wanting to be heard, or so the paintings wouldn't be what she thought they were.

"Our paintings?" Nicole's hands itched to rip the paper off them. It would be much faster than getting information out of Kallisto, who stood transfixed.

"Mine and Mom's," Kallisto finally answered. She spoke softly. "All my life, I read and reread stories of the gods and their king, Zeus. I was borderline obsessed. I take that back—I was obsessed. Of course, now I know why, but this new life is surreal. I expected to wake up any minute and it was all a dream. Each Oneiroi wove parts of the dream. A mixture of fantasy from Phantasos, nightmares from Phobetor, and everything else from Morpheus...an illusion of my deepest desires. These paintings are of gods. Once opened, I wonder if I will wake up."

"Well, I honestly don't think your dream would include a deeply distraught girl whom you are tasked to teach inventory," Nicole spoke as quietly as Kallisto had. "Come on. If you wake up from some elaborate dream, then I'm anxious to see where I am in real life. Let's open them."

Nicole watched the new god before her shake with anxiety. *Who would have guessed Greek gods could be anxious?* "Okay," was all Kallisto said before she ripped into the painting closest to her.

"See...this is all real. Very, very real," Nicole said as they both stared at an exact replica of Kallisto sitting on Pegasus with his wings to his sides. They were standing in the meadow by the waterfall on Mount Olympus. Her thick black hair draped across her shoulders. It wasn't the beauty of her full lips or the steed she sat on that made the painting the most beautiful one in the gallery...it was her eyes. Those aqua orbs were proof—she was a god—and this was no dream.

Nicole turned and looked at Kallisto, who cried silent tears. "Are you okay?"

"Yeah. I honestly thought I was going to wake up from a dream. How can I be so lucky?" She continued to shake.

"It's because of the way you think and feel that will make you a great helper of humankind. Never forget how this moment feels. It will ground you," Nicole said.

"How did you get so insightful?" Kallisto giggled and wiped the tears from her cheeks.

"Once, I was a smart cookie. Not a crumbled one." Nicole answered. "Let's see what your mom's looks like."

Thia's painting was that of a warrior. She wore a lavender peplos with a slit up to the top of her thigh, where an Atlantean dagger lay strapped to her leg. Gold bands wrapped around her upper arms, and she stood in front of Zeus' dais. She was gorgeous and lethal. The gold plate at the bottom of the painting read, "Lethal Elegance: Thia, daughter of Zeus."

"She's stunning," Nicole said.

"Yes. She is."

"How are we going to hang these in the gallery when you both live on the island?" Nicole asked.

"These paintings won't be displayed to the public for at least a century. Hermes had them commissioned to hang in my grandfather's throne room."

Nicole swallowed audibly and shook her head. "I don't think I will ever get over this. Greek gods are real. Mythological creatures are real. I'm standing here talking to the granddaughter of Zeus. How crazy is that? Now I think I'm the one dreaming."

"About as crazy as me being a Greek goddess," Kallisto said. Both girls were laughing when Morpheus walked in.

"What are you ladies . . ." Morpheus stopped and stared. "Wow. Those are captivating."

"They are," Kallisto agreed. "I now feel the enormity of my heritage."

"It is quite the heritage. Especially when you are the favored grandchild," Morpheus reached to touch the Kallisto in the frame.

"That's not true," Kallisto blushed.

"You know it is," Morpheus winked. "Has Phobetor come back?"

"We haven't seen him," Nicole answered as she cleaned up the paper strewn across the floor. "I thought he would be gone a while."

After a couple of hours with Morpheus, taking notes on artwork and memorizing the back stories of the infamous gods, Nicole sat reading the novel's last chapter. It was break time, and she needed to know who the killer of the fantasy was. Kallisto waited on a customer who was known to drop a lot of money, and Morpheus worked on the books, meaning he was reporting to Hermes off-site. Nicole closed the finished book and looked down at her watch. *Ten minutes of break left.* Decision made, she walked a couple of doors down to the bookstore, forgetting her bodyguards with the need to purchase the latest hot fantasy thriller before it sold out like its predecessor.

She stepped out the back door, to no breeze and no noise. None—at all. *Unusual, but oh well.* Looking around, she noticed no one walked the sidewalks. *What the hell's going on?* Time seemed to have stopped. She walked back into the gallery, slightly shaking, and called for Kallisto. Then, for Morpheus. *No one's there.* Then, she felt it—the pull of rapture.

"I'm not sure what the fuck is going on, but show yourself," she called again with clenched fists, nails causing the slight pain she needed to stay grounded and in control.

"No need to yell. Are you scared yet?" the disembodied voice responded. "Yes, there it is—I feel it—Your fear," the voice gave a laugh. "Would you like to know what it feels like?"

"I'm getting tired of this shit. Show yourself...coward," Nicole continued to clench her fists and parted her legs, assuming a stance for better command of the situation. *He won't force me anywhere else.*

The man who bumped into her in the doorway of the gallery appeared from around the front partition. With an evil grin that showed more teeth than were necessary, the giant of a man prowled toward her. A diagonal two-inch scar ran down his right cheek, and dark as night eyes framed by long lashes and incredibly thick, black hair hung just below his shoulders. He was eerily beautiful, with fluid movements that entranced her. She momentarily forgot to control the world he had tossed her into.

"How?" was the only word she could voice. The only one that would emerge from her mouth even though thousands ran through her mind.

"Have you not figured it out yet? You are supposed to be so smart," he continued to close the distance. With every step, she became more enchanted by his fluid movements. "I told you. One day, the deities watching you will no longer be enough. Terror is a very powerful emotion. Your fear makes me stronger. One day, you will be mine...completely mine," the deity now stood six inches from her.

Nicole tightened her fists even harder and concentrated on the pain. "I won't be that easy to control."

Like a chuckle but feral, a deep rumble emitted from his chest. He took half a step closer until his chest pressed against hers. "That night, when your fear for him and for yourself called to me, I knew you would be mine. I had never felt terror so sweet. I refuse to let you go. Not even your Oneiroi can save you." He traced a claw down her cheek, over her neck, and between her breasts—then he pulled her hips against his and growled. "Mine."

Nicole breathed in deep and heard Morpheus calling her name. She was back. *What the fuck just happened?* Nicole screamed.

CHAPTER XXXIV

PERMISSION

MORPHEUS MUST HAVE SUMMONED Phobetor because Nicole's next conscious account was waking in a giant bed curled against a warm chest with a heavy-as-hell arm draped across her waist. She knew Phobetor owned that well-sculpted arm before the scent of lavender, honeysuckle, and sandalwood had time to hit her nose in confirmation—*Damn! This feels so good.* She could tell by his slow, steady breaths—he was asleep. How long had they been here? Without much movement, she sought a bedside clock—there wasn't one. She felt for her watch and tapped it so it would tell her the time. It was almost noon. They had to be in Greece. She must have passed out. She did the math...six hours ago...*shit!*

Mindlessly, she started tracing light circles on his arm as she tried to remember what happened. Bits and pieces came back, but not much after her notetaking with Morpheus was clear. She felt Phobetor shift, and the hand of that well-sculpted arm found its way flat against the skin of her stomach, his pinky and ring finger just under the waistband of her shorts. *Shorts? How did I get into shorts?* The thought was fleeting since the index finger of his hand mimicked the circles she traced on his arm. *Oh shit, that feels good!*

Instinctively, she pushed against his body and wiggled. The large, warm hand stilled for just a second, then continued with larger strokes, and the body behind her pushed back. Moments of that special kind of torment went by before he raised the back of her T-shirt and started with light kisses down her spine. Arching, she whimpered and absorbed each touch of his lips, committing each to memory. *I'm in so much trouble.* Seconds later, her shirt was no longer an issue, and she wasn't quite sure where it went. He rolled her to her back.

"You scared me," Phobetor whispered against her lips.

"I'm sorry," she kissed him. Warm and soft, her tongue tangled gently with his. Slow. Again, she committed every movement to memory. *He tastes so good.*

He pulled back from her lips—to her verbal rejection. She could feel his smile against her skin as his lips traced an intense scorching line from her chin, down the curve of her neck, and to her breast—where her bra once was...*How in the hell?* He continued after paying homage to each of her nipples, down her stomach, taking his time, swirling his tongue in and around her naval. *Shit, shit, shit.* The burning need in her core intensified with every stroke of his tongue and each light brush of his teeth. *If he doesn't go faster, I'm going to die.* Tangling her hands in his long hair, she pushed his head, urging him. Again, she felt his lips curve into a grin against her skin. *Yep. He's trying to kill me.*

He looked up from her stomach to her eyes, with his fingers curled in the waistband of her shorts. His eyes swirled faster and darker than she'd ever seen them. He was confirming permission before going any further. Here it was. Could she allow the beautiful god above her to replace her only memory of such an act? Could she let her past go? Could she move forward? Nicole nodded.

Phobetor's sexy smirk intensified her anticipation and the desire pooling between her thighs. *He's so fucking hot!* He drew her shorts slowly down her legs, never breaking eye contact until the shorts were no longer a barrier. Again, he took his time, worshipping her body with his lips, tongue, and teeth. She could only feel. After a blinding orgasm, he crawled back up her body, looking her in the eyes, and pushed himself deep into her core. He went from slow and methodical to ravenous. They spent the rest of the afternoon in many positions of ecstasy. Leaving them sweaty and breathless.

"As much as I don't want to leave, I need to go back," Nicole whispered as she traced more circles on his chest. For the last hour, she fought against negative thoughts and emotions, refusing to allow her past to creep in and ruin the moment. So, she had bombarded him with questions about his life, which he graciously answered. When he explained his constant struggle against using his abilities to wreak havoc on mankind, she realized the god who watched over her was not only dangerous but deadly and had the great potential to be cruel. Oddly enough, that realization did nothing to deter her from wanting him—again.

"You are welcome to use the washroom while I send word to Morpheus that you will be attending classes today," he leaned down and kissed the top of her head. "My ἐξυπνος ομορφιά."

"I'm not sure what you did with my clothes," she looked around and only saw her shorts. "I'm also not sure where my work clothes went, but I can't go to classes in either."

The grin that crossed his face could only be described as mischievous. "Your clothes are—in between."

"In between what exactly?" Nicole scanned the room once more.

"Realms."

"There's an in-between realms?" Learning about realms had been hard enough to comprehend, but now there's an in-between. *Unfathomable.*

"Yes, but explaining that would take more time than you have. I placed some of your clothes in the bathing room and everything else you use to prepare yourself for classes," Phobetor pointed. "Enjoy your bath," he winked.

She had been in the bathroom a couple of times that afternoon, and her clothes nor her cosmetics had been in there, but now they were. He was right. Everything was there. He'd conjured her things from her bedroom. *Oh, to be a god.*

Amanda sat in front of the mirror, applying makeup while listening to her favorite podcasters. She noticed Nicole hadn't come home during the night and couldn't help but be concerned. She was with the notorious Phobetor. The brother, the other two Oneiroi in her life, always referred to as the one *not quite right.* It hadn't escaped her notice that the dream god was the conjurer of nightmares and fear, something in common with Nicole's captor. It wasn't a stretch to consider he could be the one they were looking for. The only problem was timing. Phobetor had been with Phantasos the day by the falls. No matter her adverse feelings toward the pain-in-the-ass god, she didn't believe Phantasos would ever harm a mortal or allow his brother to—for sport, anyway.

"Hey," Kallisto said, appearing by Amanda's door.

Amanda jumped. "Damn. Give a girl a call first. I'm glad I wasn't putting on mascara."

"Sorry," Kallisto grinned.

She didn't look the least bit sorry.

"Morpheus told me Nicole will be here in time for school."

"How is she? These Oneiroi need to learn more about proper communication," Amanda shook her head.

"I'm sure she's fine. She's with Phobetor."

"Exactly. That's what worries me. I'm not sure about him," Amanda admitted as she carefully put on her mascara.

"I trust Morpheus. He wouldn't allow her around him if he wasn't sincere about keeping her safe."

"I have some news," Amanda said, now fixing her hair.

"What?" Kallisto was scanning Amanda's closet.

"Kai finally asked me out. He's one of the last two guys on my list," Amanda said, referring to the top ten guys she should date in high school.

Laughing, Kallisto held one of Amanda's shirts to herself, seeing what she thought about it. "I didn't know you were still checking names off after . . . Michael. Can I borrow this shirt?"

Amanda knew Kallisto didn't actually mean Michael. She knew she meant Ares but would never say his name in front of her unless necessary. "Oh no, I started marking those names off as a freshman, and I'm no quitter," Amanda looked to see the shirt Kallisto was holding. "Sure, just wash it before you bring it back. I don't want the smell of Olympus all over my clothes," Amanda put on lip gloss.

Kallisto rolled her eyes.

A soft rap halted their banter. "Come in," Amanda said.

"Good morning," Nicole smiled from ear to ear. She looked—happy.

"You look," Amanda paused. "You look like you used to. Like the Nicole I've always known. Well, except for the piercings and black eyes. You look happy."

"I am," Nicole's smile lit her blushing face.

Amanda's eyes narrowed, "What happened, cousin?"

"I spent a beautiful day in Greece with a Greek god. How can I not be happy?"

"That's not all—Spill it," Amanda stood with a hand on her hip and pointed from Nicole's head to her toes. Kallisto sat on the bed and watched the volley from one cousin to the other.

Nicole rolled her eyes and sat beside Kallisto. "Don't freak out on me." She gave them highlights of her time with Phobetor.

"You seriously slept with Phobetor?" Amanda asked, making sure she understood the vague narrative correctly.

"Yes," Nicole's eyes sparkled with happiness.

Amanda and Kallisto's mouths were both agape. It took Amanda a second to comprehend her cousin had just gotten freaky with a god. "Well, how was it?"

Nicole knew they saw her exhale in relief. "It was perfect and meant to be. There's a connection with him that I can't explain."

"I understand that connection," Kallisto said.

"That's awesome," Amanda said. "But I asked you how it was. Not about your connection," Amanda smirked. All three women laughed.

Chapter XXXV

Threats

Hermes was in his library when Phobetor entered. After leaving Nicole with Kallisto and Phantasos for the day, he sought the god for answers. "I should bring Nicole here one day. She loves books," he said to the golden-winged god.

Hermes was one of the only ancient gods who had wings. Hades and a couple more had them, but rarely did they display them like Hermes tended to.

"You would have to spell her to be able to read these tomes. None are in any language used today in the mortal world," Hermes answered. "What brings you here, Phobetor?"

"I went into the dreams of your daughter's mortal consort. The deity who is after him is inquiring about another of his family members. Unfortunately, he knew an Oneiroi would be looking in, so he cut the nightmare short and said he did so the Oneiroi would not see his face. What the Hades is going on?"

Hermes hung his head. "I do not know. This god is one step ahead of us. I have no idea how he knew you or any of your brothers would be asked to investigate Anthony's dreams. Was that the only one?"

"For now. I suspect he will be back."

"Check every four or five days," Hermes ordered.

"Look, you helped me years ago. I will check a couple more times, but I do not want anything to do with whatever your family has gotten themselves into." Phobetor's eyes narrowed and flashed black, showing Hermes he meant his words.

"I understand you have no wish to be involved with the politics of the Mount, but this situation could be dangerous for my family. Whether or not I am allowed around my children, grandchildren, or great-grandchildren is irrelevant. The blood running through their veins belongs to my line. To Zeus' line. I need to know who to eliminate. No being scares my daughter or looks to harm another of her family. Never again." Hermes looked up from his desk.

"I will let you know when I know more." Phobetor vanished.

He spent the next few days watching the mortal, Anthony, from an orb while Nicole was in school. When she was not at school, he asked his brothers to keep a watch over her. Hermes was not a god to fear anything. For this deity to have him shaken was unusual, and Phobetor had a suspicion it had something to do with the god about to get out of Tartarus and Angelia's reason for hating the gods.

Nicole spent the next several days avoiding Pika as much as possible, which didn't always work out between the classes they had together and him happening by the gallery. Anxiety built up—how to let a nice guy down easily. She spent each night with Phobetor curled around her as she slept. They hadn't been together intimately since Greece, which was good with her since they were in her aunt's house. Not that her aunt knew she had a god in her room every night. Work was going great, and she was almost as good as Kallisto with her god knowledge. She had to admit the lives of the gods were pretty messed up. As far as she could see, Hades' love for Persephone was the purest of them all. She couldn't see the god of the underworld ever stepping out on his wife or her on him. However, her mother was a little much.

"Can you dust the frames in Poseidon's section? It's the only one I didn't get to yesterday," John asked her.

"Sure, no problem," Nicole answered. She loved the god of the sea. Not only because Poseidon was handsome, but there were beautiful sea creatures like sirens and mermaids. As a little girl, mermaids were her favorite fictional creatures. To find out they were real was a childhood dream come to life.

"Hey, cuz," Amanda said from between the bust of Poseidon and Athene.

"Oh, hey. What're you doing here so early?" It was two hours before closing and Nicole's first time to close with John.

"I wanted to discuss with John about working more than just the holidays."

"Awesome. About time you got off your lazy ass," Nicole joked.

"It's time I stop running from my memories and face them. I'll see you before I leave."

～⟫⟫⟫ ⟪⟪⟪～

"Hey, John. I was wondering if we could talk," Amanda asked as she approached the amusing manager. She once thought he had a thing for her. Come to find out, he was trying to make a god jealous. Little had he known that god couldn't stand her.

"Sure," John sat the reports he was reading on the desk. "What's up?"

"I was hoping I could work more. Maybe a few hours a week

"Sure. I can add you to the next schedule. Ambrose will appreciate working fewer hours," John smiled. "Have you seen Christos lately?"

Amanda felt the sting of heat on her cheeks. She hadn't thought of Phantasos' alias since January. "No. We don't really hang out."

"That's a shame. Well, I'll text you the dates and times tomorrow. The schedule is made every two weeks and sent out on Friday afternoons," John informed her.

"Thanks, John. I'm going to say bye to Nicole before I go. See you soon." Amanda made her way back to Nicole. She told her she would hang out at the bookstore and wait until she got off work.

Perusing the fantasy section of the bookstore was totally different once you learned that other realms, gods, and creatures really exist.

She purchased the first book in L.W. Phillips' latest trilogy, grabbed a coffee, and began reading. A prologue and two chapters into her novel, a man sat in the seat across from her. He wasn't just any man. Amanda knew what he was at first sight—his height and eyes gave him away. He was a god and not one she knew.

"Who are you?" Amanda said before the large man could announce himself.

"So eager and beautiful. You look like her. No wonder he finds you irresistible," the huge god smirked.

"Again, who the fuck are you?"

Amanda's hands curled into fists. After her time with Ares, she couldn't stand the gods—Kallisto and Morpheus were the exceptions. The smell of honeysuckle and lavender hung heavily around them.

"That does not matter. I want you to give your precious Oneiroi a message for me."

The god's voice was deep, and he was gorgeous, they all were, but the scar down his right cheek gave him some serious creeper vibes. She couldn't help but wonder what happened to the deity to cause the scar. *Wasn't he supposed to be perfect?*

"I'm not a pigeon. Give them the message yourself. Unless you're afraid, that is," Amanda said as she watched the god's lips twitch with a snarl.

"Tell them they will not stop me. Every time I take her, it's harder for her to return unless I allow it. I am not sure what she is, but she nor they can prevent me from what I seek. When I take her, she will be gone."

"You're the asshole who's been rapturing Nicole. Who are you?"

"No need. You will only remember my warning. See you, Amanda. Maybe one day, you can visit me too," with a wink, he vanished.

Amanda shook her head and looked around, seeing she was in the bookstore's coffee shop. *What just happened?* She looked at her watch to see Nicole had five minutes before close. From the back of the chair, she grabbed her things and hurried out the door. *Damn it!* The doors to the gallery were locked. Amanda's heart raced in fear—as she knocked while trying to text Nicole. She had the feeling someone was watching. With brief looks around her, she confirmed there was no one close. *That doesn't matter when you're dealing with gods.* She reminded herself.

"Amanda," John unlocked the door. "Are you okay? You look like you've seen a ghost."

"Not so sure about a ghost, but something. Where's Nicole?" Amanda's hands were clammy.

"She's clocking out in the back."

"Can I wait in here?" she looked around wide-eyed.

"Sure." Moments later, Nicole walked to the front.

"Amanda, are you okay?" Nicole asked.

"No." With that one word, Amanda fell unconscious.

⤜⋙ ⋘⋙

"Phobetor!" Nicole fell beside her cousin and yelled as she placed Amanda's head in her lap.

"I'll get a wet cloth," John ran to the back.

It took Phobetor only a second to appear. "Amanda? What happened?"

"I have no clue. I asked her if she was okay. She said no, then passed out." Nicole said, visibly shaken as her hands trembled across her cousin's face.

"Here," John handed Nicole the cloth. She placed it above Amanda's brow. She was clammy and white as paper. She held a book, and her purse crossed her body. Nothing seemed out of the ordinary. John told them about their interaction before Nicole walked in.

A couple of minutes went by before Amanda started stirring. Her eyes tracked from Nicole to each man squatting on either side. Her eyes were slightly bloodshot. "What happened," she asked Nicole.

"We have no idea other than you came in looking terrified and fainted."

Amanda started to sit up, and a wet cloth dropped to her lap. Handing it to Nicole, she got to her feet, strangely steady after such an episode.

"You have been in the presence of a god," Phobetor announced. Nicole and John looked at him and then back to Amanda.

"Can you call Kallisto to come," Amanda asked. "I want her here too."

Within seconds, Kallisto and all three Oneiroi were there, all looking at Amanda with anticipation.

"What happened," Phantasos asked with what sounded like anger and a hefty dose of fear in his voice.

"Not sure why you're here, but I had a visit from..." Amanda clutched her forehead. "I don't know who from."

Phantasos pushed his way to where he stood directly in front of her. Nicole could see the worry on his face, and she knew at that moment that no matter what Amanda thought about the god, he had it bad for her cousin. Concern and anger for Amanda were etched all over his face.

"Look at me," Phantasos ordered.

"Don't tell me what to do," She snapped.

"Well, this isn't getting us anywhere," Kallisto said. "Come on, let's go to the back." Kallisto pushed past the insistent Phantasos, hooked her arm around Amanda's, and led her to Morpheus' couch.

"Well, isn't this déjà vu?" Nicole said as she looked at each face surrounding Amanda, as they had not so long ago.

"All I remember is a man wanting me to tell you," Amanda looked at each Oneiroi, "something." She rubbed her forehead. "He said, for me to tell you that you won't stop him. Every time he takes her, it will be harder for her to return unless he allows it. He also said something about not knowing what she is, but whatever she is would not prevent him from getting what he wants."

"I will kill him," Phobetor's eyes swirled black.

"I will help you, brother," Phantasos' incisors lengthened.

What the fuck?

Chapter XXXVI

Visitor

Phobetor paced the floor of the office and ran a hand through his hair every time he turned to walk in the opposite direction. "This bastard must be eliminated. I have no idea who he is, and I care not, but Zeus should be warned that a god of his Pantheon will soon die. Even if I spend another century in Tartarus, the god is dead."

"I agree," Phantasos chimed in.

"Look, I have to leave for just a little bit. I will be back. I must finish what I started. Kallisto and Morpheus will see you and Amanda home." Phobetor said to Nicole before he vanished.

Phobetor reappeared on the balcony of Anthony's bedroom. He and Angelia were asleep. He placed a spell on Angelia to keep her asleep and entered her husband's mind.

Immediately, Phobetor found the memory and manifested it into the man's mind as a dream. Like before, the god sat across from the mortal in his office. Again, the mortal's face was covered in sweat.

"Now, let us finish what we started. I want to know how you feel about learning your wife is a Greek deity."

"I've started therapy. You are a figment of my imagination brought on by stress," Anthony said.

"Oh, really. Do you know this girl?" With a wave of the god's hand, a large bowl of water appeared before Anthony. Another wave started the show. Look into the water, mortal," the god growled.

The man reluctantly looked down. His eyes went wide in horror. The deity's laugh was so evil a chill went down Phobetor's spine.

"No! What is this? That's my grandchild. What are you doing to her? Stop this." Anthony demanded as he clenched his temples and squinted in an obvious effort to clear the image the god scried in the bowl of water.

"Have you ever noticed odd things about her?"

"No. She's perfect. Both my granddaughters are. Leave her alone. This is a nightmare. I need to wake up." Tears fell down Anthony's cheeks.

"This is no nightmare. She visits me often. Or did. I need to know what she is capable of. I want you to confront your wife. See, I cannot approach her. You have a week. Find out what I want to know, and only this granddaughter will be affected. If you fail me." Phobetor knew the god was grinning evilly. "I will make sure your other granddaughter visits me too."

"Why? What has Nikki ever done to you? She's a young girl."

Phobetor's blood ran cold. *It cannot be. There's no way.* He snapped his fingers, and the memory stopped. Phobetor walked to Anthony's side and peered into the bowl. There, Nicole lay on a metal table in a dungeon. Her hands and feet were cuffed, and her eyes were covered. He turned murderous and walked over to the deity. Unfortunately, this was a memory, and the god's face was veiled in magic he could not undo. "I will kill you. She is mine, and you are dead."

Phobetor flashed from the mansion to his home in Greece. He had enough sense to release both Angelia and Anthony from his hold before he vanished.

This could not be. If Nicole was Anthony's granddaughter, she was Angelia's, and that made her a demigod. *How? She does not hold a signature.* Shaking, he rubbed Hades' face on the gold coin he now held.

Phantasos beat on the doors of Zeus' home on Olympus. Probably not the smartest move for a god, but he was over this shit. Finally, a nymph opened the door and waved him in to follow.

"To what do I owe this unexpected and unwanted intrusion of my privacy?" Zeus turned from his windows as Phantasos entered the vast throne room.

Phantasos noticed the new paintings of Kallisto and Thia hanging on either side of the chaise to his right. "I have come to inform you that one of your gods will soon die. Most likely by Phobetor's hands, but he will have my blade at his side if he needs it. There will not be any compromise."

He thought he saw a flash of confusion cross Zeus' face before he locked his emotions down and smirked. "Oh? What has happened to cause such a drastic action? You know the law."

"Torturing of mortals. The god made the mistake of tormenting and rapturing the woman Phobetor has sworn to protect. Then he decided to threaten Amanda, Kallisto's best friend. The one your asshole of a son kidnapped months ago. Once we find out who he is, he will deal with all three Oneiroi and not live."

"Is this a threat?

"No threat. I promise the god will breathe his last breath. If it had been up to me, Ares would be dead. This god who is tormenting Nicole will not be given a chance." Phantasos sneered at his king, then flashed to his orb, where he watched Amanda. He shook in anger. Aggressive promises to kill one of Zeus' gods to the god king's face was not smart, but the eldest Oneiroi, while encouraging his brothers to do the smart thing, did not always follow his own advice. He needed to speak to Thia.

The god of the underworld was not in his throne room. When Phobetor arrived, the gorgons took him to the dark deity's home. Ironically, it was not black with morbid décor. It was more beautiful than Zeus' mansion. He could not help but think Persephone was the deity in charge of the home. If everyone knew where Hades lived, they would have a harder time thinking of him as evil.

"Did you know?" Phobetor asked before Hades could acknowledge him.

"Well, that is rather vague. Did I know what?" Hades sounded bored.

"That the girl I have sworn to protect is Angelia's granddaughter and Hermes and Aphrodite's great-grandchild?"

Hades threw back his head and laughed. "I did not, but that is definitely what the mortals call Karma." Hades continued to chuckle.

"Why is this so amusing to you?" Phobetor was not laughing.

"My brother has played both sides of the aisle for far too long. You can only sleep with so many women for thousands of years before wars start between the children."

"What the fuck does that mean?" Phobetor was barely holding his rage at bay. His eyes swirled black, and dark streaks traced his veins, streaking his flesh. He looked like the nightmare he was.

"There is much more to this story that I am unable to speak of. The Fates control even this. However, I will say if you care for the girl, prepare for bloodshed and let the best god win." A wide grin never left the dark god's face.

"Do you know who wants her?" Phobetor's voice was now that of nightmares, incredibly deep—more animal than man.

Hades' smile softened, and his chuckling stopped. "I do not. My best guess is that someone from Hera's line is doing this."

"Ares?" Phobetor growled in question.

"This soon after his beating? No, I doubt it. He believes in revenge, but he is a disciplined deity. He will hit when no one is expecting it."

"Nicole is a demigod. That explains her being a dream bender," Phobetor said more to himself than to Hades.

"Not all demigods have power. Especially when they have as much mortal blood in their veins as she does. Her being a bender of any kind is quite remarkable."

"I need to speak with Hermes," Phobetor turned to leave.

"What about my brother?"

Phobetor turned back to look at Hades, "I sent Phantasos to warn him that one of his gods is about to die by my hand."

"You and your brother have a death wish."

"Well. Perhaps. I hope to soon find out which god will die," Phobetor left.

⟫⟫⟫ ⟪⟪⟪

"Hermes," Phobetor yelled through the god's mansion. He did not have the time to knock. He was a dream god and never had to; it was just the polite thing to do.

"I hope you have worthy information since you are standing in my home without invitation," Hermes said, appearing at Phobetor's side.

"The god you seek is after the mortal I have sworn to protect. She is your granddaughter. What the fuck is going on?" Phobetor shook with anger.

"Explain." Hermes snarled.

Ten minutes later, Phobetor finished with his account of Anthony's memory and his sworn duty to protect Nicole, who happened to be a dream bender and a demigod.

"Who is after her and why? What could an Olympian god want with a demigod with a bloodline to such powerful gods as you and

Aphrodite? Not to mention, she is the great-great-grandchild of Zeus. He has to know he could lose his head."

"If my great-grandchild is being tormented by one in this pantheon, she has unknowingly beguiled him. Why else would a god go after a mortal with my blood so far down the family tree?"

"Let me see pictures of Angelia's true form. I only saw her once over a thousand years ago. She portrays herself as an elderly woman now."

With a wave of his hand, Hermes produces a photo of his daughter. Phobetor gasped. "That is Amanda, Kallisto's best friend, and Nicole's cousin. Your other great-granddaughter."

"No. This is Angelia. She gets her looks from her mother. Beautiful, is she not?" Longing for his daughter showed all over his face.

"Amanda could be her doppelganger. That is crazy how much she looks like her."

"Here. Take the picture. Tell my great-grandchildren they are loved, even if we never meet. I assume you will tell your charge of her heritage."

"So, help me, Hermes...if you know more than you are telling me, you will pay. I have done well controlling my dark side. That ship sailed when I saw Nicole in that scrying bowl. I will not allow any being in any realm to stop me from finding the god who chained and tormented her. That being will die, and any who seeks to protect him will follow. You had better hope I am not in armor the next time you see me. Feel free to tell all of Olympus that I and my brothers are coming. By the way—that god made a second mistake. He used Amanda as his messenger. Phantasos is also out for blood." Phobetor appeared outside Amanda's house, where everyone waited.

Before he approached them, he tried to calm his rage. He felt his eyes swirl faster and the streaks across his skin darken the more he thought about what he saw in the water. He knew if he went in looking like he did, he would scare the women, and his brothers would take a protective stance. It took him time to calm enough for his skin to go back to normal. There was not much he could do about his eyes.

"Nicole, Amanda...we need to talk. Please sit down. There is no easy way to say this," Phobetor ran his hand through his hair.

Chapter XXXVII

Revelation

"WHAT IN THE HELL is going on, Phobetor? I'm not in the mood for any more Greek god drama tonight," Amanda crossed her arms and refused to sit.

He stopped in front of Nicole and took her hand in his. This bombshell was going to be hard for the cousins to come to terms with, but keeping Angelia's secret could be dangerous for Nicole, possibly deadly. He refused to harbor deadly secrets, especially if the target was the woman he swore to protect. "Hermes asked me to check out the mortal husband of a goddess—the goddess Angelia—daughter of him and Aphrodite. Aphrodite was with Hermes briefly, and when I say briefly, I mean even for mortals. Angelia was born before Aphrodite and Ares were ever together.

He noticed Amanda stiffen when he mentioned Ares. After what she went through by the god of war's hands, he knew Amanda would have the hardest time with the information.

"I personally only saw her once in my lifetime. She rarely stayed on Olympus and renounced the gods a thousand years ago because of issues only a few know the truth about. She has not stepped foot on Mount Olympus since. She is strong. Very strong. She chose to live in the mortal realm and refused to speak to any of the gods, including her parents. Marrying only mortal men, of course, she outlived them all. It was not until Anthony, the husband she is currently married to, that she had children—two daughters. She conjured strong magic and concealed the girls from all the gods, even Zeus. I have gathered that she lied to everyone, including her husband and daughters. It worked until now. Hermes believes his great-granddaughter sparked the attention of one of the gods with great power. He does not know how this happened since she has been concealed. Hermes' great-granddaughter who gained the unwanted attention is you, Nicole." Phobetor's eyes were trained only on Nicole.

You could hear a pin drop. Everyone went still, and Phobetor could feel the shock radiate from the hand he held. Nicole was speechless.

"This can't be true," Amanda was the first to find her voice.

"It is," Phobetor told them about the memory and the scrying bowl. "I saw you held in that dungeon, gagged and tied to a metal table. You had blood around your wrists, and dirty, dried tears streaked down your cheeks. I can never unsee that. I wanted blood so badly at that moment that the inner beast I contained for over nine hundred years and fought daily to keep buried found his way out. Once somewhat calm, I went to see Hades and Hermes. All of Olympus will know before long that I am looking for and will kill the god who is responsible for your mental abduction, no matter the warning from The Fates."

"You're saying our mothers are the daughters of a Greek goddess, and they have no idea? That sounds crazy." Amanda spoke again. Nicole just stared in shock. "That means Nicole and I—"

"Here, look," Phobetor held the photo Hermes gave him out for Amanda to take.

"Where is this? I don't remember this." Amanda asked.

"That is not you. That is Angelia, your grandmother," Phobetor answered.

Amanda dropped the photo. It floated to the floor in front of Nicole. With great effort, Nicole bent to pick it up. Her eyes widened. "This can't be." She whispered.

"This explains your dream-bending abilities," Phobetor said.

"Great, she gets some cool power, and I win a lookalike contest. I feel cheated," Amanda said.

"You have looks to equal Aphrodite," Kallisto hugged Amanda.

"This is too much. Did you find out who's tormenting me and why?" Nicole asked.

"I have not. Your grandfather was given a week to let your grandmother know that he knows. The god is trying to find out how you are breaking out of his spells and how you broke from his hold the last time he took you."

"This is too much. Nicole and I need some time together—alone. We need to talk. No offense, but you guys can't understand the magnitude of what we're feeling right now. Kallisto understands . . . she can stay and keep Nicole safe," Amanda lifted her chin in preparation for protest.

"Sure," Phobetor raised Nicole's chin to look in her eyes. "I am sorry, my ἔξυπνος ομορφιά...not that you carry the blood of the gods, but this is how you had to find out."

⤙⤙⤙ ⤚⤚⤚

Once the Oneiroi vanished, Amanda spun on Nicole. "Did you have any idea about this?"

"No. Why would you think that?"

"I just have a hard time believing Aunt Kellie nor mom knew anything about this. How can they be granddaughters of Hermes and Aphrodite, hell, great-grandchildren of Zeus and have no clue?" Amanda paced the room, flailing her arms as she spoke, clearly agitated.

"You're not the only one here who feels betrayed," Nicole said.

"Look," Kallisto interrupted, whatever else was about to come out of Amanda's mouth. "I'm the granddaughter of Zeus. My mom is his daughter. They kept it all from me until they couldn't any longer, and not because I was manifesting any rare abilities. It took time to completely get over what I thought was a betrayal. But, yes, you can have the blood of the gods running through your veins and never know it. I'm a prime example of that." Kallisto looked from Amanda to Nicole. "You are far enough removed that you won't have to be a part of that world if you don't want to."

"Grandma is a goddess," Nicole said and sat heavily on the edge of the sofa, placing the heels of her hands against her eyes. "So much makes sense now."

"What do you mean," Amanda asked, still pacing.

"Remember when we all stayed with her and Poppa over the summer, and I kept having strange dreams? In one, Grandma rode Pegasus and had a crown on her head. That's all I remember now, but when I told her about my dreams, she told me never to talk about them. I was little, so I agreed," Nicole said. "There was one dream that scared me, though. One I'll never forget. It was in a dark place, and two red-eyed hairless dogs chased me until I ran into a giant paw. When I looked up, there was a gigantic three-headed dog growling down at me. I woke screaming. She rocked me in her chair as I cried myself back to sleep."

"Let's go see her," Amanda suggested.

"I'm not sure that's such a good idea," Kallisto chimed in.

"Why not? You can take us to her. It's not like she can't protect us. Apparently, Grandma's a badass goddess who can perform magic so strong that her grandfather can't even find her. She has no choice but to show her hand if we make her," Amanda began pacing again. "I refuse to pretend I don't know about her dirty little secret."

"If we're going to do this, I think Phobetor should come too. He's the one who entered your grandfather's mind, and Angelia should know the extent of trouble he may be in. He's completely mortal," Kallisto encouraged them to think beyond the betrayal and pain they felt.

"You know if he comes, Morpheus will too. He's not going to allow you to go without him," Amanda added.

"After we confront her, I want her to tell our mothers. This shit is coming out whether Grandma wants it to or not," Nicole said.

"It's ten at night here. That means it's four in the morning there," Amanda said.

"So. She's a god. She doesn't have to get her beauty rest. One of the Oneiroi can make sure Poppa sleeps deeply and doesn't wake while we discuss things with her," Nicole said.

"She used to have a couple of servants who lived in the house. The dream gods also need to check for them," Amanda added.

Plan made, the granddaughters dressed for travel. Spring in West Virginia was much cooler than in Maui. Amandas' mind reeled, and her hands shook slightly as she got ready.

"I'm sorry for snapping at you, Nicole. I pretty much loathe the gods, with a couple of exceptions, of course. To find out, I may have their blood running through my veins, no matter how little, hit a raw spot inside of me. I'm not handling this well," Amanda wiped a tear from her face. "One day, this may be okay. Today isn't it for me."

"I understand. It hits hard for me, too. Now, let's go find out what is going on and why the hell our grandmother has hidden this from everyone," Nicole hugged her cousin right before she called for Phobetor.

Moments later, all three Oneiroi appeared. Amanda rolled her eyes at the trio. "All three? Really?"

"We've made a decision. Kallisto and Phobetor are taking us to West Virginia to see dear ole grandma in all her goddess glory," Nicole announced.

"Kallisto is not going without me. That deity may be hanging around," Morpheus announced.

"We figured," Amanda said.

"All three of us are going," Phantasos added,

"Why you?" Amanda asked a little unkindly.

"Because I said so," Phantasos stepped toward her.

Amanda rubbed her hand over her face. She didn't have the energy to fight with him. "Fine."

Phobetor took them to the gates outside Angelia's home and asked them to wait while he entered the minds of all the mortals in the cabin. Once that was done, Morpheus and Phantasos flashed each of them to the sitting room to wait for Morpheus to enter their grandmother's dream state.

"Wish me luck," Morpheus winked before morphing into mist.

"Angelia," Morpheus bowed slightly. "It is nice to meet you." Morpheus manifested a clearing with nothing but grass and the sun shining on their faces. "Not sure if you know who I am. Morpheus, the Oneiroi of the gods and son of Hypnos. It seems you have been keeping secrets."

"How did you find me?" Angelia's lip twitched in contempt.

"That is a question we will answer downstairs. Your granddaughters wait for you in your sitting room."

"Excuse me. What did you just say?"

Without repeating himself, Morpheus continued. "Please get dressed and be down directly after I wake you. You will feel several god signatures when you wake. That should prove this was not just any dream. If you do not come down in a timely manner, they will come to your bedchamber. Your husband and servants are under the Oneiroi's deep sleep, so there is no need to be super quiet. This conversation may get heated." Morpheus released Angelia to wake up and watched her panic.

Chapter XXXVIII

Angelia

With magic she hadn't used in years, she dressed. Half a second later, Angelia appeared in her sitting room where three Oneiroi, her two granddaughters, and a woman who looked the same age as her granddaughters sat waiting. For the second before anyone spoke, she sensed extreme power from that girl. If she didn't know better, she would have thought the girl to be Kallisto, the mortal best friend of Amanda she had always heard so much about, but the girl sitting with the gods was no mortal.

"Nicole, Amanda, what's going on here?" Angelia asked, looking at each granddaughter in turn.

"We have questions about your—our lineage," Amanda answered her grandmother with arms crossed and no warmth.

"I see. Looks like you know a great deal if you have the Oneiroi and...excuse me, I'm not sure I know your name..." Angelia addressed the powerful girl.

Kallisto held out a hand. "I'm Kallisto, daughter of Thia, granddaughter of Zeus, and best friend to your granddaughter, Amanda."

Angelia blinked a couple of times before composing herself. "I had no idea. I mean, I thought you were mortal." Angelia shook her head, getting back to the point of the impromptu visit. "What do you know, and how do you know?" Angelia asked her granddaughters.

"Very little. Only that Poppa was visited twice by a god from the Greek Pantheon. Apparently, when you reached out to Aphrodite about there being a god signature around him, Hermes became inquisitive and protective. The same god who's been mentally rapturing me for over a year now is the one visiting Poppa," Angelia gasped at Nicole's words.

"What? A god took you. When? Why is this the first I've heard of it?" Angelia's eyes darkened from crystal blue to cobalt. "Did the god hurt you?"

"Why are you just finding out? You've got to be kidding." Amanda glared at her grandmother.

"I'll get to that later. For now, we want to understand why in the hell we are in the dark about our heritage," Nicole responded.

Amanda continued where Nicole left off. "Hermes asked Phobetor to watch over Poppa and figure out what was happening. Phobetor found out through dreams and memories that the god was looking for Nicole. Imagine his and our shock when he saw Nicole in a scrying bowl tied to a metal table and gagged." Angelia flinched at Amanda's description. "Instead of a coma, she was raptured and tortured for a week. Locked in a room where, if not for her abilities, she may not have ever returned."

"Abilities? What abilities?" Angelia asked.

Both girls ignored their grandmother's questions. "I want to know if Kathryn and Mom know anything about the world you came from or what you are—Hell, do they know what they are?" Nicole asked a little louder than was necessary.

"No. They have no idea. Nor should you," Angelia answered Nicole with obvious irritation. "If your grandfather knows, why hasn't he said anything?"

"He was given one week. In that week, he is to confront you and make you tell him what Nicole is," Phobetor interjected.

"What do you mean...what Nicole is? What abilities?"

Phobetor looks from Angelia to Nicole. "Your granddaughter is a dream bender. I found out when I was asked to heal her."

"A dream bender. Well, so much for my power concealing your ability. And here I thought dream benders were myths. Does this healing you were asked to help with have anything to do with the wreck and her newfound rebellious streak?" Angelia asked pointed-ly, looking at Nicole's hair.

"We're not sure if the deity caused the wreck or if my fear and anguish intrigued him, but my depression was not solely due to the accident. The god manipulated me for over a year. I was teetering on the edge of suicide when Phobetor saved me," Nicole admitted. She then walked to where he stood and laced her fingers with his. Angelia's mouth wasn't the only one agape at Nicole's bravado. Every deity in the room gaped.

"So, you are with this Oneiroi, the one who wields fear and pho-bia?" Angelia asked.

"I am, as long as he will have me," Nicole answered.

"That's a dangerous path you take, Nikki. He was in Tartarus for..."

"I know all about that. Please don't lecture me. I know exactly who he is and what he once was. Unfortunately, I don't know who or what my own grandmother is."

Again, Angelia flinched at her granddaughter's words. "I have only tried to keep you all safe. For a millennium, I separated my life from the gods of Olympus. The corruption on that mount is out of control. I refused to allow it to hurt my family as it did me."

"Tell us why. Why do our mothers not know they are demigods? Why are we all in the dark? Did you not think you would have to tell us? Hell, how long will we all live? What abilities do our mothers have that you are concealing?" Amanda asked each question with tear-filled eyes, needing answers. Phantasos rounded the sofa and stood behind her.

"Like I said, corruption. My story is mine. I'm so sorry; there are things I'm not willing to discuss. Just know all I ever wanted was to keep everyone safe. I never wanted a family until Anthony. I had many human husbands over the millennia, but he only made me want children. After the girls were born, my instincts were to protect them. After twenty more years, you two and the twins came along. I just wanted you to be safe and happy. I knew one day I would have to tell your mothers, and they would one day need to tell you. The gods finding you was never considered since I was able to hide us all so well, so I thought. I have no idea what abilities I conceal. Your mothers have never been out from under the magic to find out. I suppose your mothers will live thousands of years. You two and the twins, probably hundreds, if I had to guess."

"How many millennia would Mom have to live before you told her?" Amanda rolled her eyes, and her usual sarcasm dripped from her tongue in pain.

"I know you are upset with me. I get it. I love you both so very much and would do anything to protect you. Even lie to the people I love the most," Angelia confessed.

"I want to see what you really look like," Amanda insisted.

Angelia smiled, "Look in the mirror behind you, and you'll see. You and I could be identical twins."

"Show me," Amanda demanded.

Angelia inhaled and nodded in resignation. She closed her eyes for just a couple of seconds. When she opened them, Amanda was reaching for her face. Her granddaughter traced her brows and her nose, clearly in shock.

"It's true," was all Amanda could say. "How?"

"I'm sure The Fates had something to do with it. I suppose they didn't know that I aged myself. Your grandfather was awed last year when you visited. You had grown, and he couldn't believe how much you looked like me as a girl. I worked hard to be mortal. Being mortal kept you safe until it didn't." Angelia shook her head. "Everything I worked to do has crumbled."

Phobetor spoke, "To keep your family safe, you must embrace your godhood, Angelia. There is a god after Nicole. Why? We do not know. But you need to take the power back. Your husband needs to know the truth so the god who haunts him loses the upper hand. Your daughters need to know the truth so they can help protect their children. Hermes and Aphrodite deserve to meet their grandchildren and great-grandchildren, whether you believe that or not. It is time."

"This god who wants Nikki, what do we know about him? How did the deity find her?"

"He wants her to be afraid, and he needs to know why he cannot control her as he wants. He does not know she is a bender. We do not want him to find out." Phobetor answered as he stroked soothing circles over Nicole's hand.

"Okay. First, I'll speak to Anthony. After that, we need a plan. One where we can all meet as a family. I can't believe this is happening this way." Breathing in a deep, resounding breath, Angelia continued. "If my parents want to come to our realm, I will welcome them, but I refuse to go to Mount Olympus. Don't ask me to. Don't bring Zeus or any of his children or minions around me or my family. I will only meet with my parents. Is that understood?" Angelia then addressed just her granddaughters. "Girls, please understand—I love you and your mothers more than anything in the universe. I only wanted to keep you safe."

"We understand," Nicole answered. Amanda didn't look ready to forgive.

"Morpheus, please remove the sleep from my husband. I will return after I wake him. Hopefully, he will forgive me." Angelia's eyes held sadness as she flashed from the sitting room.

Chapter XXXIX

Plans

Unnerving silence plagued the room once Angelia left. Amanda was speechless, and as it seemed, so was the rest of the crew. Morpheus sat beside Kallisto on the opposite end of the couch, stroking her back. Nicole sat beside Phobetor in the oversized, comfy chair she used to curl up in and read when there over the summers of their youth. Phantasos leaned against the wall with his arms and ankles crossed. She could feel his stare on her back. She didn't want his pity. Yep, she had the blood of gods running through her veins, but no signs of anything extraordinary. Oh, wait, she was "beautiful" —so was everyone else in Hawaii. *What the hell's wrong with me? Poor, pitiful me isn't who I am. I'm a fighter.*

"Any ideas how we're going to get our parents together to tell them they are demigods and their dear ole great-granddad is the king of the Greek Pantheon?" Amanda broke the silence that was driving her crazy with their next problem and a dose of sarcasm.

Nicole sat straighter, preparing for another difficult conversation. "Well...I think we should bring my parents and the boys to Hawaii. First, the ambiance is much better, and the stress we give them can be removed by walking through paradise. Plus, I don't think I can go back to Tennessee yet."

"That's better than what I was thinking," Amanda said. "I say let's do rock, paper, scissors with every decision we must make. You know...let the chips fall where they may." Amanda stood and walked to the kitchen. "I'm getting some water. Anyone else want some?"

"Amanda? Are you okay," Kallisto asked as Amanda reached for a glass. *Of course, she would follow me.*

Amanda shrugged and thought for a second. "I'm trying so hard to hold it together. So many emotions." She rubbed the back of her neck as she walked to the facet.

"You can talk to me. You know that—right? I've been in your shoes."

"Yeah, of course I know that—" Amanda gave her best friend a hug and started crying. Kallisto rubbed her back and let her cry for as long as she needed.

Pulling away to wipe her eyes, Amanda continued. "I just keep thinking about last winter. If I had known all this, could I've prevented what happened to me? To you?"

"You can't think like that. I knew what I was, and my mom knew and had power. What happened would have happened no matter what. You need to embrace this new norm. If you don't, you might lose yourself...and that'd be a tragedy, especially since you are the best person I know."

"I'm not sure what I did to have you in my corner, but whatever it was, I'm glad I did it," Amanda squeezed Kallisto's hand. "Come on. Let's tell my family we're a bunch of freaks and then find a god and kick his ass."

⤜⤜⤜ ⤛⤛⤛

An hour went by before her grandparents came downstairs. "Poppa," Nicole cried and ran into his arms. Amanda followed suit. "Are you okay?"

"Shock can be a wonderful thing," Anthony said, hugging his granddaughters back. "Now, let's have breakfast. Has Martha been down yet?"

"No," Morpheus said. "We have not lifted her sleep yet. I do not believe we should until we have made our plans."

"I'll get breakfast," Phantasos announced before vanishing.

Kallisto raised her head to the ceiling, "Don't forget coffee!"

"This will definitely take time," Anthony shook his head. "Come on, follow us to the kitchen and help set the table."

"Sorry, Poppa," Amanda apologized. "Let me introduce you to our friends. This is my best friend, Kallisto and her fiancé, Morpheus. Phobetor, the dream god who found the asshole tormenting you, and Phantasos, the eldest dream god is the one getting breakfast."

"I was telling Amanda that I believe the best thing to do would be to take Mom, Dad, and the boys to Hawaii to tell them." Nicole started the discussion as she and Amanda sat the table.

"That's a lot of people to rapture when they know nothing of our world. Plus, the boys are so young. I think it would scare them," Angelia replied.

"True. What if we only take Mom?" Nicole rethinks. "Phobetor can help. He can take her during sleep and then heal her anxiety once she wakes. Then, we let her tell Dad."

"I like that plan much better," Angelia said, and Anthony nodded. Before any more decisions were made, Phantasos arrived in the kitchen with a feast.

"You remembered the coffee," Kallisto's eyes lit up, and they all laughed.

By the end of breakfast, Nicole could tell everything would be okay. Her grandfather kept looking at Angelia, who had changed back to the grandmother they were all used to. She knew it would take him time. But the way he looked at her, Nicole saw love in his eyes. Her grandmother's deception was out of fear and love for her family, not out of disloyalty.

"We need to keep an eye on you, Anthony. Phantasos has agreed to watch over you until we can plan a rotation between him and your in-laws, Hermes and Aphrodite," Phobetor explained. "The god you met seems to stay at bay when another god is around. We also want you and Angelia to be with your daughters and granddaughters in Hawaii. The best and fastest way is for us to take you."

"I will take us," Angelia said. Her grandfather looked at her grandmother with a mixture of shock, fear, and admiration. It didn't go unnoticed that Poppa was not as comfortable with the status quo as he would like us to think.

"Well, it seems once your mother gets to Hawaii, my house will be the headquarters of the Oneiroi and several other Greek gods," Amanda shook her head in disbelief. Like Poppa, she wasn't good with the new norm either.

"None of this is going to be easy, but we all love each other, so it will be okay," Nicole said and noticed her cousin and the eldest Oneiroi glanced at each other and then turned away. Everyone else agreed.

Kallisto and Morpheus excused themselves and left for Hawaii and work. "I need to go soon, too. I have to work from two to close. Let's all meet at the gallery at closing. Once our parents are asleep, we can get Mom and have a reunion. We'll be working with two very different time zones, making this difficult. Phobetor, can you take me and Amanda back?"

"Yes. After you are both at work and with Kallisto and Morpheus, I will speak with Hermes."

Nicole noticed her grandmother stiffen and let out a deep breath. That was going to be the hardest part of this debacle...reuniting her grandmother and the deities she called her parents. That thought reminded her that her grandmother was adamant that Zeus and the rest of the Greek Pantheon were not on the guest list. *What happened between my grandmother and Zeus, her grandfather?*

"We'll come once you get off work," Angelia stated and looked at her husband in confirmation. "We still have a lot to discuss."

Phobetor, Nicole, and Amanda appeared in Nicole's bedroom in Hawaii. "I will take you to work once you are dressed. Amanda, do you want to go with them to the gallery?"

"No. I need some time to myself. It sounds like I won't have much of that once all hell breaks loose. I'll see you when you get off work," Amanda hugged her cousin and left for her bedroom.

"Come here," Phobetor held his arms open for Nicole to step into them. "Are you going to be okay?" He held her tight, needing to feel the heat from her body. The image he received from the scrying bowl almost made him lose control. Seeing her tied down and gagged with dried tears staining her face was too much. There were bloodred streaks down her bare legs and her arms. Scratches?

"Yeah. I don't think I'm as freaked out as Amanda is."

"We need to find out who the bastard after you is. Then we can all rest, and your family can adjust to its new way of life."

"I like my new way of life," Nicole stood on her tiptoes and kissed him.

After a few minutes, he released her with a reluctant groan. "You need to get ready." Phobetor touched her nose. I'll wait here.

"Wanna join me?" Nicole asked.

With a chuckle, he answered. "Of course I do. But you will not make it to work on time if I do. If at all."

"True. Rain check?"

"Not sure what that means," Phobetor's forehead creased.

Nicole laughed. "It means we will do it later."

"I like this wet check thing," Phobetor winked and rubbed his hands up and down her arms.

"Rain check," she corrected with a laugh. "I'll be right back."

Amanda climbed into the chair by her window to think. A year ago, myths were just that...stories that weren't real. Now, every story she thought unreal, she questioned. If gods were real, sphinx and Pegasus were real...what else was? She couldn't help but be a little nervous at the magnitude of her disillusionment. First, her best friend and her best friend's mother and grandmother. Next, dream gods were literally popping in and out of her everyday life. Then, the biggest thing, her family had deep connections to the deities. Her grandmother was a full goddess. *That makes me, what a quarter deity?* Amanda shook her head and ran her hand through her hair. She couldn't help but believe if this family revelation came before last winter, she wouldn't be having such a hard time accepting it. *I need a distraction.*

After a phone call and a shower, Amanda was ready for her afternoon date with the handsome Kai Higa. *Finally, something to look forward to.* She had at least eight hours to enjoy herself without the gods, her cousin, or her grandmother.

Phobetor left Nicole at the gallery with his brother and Kallisto and flashed to his home on Olympus. He could not get over the turn of events and that image in the water. Purpose kept him from going door to door on Olympus until he found the one tormenting Nicole.

Closing his eyes, he concentrated on where to find Hermes. *There you are.* He was on the Olympian training fields training with a short sword. Darting with tremendous speed between the practice dummies, cutting and slashing. Watching the fastest god on Mount Olympus train was magnificent. He was an impressive blur of speed, strength, and deadly precision.

"Hermes," Phobetor yelled from the side of the field.

Hermes slowed and looked up, and Phobetor motioned for him. With that lightning speed, Hermes was in front of him before Phobetor had time to blink.

"Do you have information?" Hermes asked.

"Short sword, eh?" Phobetor nodded to Hermes' hand and grinned. "Where is your caduceus? Or are you tired of being the inviolable god of peace?" The caduceus was the instrument Hermes normally wielded in battle, but now he wanted blood.

"I plan on protecting what is mine this time."

"Interesting," Phobetor nodded. "Your granddaughters and the Oneiroi met with Angelia last night."

Hermes eyes widened, and he sheathed his sword. "And?"

"Shock is an understatement. Angelia will only speak with you and Aphrodite. She is adamant that Zeus nor any other Olympians know about her or her family. We need you and Aphrodite to help watch over Anthony, taking turns with Phantasos since he will be helping find the deity responsible."

"Aphrodite may tell Ares," Hermes said.

"She needs to understand that if Ares so much as steps a toe near Nicole, Kallisto, or especially Amanda, he will die. So, she may want to keep her damn mouth shut, or be a widow. Ares is not—I repeat—is not to know anything." Phobetor growled out the words and he could feel his eyes shifting to black.

"Noted. I will tell her."

"Meet us at your gallery in Maui this evening. Come in the back door after closing," Phobetor vanished.

Kai talked Amanda into going to the beach with some friends from school for the first part of their date. He picked her up from her house at two-thirty, and they joined two other couples. She couldn't get over how normal and relaxed she felt. The other girls, Shea and June—she thought those were their names—were sophomores, so they just talked about music and school. No deities or life-and-death situations. Normal teenager drama and interests. She and Kai snorkeled and watched June's boyfriend surf. Within a couple of hours, she held Kai's hand and laughed like she didn't have a care in the world. *This is what I've needed.* Six came, and Kai dropped her off at her house so she could shower, change, and pick her back up at seven. Just as she walked into her room, her cell phone rang. It was Nicole. Amanda rolled her eyes—*reality check.*

"Phobetor spoke with Hermes. He and possibly Aphrodite should be at the gallery at ten. What were you up to while we broke our backs at work?" Nicole giggled.

"Actually...Kai and I went to the beach. I just walked in. He's picking me back up in an hour, and we are going to eat and hang out."

"Do you think that's such a good idea tonight of all nights?"

"Why not? I have four more hours before I have to go back to reality."

"Okay, I guess. Should I send Kallisto for you, or are you driving?"

"I thought I would have him drop me off there. I can tell him I'm staying the night at Kalli's, and that's where I want to be dropped off."

"I haven't met him. Is he that gorgeous junior I see you eyeing in the parking lot every day?"

"He's the one," Amanda said as she held the phone and rifled through her closet for "datable" clothing—*Was the last time I went on a date months ago? With Michael?* Amanda thought. *No—it was the gala.*

"Nice. We'll see you at ten."

Amanda rubbed her temples. The gala was not what she needed to think about. "See you then."

Chapter XL

Reunited

Nicole paced the gallery floors fifteen minutes before closing, biting her fingernails. An unfortunate habit her mother could never break her from. She'd spent the last half hour looking at paintings of her family. Hermes with his legendary winged shoes, Aphrodite in all her sultry beauty, and Zeus, her great-great-grandfather, the handsome king, all hung on the walls where she worked—*Has to be fate.* As she went from painting to painting, she remembered the tales Morpheus told her in her first few days at work. Not all of them held her family in high regard. *How am I supposed to fit in with them?*

Phobetor was the first to arrive, followed quickly by his eldest brother, Angelia, and Anthony, who was a little green from his first zone-hopping with a god, having gone from the East Coast to the middle of the Pacific Ocean in mere seconds. The god that *rezoned* him was his wife, which did not seem to help in the slightest.

"Hermes and Aphrodite should be here any second," Phobetor told Angelia, knowing she had to be as nervous as her granddaughter.

"Where is Amanda?" Phantasos looked the room over.

"Uh, she'll be here soon."

"Should I get her?" He offered, looking from Nicole to Kallisto.

"No. She knows to come here. She still has a few minutes until we officially close," Nicole gave Phantasos a forced grin, then looked to Kallisto with wide eyes and whispered, "I refuse to be the one to tell him."

"I can hear you. Tell...me...what?" Phantasos emphasized the last three words.

"A friend of hers—

Before Nicole could finish her sentence, Hermes and Aphrodite emerged from thin air. The air felt thick and crackled as Angelia looked at her parents for the first time in a millennia.

Nicole was surprised at how tall they both were. Hermes had to be at least six-eight, and Aphrodite was at least six feet, if not more. Both were shockingly gorgeous, with blonde hair and blue eyes, *just like Amanda's.* She supposed the new deities were waiting for their daughter to make the first move since she was the reason they hadn't seen each other.

"Mother...Father," Angelia bowed her head slightly. They both bowed their heads in turn. "This is my husband, Anthony. It's been a long day for him, and the overwhelming surprises keep coming." Anthony wore the look of shock that Nicole felt. "This is my grand-daughter, Nicole—Where's Amanda?" Angelia looked at Nicole, then at Morpheus.

"I'm here," Amanda raised her hand in greeting as she entered the room. "Saving the best for last," She winked at her great-grandparents.

"And this is my granddaughter, Amanda." Angelia continued, and Amanda winked—again.

"It is my pleasure to meet you both," Aphrodite acknowledged them with a slight bow of her head.

"So, you're the great *grandgods.* Tell me, what did you do to my grandmother that made her deny you and her home for a thousand years?" Amanda asked without any pretense.

Nicole's eyes flew wide, and she could have sworn the "cough" Phantasos projected sounded like, *Damn.*

"We did not come to rehash the past. We are here to meet our grandchildren and great-grandchildren for the first time and help you find the deity who is tormenting the family," Hermes leveled his gaze on Amanda. What he didn't realize—Amanda didn't care who or what he was. However, she cared about her mom, aunt, cousins, and grandparents.

"Well, once everyone has met, I want answers. It's after four in the morning in Tennessee. We need to get this party started," Amanda looked from her grandmother to the deities before her. "Nicole, Grandma, and Phobetor should go to Tennessee to get Aunt Kellie. I'm sure Phobetor can prepare her for the shock by going into her dreams first. Me, Kallisto, and Thia can talk with my parents. Kallisto, do you mind calling your mother?"

"On it now," Kallisto pulled her cell from her jeans pocket.

"Everyone else can wait on us upstairs in either mine or Nicole's bedroom. Once we have Kellie and my parents gathered in the living room and smelling salts for all the shock and fainting I'm sure will happen...we can give them another *surprise* by bringing the rest of you in—any objections?"

"Well, you're nothing if not detailed," Angelia grinned. "We have our marching orders. All heartfelt reunions can wait until we are all together." Angelia said sarcastically.

Amanda grinned back at her grandmother and then turned to Kallisto. "Can you take me home? They can follow." Gesturing to Hermes and Aphrodite, who both looked stunned at Amanda's tone.

"How did you get here?" Phantasos addressed Amanda with a quizzical glare.

"A friend brought me," she grinned sweetly back at him.

"Sure," Kallisto interrupted the exchange, which could have become a problem. "Morpheus, can you show them?" Kallisto looked between him, and the two intense gods that stood in front of them. He nodded once.

⟶⟩⟩⟩ ⟨⟨⟨⟵

"Nicole, I will take you and Angelia into your mother's dreams once I have you outside your home. Mortals tend to have an easier time with the unknown and fantasy while they are dreaming. You can both speak to her there and prepare her for waking. I will have already placed your dad and brothers in a deep sleep. Do not worry. I will lift it when we are about to return to Hawaii," Phobetor instructed.

"This isn't going to be easy, is it?" Nicole asked him.

"No. It will not be easy. Angelia, you should tell her why you kept this from her before she wakes. She will be upset in her dream state, but nothing like when she wakes."

Angelia nodded in understanding. "I'm truly sorry, Nikki. This was never my intention."

"I know you are," Nicole squeezed her grandmother's hand.

"Ready?" Phobetor asked. They both nodded. Seconds later, all three stood by the streetlamp outside Nicole's house.

"Your father and brothers are in a deep sleep. Nicole, you will want to take over the dream out of instinct. I need you to—not. I can help your mother if I maintain control. I can heal like my father."

"I understand," Nicole said.

⟶⟩⟩⟩ ⟨⟨⟨⟵

Phobetor created the dream setting of the backyard of Nicole's house. It was beautiful, with an inground pool, flowers starting to bloom everywhere, and a koi pond with a small waterfall where her mother sat and drank her coffee on the weekends. Nicole was shocked he knew just where to place them.

Nicole's mother sat by the pond, sipping her coffee in deep thought. "Mom," Nicole felt her mother's surprise like it was her own.

"Nicole? Oh, I've missed you," her mother stood and hugged her tightly. She could feel the emotions flowing from her mother. She could feel her happiness. Nicole shook her head. *This is weird.* She had never experienced dreams this way. Strangely, she felt everything—all their emotions.

Nicole heard Phobetor in her mind...*your abilities that seeped through the concealment magic are stronger now because you are physically closer to your grandmother. It will be interesting to see you at full strength once she lifts the magic.* She just stared at him.

Shaking her head, she dispelled the shock of the assailment of her ability and continued with the task. "Mom, I have a lot I need to tell you. Grandma is with me to help." Angelia stepped from around the pool house.

"Baby girl," Angelia hugged Kellie when she got to her.

"This is so strange," Kellie said as she hugged her mother back.

"You are in the dream of an Oneiroi—a Greek dream god," Nicole said. Phobetor stepped out next.

Kellie gasped at the obvious, not normal human. In this state, his eyes were dark, and his skin had a slight glow—he looked and moved like something ethereal. There was no denying he was something—different. Nicole did what he asked and allowed him to remain in control, refraining from taking the lead like she had so many times before in her dreams. She couldn't help but appreciate the all-consuming presence he exuded and grinned to herself.

"This has to be the strangest dream I've ever had," Kellie stated, looking between them as she sat back in her chair.

Angelia sat by her daughter. "What I am about to tell you will not only come as a shock, but you will think that you have gone crazy," Nicole watched her mother shift in her seat, already uncomfortable with her dream.

"I never told you about my family. Well...I told you they were not in my life because they kicked me out when I was young. That isn't the truth. I hadn't seen them for more years than you are prepared to comprehend possible." Kellie continued to look at her mother like she was crazy.

Phobetor manifested a glass of water in Angelia's hands. She nodded to him in thanks. Kellie's eyes widened, so Nicole moved behind her mother and placed a hand on her shoulder, lending her strength—and to catch her if she fainted.

"There's no easy way to say this, so I will just say it. Then, we will spend the rest of the time convincing you that you are sane. After that, you will wake, and we will confirm that you are not insane and heard us correctly while in your dream-state—and then you'll probably go into shock," Angelia told her daughter as she took a sip of water, vying for time. "I was born in what we call another realm. In that realm is Mount Olympus, where the Pantheon of the Greek gods you know from mythology resides. All myths are steeped in truth. It so happens that Olympus and its gods are real. And . . . I am one of them."

"This is the craziest dream ever. No more caffeine or epic movies before bed," Kellie laughed and took another sip of her coffee. "This is great. My mom's a god. I guess that makes me one, too," Kellie snickered.

"Half god, known as a demigod. I suppressed your abilities when I found out I was pregnant with you. I did the same with your sister. I don't know what your abilities are."

"The magic grandma used is strong; however, some of my abilities seeped through. I'm what is known as a dream bender. I'm mostly mortal with the ability to control my dreams. Even overshadowing those of an Oneiroi if they go into my dreams," Nicole added.

"I needed to see you, Nikki, but this dream needs to go. This is just too much, even for a dream," Kellie said just before everything went black.

"What in Hades happened," Phobetor said. "Did you—"

"No! You said not to. Why would I take us out before we were sure she would be okay?"

⟫⟫⟩ ⟨⟨⟨

"She did it. Your mother. I bet she, too, is a bender," Phobetor said seconds before they were flashed to the living room of Nicole's home—all four of them.

Kellie was wide awake, staring at her mother, her daughter, and the Oneiroi. Angelia realized what happened about the same time Phobetor did and flashed them all together.

"What. The. Hell?" was all Kellie said before she fainted.

"Amanda was right about the smelling salts," Nicole closed her eyes and took a deep breath. Seconds later, her mother was awake and shaking uncontrollably. "She's in shock."

Chapter XLI

Family

After an hour of cold compresses and a lot of convincing, Nicole, Phobetor, and Angelia returned to Hawaii with Kellie, where more cold cloths were needed. Kathryn and Alaric were doing slightly better. It helped to have Thia and Kallisto there since they had just gone through similar circumstances.

"We want to introduce you to your grandparents," Angelia said to Kellie and Kathryn. Your girls met them briefly tonight. I saw them for the first time in many...many years."

"Who are your parents," Kathryn asked her mother.

"Please don't pass out again," Nicole pleaded to her mother.

"My parents are Hermes and Aphrodite," Angelia said.

"Our grandparents are the Greek gods Hermes and Aphrodite?" Kathryn's mouth hung open. "This is just nuts."

"*The* Hermes and Aphrodite? Kellie asked.

"I wasn't very impressed," Amanda interjected. "Obviously, they're not that great, or we wouldn't be in this situation right now."

"Amanda," Angelia scolded her granddaughter.

"Just telling it how it is," Amanda shrugged.

"Hermes, Aphrodite," Angelia spoke as if they were standing beside her. A second later, the two gods manifested in front of the family they dreamed of meeting one day.

⊰⊱

"We should give this family time to meet and reunite. No one will bother Nicole with three such gods as these with her. Let's go home and have breakfast," Thia said to her daughter and the Oneiroi.

Kellie whipped her head to Thia. "What do you mean no one will bother Nicole?"

"That's why we are all together. There's been some problems, but we need to take this a little at a time. I'm going to explain." Angelia said to her daughter. "We will call you back when we start the planning phase," Angelia looked to Phobetor. He nodded, and everyone who wasn't family vanished.

⊰⊱

"This may not be what you want to discuss, but we deserve to know why you kept this from us," Amanda demanded, standing before her new extended family, undaunted by their obvious power. It radiated off them like lightning slashing through the sky. She spared a moment to wonder why she didn't feel that same crackle in the air from the gods she knew and hung out with daily. The Oneiroi alone were extremely powerful, and Thia was Zeus' daughter, for god's sake.

"Very well," Angelia exhaled in irritation, not at all seeming very godlike. "There was a god who treated me very unkindly. And when I say unkindly, I mean cruelly. No one would do anything about it. Well, let's just say what was done was a political farce, and I saw where everyone's loyalty lay. I will never go into the details. Those are my crosses to bear. Do not ask me to elaborate."

Amanda noticed Hermes and Aphrodite flinch and look away from their daughter in...shame? "We wronged you and let you down," Hermes answered. Aphrodite continued to look away.

"Yes, you did. But that was a thousand years ago. What happened will never be completely forgiven," she stared pointedly at her mother, "but if none of the other Olympians bother my girls, grand-children, or any of our spouses, we can continue some sort of truce. After all, my family deserves to have the power they were born with. I should have never suppressed it." Angelia turned to her daughters. "I had lived among mortals for so long, it felt right—at the time. I was wrong. I can't change what I did. I can only ask for forgiveness and move forward. I don't want to live without my children as I have lived without my parents."

"I forgive you, Grandma, but I can't live with Aphrodite being my great-grandmother after what her husband did to me and Kallisto. Do you know what he did?" Amanda asked the goddess as she looked directly into Aphrodite's eyes.

Aphrodite hung her head, and Amanda felt the crackle leave her. *Yep, my friends have been suppressing that shit.*

"I know only that the Oneiroi, Phantasos severely beat him on his father's orders. He and I are married, but that holds a different meaning for gods who never die. We do not live together. We are bound by fate."

"Well, mortals tend to view marriage as a lifelong commitment to one another—a bond of love and loyalty. You're husband kidnapped us and, long story short, beat me unconscious after weeks of torment and torture. Forgive me if I assume your loyalty lies with your husband and not us."

Tears welled in Kathryn's eyes, and anger simmered in Alaric's. It was the first time her parents heard of their daughter's torment and torture.

"Why was this man...god—whatever the fuck he is—allowed to live?" Alaric smoldered, fists clenched, and eyes large with anger. Amanda was suddenly worried he might have a heart attack. "Why didn't we know?" He growled out his anger as tears fell down Kathryn's face.

"Dad, it's okay. I'm okay," It was better to lie than watch her father lose it when nothing could be done.

"I learned of this last night. I threw up when I found out. This is one of the reasons my family will gain their abilities as the demigods they are this evening," Angelia said. Katheryn and Alaric now stood on either side of Amanda. "The other reason is that a god has been mentally rapturing Nikki and tormenting her since the wreck over a year ago. This, too, was news to me."

"What?" Kellie turned to her daughter with shock and fear in her eyes. "What does that even mean?"

Another wave of shock went through the room. Amanda knew Hermes' and Aphrodite's power surged with the new information.

"When she was in a coma, she was actually being held mentally by a god. Nicole is what we call a dream bender," Angelia continued. "My magic is quite powerful, but Nicole's is too. What we think is the abilities that were seeping from her left a signature. One this god found and clung to. We need everyone to help find out who is doing this and put a stop to it. I won't allow another member of my family to be harmed."

"How are we to stand up to gods? I feel the power coming off them sitting here," Kathryn pointed to her grandparents. "We are no match."

"Each of you will have a signature once I lift the magic. Hopefully, you will also manifest your abilities. Kathryn and Kellie will most likely be the strongest since they are half-gods. We know Nicole is a bender, but we are unsure how strong she will become. Amanda," Angelia turned to her. "We don't know what yours will be or how long it will take them to come in. There is a chance you will be without. Not all demigods have power. You carry your great-grandmother's beauty and are my doppelganger, but doppelgangers don't always manifest power."

"Great. Odd girl out," Amanda crossed her arms.

"This is a lot to digest. I'm still wearing my work clothes from last night. Can we call for a break and let me shower and change? Plus, I need some time with Amanda . . . alone," Nicole said.

"Sure, honey," Kellie walked to her daughter and swept the hair off her shoulder as she squeezed her tight in a side hug.

"I think we've had enough time to meet. This family debacle isn't going to fix itself in one day. We should let the others know we are ready. We need to work together to find the god responsible for rapturing Nicole and tormenting my husband. Let's meet back here in two hours," Angelia suggested. Collective nods came from around the room.

Nicole went to shower and change, then to see her cousin who lay across her bed staring at the ceiling. "Have you been laying here the entire time I've been getting ready?"

"Yep," Amanda replied, still staring at the ceiling.

"Wanna talk about it?"

"Nope."

"Me neither. Instead, you wanna talk about your date with Kai?" Nicole smirked when Amanda finally turned and looked back at her.

"I had the most fun I've had since before Kallisto's dad went missing last year. *Since immortals became real.* It was easy. Crazy how easy mortal life is when immortals aren't screwing it up," Amanda returned to looking at the ceiling. "I almost didn't come to the dysfunctional family reunion this morning. I actually came very close to staying the night with the Shea chick that's going out with Kai's best friend, Mike."

"I'm glad you didn't. Not only because several gods would be looking for you, but Phantasos was already asking where you were. I'm not going to be the one who tells him you were on a date."

"Phantasos can kiss my—"

"How did things go?" Kallisto interrupted. She appeared in Amanda's room, cutting off whatever colorful things her cousin was going to say.

"Damn it, Kallisto," Amanda said as she grabbed her chest. "Can't you call and give us a warning before you do that?"

"Sorry. But how did it go?" Kallisto asked again.

"Let's just say we're still a dysfunctional bunch but on the path to at least working as a unit to find who is doing this to me and strong-arming Poppa," Nicole responded.

"How are your parents?" Kallisto took a seat on the bed and looked between the cousins.

"They're not doing great. Hell, when Grandma mentioned our kidnappings last year, I thought my dad was going to have a heart attack. I've never seen him so mad and red-faced," Amanda said as she looked at her phone.

"So, you and Kai?" Kallisto looked at Amanda. Her abrupt subject change had Nicole blinking.

"That's who just texted me. He wanted to see if I wanted to hang out this afternoon."

"It's only ten thirty in the morning. Surely, we'll be done by three—right?" Amanda asked them.

"If not, you could still go. But I'm not telling Phantasos—you have to," Nicole said.

Amanda rolled her eyes. "It's none of that asshole's business. He's overprotective because if something were to happen to me, life would be hell for Morpheus and, in turn, him since Kalli and I are best friends. We basically hate each other." Amanda said as she texted Kai back and forth.

"If you say so," Nicole gave Kallisto raised brows and shook her head. "Still, I'm not telling him. He's too big to be getting mad at the messenger."

"But to answer your question, Kai was great. Easy to be around, funny, and boy, can he kiss," Amanda truly smiled for the first time in days that Nicole could remember. "We went snorkeling, then changed for dinner and putt-putt golf. We talked a lot. It was nice."

"I'm glad," Kallisto said. "It's time to join the group again. Will Hermes and Aphrodite be there?"

"I suppose," Nicole answered, and Amanda rolled her eyes.

Chapter XLII

Bait

Everyone, including the great-grandparents, gathered in the living room at Amanda's house. Nicole emerged freshly showered and greeted Phobetor with a wide grin, and he returned it with a chaste kiss in front of everyone. Neither cared as several raised brows watched their exchange.

"Let me see the whole thing," Kellie gestured to Nicole's back where your new tattoo rested with its top barely cresting over her tank top. Nicole lowered her tank enough to show the art in its entirety.

"Explain its meaning," her mother said.

"Those are Chase's birth and death dates in Roman numerals. The lion, I'm not sure. It just came to me. Isn't it beautiful?

"May I see?" Aphrodite asked. Nicole turned her back to everyone while holding her tank just under the tat.

Aphrodite went very still. "The lion is beautiful. Who is Chase?" she asked, very interested in Nicole's new ink.

Nicole let her tank rise back, covering the majority of the artwork and looked between her mother and Phobetor. "He was my first love. The guy who died in the wreck I was in over a year ago. Ironically, he's the reason I'm here. The catalyst for my new life."

"And the lion? You said meant?" Aphrodite continued with questions.

"I just liked it."

"This was the wreck in which you were unconscious for a week?" Her great-grandmother continued with what felt like an interrogation.

"Yes. The *coma* —better known as when a god held me mentally captured for a week," Nicole's anger evident in her tone.

Angelia cleared her voice, calling everyone to start with the planning. "Phobetor, will you tell us what you've found out about the immortal rapturing Nikki?"

"We narrowed it to a god and not a creature capable of rapture. Nicole remembered a few details. Never his face but smells and the voice of a male. He enjoys her fear, terror, and possibly her pain. He is infatuated with her, to the point of going to Anthony and telling him of his wife's heritage and strong-arming him into facing her. He wants Angelia to divulge Nikki's abilities. Apparently, he does not understand how she has been able to break from his hold after being with him for a while. I am sure he has not thought of her being a dream bender since those are wildly considered myths—were considered myths."

"The more knowledge and understanding this god has, the easier he can take and keep her. He has not taken her physically—yet. We are not sure if he cannot or is unable to because of Nicole's unique abilities," Phantasos interjected. "The Fates acknowledged she is in danger and the death of the god we seek will cause war."

Nicole watched Aphrodite stiffen at Phobetor's words. "You plan on killing the god responsible for this?" Aphrodite questioned.

"Yes. The god will die by my hands." Phobetor announced. "I saw her tied to a metal table. He tortured her for a week, feeding on her fear. He made fear, depression, and anxiety take hold of her, causing her to contemplate taking her own life. We have watched her every minute because he continues to rapture her mentally."

"He paid a visit to Amanda," Phantasos' words were guttural. "He will die."

"What about the war The Fates warned of?" Hermes asked.

"We have never been afraid of war," Phobetor answered.

Nicole interrupted, "We need to use me as bait and bring him to us. It's the fastest and best way."

Phobetor's head swung in her direction. He growled his disagreement, then barked out, "No!"

"Listen," Nicole continued speaking, looking at everyone except Phobetor. "Once Angelia lifts the magic over us, I will be stronger. You got to me before—you can do it again," She spoke quietly and finally turned to Phobetor.

"I'm with Phobetor," Nicole's mother said, visibly shaking.

"Please, before we make a decision, let grandma lift the magic so we can see," Nicole pleaded.

"I will lift them now," Angelia said before the Oneiroi or Kellie could object. Angelia closed her eyes and became very still. Seconds went by, and nothing seemed to happen. Then the room started to vibrate. Glass shook in the kitchen. Kathryn and Kellie began to light up. Their eyes glowed white, and their skin shimmered. Next, Nicole and Amanda did much the same. "I kept the magic on the twins. I don't think John would handle the boys glowing very well," Angelia said.

Kathryn and Kellie looked at their hands and at each other. "I feel like there's a light radiating through my body. It's the only way I can describe it."

"Me too," Kellie responded.

"Me too," Nicole looked at her hands and then at her mom.

"I feel nothing different," Amanda announced.

"It will take several days, possibly weeks, to fully come into your gifts. Don't fret, sweetie, you have a long time," Angelia addressed her granddaughter. "However, you are even more radiant with divinity flowing freely through you. Unfortunately, every male will be pining for you if we don't mask your divine perfection."

"I think we need another plan just in case the one with Nicole does not work well," Hermes suggested.

"I agree," Aphrodite seconded.

"We can mask our presence and watch for when the being returns to Anthony," Hermes said. "Is that okay with you," he looked at his daughter and her husband.

"We will do anything to protect our grandchildren," Anthony said. He looked a little less green than he did when he first arrived.

"Now we have a few plans in place. I would like Mom and Dad to stay for a few days before going back. Kellie, I know you need to get back quickly," Kathryn said.

"We have placed memories in John and the boy's minds. They believe you were on a business trip for two days. They will not remember yesterday as you do. Be careful when speaking of anything between Friday morning and when you return," Morpheus explained to Kellie. "I will take you back."

Kellie said her goodbyes to her parents and Nicole. Morpheus vanished with her moments later. Kallisto and Thia went home.

"I'll be back this evening," Amanda announced to her mom and dad after Aphrodite and Hermes departed, tentatively hugging Angelia. She and Nicole were not ready for hugs by the gods they just met, whether family or not.

"Where are you headed," Phantasos asked.

"Not that it's any of your business, but I have a date," she smirked. Phantasos became rigid. "With?"

"Oh shit," Nicole said under her breath to Phobetor.

⟫⟫⟩ ⟨⟨⟨⟨

"None of your damned business," Amanda repeated, arms crossed, gearing for a verbal battle. *He has some nerve.*

"Just be careful, honey," Kathryn said.

"Are you sure you need to go anywhere alone?" her dad asked.

"Exactly," Phantasos agreed.

"I don't need a babysitter. Nicole does. I'm fine. I'll be back later," Amanda told her dad. "Don't you dare follow me or watch over me with that orb thingy," She growled and pointed a finger at Phantasos.

His lip twitched in a snarl. Her phone pinged. "Kai's here," Amanda announced and gave her mother a kiss on the cheek and her dad a hug, then walked out the front door. She felt the heat of Phantasos' rage and his scorching stare on her back before the door closed behind her.

⟫⟫⟫ ⟪⟪⟪

Phantasos bowed his head to Kathryn and Alaric before he vanished.

"Well, that was quite interesting," Angelia smirked.

"The Fates can make life difficult with their half-warnings and riddles," Phobetor said.

"I want to find out if I'm stronger," Nicole looked at him. "Can you place me in a deep sleep and dream walk with me?"

He now trusted her completely. For an Oneiroi to go into a dream without power was not something taken lightly. This would be the ultimate test of his trust and faith in her.

"Yes. Just go easy on me." He winked.

Chapter XLIII

Uncovered

Nicole and Phobetor worked on her enhanced, unsuppressed abilities for the next three days. With each dream, she became stronger. Controlling the divine hum that radiated through her body became easier. Her senses became extremely heightened, and her power was evident for all to witness. She felt all emotions, which proved a little disconcerting. When Phobetor took her in a dream of his creation, she could still only take partial control, changing minor things, but she could never gain total control. However, she was in complete control if he went into a dream she conjured. As much as he tried, he was unable to take control of the dreams she manifested.

"My fear is we do not know how strong this god is. He could learn from his mistakes and regain his control as I can," Phobetor said to Nicole as they discussed the dream they had just emerged from.

"What if you take me to another realm to see if I can turn that into a dream state I can control, like I did with the graveyard?"

"Good idea. There is very little difference between psychological rapturing and dreaming. That is why you were able to change the setting and remove him. You should think of a place you want to go so you are not making that decision when bound and scared." It was all Phobetor could do to say those last words. Even thinking of her bound and afraid made his eyes swirl black and the veins in his forearms lined in obsidian streaks.

"Look," Nicole touched his arm. "This will work. We need to stop him before he hurts me or goes after Amanda. Now that our powers have been awakened, he can sense our signatures."

"So can the rest of the immortals," Phobetor said.

"Well, I won't go until I know I'm strong enough. We still have a few days before he returns to my grandfather. Until then, a girl has to go to school and work," as she raised to her tiptoes and kissed his cheek. He grinned mischievously, swept her up from the floor, and made sure she thought about him all day. Their kiss lasted longer than necessary to encourage her thoughts in his direction. She was running late for school.

The school day went by fast. She finally told Pika the day before that she only wanted to be friends. He wasn't at school, so she hoped he was absent because he was taking care of things while his parents were on another island and not because he was irritated with her. Amanda hung out with Kai every chance she got, and Phantasos hadn't been around since he left Amanda's Sunday afternoon. Her grandparents were staying in Maui until the week given by the deity was up. Everything seemed to be going well since the unveiling of their heritage.

"Can you and Amanda start unwrapping the paintings brought in this morning?" Kallisto asked Nicole when she got to the gallery. "Amanda ran next door to see if they had a stepladder we could borrow. We need two, and Morpheus forgot to pick another one up."

"Hey, a god never forgets," Morpheus scoffed.

Kallisto's brows rose. "Well, being that I'm a goddess, I know better," Kallisto said as she grinned and kissed his cheek.

"All four paintings?" Nicole asked, pointing to the wrapped art.

"Yeah. I'm not sure what they sent," Morpheus answered.

Amanda returned in time to help with the unwrapping of the two largest canvases. The largest, an 80"x36" horizontal painting, was the first to be opened. It intrigued them, being it was so big. "If you hold it steady, I'll start unwrapping this end," Nicole looked at the large painting, sizing it up.

"Okay. Wanna take bets on what it's of before we start unwrapping?" Amanda grinned.

"My guess is it is a panoramic of Olympus," Morpheus said.

"I say it's all the Olympic gods standing side-by-side, hands on their hips, like the prints of superheroes," Nicole giggled.

"It's all my grandfather's courtesans in one painting," Kallisto smirked.

"I can't believe you went there," Amanda laughed. "I think it's of all the mythological creatures."

"Let's find out." Amanda held one end as Nicole started removing the paper. The frame made the painting incredibly heavy.

It was an epic battle. The Greek Pantheon against one Nicole had no clue of. Ares led the battle in full armor with his sword raised. Many gods and creatures followed him. Zeus, Poseidon, and Hades stood on the top of a hill overlooking the battle as if bored. Some of the gods and creatures Nicole recognized were Hermes with his caduceus, Apollo and his bow, Heracles with a bow and sword, Eros with a bow, three cyclops, many centaurs with bows, and one Cerberus—*who is that?*

"Morpheus, who is that?" Nicole pointed to a beast with the head of a lion and the body of a large man who was first in line to battle the other Pantheon. Alongside the beast was another giant of a man.

"That's Ares' sons, Phobos and Deimos. They always accompany Ares in battle. They spread terror and panic amongst the enemies. Phobos is the one with the head of a lion."

"Does he always have the head of a lion?" Nicole asked, her mood completely changed as she looked upon the battle scene before them.

"No. He looks very similar to Ares when not in battle," Morpheus explained.

"His lion persona looks a lot like my tattoo, don't you think?"

"It does. Did you say terror?" Amanda asked. "Could he be the one?"

"Phob—," Nicole started to summon.

⟫⟫⟫ ⟪⟪⟪

Phobetor appeared before Nicole finished calling his name. He had been watching and came to the same realization. "Phobos!" The name came as a growl deep in Phobetor's chest.

"We don't know that for sure. You can't go killing gods you're not sure of," Nicole placed a calming palm on his chest.

"Sure, I can," his eyes swirled black, and his skin began to streak. His words came out deeper than she'd ever heard.

"Easy now, brother. I agree this is suspicious; however, you need to make sure. He hails from a bloodline that will hunt you down if you kill him. Especially without proof," Morpheus tried to calm the beast inside his brother as it struggled to make an appearance.

"Proof? Let him deny it to my face," Phobetor growled.

"You are not capable of facing anyone right now," Morpheus continued.

Nicole watched as Phobetor tried to gain back his control. "He's really changing into a creature I don't know, isn't he?" She wasn't sure if she was asking herself to verify or anyone who would answer.

"I felt his anger," Phantasos appeared beside Morpheus, ready to help control the beast.

"Yes. He has a nightmarish form just as I morph into mist," Morpheus answered Nicole's question. "His form can be pliable unless provoked, then there is rarely any give. As you can see, he is provoked."

All three women watched as two brothers worked to calm the third. Nicole could tell they had practiced calming the beast but were not getting very far.

"Let me help," Nicole wanted to comfort Phobetor. Unlike Amanda and Kallisto, she wasn't afraid of the transformation taking place before them.

"Not sure that is wise," Phantasos looked between Nicole and Phobetor.

"I'm not afraid of him. He won't hurt me." Nicole walked to Phobetor and the beast fighting to be released. "It's okay. Calm down so we can talk," she placed her hand on his chest again and held it there this time. A few minutes passed before the obsidian-streaked veins returned to normal. His eyes continued to swirl black like they were made of liquid, but his breaths came slower. "That's better."

"We need a plan," Morpheus suggested after explaining to Phantasos what caused Phobetor's intense reaction. Phantasos went still when Morpheus told him who was suspect number one on their short list of suspects.

"Ares' son," he said aloud with a snarl of his lips.

"Again, we do not know that for sure. This is just a painting. What motive does he have?"

"I can think of several," Phobetor's voice came out gravelly.

"Who is this Phobos' mother?" Amanda asked. The Oneiroi looked at each other before Phobetor answered.

"Aphrodite."

Nicole and Amanda looked at each other with surprise and aversion. "You've got to be kidding," Amanda said, looking disgusted, "You're quite the carnal bunch, aren't you?"

Ignoring Amanda, Phantasos said, "We know who we are most likely looking for. This will dispel his concealment ability. He will no longer be able to hide his face from us."

"Phobetor, you need to be okay with me luring him into rapturing me," Nicole touched his chest again.

"No!" he growled, his eyes dancing faster with black liquid.

"You have no choice. This is my choice, and you need to accept it," She continued to touch him as she looked straight into his eyes, standing up to the beast barely contained. He scowled.

Minutes ticked by as his jaws worked until he finally yielded. "Fine, but you must listen to us," he gestured between himself and his brothers. "We need plans. A plan on what to do when he takes you, and one as backup in case the first one does not work."

"I can agree to that," Nicole said.

Chapter XLIV

Raptured

THE REST OF THE evening was spent planning best- and worst-case scenarios. Phobetor was anxious—a feeling he was not accustomed to and not sure how to handle. He needed Nicole safe. Allowing Phobos to take her was the opposite of safe. According to the plan, he was to watch over her until her classes were over. She, John, and Amanda were closing, so no gods would be around while she worked. Unfortunately, this part of Nicole's disturbing plan left her open and vulnerable to the whims of her tormentor.

Phobetor leaned against Amanda's car in the school parking lot, waiting to hold Nicole one more time before she would be without the security of a god. Amanda arrived first and looked at him with sadness and worry in her eyes.

"I don't like this either," Amanda admitted as she climbed into the driver's side. All Phobetor could manage, without losing it, was a nod.

For extra protection, John and his brothers knew of the insane plan, and so did most of Nicole's family. They had not told her great-grandparents, not knowing which side Aphrodite would fall on. How could they ask her to choose her great-granddaughter over her son, even if he was a sadistic ass? He also chose to keep it from Hades and Zeus. If he was going down for killing another god, he wanted to make sure no one would stand in his way. Only those he trusted with Nicole's life were privy to the plan.

"Phobetor? I wasn't expecting you in the flesh, but I'm glad you're here," Nicole said as she approached him.

Her smile was wide, and he committed it and every inch of her to memory. She had healed. She still had black and purple hair and piercings, but her soul was whole again. *Would Phobos take her back to that dark place of self-loathing she escaped from? Will I be able to get to her in time? Can I save her?* So many questions raced through Phobetor's mind. He knew it was very likely that Zeus would have his head for what he was about to do, but as long as Nicole was safe, he did not care.

"I had to try and talk you out of this one more time. Plus, I just needed to hold you for a moment."

Phobetor wiped the tear sneaking down her face at his words, then commenced kissing her long and deep. Not caring about the dozens of onlookers. After their kiss, he held her out a little, memorizing every square inch of her face.

"The first time I saw you—you were asleep. When I looked at you, I knew then you would be mine. When I went into your dream, you scared me. That was the first time I ever remember being truly afraid. I told Phantasos I could not heal you—the entire time, knowing I would not allow anyone else to do so. I fell in love with you, my έξυπνος ομορφιά, my clever beauty. I beg you to be careful."

Now, several tears rolled down her cheeks. "I love you, too. I'm stronger now. Not just because I'm a demigod but because you healed me and made me want to be strong again. Plus, you taught me how to manipulate my power. I'll be okay. I promise."

The parking lot was empty before they finished saying goodbye. Phobetor vanished with a last kiss to the tip of her nose and awaited the message that Nicole was taken.

Amanda watched the heart-wrenching scene outside her car play out before her. When Phobetor vanished, she noticed she was crying. Nicole climbed into Amanda's car, wiping tears from her eyes as Amanda did the same.

"You two just ripped the heart from my chest," Amanda sniffled as she drove to the gallery.

"It feels weird not having a watcher. I feel so...empty," Nicole confessed.

"If you can give me a sign that you're about to hit the floor, will you?" Amanda asked. "I want to catch you if I can."

"The way your mind works scares me sometimes," both girls laughed.

Amanda felt a slight tingling—maybe they watched her instead of Nicole.

Once in the gallery, she and John watched her cousin's every move. *I don't like this shit.* Amanda was scared for Nicole. This wasn't how she thought they should be going about this. No one asked her, though.

"You know, you two watching me so close will give me a complex," Nicole laughed. "There's a chance the god won't come, and those customers need help." She pointed to the young man and woman who walked in.

It was almost closing time, and nothing had happened. The bell on the door chimed while Amanda dusted the paintings around the corner. "I'll be with you in a moment," she said to the customer entering.

"I am in no hurry," came a deep Greek accent—one she didn't recognize.

Amanda dropped her duster and rounded the corner. There he stood. Now face to face with *him*, she remembered his threat. She knew it was the god from the painting, even if he wasn't in his lion form—Phobos. Everything from his baritone accent to his thick arms and incredible height made the hair all over her body stand on end. *Fight or flight* went through her head.

"You're not supposed to be here. *Not in the flesh*," she said to the giant of a man with long dark hair and catlike eyes.

He threw back his head and laughed. "Did it ever cross your mind that I can feel Nicole's power? It is—strong. Very strong—not one to be trifled with. Why would I take her, when I can have you?"

"No!" Amanda screamed and turned to run.

Phobos roared with laughter. "You have not been in the gallery for a while now. You are in another place altogether. Unfortunately, I could only take Nicole mentally, never body and soul. You, however." He grinned and showed long fangs. "You, I could take—and did. Tell me, how afraid are you?"

⊱⊱⊱ ⊰⊰⊰

He waved a hand, and they were outside the dilapidated mansion where she and Kallisto were taken months ago. Flashes of Ares' hands around her neck went through her head, and hot white anger engulfed her.

"You and your father are some sick fucks," Amanda spat in his face.

He slapped her hard, leaving blood dripping from her nostrils. "Naughty girl. Just so you understand, I do not want your anger—I want you terrified, and I always get what I want."

"Just like your dad," she felt and smelled the copper tang of blood. Using the back of her hand, she wiped it from her face.

"My father knows nothing of this or of your cousin. Now that you mention him, he will be mad that I took you. You see—" Phobos' hands were now giant lion paws, and he traced one claw down her face. She felt the sting of the cut and a trickle of wet heat run down her cheek. "He has it bad for you. If you were not mine now, you would be his someday. Who knows, we may share once he finds out," his laugh sounded animalistic, between a growl and a purr.

Amanda screamed as his head shifted into the dark-maned lion she saw in the painting, and his hands manifested into the large claws of a lion. His hands and head were the only things turned. His body was still of the giant, muscled man. His feline eyes were red, and his fangs were even larger. She kicked and fought as he backed her toward the mansion's steps. *This wasn't the plan. They won't be able to find me.* This wasn't the mental warfare they readied for...*this was physical.* Fear gripped her chest, and she heard him purr with satisfaction.

"Fighting me will do you no good," His words came out as deep guttural hisses. Phobos grabbed her around the waist and took her inside the mansion as she fought.

The smell of the dank mansion hurled Amanda back to January, where Ares assaulted her and held her best friend's life over her head, causing her to almost give in to his demands. Instead, she fought him, and he nearly killed her. *It's all happening again.* Fear of the monster's spawn, who held her tight as he took her deep into hell, caused bile to surface in her throat. The darkness of the house only added to her fear. It made the god's touch, the sound of his breath, and the hardness of his grip more sinister if that were possible. *Will he beat me? Will he make me* . . . Her body was racked with uncontrolled tremors as she thought about the possibilities.

"No reason to shake so. Not yet anyway," Phobos' voice was quiet yet boomed through her ears.

"Why? Just let me go," she sounded small, almost childlike when she begged. That pissed her off.

"That. Is. It—More. Fight me more." That time, his words were accompanied by a deep rumble from his chest. There was no mistaking it for pure pleasure.

Moments later, she was slammed down on a cold, hard surface, taking her breath. Phobos pulled at her wrists and shackled them to the corners above her head. Next, he shackled her ankles to the opposite corners of the slab. She was spread eagle on her back, in the dark, with a monster and no power to escape.

"You bastard," Amanda's words still held fear, but this time she managed anger.

It was only a second in time. After the slur left her lips, he split them with one swipe of his paw. That put an abrupt end to the anger, as nothing but terror coursed down her spine.

"I suppose I found your fear button. Pain it will be," Phobos announced right before he bent two of her fingers backward. "This will be fun."

Amanda screamed.

⤐⟩⟩ ⟨⟨⤛

Angelia was worried about both her granddaughters. Amanda was clutched in the hands of an insane deity, and Nicole was going crazy, worried for her cousin.

"Find her!" Nicole screamed at the Oneiroi. "Find her," she begged over and over. "This was never the plan. What have I done?"

In the gallery stood the three Oneiroi in their leather fighting gear. Angelia, her parents, Kallisto, and Thia all stood with them, waiting to find the location of Amanda and her tormentor. They didn't tell Kathryn or Kellie since they were in no place to help and would be in the way. Since Phobos physically raptured Amanda instead of Nicole, Angelia went to her parents to get them to help search.

She begged her parents with tears in her eyes. Aphrodite looked pained but chose Angelia and her granddaughter. . . this time.

"He won't kill her because he needs her fear and terror. You didn't do this. How were we to know he would take Amanda instead?" Angelia said to Nicole as she tried to calm her grandchild. They had already searched for over six hours and found nothing.

"We need more help," Phantasos said, barely hanging on to his sanity as he paced the gallery floor, running his hands through his thick blonde hair.

"I will ask Hades for help. I do not trust Zeus to choose Amanda over his grandson," Phobetor said seconds before he rubbed the coin given to him by the king of the Underworld.

"To what do I owe this—dishonor," Hades grunted and glowered at Phobetor as he made his way to the dais.

"We believe Phobos took Amanda, your niece's best friend. The same girl Ares took a few months ago."

Hades stood up from his throne. The gorgons on either side of him hissed. "What do you mean you *believe*? Do you not know?"

"We are almost positive it was Phobos, but if it is not him, another god from Olympus took her. We have several gods looking for them now. But there are so many realms. We would rather not ask your brother for help since Phobos is his grandson and Ares' son."

"I see." Hades looked at his minions on either side of him. "I will send the gorgons with you. They have an uncanny ability to sniff out prey. If you have not found the girl soon, come back here before you go to Zeus. Understood, Oneiroi?" Hade's eyes flashed red.

"Thank you." Phobetor found himself standing back in the gallery. Only now, he had two big-ass gorgons with him. Everyone, including Hermes, gave them a wide berth. No one looked them in the eye.

The tongues of the gorgons and the snakes attached to their heads flicked out over and over as they glided around the gallery, gathering scent. All the gods watched in silence.

After twenty minutes, one spoke, with a hissing high-pitched sound. "We found them. She is with the god Phobos, as you thought."

Aphrodite flinched, then she stood up straight and announced to the group. "He chose his path."

The serpents told the gods standing before them where to find Amanda. Phantasos looked at Morpheus. "Same place. I will kill Ares, too, if he is part of this."

Moments later, all the gods, Nicole, and the gorgons were gathered on the overgrown lawn of the eerie mansion.

"There are other creatures in this realm," Morpheus warned. "Kallisto, Nicole, you two stay close to me."

"Come out, Phobos. We know you are in there," Phantasos yelled, again pacing.

Phobetor stood between his brothers, he and Phantasos, in their battle forms and armor. Phantasos' fangs were on full display. His massive wings had been out since their boots touched the tall grass. Morpheus was only to fight if he had to. He was to keep Nicole safe. Phobetor's eyes swirled, and all his veins were lined in black. Smooth black wings burst from his back when Phobos walked out onto the second-floor balcony.

"They have wings?" Nicole's voice shook with shock. Phobetor's wings looked like those of a dragon, smooth with black veins steaking through them. Phantasos' were like black angel wings, but with such tiny feathers, they looked smooth to the touch. "What the hell?"

"I am the only one who can morph into mist. How did you think they kept up with me?" Morpheus grinned down at her.

"You brought so many to the party. Even my mother," Phobos snarled. "Nicole, did you miss me? Would you like to join me and Amanda? We are becoming almost as close as you and I were."

Phobetor growled. "Do not look or speak to her."

"You have done this to yourself, son. If they kill you, I will mourn the god you once were, not the one you became," Aphrodite spoke as she looked up at her son with sadness.

"I guess the fastest god wins. If I get to her before you get to me, you will never see her again," The lion roared so loud that everyone covered their ears. Phobetor flew as fast as an arrow to the balcony just as Phobos vanished.

Loud, as if by speaker, making sure the lion heard him, Hermes projected his voice, "I have made it where no one can leave this place, Phobos. You need to put a stop to this madness. The Oneiroi are not known for their mercy."

Flashes of Phobos leaning over Nicole as the beast licked blood from her face, paralyzed Phobetor once he reached the balcony. His breathing became rapid as he fought the horror of what else the god of fear had done to her. *Fight this.* He thought as he leaned against the wall, while horrible visions continued to invade his mind. Phobos used his powers. The same ones that helped win battles.

Phobetor heard a gorgon hiss out somewhere on the lower level, "Come out, kitty-kitty. We can taste you." He shook the fear from his spine, folded his wings, and continued searching the top floors of the structure.

Each room held feelings of dread and torture. *This has been Ares and his son's torture house for centuries.*

Chapter XLV

Wrath

Phantasos burst through the front door, short sword in hand, followed by the gorgons. A wave of panic hit him on his chest. *What if I find her dead?* The pain of that thought bent him over, and he vomited. *This is Phobos' doing.* Phantasos fought the terror in his head of Amanda slain on a metal table.

He worked clearing the first floor. It was only a minute before he heard a familiar voice. Lounging on a chaise, the sphinx laughed.

"She might just die this time, dreamer." Her shrill laughter died when she saw the gorgons.

"We have this handled," hissed a gorgon. "You continue forward."

On high alert, he worked his way down a familiar corridor. He was in the same corridor where he and Morpheus found Amanda and Kallisto held hostage by Ares. Memories, both true and false, worked through his mind—the truth of how he found Amanda beaten to unconsciousness and false flashes of her beaten to death instead of almost comatose. Phobos continued his mind fuck. The corridor ended, and he had no choice but to turn around. Amanda was not there.

He made his way back to where the Sphinx had been. Traces of her blood marked the exact spot. *Good.* He and his brother fought together for centuries. He knew Phobetor would continue up, so he went down. He slowly opened the door to the basement and gradually descended the staircase. Another wave of fear struck him, almost bending him over with physical and emotional pain. This time, he saw both Amanda and Nicole. They hung by their wrists from the ceiling with thick ropes. Bloody whip marks marred their naked backs and limbs. He tightened his hand around the hilt of his sword, grounding himself, and willed the images to disappear.

"Why are you hiding? Come out and fight like a god," Phantasos said loud enough for the god to hear him if he were in the basement.

"I smell him," a gorgon hissed from the top of the stairs. Phantasos dared a glance up to her. The creature's grin dripped with blood. *That's where the sphinx went.*

Phobetor, Phobos is in the basement. The mental connection the Oneiroi had when fighting was another perk of the trio. Phantasos felt when Phobetor materialized two steps above him. They continued down, taking each step with caution.

Phantasos heard his brother grunt in pain and turned to see him pressing the heels of his hands into his eyes and breathing heavily. "Get the fuck out of my head," Phobetor hissed through clenched teeth.

"Ground yourself, brother. He will not stop. This is mental warfare," Phantasos schooled his younger brother as he watched Phobetor push the images he was fighting from his head. After Phobetor reinforced his mental shields, they continued down the long staircase.

Once all the way down, Phobetor went left, and Phantasos went right. There was a long hallway with at least six dilapidated doors. Slowly, Phantasos opened each and scanned for Amanda and Phobos. After three rooms and no luck, he caught sight of a flicker of light. Bracing himself for anything, Phantasos walked into the dark room with one tiny light hanging in its corner. The light illuminated his worst fear, a metal table in the middle with leather wrist and ankle straps, shackles lining the damp walls, and Amanda with her back pressed to Phobos' chest. His claws circled her neck, and an evil grin crossed his feline face. Phobos' fangs looked even longer in the dull light. Amanda was wide-eyed and horrified. He could see her trembling against the beast.

"You cannot kill me before I rip out her throat," Phobos rumbled as he pressed his nose to Amanda's neck and inhaled. "Now I know why my father wants her so bad," he then licked her neck from her collarbone to her ear.

Phantasos watched tears stream down her terrified face, then noticed one bead of blood flowing in the mix of them, dried blood on her swollen lips, and she held her right hand protectively to her chest.

"What did you do to her face," Phantasos shook with anger.

"Oh? This?" He traced the slice down her cheek, opening the wound further with a claw. "It is just a little blood and a mark to remember me. It is not the face you should concern yourself with. I have so enjoyed her fear," Phobos purred. "Even if it cost me some bruising," Phobos' laugh made Amanda cry harder. "You should be proud of her. She refused to be terrified at first and made me work to get her there."

"You will die this day," Phantasos told the lion. He felt energy radiating off of Phobetor as he walked up behind him.

"We will see," Phobos licked the tears and blood from Amanda's face, purring loudly as he did it. "Curious, have you tasted her blood, Oneiroi? You see, this line on her face gave me my first taste. I was unable to hold back after that." Phobos used his other paw to grab Amanda's breast, and her tears streamed faster.

"I will never drink from her," Phantasos shook with rage. "Now, get your fucking paws off of her." Phantasos knew if he made a move toward the beast, he would kill her.

The lion grinned. "That truly is a shame. Do you not want to know why my father covets her?" Phobos licked the tears and blood from her face again as Amanda whimpered.

"He covets what he will never have."

"Never say never, Oneiroi. Ironically, it is me, his son, you must worry about. What I want from her is much worse." Phobos continued his unwanted ministrations on Amanda's breasts and ground his hips into her backside.

A trance came over Phantasos as he watched the god grope her. The vision was Amanda being *taken* by both gods, Ares and Phobos, in all the ways she could be. The visions caused him to pause for the first time in his life. Terror gripped his soul, and he could not move.

"Shields brother!" Phobetor yelled behind him.

Phobos roared in pain when Morpheus materialized beside him and, in one fluid motion, grabbed the paw from around Amanda's neck and severed a digit, causing Phobos to fall to one knee beside his detached claw. Morpheus' eyes glowed red with anger as he kicked the god in the side, knocking him off balance. A combination of the commotion and the anguished sound from Amanda's lips pulled Phantasos from the trance the lion weaved.

Phobetor rushed to grab Amanda, moving her to safety as Phantasos rushed forward and plunged an Atlantean steel dagger deep into Phobos' chest where his heart once beat. He then pulled the dagger out and watched blood pour from his torso.

"You see, lion, you cannot defeat us," Phantasos spat. His words were as strong as his actions, but inside, he was still reeling from the visions Phobos had gifted him.

Phantasos lifted the god's face to his. The dying god grinned and said, "My father will fulfill his part of the vision."

Phantasos stabbed him in the chest again and then cut a deep line down the beast's face just before dropping him back to the floor. He looked at Amanda as he wiped the blood from the dagger onto the lion's sleeve. *Fear.* Amanda's face was full of fear. *She sees me for what I am and fears me now.* Phantasos thought.

"Someone should call his father. Ares needs to see what happens when they mess with what is not theirs," Phantasos walked back up the stairs, refusing to look at Amanda again.

Phantasos walked back to the porch and took a deep, cleansing breath. "Your son is dead. It was me who killed him. Tell your husband that," Phantasos addressed Aphrodite. She collapsed in tears. No matter that Phobos was evil, he was still her son.

⟶⟫⟩ ⟨⟪⟵

Nicole ran to her cousin when she saw her cradled in Phobetor's arms. "She's in shock," he told her.

Angelia manifested a bed on the lawn for him to lay Amanda. "Call a healer," she beckoned Hermes. He vanished for seconds and returned with a nymph and Hypnos.

"This child has been through enough. She has physically survived the attacks of two powerful gods. I am not sure she will mentally or emotionally survive this time, even with my help," Hypnos warned, looking at his sons. "Mortals and gods do not mix."

"She's my granddaughter," Angelia told him.

Hypnos' brow rose. "She is still more human than god. I feel no magic in her—and no signature. Prepare yourselves for the fallout."

"I just released the concealment on my family. She hasn't had enough time," Angelia's tears dripped onto Amanda's chest.

⟶⟫⟩ ⟨⟪⟵

Amanda's body hurt, and her head rang with pain. Opening her eyes wasn't an option. She listened to her grandmother talk with who must be Hypnos. *They had wings. He had fangs.* Flashes of Phantasos' and Phobetor's god forms whirled through her head. *A man with the head of a lion hit and licked me...flung me around...he killed him...* Her thoughts came in spurts. Not continuing with one thought before another surged through her mind. *He has wings.*

"I'm going to throw up," she said to anyone who would listen.

"Here," someone handed her a cold, wet cloth.

"What have you done!" a deep voice boomed. A voice Amanda would never forget. The same voice that haunted her almost every night between laying her head on her pillow and opening her eyes in the morning. The voice was that of the man in her nightmares. *Ares.* She forced her eyes open, and yellow spots flashed in her periphery before they focused enough to see her nightmare standing in the doorway.

"Who killed my son?" Ares bellowed. He stood in the doorway of the mansion, cradling his son's body. His eyes glowed bright red—he, too, had wings and fangs.

No! Please, not him. Amanda thought as terror ripped through her.

"He took a demigod and tortured her repeatedly, and then he took her cousin and did the same," Aphrodite answered her husband's roar of pain and flashed to his side.

"My son was murdered because he played with two demis? A god was destroyed because of the lives of mortals?" Ares roared.

"Yes. He tortured the granddaughters of Angelia. And I plunged an Atlantean dagger into his chest," Phantasos walked closer to Ares, his wings and fangs still on full display and the Atlantean steel clutched in his fist.

"You need to take your son and leave us, Ares," Angelia walked to stand beside Phantasos. "There's no need to make this tragedy worse. Your son tortured my granddaughter for over a year. Then he took my other granddaughter, Amanda, and did the same, knowing his fate when caught."

Ares grinned at Angelia. "My dear Angelia. You wear the face of the elderly. Show yourself."

"No. Leave us," Angelia demanded.

Hermes and Phobetor walked to stand beside Phantasos and Angelia. Each ready to fight.

"Where is your doppelganger? Oh, never mind, I see her," Ares winked at Amanda and flashed his son's body and Aphrodite from the scene. Then he descended the steps to stand in front of Angelia. "What has it been? A thousand years or so since—well, you know when."

"Leave, or this will get very messy when I summon Zeus," Angelia said.

"You." Ares pointed at Phantasos. "I will have your head for this. After we finish the mourning period, you will die by my hand." He looked between Phantasos and Angelia, then straight at Amanda and grinned. It was the same malicious grin he had given her when she refused him all those months ago. Ares licked his lips seductively and winked at Amanda before he vanished.

Phantasos turned and looked at her with concern in his eyes, and she briefly wondered why. She also wondered about his fangs, which had faded back to normal. Right before Hypnos touched her brow, and her world went black.

Epilogue

It was Monday, three days after the shit hit the fan. Amanda's parents were beside themselves and refused to let her go to school for a few days, so she sat on her bed and read up on mainland universities. She told her parents she no longer wanted to attend college in Hawaii. Unless her mother told Thia about her new plans, Kallisto didn't yet know. Telling her best friend that she wasn't going to university in Hawaii because of her divine acquaintances was going to be one of the most difficult things she would ever do. She and Kallisto spent the last ten years closer than sisters, often referring to each other's parents as Mom and Dad. The plan had always been that they would go to college together, room together, and always be there for each other. Plans change.

The only divine beings she'd seen since that night were her mother and Nicole. She asked everyone to stay away, even Kallisto and her grandmother. Amanda didn't blame Kallisto, not completely anyway, but it was because of her that she met the gods. And if they were to remain such close friends, the gods would always be around. Amanda knew she didn't want that. The lies of her grandmother had left her powerless in Ares' hold. She knew her grandmother loved her, but she needed time. How she wished she could go back to the days before she knew the truth of the gods and other realms. Unfortunately, that was impossible since her mother was a demigod. Amanda wiped away what had to be the millionth tear.

Once Nicole went back to Tennessee at the start of summer, she wouldn't have to deal with any of the gods. Amanda's mother promised to have their concealments back in place, effectively removing any immortal signatures from them. However, she didn't think for one minute that if Ares wanted her, he wouldn't be able to find her. She knew better than that.

Her father asked her to join him in South Africa before leaving on his trip that morning. He bought her airline tickets and laid them on her bedside table before she woke.

The reality of Phantasos was too much for her to process. She watched him kill and was happy about it. That was also too much for her to process. Amanda could not wrap her mind around being happy someone was dead.

Most of the time, she did a good job not thinking about the eldest Oneiroi. But he was always in her dreams, figuratively. He never actually visited them. For that, she was grateful. Most of all, she could not come to terms with the fact he had wings and fangs. For some reason, those two things scared her the most.

⟩⟩⟩⟩ ⟨⟨⟨⟨

Nicole and Phobetor sat wrapped in each other's arms with the balcony doors open to the lights of Athens.

"Have you seen him?" Nicole asked.

"Phantasos? No. He sent word that he would not be around for a while and for me and Morpheus to work our own damn dreamers," Phobetor smirked. "I am sure he is training. Mourning for the gods lasts for a year or so. It probably seems like a long time for a mortal, but it is a short time for us. I know he met with Zeus, but I have no idea what was said. I just know Phantasos is not in a good place. I can feel his pain."

"He should be happy he put an end to the one who was tormenting me and took Amanda."

"The Fates seem to have dealt him a tough hand. Also, to kill a god means death. He knew that and still plunged an Atlantean dagger into Phobos' heart. A dagger he borrowed from Zeus' daughter, Thia."

"He planned to kill Phobos before he took Amanda?" Nicole asked.

"When we assumed he would take you. He ensured he took the hit so I was not doomed to the same fate as he is now. He protected me," Phobetor answered.

"Why would he do that?" Nicole sat up and looked Phobetor in the eyes.

"He saw me with you."

⤜⤜⤜ ⤛⤛⤛

Hades heard the boom when he entered Tartarus, so he dismissed his gorgons and waited on his throne for the giant. It took only minutes before the throne room doors burst from their hinges. Wind whipped around the titan's cloak as he strode toward Hades.

"What the hell happened?" The being shouted.

"Maybe you should be asking Zeus that. It did not happen in my territory," Hades feigned indifference.

With one hand, the man walked up the dais to the throne, picked up the god of the Underworld, and flung him into the stone wall behind the dais.

"You were given the missive to keep her safe. She has not been safe in a very long time, Hades."

"She is safe. I now have all three Oneiroi at my beck and call. One is in love with her and never far away. She is safe."

Hades wiped the blood from his nose. Never had anyone touched him in anger, let alone tossed him around. His jaws gritted in rage, but he was not foolish enough to retaliate. It would only take one word from this being, and all would be gone.

"What would happen if the god of the Underworld were to die, Hades?" The deep voice asked.

"Before Zeus got a handle on things and assigned someone in my place, evil beings of all sorts would be released into the universe. All realms would suffer."

"Remember that. Only so many true immortal beings are left; you are not one of them. If I have to show my hand, you will die. Now get up. You look weak on the floor."

The End
(Or Not)

Thank you for reading Dream Healing!

Book II of the Oneiroi Trilogy

Sign up for L. W. Phillips's author newsletter. This is where she finds her ARC and BETA readers; there are always giveaways!
http://eepurl.com/ii9BAb

Continue for a sneak peek of Book III in the Oneiroi Trilogy, <u>Dream Sacrifice!</u>

DREAM SACRIFICE

CHAPTER I

South Africa

"Just a doppelganger. It's been two months, and I'm still just a doppelganger," Amanda informed her reflection. The day before her second kidnapping, her demigod abilities were released from her grandmother's concealment. Angelia, her grandmother, better known as the Greek god who never told her daughters or grandchildren that they were descendants of Zeus himself. Amanda was the great-great-grandchild of the king of the gods. So were her cousins, Nicole and Nicole's five-year-old twin brothers.

Nicole's abilities manifested before their grandmother released them. However, they were miniscule. She was a dream bender and became even more badass once her concealment was removed. It was pretty cool, actually. Unfortunately for Amanda, she just looked damn good. Her grandmother was the daughter of Hermes and Aphrodite and got her godly good looks from her mother, not that Hermes looked unsavory. None of the gods did. They were all extraordinary-looking and—hot. But Aphrodite was the elite when it came to looks and sensuality, and Angelia looked just like her mother—and Amanda was Angelia's doppelganger. "Spitting image," her aunt Kellie from Tennessee said.

When the concealment was undone, Amanda's beauty intensified. She had always been gorgeous and still looked like herself, but she was now—more—luminous, radiant, stunning.

It has taken Amanda a long time to come to terms with everything the first part of the year dealt her. But she was finally starting to come out of the fog. It helped her to distance herself from the gods who invaded her personal space, even if that meant distancing herself from her best friend, Kallisto. That was hell, she wouldn't lie. However necessary. She'd made a deal with her mother and cousin that they had to stay away from her when they wanted to be around the gods or practice their own abilities. That proved easier since she left for South Africa with her dad after graduation. Begging wasn't usually in her repertoire, but she needed to get away, and what better way than to go with the only *normal mortal* in her life to another continent? Not that the gods couldn't get to her if they wanted. Hell, they could watch her from those damn orbs she despised.

She spent her days either at the camp or shopping in the city. Her dad ran the biology department of their local university in Hawaii and was the lead marine biologist on a three-month grant to study great white sharks off the coast of Africa. Unfortunately, he spent days at a time on a ship, and she didn't see him a lot, but he still provided her with the means to finally get away before she started college in the fall.

Occasionally, she spoke to Kallisto, but things had changed, whether either of them wanted it to or not. It only took three immortals to rattle their relationship. Ares, the god of war who kidnapped them both last January; Phobos, who took her two months ago, and Phantasos—she didn't want to think about him. Didn't want to was one thing—did anyway was another. Her thoughts often strayed to him. The look in his eyes when he wiped the dagger on Phobos' shirt sleeve after ripping it out of the stab wound he had inflicted moments before, killing the god who had tormented her and her cousin, terrified her. She was grateful but couldn't forget the haunting look in his black eyes or the wings and fangs that came with it. It was her first time seeing him in what she could only think of as his battle state. She refused to believe the wings and fangs were his natural form, and he manifested the one she was accustomed to seeing, only in her presence.

"Okay, Amanda," she chastised herself. "Get off your ass and go shopping."

She grabbed her backpack and cell phone and took off to the street market, where she would meet up with Annika, whom she met the week before while shopping. The two of them hit it off. They both loved the market, books and being happy with their mundane mortal selves. It was an easy friendship with laughs and no drama—no gods.

"It came in yesterday," Annika held up the book she'd ordered on Amanda's recommendation.

"Great. Don't ask me questions about it. I'm not a spoiler of literature," Amanda grinned. "Are you looking for anything in particular today?"

"No. Not really. If I find something I can't live without in the States, I'll get it," Annika spoke with a British accent. She had gotten into Harvard in hopes of becoming a cardiologist one day. Crazy smart and very pretty, she stood only five feet tall and had long, black curly hair with eyelashes you could see a mile away.

"I'm looking for a vibrant scarf to wear to dinner with my dad. He's coming ashore tomorrow and told me he'd take me to his favorite place for dinner," Amanda said.

"Well, vibrant will not be a problem," Annika waved her hand around, emphasizing the bright colors of the market. Oranges, blues, reds, purple—so colorful were the markets in South Africa. The ambiance those colors invoked made shopping in the markets enjoyable.

"True," Amanda laughed. It wasn't just the bright colors that allured her. The aroma of the spices, purses, blankets, and friendly faces made the markets Amanda's favorite thing to do on the weekends. She could and often did visit them for hours.

After a couple of hours shopping—she found the perfect scarf—they ate and then sat and did what she thought to be most fun—people watch and gossip.

"So, tell me more about this book you're writing," Annika said as she sipped from her berry shake.

"I haven't really written much since I've been here," Amanda admitted. Actually, she'd never written anything down. The book was the white lie she'd told her new friend. She needed some way of expressing what she'd been through, and she couldn't tell her the truth.

"Well, you have to promise me that I will be the first to read the finished product. I can't wait to find out if Angie hooks up with the eldest god."

Amanda spat her drink out in shock.

"Are you okay?" Annika laughed.

Cleaning her reddened face from soda, Amanda responded, "Why would you think those two would ever be a thing?"

"Isn't it obvious? I thought that's where the book was going," Annika looked confused.

"No. Angie hates him, and I'm pretty sure he hates Angie. It's getting late. I better get back since Dad will be in soon, if not already," Amanda said while she hastily gathered her spoils and threw them in her backpack.

"Did I say something wrong?" Annika asked.

Amanda exhaled and reminded herself that her new friend didn't have a clue the unrealistic stories were not made up.

"No. Not at all. I just forgot Dad was coming in, and I haven't seen him in two weeks. Since I've only been here three, it feels like forever."

Annika didn't look convinced. "Call me when he goes back out, and we can hang out more. I won't leave for two more weeks. You?"

"I'm not sure. My friend is trying to get me to visit her in Greece before I go back to Hawaii. I haven't decided yet."

"Greece? Sign me up," Annika smirked. "Grecian men are gorgeous."

Amanda laughed and waved, "See ya soon."

Three more weeks and she would have to make some decisions. Before school was out, she sent late admissions requests to a couple of mainland universities, hoping she could get out of Hawaii for a while. Her mother called a couple of days before, and she received a letter that she had gotten in at USC. That phone call rocked her world. Yes, she wanted and needed to get out of Hawaii. She needed to separate herself from her best friend. Not because she didn't love her but because of the baggage Kallisto came with. Amanda accepted the offer to USC, but would she be content plunged into a new life? Three weeks—she had three weeks to make her mind up.

Amanda stopped right before she was free of the market because she felt it. Someone or something was watching. It wasn't the first time since she'd been in Africa that she felt the watcher, the god—but it had been a couple of days since the last disturbing incident. Unfortunately, unlike her cousin, she couldn't tell who the watcher was. Was the being friend or foe? She turned in a complete circle and looked for the deity. No one stood out to her. Deciding to face the being if he or she materialized, she continued her walk to the campsite. She was confident Ares wasn't the pursuer since he was still in mourning. She thought most likely it was Kallisto or one of the Oneiroi—*Phantasos, maybe.*

The thought of the eldest Oneiroi took her musings down the path of her friend Annika's opinion of the *book* she was writing. How she thought the heroine and the eldest god would ever get together was beyond her.

Back at the campsite, Amanda stretched across her bunk with a book she picked up at the airport on her trip to South Africa. She had read a lot since her last abduction. Books took her mind away from the memories, away from the terror she endured, and into a fantasy world. She made sure she steered clear of mythology—no stories of the gods. After a few minutes of reading, she felt the watcher fade away.

Two and a half months. That's how long it had been since he killed Ares' son, Phobos.—since killing Nicole's year-long tormentor. The one who kidnapped Amanda instead of Nicole. The one who marked her face with his claw. Two and a half months since he spoke to Zeus and made a deal with the devil himself, Hades. Phantasos trained and meditated every day since. He prepared for the day Ares would avenge his son's death. The day Ares would come for him. When he was not training, he watched—her.

He could not help but be a little amused at Amanda's refusal to acknowledge him. He knew that she recognized a deity watching her. The old Amanda would have called him out on it. The girl curled up on a makeshift bed reading a book; she would not. This new Amanda refused to yell in protest and demand her watcher materialize. Not that he would. He, too, had changed since Phobos. Zeus gave him no choice but to change.

After he killed Zeus' grandson, the king of the gods summoned him to his throne room. It was the first time Phantasos had seen the king in a rage. A rage directed at him because directing it at himself would be counterproductive. After all, it was the god king's fault that all hell broke loose. He chose to allow Ares and his sons to torment others.

"You killed my grandson!" Zeus shouted and hit the floor with his staff hard enough that it caused a fissure in the marble floor of his throne room.

"Your grandson tortured and tormented two of your great-great-granddaughters and the husband of your granddaughter. He would have killed Amanda," Phantasos yelled back, not caring if the god-king before him struck him down with his lightning.

Zeus shook with anger and grief. "You should have brought him to me."

"He had gone mad. There was no saving him. Ask Aphrodite and Hermes," Phantasos responded. "If you will not, believe me, believe Aphrodite. She loved her son but knew he had to be put down."

"No matter. Ares will come for you. May the best god win. I will not stop him from ending your existence."

Zeus then turned his back to the Oneiroi, and Phantasos vanished from Zeus' sight.

After days of contemplation, he decided he needed some help protecting the ones he loved. That was when he made a deal with Underlord himself, Hades. Once he agreed with Hades' terms, he knew he had made a deal with the devil. Hades now owned him. The dark king had all three Oneiroi in his grasp. *Zeus had better be careful.*

Acknowledgements

I want to thank God for giving me the gift of gab and perseverance; it definitely took both to finish this book on my self-imposed crazy timeline.

Second, I want to thank my BETA readers! Especially my besties, Kellie and Nikki! (Those two names look familiar?)

Third, thank you, JoAnna, for being an amazing BETA reader and creating awesome merchandise. Here's to the word beautiful and the shaking of a head—inside joke. JoAnna understands.

Fourth, Rowan Magennis for the best cover art an author could ask for. She did it again! Absolutely AMAZING artist!

Fifth, my daughter, Allison—she is my biggest fan.

Last but not least, my husband—Ty, thank you for putting up with me for the last year and a half as I race to the finish line of not one but two books. Thank you for cooking and maintaining some semblance of home while I sat behind the computer playing with gods and timelines.

Thank you for helping make my dream come true!

L. W. Phillips is a businesswoman with a secret—well, with everyone reading this, she *had* a secret. For years, she figuratively wrote all day. She went through each day thinking of her actions and reactions and those of others as scenes in books. Finally, she decided to write some of these *scenes* down. Those scenes took on a fantastical vibe, and of course—she had to add in Greek gods. She woke one morning with a full-length novel—well—it was actually four months later after her first words went on the screen.

Sometimes, her musings are more cartoonish, especially living with three Schnauzers and a Poodle. Please don't get your hopes up; no comics from her—she can't draw a stick figure. Along with her pups, she has a husband and three children—two grown and one teenager. She breeds crested geckos and runs a dental company. When does she sleep, you ask? She doesn't.

Her escape is the world of fantasy. Reading and writing relax her. Young adult fantasy is her favorite, with adult fantasy and historical fiction following close behind. Her favorite tropes are enemies to lovers and forbidden love.

Her motto is never give up and always follow your dreams!